W9-CEJ-056

Don't miss the previous Ruby Redfort adventures:

Ruby Redfort Look Into My Eyes
Ruby Redfort Take Your Last Breath
Ruby Redfort Catch Your Death

LAUREN CHILD first introduced the character of
Ruby Redfort in her three award-winning, best-selling
CLARICE BEAN novels. Since then she has been inundated
with letters from fans asking for the RUBY REDFORT books.
Those letters worked, because this is
number four in the series.

Lauren is also the creator of the **CHARLIE AND LOLA** books,
as well as associate producer on the TV show of the same
name. Her books have won many prizes, including the
Smarties Prize (four times), the Kate Greenaway Medal,
and the Red House Children's Book Award.

The RUBY REDFORT series features codes and puzzles
created with the help of super-geek consultant Marcus du
Sautoy, Simonyi Professor for the Public Understanding of
Science at Oxford University and all-around genius.

LAUREN CHILD

FORT

FEEL THE FEAR

CANDLEWICK PRESS

This is a work of fiction. Names, characters, places, and incidents are either products of the author's imagination or, if real, are used fictitiously.

Copyright © 2015 by Lauren Child
Series design by David Mackintosh

All rights reserved. No part of this book may be reproduced, transmitted, or stored in an information retrieval system in any form or by any means, graphic, electronic, or mechanical, including photocopying, taping, and recording, without prior written permission from the publisher.

First published in Great Britain by HarperCollins Children's Books, a division of HarperCollins Publishers Ltd

First U.S. edition 2016

Library of Congress Catalog Card Number 2015937234
ISBN 978-0-7636-5470-2

15 16 17 18 19 20 BVG 10 9 8 7 6 5 4 3 2 1

Printed in Berryville, VA, U.S.A.

This book was typeset in Eames Century Modern.

Candlewick Press
99 Dover Street
Somerville, Massachusetts 02144

visit us at www.candlewick.com

For **Cousin Phoebe**
and **Cousin Lucy**

"**Fearlessness is often regarded as one of the keys to freedom. But does fear not serve a purpose? Is this deeply primal emotion not there to guide us, to help us sidestep danger and prompt us to take a safer path?**

The question should be asked: Is it always a positive quality to be fearless?

Why do we fear fear?"

DR. JOSEPHINE HONEYBONE, *founder of the Heimlich Good Emotion Institute, from her thesis,* The Worthy Emotion

Fall

ONE BRIGHT SUNNY DAY IN OCTOBER, a woman looked up to
see a five-year-old girl wriggle out of a tiny fifteenth-story window.
As far as the woman could make out, the child was lured by the
desire to reach a yellow balloon that had become snagged on the
ironwork of the building's fire escape. The girl seemed unaware
of the life-threatening drop that yawned beneath her and, without
concern, edged forward on hands and knees. She paused when
she encountered a hole in the rusting metal walkway — then put
her hand through it as if to make sure the gap was real.

The woman on the sidewalk held her breath.

The child reached out across the void but could not quite
grasp the long pink ribbon that tethered the balloon, and it gave
a mocking nod, turning to reveal its printed smiley face. The
girl, who was attending her cousin's birthday, wondered if the
balloon had floated in from some other celebration. Because
this balloon was different from most: attached to its string was a

brown paper tag, like an old-fashioned luggage label. The child began to wonder if the tag was a message, a greeting from some faraway place.

What was it trying to tell her?

All at once the little girl stood up quite straight—then she confidently stepped onto the metal beam that had once supported the fire escape, her fingers almost within touching distance of the balloon now, but not quite. For one whole minute the child stood completely still, and then, very slowly, she took her hands from the safety rail, spread her arms wide like a tightrope walker might, and continued to pursue the balloon by stepping one foot exactly in front of the other along the narrow iron strut that jutted from the building.

The woman on the sidewalk gasped, unsure if she should call out or if her cry might cause the girl to lose her balance and fall. She could neither run for help nor warn the child—so she just stood there rooted to the ground, waiting for tragedy to play out.

The girl, unaware of the woman's dilemma, was interested only in the label tied to the balloon's string. *What did it say?*

She grabbed for it, but as she did so, her foot slipped, she toppled forward, and, with the yellow balloon in hand, fell toward the earth.

The woman on the sidewalk covered her eyes and screamed, and a man walking his dog froze.

As the child fell, she thought about Agent Deliberately Dangerous and his amazing floating cloak — a gravity-defying garment that always brought him safely back down to earth. She thought about what she had eaten for breakfast: a bowl of Puffed Pops and two whole glasses of banana milk. Was this enough to make the difference between floating like a leaf and plummeting like a stone? She thought about what noise she would make when she hit the sidewalk. Would it make a *boing* sound like that Looney Toons dog, or would she land, catlike, on her feet?

And just as it seemed she was going to smack down hard on the pavement, something amazing happened. A truck drew up — it belonged to the Twinford Mattress Company — and the little girl landed with a puff, plumb-square in the middle of it. Of course all of this happened in the space of 3.2 seconds, but it played out in cartoon time.

A couple of blocks away, when the truck stopped at a red light, the child climbed out unnoticed and walked back to the party, balloon in hand.

When she got to the street corner, she paused to examine the tag. Disappointingly, there was no message; it was entirely blank, except for an image of two eyes tightly shut. Still, she untied it from the balloon's string and tucked it in her pocket. She had gone to a lot of trouble to get it, and in any case, who knew when a brown label might come in handy?

She let go of the smiling balloon, and it climbed back into the sky until it was so high it was no longer visible.

The woman from the sidewalk searched and searched, but there was no sign, no visible trace of the girl who had fallen from the sky.

An Ordinary Kid

WHEN RUBY REDFORT WAS YOUNGER, she and thirty-three other participants were asked to watch a film that showed six people — three in white T-shirts and three in black T-shirts — throwing basketballs to one another. The task was to count the number of times the players in white passed the ball.

Ruby counted sixteen passes.

This was the correct answer.

She also noticed the gorilla.

Or, more accurately, the man in the gorilla suit who walked across the basketball court, stopped, beat his chest, and strolled out of the shot.

Fifteen of her co-watchers noticed this too.

Ruby *also* noticed that one of the three players dressed in black departed the game when the gorilla appeared.

Five of her co-watchers noticed this too.

Ruby noticed the curtain in the background change color, from red to orange.

Zero of her co-watchers noticed this.

The psychologists conducting the experiment declared that Ruby was a remarkably focused individual but also had an extraordinary ability to see everything all at once.

Aside from the things Ruby had spotted in the content of the film, she had *also* noticed one of her co-watchers (the one with the mole on her left cheek) sticking a piece of chewing gum (the brand was Fruity Chews) under the adjacent seat, another (the guy with hay fever) knocking over his glass of water, and a third (a woman with a Band-Aid on her fourth finger) anxiously twisting her earring (she was wearing mismatched socks, very slightly different shades of green).

Not that *any* of these three observations had anything to do with the experiment Ruby was taking part in.

Some several years later . . .

CHAPTER 1
A Nice Glass of Milk

RUBY REDFORT LOOKED DOWN.

She could see the traffic moving like little inching bugs, far, far beneath her feet. She could feel a hot breeze on her face and hear the muffled sounds of car horns and sirens. It was a day like most of the days had been that summer — too hot to be comfortable, the sort of heat that brought irritability and rage and left a sense of general malaise.

Ruby surveyed the whole beautiful picture that was Twinford City — all detail gone from this height, just the matrix of streets and buildings, huge skyscrapers punctuating the grid. Outside the city, the big beyond: desert to the east, ocean to the west, and mountains marching north. From up here on her ledge, she could see the giant blinking eye that was the logo of the city eye hospital, with its slogan beneath it: "The Window to Your Soul."

The eye-hospital sign had been there since 1937 and was something of a landmark. People actually traveled downtown to have their picture taken with the neon eye winking above them.

As Ruby sat there on the ledge of the Sandwich, she was contemplating recent events, and the various ways she had almost met her death—the past couple of months had offered a range of possibilities. Death by wolf, death by gunshot, death by exposure, death by cliff fall, death by fire. In one way it didn't make for happy reminiscing, but in another it sort of did. She was alive, after all, because somehow she had dodged bullets—metaphorical and literal—and was now sitting calmly watching the world go by. It was unlike Ruby to dwell on things, but Mr. Death had come so close to knocking at her door that she found herself fascinated by the very thought of it.

Now here she was sitting on the window ledge of a skyscraper, with news of an approaching storm on its way. Some would regard this as a risky activity. Ruby did not. Disappointingly, as far as she was concerned, at this exact moment there were no gusting winds, no adverse weather conditions, not even a stray pigeon looking to take a peck out of her. She judged her spot on Mr. Barnaby H. Cleethorps's windowsill to be no more dangerous than sitting on a park bench in Twinford Square. Well, that wasn't quite true; there was the danger that Mr. Cleethorps would finish his meeting with her father early and they would both give her grief for parking her behind on the ledge of his seventy-second-floor window and playing fast and loose with gravity. But it was hardly the high-octane excitement Ruby had become used to during the past five months as a Spectrum agent.

Ruby was in the Sandwich Building—or rather sitting on the outside of it—because her father had insisted on bringing her to work with him.

"Until that cast comes off your arm, honey, I'm not letting you out of my sight."

Her father had become rather overprotective since Ruby's accident, and he would now only trust her care to his equally jittery wife, Sabina, or the housekeeper, Mrs. Digby. A broken arm, an injured foot, singed hair—how close his only child had come to being burned to a cinder!

Forest fires are very unpredictable. *What was she even doing out there on Wolf Paw Mountain?* Brant Redfort had asked himself, and indeed anyone and everyone who had walked through the door, in the days after the incident.

Brant, as a consequence, was now plagued by fear: he was waking up at four a.m. contemplating the horror of life without his girl. The thought was making him crazy. His fearfulness spread to his wife like a contagious disease, and now for the very first time in Ruby's thirteen years, her parents wanted to know exactly where she was and exactly what she was doing at all times. Ruby was going "nuts," as she so delicately put it.

"Let them worry," advised Mrs. Digby, a wise old bird who had been with the family since Mrs. Redfort was a girl. "They've never had the sane sense to worry before; it will do them the power of good to employ a little imagination."

"Why?" asked Ruby. "What's the point of them getting all torn up with terror? What good is it gonna do them?"

"They're too trusting," replied Mrs. Digby. "They don't see the bad in things like I do." Mrs. Digby was a big believer in seeing the bad in things—think the worst and you will never be disappointed. It was a motto that had stood her in good stead.

So for now Ruby was doing what her parents wanted; she was biding her time and looking forward to the day when she could lose the arm cast and get her parents off her case.

Ruby's father was in advertising—the public relations, meet 'n' greet, shake-you-by-the-hand side of the business. Being friendly to the big clients was an important job, and Brant Redfort was very good at it. Typically, therefore, Brant searched for a tie that might appeal to the client—in this instance, Barnaby Cleethorps, a conservative fellow but a jolly sort. Brant had picked out one that was patterned a little like a red-and-white checkered tablecloth, scattered with tiny picnic things. Just the ticket, he had winked at himself in the mirror.

As Brant came down for breakfast that morning, he caught sight of his daughter, lounging on the patio table, banana milk in one hand, zombie comic in the other, her T-shirt bearing the words *what are you looking at, duh brain?*

He sighed. It seemed unlikely that Ruby would be following him into a career in public relations.

"Now, be careful, Ruby," warned her mother. "There are some unsavory types downtown."

"You do know I'm going to Dad's client's office, don'tcha?" said Ruby, sucking down the dregs of her banana milk.

"Say no more," muttered Mrs. Digby, who had a notion that the advertising business was rife with unsavory types.

Brant kissed his wife on the cheek. "I'll keep an eye on her, honey — never fear. What possible harm can come to her in Barnaby Cleethorps's offices?"

Sabina kissed her daughter and hugged her as if a month might pass before seeing her again.

"Mom, you gotta chill," said Ruby, disentangling herself from her mother's embrace and stepping into the chauffeur-driven, air-conditioned car.

They arrived on Third Avenue and took the elevator up to

the seventy–second floor. Mr. Cleethorps greeted them — "Nice to meet you, young Ruby"— and pumped Ruby's good hand so hard, she thought it might come loose from its socket. "I see you have been in the wars, but I understand from your father that you're quite the brave little lady."

Ruby smiled the smile of a five-year-old, which was obviously what Mr. Cleethorps had mistaken her for. "How about a drink for our small guest," he said. He turned to his assistant, who nodded and smiled and went off to find something suitable — Ruby suspected milk.

As it turned out, she was right. She rolled her eyes. Ruby was not a fan of milk, unless it was flavored with strawberry, chocolate, or her particular favorite, banana.

Once alone, Ruby set about finding a good place to dispose of her beverage. There were no plants in the reception area, and it didn't seem like good manners to tip it into one of the ornamental glass vases. She scanned the room further, and that's when she noticed that a section of the window in the waiting area could be opened. She stood on a stool, reached up, and pulled on the latch. She pushed the window open, and a fresh breeze blew in and Ruby couldn't help wondering how nice it might feel to sit out in that pollution-free air. . . .

And that's how Ruby came to be sitting on the ledge of a very tall building, seven hundred feet above street level, wiggling her toes and contemplating the whole big picture. She felt truly calm sitting there on the edge of nowhere. Ruby Redfort had no issue with heights; she'd never suffered vertigo, never felt that strange desire to let herself fall. Fear had never dominated Ruby's actions, but now fear wasn't even playing a part. It seemed she had reached a state of fearlessness.

Ruby picked up the glass and flung the milk from it, watching it disperse into tiny droplets that disappeared into the air. She placed the empty glass carefully on the ledge and decided she wouldn't mind taking a little wander around the building, see her dad schmoozing Barnaby Cleethorps — why not?

The ledge was relatively wide, and it was easy to walk to the south corner window and peek into Mr. Cleethorps's office. A slide presentation was obviously in progress, since the slatted blinds were all pulled down, and Ruby could only observe what was going on by peeking through the gaps. A number of the Barnaby Cleethorps team were gathered around looking at designs prepared by the creatives at her father's agency. There, projected onto the screen, was the slogan the ad agency had spent weeks fine-tuning: "You Have to Feel It to Believe It!"

Ruby could see Mr. Barnaby Cleethorps's face, and it was not a happy one. She adjusted her position on the ledge so she could see her father's expression. As always, he looked remarkably cool, not in any way flustered, but she knew he must be feeling the strain, because he was heading toward the window, and when her father was feeling tense, his response was usually to let in some air. Tension brought on a sort of claustrophobia—too much stress in one room made it difficult for him to breathe.

Ruby ducked down, making herself as small as she could. Not that Brant could have seen her through the venetian blind, but she didn't want to take any chances.

The opening of the seventy-second-floor window might have helped Brant Redfort regain his calm, but for his daughter it had entirely the opposite effect. The problem was that Ruby had not anticipated *how* the window might open; she was expecting it to hinge in the middle, when in fact this huge window was of the pivoting variety, and as her father yanked it open, Ruby was flung out into thin air. She landed in—or, more accurately, dangled *from*—one of those window-cleaning cradles that travels the length and breadth of skyscrapers, allowing maintenance guys to squeegee the acres of glass. Luckily there were no maintenance guys in it now, though *unluckily* it meant there was no one to pull Ruby back in.

Now, suspended seven hundred feet above the downtown

traffic that crawled and tooted beneath her, she could see the irony of the situation — her father, intent on keeping her safe, had almost brought about her demise.

But at this precise moment she was struggling to see the funny side.

CHAPTER 2
Small Talk

HANGING THERE BY HER FINGERTIPS, Ruby looked down at the map of streets. She could see the city's famous old movie theater, the Scarlet Pagoda; the Japanese garden in front of it; the lampposts decked in bunting and lights to celebrate this year's Twinford Film Festival: A Date with Thrills.

The festival was to be a celebration of romantic thriller movies of the kind that she and Mrs. Digby loved, and the situation Ruby currently found herself in was no doubt one seen in many of these pictures.

Only, for Ruby, this was no stunt; there was no safety net, and she needed to get a grip before someone raised the alarm. She heaved herself into the window-cleaning cradle and found the controls that would carry her back to her original window. She knew which one it was because it had an empty milk glass sitting in front of it.

She was just clambering out of the cradle when she heard a voice.

"Hey, kid, would you come in from there?"

Ruby looked up to see a tall, well-groomed man in a well-cut suit standing in the room. He appeared moderately anxious.

"Am I making you nervous?" asked Ruby.

"The only person making me nervous is the meter maid on Third Avenue, where I'm double-parked."

"Geez, Hitch, why don't you just find a parking spot like a normal person?"

"You think it's easy parking in this city?" Hitch replied.

Ruby sighed, swiveled herself around, and dropped back in through the window. She landed on the long elegant coffee table, the main feature of the sleek reception room. Pens went skidding across its surface and a bowl of marbles overturned, its contents spinning in all directions and disappearing under furniture.

Hitch rolled his eyes. "Good going, kid."

"OK, OK," said Ruby, gathering up the pens and plonking them back in their pen pot. "Don't have a total baby about it, man."

HITCH: *It's not me who's going to have the "baby."*
Mr. Barnaby H. Cleethorps is a very particular man.

RUBY: *What's he gonna do, dangle me out of the window by my toes?*

HITCH: *Probably.*

RUBY: *Boy, this guy must really like his pens tidy!*

HITCH: *You better believe it, Redfort.*

RUBY: *So what are you doing here? You back from summer vacation?*

HITCH: *Something like that.*

RUBY: *Where have you been, anyway?*

HITCH: *It's classified.*

RUBY: *Your vacations are classified?*

HITCH: *I wasn't on vacation.*

RUBY: *But you just said you were.*

HITCH: *No, I didn't; you did.*

RUBY: *Boy, have I missed small-talking to you. So where are we going?*

HITCH: *Elevator.*

RUBY: *You know I can't leave — my dad won't let me out of his sight.*

HITCH: *I've cleared it; your father has entrusted me with your safety.*

RUBY: *He clearly doesn't know your safety record — so what are we doing?*

HITCH: *I'm going to have a cup of coffee, and you are going to be grilled.*

RUBY: *Huh?*

HITCH: *Our boss, she wants to talk to you.*

To the outside world, Hitch was the Redforts' household manager, but to the few in the know, he was actually a highly trained Spectrum agent, living undercover at the Redfort home, stationed there to mentor and protect Ruby Redfort, Spectrum's youngest recruit. Their boss was LB, head of Spectrum 8.

They took the elevator down to street level. It wasn't the quickest ride, since the building was an old one and the elevator cars were far from state-of-the-art.

"I thought I was on sick leave," said Ruby.

"Not anymore," said Hitch.

"Anything going down at Spectrum?" asked Ruby. "A new case?" Ruby had been a Spectrum agent and expert code breaker since April, and in that time she had worked on three cases. All three had nearly gotten her killed. But then evading death sort of went with the territory.

"Don't ask me. I'm just the bozo driving the car," replied Hitch.

Ruby gave him a look, aware that if anyone was going to

know anything, then it was Hitch. But that said, there was no point trying to get him to talk; if he didn't want to, then he never would. That was the thing about Hitch: he kept his mouth shut. **SPECTRUM RULE 1: KEEP IT ZIPPED.** He had to: as one of the highest-ranking agents at Spectrum 8, he was trusted with heavily classified information. He didn't squeal for anything or anybody.

So how had a top-notch spy wound up working undercover as bodyguard to a thirteen-year-old kid? Hitch, for one, asked himself this question practically every day.

They strode out of the Sandwich Building and saw a meter maid busy studying Hitch's car.

Where to start? He was parked in a tow zone, facing in the wrong direction, one of the wheels up on the sidewalk, the vehicle abandoned for twenty-one minutes. This was going to be one long ticket.

Hitch just raised an eyebrow. "Wait here, kid."

The meter maid had her hands on her hips, like she meant business. She looked ready for a fight, like she was thinking, *Here he comes, another bozo who doesn't want to take responsibility for his own dumb actions.*

Hitch strolled over, and the meter maid crossed her arms — a defensive move.

Hitch leaned against his car and began talking—well, not so much talking as chatting. The meter maid shifted her weight and relaxed her arms so she now stood with one hand on her hip—was she actually smiling?

Man, you're good, thought Ruby. Hitch could talk his way out of a maze.

The conversation, for that's what it had become, went on for some time. *What is he telling her?*

The meter maid looked over to where Ruby stood, then she stuck her ticket pad back in her pocket. She laughed and nodded.

She raised an arm as if to high-five Hitch. He wasn't the high-fiving type, Ruby knew that, so instead he gave her a kind of salute. Happy with that, the meter maid walked off whistling a merry tune.

Ruby climbed into the car. "What did you say to her?"

"Just explained what a great kid you are," replied Hitch as he slid into the driver's seat.

"Yeah, right—apart from that?" said Ruby.

"I said I could get her courtside tickets to the Twinford Sneakers play-offs."

"And can you?"

"Sure—the organizer is an old friend of mine."

"I thought you secret agents didn't have friends."

"No, you're thinking of tax inspectors," said Hitch, starting the engine. "I've got more friends than I can handle."

"Funny," said Ruby, "I've never met any of them."

"They're all the shy and retiring type," said Hitch.

Ruby looked at him. "You sure they're not the invisible, imaginary type?"

"Oh, they're just quiet," said Hitch. "A game of cards and an early night."

"Sounds like a hoot — wish I could meet 'em."

"Ah, you wouldn't like 'em, kid," said Hitch. "Not one of them has an interest in bubble gum."

CHAPTER 3

-8

IT WAS NO REAL SURPRISE TO RUBY that Hitch himself was bringing her into HQ today. Sure, she had been into the building's hub many times and worked endless long hours in its secure surrounds, but even so, knowledge of the "way in" was not a given. The spy agency's entrance moved frequently, and Ruby was not among the privileged few informed of Spectrum 8's plans and architectural changes. Hitch was her link to this underground world, and without him, she could very easily find herself shut out in the cold. You mess up, you're out for good.

Last time Ruby had visited was by way of the toddler playground in the middle of Central City Park, and to Ruby's huge annoyance *and* humiliation, Vapona Begwell — fellow pupil, school-yard enemy, and major irritation — had observed her crawling into the kids' caterpillar tunnel. Ruby still hadn't lived it down, and Bugwart (as Ruby called her) wasn't about to let anyone forget it — ever.

Of course, Vapona had no idea what "Little Red Ridingfort" was actually doing in the caterpillar tunnel, and she never would. To tell the secret of Spectrum was forbidden. That said, there was one person outside the organization who did know, and he was Clancy Crew, the most loyal ally a schoolkid could have, and Ruby Redfort's closest friend. He would part with body parts before divulging a sworn-to secret.

"So where is the Spectrum portal this time?" asked Ruby.

"If I told you it was the toddler playground, what would you say?" replied Hitch.

"You have to be kidding!" said Ruby. "You're telling me I have to walk into the little-kid playground and crawl into that tunnel *again*?"

Hitch said nothing.

"Man, I bet this was your idea. You get a big kick outta this, don't you? Humiliate the kid, watch her street credibility sink below zero—I bet you're laughing all day long."

Hitch looked at her out of the corner of his eye.

"You really serious about this?" asked Ruby.

"Nah, I'm just messing with you, Redfort. You should see the look on your face. You know, you can really whine when you want to."

"You shouldn't kid around with people that way. It interferes with a trusting relationship."

"You shouldn't get wound up so easily, Redfort. You'll get a reputation for being flighty."

Ruby glared at him.

It had been around five months now since Hitch had walked through the Redforts' front door and taken up work in their stylish modern home under the guise of household manager. Ruby's mom still insisted on introducing him as the butler, even though Hitch had on many occasions more than hinted that he would prefer her not to.

This kind of undercover work would ordinarily be beneath someone of Hitch's status, but Ruby Redfort was no ordinary assignment. The reason: she was the brightest code breaker to step into Spectrum since the late Bradley Baker. Bradley Baker had begun his career as a boy, had died a man, and was to this day a hero mourned by every agent at Spectrum. Bradley Baker was a legend and — to Ruby — a pain in the derriere.

It was hard to outdo a dead super-agent, but Ruby was certainly in the business of trying. She was ambitious — not just determined to *outclass* Baker's code-breaking ability but also to become at least as good a field agent. Whether she would or not remained to be seen.

So Hitch, for now, was her official protector. He had been a field agent for a long time now and was highly trained in many disciplines. It hadn't exactly been his idea of a whole bunch of fun. Watching over a schoolkid was not without its frustrations, particularly a schoolkid with a big mouth. But Ruby had grown on him. That was the thing about her — you just found yourself wishing she were there even when you wanted her to go jump in a lake.

She was sharp as a tack and keen as a knife, determined, hardworking, loyal, and — luckily — pretty funny as well. There were few Spectrum agents Hitch could say all that about.

Hitch's watch beeped. He took the call through his earpiece, and Ruby had no idea what was being said. All she knew was that three seconds later, they were heading back in the direction they had come and were now making their way once again to the downtown city center.

"What's the deal?" asked Ruby.

"I guess Spectrum is ramping up security," said Hitch. "They've moved the 'way in' again."

"Something happened?" she asked.

"Something's always happened," he replied.

Downtown, all the buildings were tall, even the short ones. Imposing stone department stores, offices, government buildings, banks, and apartment buildings. Skyscrapers rose up hundreds of feet, and when you looked up, the city tapered away into blue. The older Twinfordites often referred to this part of the city as Mini Manhattan or Little L.A., because it bore a certain resemblance to both: a sort of mixture of uptown New York and downtown L.A. Although in terms of square mileage it was not on the same scale as either.

The buildings were by and large attractive, many dating back to the 1920s and '30s. There were newer ones, of course, all glass and steel, but when one stood in just the right spot and looked up beyond the modern street signage and billboards, one could imagine Twinford City past. This was why downtown Twinford was often used for feature films depicting another age, when 1930s mobsters screeched through the streets and elegantly dressed couples danced through the night.

This part of town was an area that Ruby loved — it was exciting somehow to lose one's self, to become anonymous, in the crisscrossing streets, ant-like to someone looking down from the top of the gargantuan architecture.

Hitch parked underneath the building known as the Schroeder, in a single empty space among the seemingly endless rows of stationary cars. There was nothing to indicate that this one lone parking spot had been reserved for Hitch's silver convertible, but Ruby got the impression that somehow it had. The parking ramps spiraled down below them, and Ruby wondered just how many vehicles were sitting under this vast building.

"Fifteen hundred," said Hitch, as if reading her thoughts. "Fifteen hundred seventeen if you count the maintenance team's trucks. All parked on three underground levels under seventy-seven floors of concrete, steel, and glass. Makes the mind boggle, doesn't it?"

"Makes the mind wonder if you shouldn't get out more," said Ruby. "Maybe call up some of those 'fun friends' of yours, live a little."

They climbed out of the car and walked across to the elevator. Someone had scratched a tiny image of a housefly next to the "down" button, and there was a trail line etched into the steel of the doors as if the fly had just buzzed out. The doors opened, and Ruby and Hitch stepped in. When Hitch snapped open what seemed to be an invisible panel and pressed some digits, the doors behind them closed and the doors in front of them opened. They exited. On the other side was a dusty old service elevator. Hitch clanged open its accordion metal gate, and they stepped into the rough wide box. He punched the button marked "−8," and a second or seven later, they began to move unsteadily toward the bottom of the elevator shaft, the dark lit up by a single naked lightbulb that swung above them, casting eerie shadows as they descended.

How many would guess that this tired-looking elevator with its stingy light source might lead to one of the world's most sophisticated intelligence operations? Well, Ruby Redfort might; she had seen it all before.

CHAPTER 4
Avoid the Sharp End

WHEN THE DOORS OPENED, they were in a very different space: huge, subterranean, and sleek. No dust, no cobwebs, no bugs — of either variety.

"So what exactly does our boss want to talk to me about?" asked Ruby.

"It's not my business to say," said Hitch.

Ruby hadn't seen LB, the head of Spectrum 8, since before the whole Blue Wolf mission had kicked off.

The thing was, by the time Ruby had been helicoptered off Wolf Paw Mountain and rushed to the emergency room, LB had had her own crisis to take care of; she'd been called away on urgent duty and unable to attend Ruby's official debrief. That task had been passed to another agent.

"Will she be in a good mood, d'ya think?" said Ruby, knowing this was about as likely as LB showing up in a pink pantsuit (LB only ever wore white).

Hitch didn't answer. He just pointed to a waiting area, with sleek white chairs.

HITCH: *Wait here, kid.*

RUBY: *OK.*

HITCH: *Here? You got that?*

RUBY: *Uh-huh.*

HITCH: *That's a yes, right?*

RUBY: *Uh-huh.*

HITCH: *You'll be called in about fifteen, OK?*

RUBY: *OK.*

HITCH: *Don't move.*

RUBY: *Got it.*

Fifteen minutes, thought Ruby. *Enough time to drink a soda.* And she walked off in the direction of the Spectrum cafeteria.

She got herself a can of Fizz and sat down on one of the stylish chairs arranged around one of the many cool-looking tables, all lit by low-hanging lights. The effect was cozy and conspiratorial. The Spectrum cafeteria was no ordinary work cafeteria—like all things Spectrum, it gave the impression of being very pleased with itself.

Ruby took out her book of rules, a small magenta notebook

with the word **RULES** printed in bright-red letters across the front.

She'd had this book of rules since she was four years old, and it had grown into quite a list over the years. Seventy-nine of them, in fact. Now she had a new rule to add.

RULE 80: DON'T STAND ON A WINDOW LEDGE IF YOU AREN'T COMPLETELY SURE WHETHER THE WINDOW OPENS INWARD OR OUTWARD.

OK, it was quite a specific rule. But a useful one. She'd improve on it later, give it a bit more pizzazz.

"You look better."

Ruby looked up to see Dr. Harper, the Spectrum medic who had treated her when she was brought in from Wolf Paw Mountain.

"Better than what?"

"Better than what you looked like the last time I saw you."

"Yeah, well, last time you saw me, I had the flu, plus an injured foot, a broken arm, and I'd nearly died of being burned to death."

"Yes, your hair doesn't look so good," said Harper, making a face. "Still a bit . . . crispy. So is the arm giving you any trouble?"

"Nah, not really," said Ruby. "But it itches like crazy."

"Yes, that's healing for you," said Dr. Harper. "Itchy."

"Anything you can give me for it?" asked Ruby hopefully.

"Yes," said Dr. Harper, reaching into her top pocket. "This." She handed Ruby a yellow pencil.

"Thanks," said Ruby. "Does it come with any directions?"

"Yes. Avoid the sharp end," replied Dr. Harper.

"How about my foot?"

The doctor gave it the once-over and declared it "good to go."

"You sure?" asked Ruby.

"Trust me — I'm a doctor," said Harper.

"And there I was thinking you might be a comedian. What about my arm?"

"Oh," said Dr. Harper, "that's healed too. I'd cut you out of that cast right now, but I've got to be somewhere." She looked at her watch anxiously.

"A medical emergency?" asked Ruby.

"A table for two at the Twinford Grand," said Dr. Harper.

"You won't help me out of this thing because you've got a lunch date?"

"Did no one ever tell you lunch is the most important meal of the day?"

"That's breakfast," said Ruby.

"Oh, dear, I missed breakfast," said Dr. Harper. "So, I guess it's twice as important that I don't miss lunch."

"I'm glad I'm not *dying*," said Ruby.

"No one dies of an arm cast," said Dr. Harper.

"And you *say* you're not a comedian," said Ruby.

"See you next fall," called Dr. Harper as she made her way out of the cafeteria.

Before Ruby had a chance to get back to her thoughts, a voice came through the cafeteria intercom system. *"Redfort, Ruby, report immediately to Spectrum 8. Agent in charge, office situated on black-and-white level. HQ."*

The voice belonged to the Spectrum information announcer, a person Ruby had never actually laid eyes on but imagined would not be someone you would want to wind up on a desert island with.

She guessed the owner of this voice resided in the same general department as Buzz, the mushroom-like woman who manned the fifty-plus telephones in an office just off the central atrium. Why he couldn't just say, "Ruby Redfort to LB's office, pronto," Ruby didn't know.

She finished her drink and slowly got to her feet, then sauntered off to find LB.

"Howdy," she said as she passed Buzz, who was as usual on the phone and talking to who knew what. Buzz blinked at her, pointed to her watch, and continued her call.

As Ruby approached LB's office, she could see that the door was slightly ajar, and as she got nearer, she could hear fragments of a discussion, the voices semi-hushed. She could only pick up words at intervals, so they were separated from their meaning:

"apparently removed without authorization . . ."

". . . from the Department of Defense?"

"that's what we've been told"

"highly classified?"

"affirmative . . ."

"but how could anyone make it in?"

"entered via an air vent . . . I know it seems impossible"

"nothing else tampered with?"

"No sign of anything else missing, no sign of anyone or anything anywhere else in the building."

"You worried about our security?"

"Always. I'm . . ."

". . . but only an idiot would attempt —"

She knocked, and the conversation stopped dead.

"Come in," said LB, her voice sounding even more gravelly and drawn out than usual. "And close the darned door, Redfort."

Ruby pushed the door shut behind her and walked over to

the empty seat next to Hitch. He tapped his watch and gave her a look to say, *Why in the world of reason can't you follow orders?* She slung her satchel across the back of the chair and slumped down. Then she looked from LB to Hitch.

Hitch's brow was ever so slightly furrowed; LB seemed not quite as composed as usual. In her hand was an object that she was turning over and over: a smooth rectangle of clear plastic or Lucite, the shape and size of a key tag, perhaps. But the thing attached to it was no house key, or at least, if it was, it was a pretty state-of-the-art locking device. When LB caught Ruby's gaze, she frowned and slipped the thing into the pocket of her white jacket.

"What's with you guys?" asked Ruby. "Did your kittens get run over or something?"

Hitch raised an eyebrow. "I *wish* the problem were a simple case of a couple of flat cats," he said, "and I speak as a cat lover."

"Must be serious, then," said Ruby. "So you gonna tell me about it?"

"No," said LB.

Ruby shrugged. "OK. So anything you *do* wanna share?"

LB gathered her papers into a neat pile and then peered at Ruby through her large white-rimmed soft-tinted glasses. Today she looked tired. *Working late? Or is she not sleeping so good?*

"So. You did well, Redfort. It's a pity that you couldn't manage to secure the wolf, but you prevented the suspect from acquiring it and that is *something*."

LB was referring to the previous case Ruby had been assigned to, when she had indeed done well, albeit in a messy, skin-of-her-teeth sort of way. She had used her code-breaking and detective skills to figure out who had let loose a load of rare wild animals from a zoo owned by a private collector. She had discovered that the zookeeper was to blame, though he had later been murdered by those who had commissioned the crime.

The perpetrators had been a young woman, believed to be a perfumer, named Lorelei von Leyden, and her mysterious sponsor, about whom they knew nothing other than that—based on her accent and the location of her initial coded message—she was Australian. Both were prepared to kill more than once to get their hands on the cyan scent—an intoxicating perfume extracted from the near-extinct cyan wolf. The scent was the stuff of myth and legend; a few drops were worth a small fortune.

The only problem was some of this scent had been successfully stolen.

"Unfortunately," said LB, echoing Ruby's thoughts, "they got away with it. So while I can congratulate you for cracking the case, I can't help but feel it is a shame that you managed to let the vial of cyan get into enemy hands and the two main assailants disappear into the wide blue yonder. But there we are: amateur hour, I daresay, comes to us all."

LB had an unfortunate way of turning what might first be construed as praise into something rather more approaching a dressing-down. Fortunately or unfortunately, Ruby had become accustomed to it and didn't let it bother her.

"Going back to the events of that particular encounter, can you repeat again exactly what it was that the Australian woman said to you before she encouraged you to walk off that cliff?"

"I'm unlikely to forget," said Ruby. "I thought they were gonna be the last words I ever heard." This was no lie.

Ruby paused for a second, concentrating so she might recall it perfectly, and then said, "She asked me to hand over the vial of cyan — she had a gun, so I did. I guess I thought she was intending to sell it for its perfume value, since it's worth a lot — so I said, *'All this so you can make some money out of some stupid fragrance.'* And she said, *'Is that what you think this is about? No, sweetie, this is not about some high-end perfume counter cluttered up with rich folks wanting to waste their money. This is about something important, more important than you could ever imagine.'*"

LB said nothing, but stared straight ahead into the middle distance as if trying to focus on something that was too far away to see. No one spoke, and the silence was only broken by the sound of Buzz's voice coming through the intercom.

"Agent Farrow from Security is here to see you."

LB nodded. "I'll be one minute." She turned back to Ruby. "Well, Redfort, I recognize that you showed great initiative and courage when you went into the mountains to recover the cyan wolf, but . . ."

She paused. Ruby looked over at Hitch; his face betrayed nothing.

"*But,*" continued LB, "you also headed into the field alone and without backup. You ignored direct Spectrum orders. And you would not be alive today if one of our agents hadn't risked his life to haul you out of there."

Ruby opened her mouth to protest.

LB raised her hand. "As I said, you displayed good qualities. But you also took unacceptable risks. So as of this moment, you are off the field agent program. To put it in terms you might understand, you're grounded, Redfort."

"You have to be *kidding,*" said Ruby.

"You think I have *time* to kid around?" said LB. Her eyes were steel — nothing about her suggested that she ever kidded around. "You will be permitted to take one further test, and your results will be evaluated. The outcome will determine your future field-agent suitability." She looked over at Hitch. "You can thank your colleague here for this chance. Be ready for it. There will be no warning; if you fail to show, you fail the test."

LB stood, gathered her papers, and exited the room. Not another word spoken; silence but for the swish of her elegant white skirt as she padded barefoot down the corridor.

When they were alone, Ruby turned to Hitch. *"Grounded?"*

Hitch looked her square in the eye. "Be more grateful," he said. "LB was ready to kick you off the field training for good and always."

"Why? I cracked the case."

"You solved *part* of the case," said Hitch. "But you let the bad guys get away. And you nearly died in the process."

"Nearly dying is a sackable offense?"

"Redfort, we can't afford to lose good code breakers, nor, for that matter, agents. A lot of investment goes into training you. And when you play fast and loose with your life, every last one of our lives is also at risk."

Ruby said nothing.

"Besides," he said, "do you have any idea how difficult it is to find thirteen-year-old schoolkids who can crack a code?"

She looked at him. "Yeah right," she said.

They left Spectrum, rode the elevator back to ground level, and were once again in the Schroeder parking garage. They climbed into the car. "So who's the idiot, anyway?" asked Ruby.

"What idiot?" asked Hitch.

"The idiot you were talking about when I arrived."

"*You are* if you think I'm blabbing to a schoolkid."

"Worth a shot," said Ruby.

"Which is what Spectrum might think if I go ahead and repeat classified information without authorization."

"They'd *shoot* you?"

"They might consider it."

"Really?"

"No, Redfort, not really, at least I doubt it, but they might fire me."

"That would suck," she said.

Hitch nodded. "Yes, it would. I'd have to go and get a *real* job." He shuddered.

"I'm sure my parents would keep you on."

"Yes," said Hitch. "That's exactly what I'm afraid of."

Meanwhile,
via a secure transmitter line,
a man and woman were
talking. . . .

"So you have the 8 key?"

"No."

"No?"

"No."

"Why not?"

"It can't be done."

"Everything can be done."

"You don't understand. The subject has kept it safe. Security has been increased since I acquired the other two items —"

"Why two items? I only instructed you to bring back one."

"I took something for myself. I saw it in their lab as I was leaving and thought I could use it."

"Use it for what?"

"It's personal."

"I'm not paying you to steal 'useful' items for yourself. I don't want you attracting attention by busting into labs and taking what you want."

"Relax. They won't even know I took it; they won't even know I was there."

"Just don't get distracted, Birdboy. You need to keep your eye on the ball."

"I'll get what you want, but you need to give me time."

"I don't have time. I need it now!"

"It's not easy to access."

"Of course not. I wouldn't need you if it was."

"It's more difficult than I thought."

"I thought you were supposed to be brilliant."

"I thought you were supposed to be dead, Valerie."

"You see? Everything's possible."

"Becoming *undead* is possible?"

"It would seem so."

CHAPTER 5
A Little Off Balance

HEY, RUBE," SAID HER FATHER, LOOKING UP. He was in the living room and looking weary. He was lounging back in his chair, the one he liked to sit in if his day had been tough. Mr. Barnaby Cleethorps had obviously been a handful. Hitch was mixing a drink at the bar.

"Good trip to the dentist?" asked Brant.

"Uh?" said Ruby. "The dentist? Umm . . ."

"That's OK, honey—dumb question. When does one ever want to go to the dentist, right?"

"When one has a cavity?" said Ruby.

"So you had a cavity?" said her father.

"False alarm," said Ruby, wondering why Hitch hadn't briefed her about the "trip to the dentist."

"Hitch was with you the whole time, of course?" her father asked anxiously.

"Oh, yeah, he was there, all right." She flashed a look at Hitch. "*Weasel,*" she mouthed.

Hitch handed Ruby a glass of lemonade and whispered as he passed, "Just keeping you on your toes, kid. Keep sharp and stay alive."

"What a lovely sentiment. I'll be sure to write it in your next birthday card," hissed Ruby, giving him a death stare.

Brant Redfort looked at his watch. "Do you think supper's ready?"

"I hope so. I'm starving," said Ruby.

"You didn't eat lunch?" Brant asked, alarmed.

"Yeah, sure I did. I'm just sorta double hungry these days. Probably the healing process; one needs to eat twice as much."

Brant Redfort looked troubled. "I'll talk to your mother about it; can't have my girl's healing process compromised," he said, ruffling her hair. She tried not to growl at him—she hated the hair-ruffle thing—but her father looked so tired she didn't want to give him a hard time.

"So what else happened today?" he asked.

"The doc said I could finally get this lump of plaster sawed off," said Ruby, holding her cast up.

"That's swell news, honey."

"I wanna do it as quick as possible," said Ruby. "Tomorrow would be good, you know what I'm saying?"

"The Scarlet Pagoda! Absolutely. You'll want to look your best for tomorrow night's theater fund-raiser."

"That's right, Dad. Looking my best is what I live for."

"Look, I'll call Dr. Shepherd. I'll bet he can wriggle you onto his list — get one of his guys to do it. I don't want just anyone sawing into my Rube's arm." He mussed her hair again and picked up the phone.

"Hello, Frank. Brant here. . . . Very well, thank you! And you? . . . And Wallis? . . . And the kids? . . . And your parents? . . . Your sister Betty? . . . Glad to hear it. The thing is, Ruby needs a plaster cast removed pronto, and I was wondering if you could slide her in tomorrow, get one of your best guys to do it? . . . Swell, Frank, I appreciate it. I'll wait to hear from you." He hung up. "Looks like you're all set for tomorrow night's costume shindig. All of fashionable Twinford will be turning out for it. And you know we Redforts have to be there looking like a million dollars."

Ruby did know. Her parents were nice — more than nice. They were very, very likable, friendly, sociable, popular people. Take this Scarlet Pagoda fund-raiser, for example. Mr. and Mrs. Redfort were right at the top of the invitation list. If they hadn't been able to make the date, then there was a good chance that the date would have been changed to fit with their social schedules. They were fun folk, influential, and they always gave generously.

Their daughter, Ruby, was also popular, but in a totally different way and for totally different reasons. For one thing, she did not go out of her way to be friendly. She was never willfully unkind or unfair, but she didn't feel the need to be liked for the sake of being liked. She felt no motivation to be popular and perhaps for this very reason, she was. Magnetically so.

"Thanks, Dad," said Ruby, heading toward the stairs.

"No problem," said Brant. "Soon that arm cast will be behind you and you'll be back playing Ping-Pong with your pals."

Brant Redfort was unaware that Ruby *had* been playing Ping-Pong with her pals *and* doing numerous other things she always did. She wasn't going to let a broken arm cramp her style, and she wasn't afraid of a little pain.

Ruby went on up to her room, closed the door securely behind her, and pulled at a wooden slat that concealed a secret compartment where she kept one of her yellow notebooks (the other 624 were hidden under the floorboards, and not a living human soul had ever read one word of what she wrote). It was in these that she noted down everything of interest and anything that *might* one day be of interest. Her **RULE 16** being **EVEN THE MUNDANE CAN TELL A STORY** and her **RULE 34** being

YOU NEVER KNOW WHEN SOMETHING IS GOING TO COME IN HANDY — this included seemingly useless information.

Ruby picked up a pen and wrote:

```
What is the test I have to pass? How can I
find out? Need to be prepared.

What were LB and Hitch talking about,
exactly? Something removed or possibly
stolen? From a high-security location?

LB looked edgy, off her game. Why?
```

Ruby didn't know the answers to any of these questions, but one thing was for sure — she was going to try to find out. There was no *way* she was going to put up with this whole *grounded* deal.

Later, at dinner, Ruby was listening to her parents discussing the proposed renovation of the Scarlet Pagoda. Tomorrow night's party was in aid of this cause. There would be a high-end raffle, and some of the prizes were quite spectacular; Sabina, for example, had her heart set on winning the Ada Borland portrait — Ada Borland being a world-famous photographer who had offered as one of the prizes the extreme honor of photographing the winner or their loved one. Sabina had bought approximately fifty-two raffle tickets to date.

Aside from this highlight, Sabina was in charge of commissioning the famous Twinford sculptor Louisa Parker to create a piece of art that might stand in the Japanese garden in front of the theater once the restoration work was completed. There had been much discussion among committee members about who the sculpture should represent. No one could agree, most feeling it should be either the person donating the largest sum of money to the theater fund or someone of influence in Twinford society, but everyone hoped the resulting sculpture would be a lot more attractive than Mayor Abrahams's recent statue, which loomed down from the Skylark Building and scared the living daylights out of everyone who saw it.

"It should be a sculpture of someone who performed at the theater during its heyday," said Sabina.

"How about a star from a film shown there when it first became a movie theater?" suggested Brant.

"Or," said Sabina, her eyes lighting up as the flicker of a very good idea came to her, "how about someone whose film was *set* in the Scarlet Pagoda and then later *shown in* the Scarlet Pagoda?"

"You mean thingy?" said Brant.

"Yes, what's-her-name," agreed Sabina.

"Yes, the film star being honored this year . . ." said Brant.

They both looked at Ruby.

"Margo Bardem," said Ruby. "Her career began in the Scarlet Pagoda as an assistant hairdresser and makeup artist. She got spotted and stepped in to replace the main actress in her debut movie, *The Cat That Got the Canary,* produced and directed by George Katsel, who later married Bardem. It was both filmed on location in the Scarlet Pagoda and premiered there in 1952."

"Ruby, you are like a sitting encyclopedia," said her mother, clapping her hands together.

"I read the film festival publicity flyer," said Ruby.

"I just hope we raise enough money to rescue that beautiful building," said Brant. "Can you imagine a Twinford without the Scarlet Pagoda?"

"I'm not sure the wrecking ball wouldn't be such an unwelcome idea for that old pile," said Mrs. Digby as she entered the room with a large casserole dish.

"Oh, Mrs. Digby!" exclaimed Sabina. "You surely don't mean that."

"When you've grown up in a rotten falling-down old shack during the Great Depression, I tell you, you set your sights on something wipe-clean and fungus free."

Sabina was speechless.

"I'll tell you something for nothing," said Mrs. Digby, heaving the huge dish onto the table. "You wouldn't get me stepping one little toe into that Scarlet Pagoda, no siree, thank you for asking."

"Whyever not?" asked Sabina.

"The spirit world is why not," said Mrs. Digby folding her arms.

"You're not serious, Mrs. D. You surely don't believe that old hokum about hauntings?" said Brant.

"Call it what you will, but don't expect me to be there."

"But you love those old movies," said Ruby. "Just think, you might even get the chance to meet some of your screen idols."

"I'm not risking it," said Mrs. Digby. "I might find myself face to face with the paranormal."

"Are you for real?" said Ruby. "You actually believe in all that?"

"I most certainly do," said Mrs. Digby. "Kicking and screaming is the only way you'll drag me in there."

"So we can't interest you in a free ticket to the costume show tomorrow night?" asked Sabina.

"You most certainly can't," said Mrs. Digby.

"So who on earth should we invite at this short notice?" said Sabina.

"Ask Elaine Lemon," said Brant.

"Good idea," said Mrs. Digby. "She'd scare the pants off any ghoul going."

At which point the telephone rang.

Ruby left the table and answered the phone. "Hello, Clance," she said. He often called during supper: he couldn't seem to get the hang of the fact that not everyone ate at the exact same time as his family.

"Hey, how'd you know it was me?" said Clancy.

"Because I'm midway through dinner and you often call when I'm midway through dinner," replied Ruby. "It's a probability thing. The likelihood is it will be you — you or Mrs. Lemon."

"Is that so?"

"Yes."

"Do you want me to hang up?"

"Not now that you've already interfered with my whole digestive process."

"Oh, OK."

"So why did you call?"

"I wondered if you got my message."

"What message?"

"The one I left in the tree."

"What did it say?"

"Call me immediately."

"So, obviously not."

"That's what I thought."

"So why did you want me to call?"

"To see if you might wanna meet up, no big deal or anything."

"Why didn't you leave a message on my answering machine?"

"I'm not sure." Pause. "Force of habit?"

"Ruby, honey," called her mother, "could you maybe put down the phone and come back to the table. It's such a shame when the family dinner is interrupted by the telephone. And it plays crazy potatoes with one's digestion."

"You hear that, Clance? Now you've upset my mom's digestive process too."

"Extend my apologies," said Clancy.

"You can extend them yourself if you wanna come over."

"Nah, I feel like sitting up a tree."

"Look, how about I see you in twenty minutes on Amster Green. I need to get out, stretch my legs, and get some decent conversation."

"I thought your folks wouldn't let you out on your own," said Clancy.

"I'll bring Bug," said Ruby. "You know what they say: you're never alone with a husky at your side."

"Who says *that*?" muttered Clancy as he hung up the phone.

Ruby sat down at the table.

"What's that on your face?" asked her mother. She was peering at her now, fork in hand, studying her daughter's face. "Is it a bruise?"

"Probably dirt," said Ruby. "I might go take a shower."

But Sabina reached out her hand and began rubbing at Ruby's cheek.

"Ow," cried Ruby.

"That's not dirt," confirmed Sabina. "You're probably anemic, people bruise easily when they're anemic—and they become anemic when their body is under stress."

"OK, OK, I promise I'll stop being anemic if you lay off rubbing my face," said Ruby.

"A good healthy diet is what you need, young lady. Plenty of . . . what's it called, Brant?"

"Iron," said Ruby.

"I'll order some in," said Sabina, dropping her napkin and leaving the table. "Tomorrow is the Scarlet Pagoda costume benefit, and I don't want you looking like one of the exhibits."

CHAPTER 6
A Stroll with a Husky

RUBY WAS RIGHT — her parents did agree to let her take a walk with Bug at her side. It was of course "thanks to that dog" that Ruby was alive at all.

If he hadn't come running back to alert the fire crew to her plight, then she wouldn't be here today with a broken arm, injured foot, and badly singed hair. Sabina had told all her friends the story of their hero dog. This account of Ruby's rescue was true, of course, minus a few key details.

Ruby and her ever-loyal husky set off down Cedarwood Drive and at the corner turned right onto Amster Street. On her way to the green, Ruby dropped by Marty's mini-mart to pick up some bubble gum. Ordinarily she would carry a pack with her, but she had been unusually careless and her dad had found her stash of Hubble-Yum under the couch while she was in the hospital getting her arm fixed up and had disposed of it. Her father was waging a one-man war against bubble gum.

Ruby came out of the mini-mart and noticed a kid with a styled-unstyled look. He was standing there with two other boys but he sort of looked like he might be waiting for someone. When she passed him, he half turned around like he might say something to her, but he didn't. Instead he jumped on his skateboard and grabbed the bumper of a passing truck and was carried off into the traffic.

It was kind of impressive — dangerous, sure, but practical in a cool sort of way. Skitching was something she needed to try.

When Ruby reached the green, she looked up at the old oak and searched for some sign of Clancy. She could see the bike that had once been hers and was now his, but he was not visible. She whistled — two short, one long — and immediately the whistle came back, one long two short. He was already up high in the tree's branches.

Bug lay down on the grass — he knew the deal — and waited patiently while Ruby set about climbing. It took longer than usual, what with her arm trouble, but she was a good climber, so she made it OK.

Ruby and Clancy Crew sat side by side on the old oak's highest sitting branch. From here they looked down on Amster Green and its surrounding shops. The leaves were so plentiful that no one could see Ruby and Clancy from the sidewalk. The two of them used the tree not only for hanging out in, but also as a good place to hide coded messages for each other. Even if someone was smart enough to find the origami notes in the knots of the tree's bark, they certainly wouldn't be smart enough to decipher them.

The sun was still hot considering the time of day, so the foliage provided welcome shade. Though summer vacation was nearly over, there was no sign of summer's end or of fall's beginning anywhere on the horizon — not a frost-curled leaf or a gusty breeze. Certainly no one yet believed that it was ever going to be any different, any cooler. It seemed no Twinfordite could remember back to when the weather had been anything less than 80 degrees. It had been a remarkable summer. The best of it had meant beach time and barbecues and long social evenings, swimming in backyard pools and hanging out late into the night, but no one could deny that this had come at a cost — the heat wave had exhausted the city and left forests ravaged by fire. The fire services had been on red alert and crime had been a little higher too, something to do with the temperature boiling people's minds, or so the psychologists said.

"My mom doesn't think the weather's ever gonna break," said Clancy.

"Yeah, well, your mom's wrong," said Ruby.

"Well, duh, of course I know that. I'm just making the point that it's hard to imagine. It just seems so normal, being hot all the time, never having to remember a sweater, for instance."

"Yeah," said Ruby, "but any day now it's gonna break, and when it does, you'll be needing more than a sweater." She scratched her broken arm by sliding the yellow pencil under the cast and moving it from side to side.

"I can't wait that long," said Clancy.

"Chew on some ice or something," suggested Ruby. "Oh, boy, will I ever be glad to get this cast removed."

"When are they hacking it off?" asked Clancy, who was hoping to be there when the nurse cut through the plaster with the electric saw thing.

"Tomorrow," said Ruby. "They warned me when I had it put on that my arm might be all withered and hairy and not the same as the other one."

Clancy stared at her, his mouth forming an O.

"Don't look so excited about it," said Ruby.

"I wasn't looking excited, I was looking interested. I mean, mismatched arms — could be cool."

"Well, the hairiness is temporary."

"Shame," said Clancy. "Hey, have you been watching that show?"

"What show?"

"That illusionist guy, Darnley Rex," said Clancy. "He has a new show, you know, magic and stuff. Boy, does it ever do your head in."

"It's all about planting an idea in your brain. It's all done with words, that's what you gotta remember," said Ruby. "Before you know it, they have convinced your mind to think you are seeing something else or even are something else, and the next thing you know you are clucking like a chicken."

"I sorta wish it was magic, though," said Clancy. "I mean I know it isn't, but wouldn't it be crazy if it was?"

"I don't know," said Ruby. "If Darnley Rex could get the whole country clucking like chickens, then he could take over the world. Not a happy prospect."

A minute passed before Clancy ventured, "So have they given you a medal yet?"

"Who?" said Ruby.

"Spectrum. Has Spectrum awarded you a medal?"

"A medal for what?" said Ruby.

Clancy looked puzzled. "For nearly being burned alive in a forest fire, of course."

"Why would they do that? People don't just go around getting medals for not getting burned alive in forest fires. Otherwise everyone and anyone would get one.”

“OK, not just for not getting burned alive, but how about all that other stuff you did?”

“That’s what I’m paid for. That is my actual job,” said Ruby. She paused. “Though, maybe not for much longer,” she added.

“What?”

“Spectrum. They’ve taken me off field training indefinitely.”

“Indefinitely?” said Clancy.

“Well, unless I take this test and pass it. Fail and I’m out, stuck at a desk for the rest of my career, like old Froghorn. It’s kind of a last-chance-saloon kind of deal.”

“You’re not serious!” said Clancy. He was flapping his arms now. “You cracked that whole wolf case! They should be giving you a medal to show their appreciation for a job well done and all that, like in the army, not —”

“Look, Clance,” Ruby interrupted. “A: this ain’t the army, and B: it wasn’t a job well done. I’m bummed about it too, but I think what you gotta understand is that it isn’t really a thanking-with-a-medal-type situation — I mean, there’s no ‘thanking’ in secret agenting. You do well, you get another assignment; you louse up, you get your marching orders — that’s about it. I pulled it outta the bag with the whole code-breaking-and-case-solving thing, but I loused up my survival training, nearly got myself killed, and worse — lost what was left of the cyan perfume. It's not medal-worthy stuff. So . . . I guess I'm lucky I'm even getting another chance."

She didn't feel lucky, though. She felt royally mistreated.

"What's the test?" Clancy asked.

"No idea."

"But you'll pass it, right?"

"I sure hope so," said Ruby. She didn't want to think about what she'd do if she got kicked out of the Spectrum Field Agent Training Program. Sure, she got a big buzz out of code breaking, but she lived for the thrill of working as a bona fide all-action agent.

They climbed back down the tree. Ruby was quicker on the descent, but when she made the final jump from the low branch to the ground, she stumbled and found she was unable to steady herself. She thumped down on the grass and landed awkwardly on her shoulder.

"Rube, you sure you're ready to go back to work?" asked Clancy.

"Sure, I'm sure — never felt better, considering." She dusted herself down.

"Well, that's great, Rube, but have you considered that this traumatic event may have had a traumatic impact on you? Subconscious and all—but there nonetheless?"

"Have you been reading your aunt Tatum's psychology books again?"

"I'm just saying."

"Clancy, you're overthinking stuff. I am totally A-OK, except for I have a very itchy and possibly hairy arm."

"I hate to be the one to notice, but your balance is a little off too, like you're not so sure of yourself," remarked Clancy.

"My balance is good, better than good—great. It's just this cast throwing me off."

Clancy looked at her hard. "If you say so, Rube, then I believe you."

He didn't believe her, not for a minute. Ruby knew that, but she didn't want to discuss it further. Talking about this kind of stuff was fine when it related to other people; in fact she found it fascinating. Talking about this stuff in relation to her was very tedious.

When she got back home she went straight to her room and on up to the roof, where she could sit in private and think her own thoughts undisturbed. What she was thinking about was the Spectrum test. What would it be? Survival? Agility? Strength?

And what would happen if she failed?

It was too awful to contemplate.

She stared up into the starlit sky and searched for meteors. It was the end of the season but she couldn't help looking, and Ruby's patience knew few bounds. It was like a sort of meditation, looking up into the infinity above her, and it allowed her to think. She heard the soft padding feet of her dog.

"Hey there, boy." She scratched him behind the ears. "What's next for old Ruby Redfort, do you think?" She looked at the husky like he might answer back.

Three cases and five months into her agent career and she already felt like she had always done the job — she certainly wasn't ready to give it up.

She thought back to the past month's events — the meeting with the Australian, her close encounter with the perfumer Lorelei . . . There was more to that whole conspiracy than she could fathom. Why had the Australian woman commissioned Lorelei to steal the cyan scent? What was she planning to do with it? Where were they now? What did they really want and when would they resurface? Perhaps never, though this seemed unlikely — in every thriller she had ever read, the evil genius always came back for a curtain call.

Ruby found herself actually longing for this to be the case for these two, and she wished with a strange hope that it would be sooner rather than later. . . . Her curiosity made her want it so.

As Ruby gazed up at the dark sky, her hand on Bug's warm head, she heard distant sirens, lots of them, drifting through the night air from downtown Twinford. They sounded like a warning cry of things to come. And as Ruby listened, another alarm sounded in her mind, and she was suddenly almost able to hear LB's voice, the words sharp and unequivocal: *Too much curiosity can be fatal.*

It was a warning Ruby had been given on many occasions and had always ignored. Would she heed it this time?

History suggested not.

**High
above the
howling sirens . . .**

. . . above the slow-turning red-and-white lights of emergency vehicles, a tiny figure walked across the barely illuminated sky. He trod the air between two colossal buildings, his feet feeling the invisible path, skywalking.

The sirens and lights were not for him. Farther down the street, a building was burning.

Well, it was none of his concern.

When he had crossed the void, he stepped lightly onto the rooftop and vanished as if he were a mere figment of the imagination.

CHAPTER 7
The Wake-Up Call

RUBY REDFORT WOKE TO THE SOUND of the telephone. At least, she thought it was a telephone. She stumbled out of bed and staggered to her feet. But she couldn't seem to locate the ringing. She had a lot of phones — a whole collection of them. One shaped like a shell, one a lobster, another a squirrel in a tux. There was also a donut, a hamburger, a few shaped like telephones, and a whole lot more.

As Ruby scanned the room, trying to work out where exactly the noise was coming from, it slowly dawned on her that the sound was no ringing phone and in fact was almost certainly emanating from her watch, which was tucked away in her desk drawer. The watch was no ordinary Timex, Ingersoll, or Swiss. This watch was custom-made, multifunctional, radio equipped, and though often referred to as a Rescue Watch, its official title was the Spectrum Escape Watch. It had once belonged to Bradley Baker when he was a kid.

Now it belonged to Ruby.

Ruby picked it up and switched it to speak mode.

"So how's the broken arm doing?" came a perky voice.

"You woke me to ask me that?" said Ruby.

"It's ten a.m.," said the voice.

"I wasn't aware," said Ruby.

"Perhaps you should set your alarm."

"I don't need to. I've got people like you bothering me."

"So the arm, is it giving you any trouble?"

"Yeah, it's preventing me from sleeping."

"How's that?"

"People keep calling to ask how it is."

"Is that so," said the voice. "And how is it?"

"Itchy," said Ruby.

"That's a good sign," said the voice. "Means it's healing."

"So people keep telling me. By the way, do you mind giving me some idea of who you are?" Ruby asked.

"Oh, I'm sorry. Did I neglect to say?"

"Uh-huh." Ruby yawned.

"I'm Agent Gill. LB asked me to coordinate your field test. Just wanted to say hi."

"Hi back," said Ruby, scratching her arm with the yellow pencil. She tottered into the bathroom and examined her face in the mirror. "So this is a survival test?" she asked, fake-casually.

"I can neither confirm nor deny," said Gill. "When's the cast coming off?"

"Today," said Ruby.

"That's good because you're going to need both arms for this; fitness is key."

"Isn't it always?" said Ruby.

"That's correct, so you might want to get back on your bicycle and put in some miles. Give yourself a bit of a workout."

"I would, only I don't have a bike," said Ruby.

"Sure you do—I've seen you riding around. Yellow, isn't it?"

"Green," said Ruby.

"That's the one," said Gill. "Yep, you got to get back on that green bike of yours."

"It's blue," said Ruby.

"You just said it was green."

"Not anymore."

"How so?" said Gill.

"I sprayed it Windrush blue and gave it to my pal Clancy."

"That was nice of you," said Gill.

"Yeah, maybe, but it leaves me walking, I guess."

Gill sighed down the end of the phone line. "That's what you get for being nice."

"Tell me about it," said Ruby.

"My advice: take up jogging," said Gill.

"You woke me to suggest I should take up jogging?"

"No," said Gill, "I woke you to inform you that you'll be contacted any day soon, maybe in the next few hours. You need to be on standby."

"You contacted me to tell me that you'll be contacting me?"

"Correct, I'll be contacting you," said Gill, and hung up.

Ruby's watch vibrated. She looked at the words that appeared on the glass that covered the dial.

Be prepared!

"I'll count the hours," muttered Ruby. The truth was that despite her sarcastic tone, she really was counting the hours. Life as it had been before Spectrum recruitment now seemed humdrum. Sure, she could happily live a week or two without the thrill of spy agency work: her friends were amusing, her family likable; there were books; there was music, museums, galleries, movies, diners, roller skates, the great outdoors, the great indoors, and then there was TV, and of course Ping-Pong—all available to entertain, occupy, and stretch her curious mind. But Ruby was no ordinary thirteen-year-old; her mind needed a lot of stretching and occupying.

As Ruby set about looking for things to wear, she noticed a note, clearly pinned on her door by Mrs. Digby. It said:

DON'T FORGET THE DO TONIGHT! 6:30 SHARP. MAKE
SURE YOU'VE WASHED BEHIND YOUR EARS (WITH SOAP).
P.S. YOUR MOTHER HAS BOUGHT YOU A DRESS
(YOU'RE NOT GONNA LIKE IT).

Ruby rolled her eyes and began the search for her Yellow Stripe sneakers and a fresh T-shirt. Her eyes settled on one — red with black text, the words pleading: *please tell me I'm not awake.*

Ruby had many T-shirts, all pretty similar in tone, all bearing slogans, statements, or questions, some funny, some impolite, some funny and impolite. They caused her mother great consternation, but Ruby wasn't the sort of kid to let someone else's opinion get in the way of her wardrobe, particularly not her mother's.

"You'll appreciate me one day," Sabina would often say.

"Mom, I appreciate you now," was always Ruby's reply. "It's just these outfits you keep buying me are causing me to appreciate you less than I would if you didn't buy them."

The intercom in Ruby's room buzzed. "Yuh huh," said Ruby into the speaker.

"This is your housekeeper—you know, the wretched old lady who attends to your every need?"

"Hello, Mrs. Digby. What can I do for you?"

"Just reminding you about tonight," said the housekeeper. "Your mother and father want you hosed down, dressed, shoes shined, standing at the front door by six thirty sharp."

"You already told me that in your note—anything else you wanna repeat?"

"Yep, six thirty sharp—be there or be in peril."

Mrs. Digby had been housekeeper to the Redforts for just about ever and she knew Ruby inside out and back to front. And one thing she was sure as eggs is eggs about was that Ruby Redfort would never be winning any punctuality award. She was a terrible timekeeper.

The buzzer buzzed again. "There's a note from your father, stuck to the refrigerator."

"And?" said Ruby.

"And what?" said Mrs. Digby.

"And what does it say?"

"If you got your lazy self down here, you could see for yourself."

The housekeeper hung up, and Ruby went downstairs to find something to eat.

The note was still on the refrigerator. It read:

Dr. Shepherd has found time for you in his
schedule. Be at the St. Angelina hospital at
1:15 p.m. My chauffeur, Bob, will pick you up
from the house at 12:30 and bring you home.
Do not take the subway. And seriously,
honey, don't be late — the guy is
doing me a big favor here.
Love, Pop

Ruby looked at her watch; she had more than a couple of hours before she needed to be there. Time enough to check out the vintage store on Amster and find a dress she might want to wear to the evening's event. Obviously she wasn't going to wear the dress her *mother* had picked for her. But maybe if she wore *a* dress, it would make Sabina happy.

She got lucky — the dress she particularly liked fit perfectly, or at least would once she applied a little tape to the hem. She also found a cool-looking old paperback thriller that she thought might be an OK read. Her dad had booked his chauffeur to pick her up way too early. She still had plenty of time, and she would rather read her book in the sun than in an air-conditioned waiting room. She would make a call.

As she was leaving, she caught sight of a pay phone in front of the store. She dialed her father's number and was put through to his personal assistant.

"Hi, Dorothy. Sabina Redfort here. Look, I've decided to drive Ruby to the hospital myself. You know how it is with kids — I just want to be sure she gets there on time and I know Bob's a wonderful chauffeur and all but can he wrestle a teenager into a car on time? I doubt it." (Ruby laughed in exactly the way her mother would.) "Yes, Dorothy, I hear you! So if you could cancel Bob, I would be very grateful. Oh and don't tell my husband — he will think I'm being a worry worm. . . . It's wart? Really? Worrywart?" (She laughed again.) "Bye, bye, bye."

Ruby's impersonation of her mother had gotten so good over the years that not even her mother could tell the difference.

Ruby sat down on a bench, leaned her back against the wall, and smiled to herself. She wasn't sure how she was going to get to the hospital with no bike, but she'd solve that problem later. She opened her new book, *No Time to Scream,* and began to read.

Ruby quickly lost track of time; the book was a lot more engrossing than she had expected it to be. She had almost read the whole 275 pages when she sensed someone's gaze and looked up. The kid from yesterday evening, the one standing outside the mini-mart with the styled-unstyled hair, was standing on top of the pay phone, as if no one was going to mind, or perhaps he didn't care either way.

Ruby thought about him on his skateboard, hitching a ride from that truck; she really should try that. He was one of those kids who knew he was good-looking — only today he looked awkward and was fiddling with his key chain, which he had looped to his pocket, a self-conscious tough-guy look that wasn't really working for him. He seemed to be preparing to smile, to say something, even.

"Hey," he said.

"Hey back," replied Ruby. She was busy trying to find her hat, which was somewhere in her satchel. "By the way, I think that lady wants to make a call." She indicated the elderly woman who was clearly working up the courage to ask the boy to step off the pay phone. He shrugged and jumped down.

"So what's your name?" asked the boy.

"I believe it's traditional to introduce yourself first before asking a personal question like *What's your name?*"

"*What's your name?* is a personal question?" said the boy.

"It is to me, unless of course you are a law-enforcement officer, or person in a position of ultimate authority, and if you are, I guess

What's your name? would be a demand." She paused without looking up. "*Are* you in the whole law-enforcement business?"

The boy sounded flustered when he replied, "Am I what?"

"In law enforcement?" said Ruby.

"Uh, no," said the boy uncertainly.

"Didn't think so," said Ruby. She resumed her satchel rifling. "So what is it?"

"What's what?" said the boy.

"Your name, buster."

"My name?"

"What? You got amnesia? Or you in the witness protection program?"

The boy actually smiled at this, surprised, like he had never met a girl before who wasn't falling over herself to get his attention.

"My name . . ." announced the boy. He was about to disclose this piece of information when Ruby caught sight of something alarming—it was the clock above the pharmacy door.

Darn! The hospital, her appointment. She was late.

"Look, I'm sure you got a really nice name, buster, and I'm sure it suits you and all, but tell me next time because I gotta scoot." She had jammed on her hat, finally retrieved from her bag, and was already hailing a cab, opening the door, and climbing into it.

The kid with the hair watched as the taxi joined the other cars, all waiting for the lights to change from red to green. Glancing down, he saw Ruby's book on the bench.

"Hey, your book!" he yelled. He began to run, zigzagging through the moving traffic, but the lights had changed and the cab was picking up speed.

"Keep it for me," she shouted back. "I want to know how it ends."

CHAPTER 8
Not a Nickel

THE RADIO WAS TUNED TO TTR, Twinford Talk Radio, and the local news debate was blaring out. First a story about the mayor's statue, newly commissioned by the mayor himself — it had upset a lot of Twinfordites.

"*IT'S JUST SO UNSPEAKABLY UGLY,*" said Roxy from North Twinford.

"*I HAVE TO SAY, MY TODDLER CRIES EVERY TIME WE PASS IT,*" agreed Judy from Midtown Avenue. "*I FEEL LIKE THROWING A BLANKET OVER IT — YOU KNOW WHAT I'M SAYING?*"

"I sure as heck do, Judy," said the cabdriver. "It's just about the ugliest thing I ever laid eyes on." The driver looked at Ruby in the rearview mirror. "You a fan?"

"I'm into horror if that's what you're asking," said Ruby. The sculptor who had attempted to capture the mayor in stone had clearly been going for some kind of modernist vibe, but the result was pure nightmare.

"I hear you, kid!" said the cabdriver, punching the horn. He stuck his head out the window. "Get outta my way, lady!"

TTR had moved on to another story about the predicted storms, which despite regular weather updates had yet to ravage Twinford.

"*I MEAN, THEY KEEP TELLING US THIS HURRICANE IS ON ITS WAY, BUT THERE ISN'T ENOUGH WIND TO FLY A KITE. I PROMISE YOU—I'VE TRIED*," said Steve from Ocean Bay.

The other big debate was about a presumed robbery that had taken place on the twenty-sixth floor of the Lakeridge Square apartments. Presumed, because nothing had actually been reported missing yet. "*LAKERIDGE RESIDENTS TARGETED BY HIGH-RISE THIEF*," announced Ted, the show's host.

"I'll bet it has something to do with that skywalker," said the cabdriver.

"What skywalker?" said Ruby.

"Some clown's been spotted walking between those fancy apartments in the city downtown," said the cabdriver. "Doesn't worry me. I live on the ground floor of a low-rise out in East Twinford."

"What, you mean he's been seen walking on roofs?"

"No, walking on the air is what I heard," said the cabdriver. "Just strolling between the buildings."

"Sounds unlikely," said Ruby.

"*SO HOW IS THIS GUY DOING IT, ALICE? HIGH WIRES OR SUPERPOWERS? AND WHAT DO YOU THINK THE TWINFORD POLICE SHOULD BE DOING ABOUT THIS GUY, IF ANYTHING?*"

"*DO YOU KNOW WHAT I THINK?*" said Alice from East Twinford. "*GOOD LUCK TO HIM! I WISH I HAD THE MONEY TO LIVE IN THE LAKERIDGE BUILDING. THESE RICH FOLKS HAVE MORE MONEY THAN THEY CAN HANDLE. WHAT DO THEY CARE IF SOME THIEF BREAKS INTO THEIR APARTMENT AND STEALS ONE OF THEIR VALUABLES? THEY SHOULDN'T HAVE ALL THIS WEALTH — IT'S NOT RIGHT. IF I HAD MY WAY, I WOULD —*"

"*THANK YOU FOR THAT INTERESTING POINT OF VIEW, ALICE. BUT I MIGHT JUST CUT YOU OFF THERE,*" said Ted.

It was an intriguing discussion, and Ruby was disappointed when the radio show moved on to the less interesting subject of bathroom lime scale. She tuned out and instead let her thoughts drift as she watched the city flick past the cab window. It was only when Ruby had traveled halfway to where she needed to be that she realized she wasn't going to have enough money to pay for the entire cab ride. Heck, she didn't have enough to pay the distance she had already traveled. She had spent her money on the dress and the book, and now she was short.

"Look, man, you're gonna have to pull over. I'll step out here," Ruby said to the driver. "I'm outta funds."

The cab screeched to a halt.

"Unless . . . I don't suppose . . ." Ruby ventured, handing him every nickel and dime she had, "you might wanna help out a kid with a busted arm?"

"Scram," said the driver, pointing his thumb in the direction of the sidewalk.

"Thanks for your kindness, sir," called Ruby as the cabdriver pulled away. "I'll remember you in my will!"

Ruby arrived at the hospital almost a half hour late and was met by a sour-faced nurse. Her name tag read NURSE DRIVER.

"You're late," she said.

"Only twenty-seven minutes," said Ruby.

"Late is late," said the nurse.

"Too late?" asked Ruby.

"Dr. Shepherd is gone," said Nurse Driver, hands on hips.

"Really."

"Dr. Shepherd is a busy man."

"Sorry," said Ruby, giving her the old Ruby Redfort sad eyes. "I had such trouble getting here. First of all I —"

Nurse Driver raised her hand to stop the tide of excuses. "If you promise not to say another word, I'll see what I can do." She made a few calls and told Ruby to sit it out on the hard plastic chairs in the waiting area.

Ruby picked up a crumpled copy of the *Twinford Mirror*. On page two was a piece about the Lakeridge break-in. Mr. Baradi was quite shaken up to find the front door to his twenty-sixth-floor apartment wide open when he arose at 6:20 a.m.

```
"It was unlocked from the inside," he
explained to the police from the 24th
Precinct. "I ask you," he continued, "how
in the name of rigatoni did that happen?"
Nothing so far has been discovered missing,
but the search continues.
```

Forty-five minutes later, Nurse Driver ushered Ruby inside a small white box of a room and informed her that someone would see her presently. One hour and thirty-one minutes later the door still hadn't opened. Ruby read all the notices and information pinned to the walls, first in English and then in Spanish and then in Braille. At last the door opened.

"So, want to get that thing off?" said the technician, pointing at her arm.

"Umm, yeah, that would be nice. Don't get me wrong, it's been great, but I oughta be getting back to my parents or they might decide to rent out my room."

The technician didn't rise to Ruby's sarcasm. "Is that a yes?" she said.

"Yes," said Ruby.

"A yes, please?"

"Yes, please, ma'am," said Ruby.

"Better," said the technician, who then set about her task, and soon enough Ruby's arm was free of its plaster casing.

"You got any advice for me?" asked Ruby, pointing to her newly liberated arm. It felt weirdly drafty, now that the cast was off.

"Uh-huh," said the technician. "You might want to relax that attitude of yours. It's not good for your future health."

Ruby smiled at her. "Seeing as how you're a medical person, I will bear that in mind." Then she thanked the technician, offering her a cube of bubble gum, which the technician accepted, and then Ruby strolled back down the corridor and out of the hospital.

Ruby took a taxi home and alerted Hitch to her cash-poor circumstances; he came out to settle up with the driver—and her father was none the wiser.

Ruby walked into the kitchen to find her mother having her hair put up into an elaborate sort of do. Sabina was turning the pages of the latest copy of the *Whispering Weekly,* a sort of gossip and fashion journal. The gossip was about celebrities: mostly actors and singers, and the fashion was almost all about how the celebrities looked disastrous in their chosen gowns. **FAMOUSLY FABULOUS? OR TRAGICALLY TERRIBLE?**

There was one whole section dedicated to mishaps: close-ups of runs in stockings, pimples, aging skin, or bad hair. Tammy the hairdresser kept leaning over Sabina's shoulder and tutting sympathetically and occasionally even turning the pages. The story Tammy was most interested in was about the actress who had had the misfortune to use a brand of makeup known as Face Flawless. Evidently the actress had attempted to conceal her blemishes so that she might look picture-perfect for her film premiere. The only thing was, Face Flawless used an ingredient in its formula that reacted badly under flash photography. The result was far from flawless: all the areas it covered glowed white. Poor Jessica Riley, her face was just a mess of circles and powdery blotches.

"My heart goes out to her," said Tammy, making a sad face. "They shouldn't print these stories." She waited for Sabina to turn the page. "I mean, look at her," she said, pointing a comb at a singer who had been snapped in an ill-fitting bathing suit. "Poor thing — gosh, though, she might want to think about shrinking those thighs."

"I'm sure she feels a lot better knowing that twenty million people like you all pity her," said Ruby.

Brant Redfort walked in. "Oh, Ruby, you look different."

Sabina looked up from the magazine. "Yes, you do. Why, I wonder . . . ?"

"Could it be my . . . arm . . . ?" said Ruby.

"Yes!" said both her parents at once.

"We should celebrate!" said her father.

"You know me, I love to celebrate," said her mother, clapping her hands together. "Hitch!" she called. "We're celebrating! Could you rustle up something celebratory?"

There was a long ring from the doorbell, followed by another and another.

Mrs. Digby answered to find Clancy hopping from one foot to the other.

"Jeepers child, keep your shorts on."

"Sorry!" called Clancy as he ran up the stairs two at a time.

Clancy had biked over especially to see the arm.

"It's not as hairy as I'd hoped," he said when Ruby showed it to him, "but it is definitely hairier than the other one."

Ruby rolled her eyes. "Boy, do you live a sheltered life."

"Hey, Clancy," said Sabina, "how come you're not all scrubbed up for the Scarlet Pagoda benefit tonight? It's a dressy affair, you know."

Clancy's face immediately dropped. "Because I'm not going is why."

"What? Are you insane?" said Ruby. "Have you actually lost your whole complete mind?"

"My dad has a last-minute ambassadorial dinner tonight, so I am strictly on family duty."

Ruby folded her arms.

"Look, no one's as bummed about it as I am," said Clancy. "I really wanted to be there. I mean, aren't they showing costumes from *The Crab Man Cometh*?"

Ruby's parents looked blank, but Ruby nodded.

"You sure you don't want to come with us, Clancy dear?" asked Sabina.

"Good thinking, honey," agreed Brant. "Come with us."

"You gotta come, bozo," said Ruby. "They'll have all the costumes that have appeared in every horror movie you love — and other films too, the cool ones, not the schlocky stuff."

Clancy let out a pathetic laugh. "I know! It's not like I haven't been looking forward to it for weeks. But you think my dad is gonna let me off to go to that when he's got Ambassador Sanchez coming? She has eight kids, get that? Eight!"

"So?" said Ruby.

"So," said Clancy, "my dad only has six kids."

Ruby looked at him. "Is this a competitive thing?"

"You bet it is. Do you know how difficult it is for women to make it in the political arena?"

"You're preaching to the choir," said Ruby.

"So Ambassador Sanchez makes my father look like a lightweight. At least that's how my dad sees it. Sanchez is the queen of the career family — I mean, heck, she even baked her own cake when the president dropped by last month. She is a single mother of eight and an ambassador who bakes cakes for the president."

"She sounds super," said Sabina.

"So your dad's gonna fight back?" said Brant.

"Oh, he's fighting back, all right," said Clancy. "He's determined to at least look like this really great dad who spends his time looking after his great kids while he does a really great job of doing his great job. So he wants us all there."

"What about his really great wife?" asked Sabina, sipping on one of the celebratory drinks Hitch had just rustled up.

"She's having her hair done," said Clancy. "She had it done yesterday too."

"Well, you know what they say: great hair opens doors," said Brant.

Clancy scrunkled his nose at this, perhaps trying to work out the truth of the statement. "Maybe . . . Anyway, he wants us all there with good hair, while he is busy making Twinford believe his career is really great and we are great and he is great and Twinford can be great. You get it?"

"I get it," said Ruby. "You can't come because you are all busy being great and getting your hair done."

Clancy nodded. That was about the size of it.

CHAPTER 9
The Scorpion Specter at the Scarlet Pagoda

RUBY WAS LOOKING FORWARD TO THE EVENING. Not so much the "do" itself — all that party yakking was sure to be a total yawn — but the costumes, *they* promised to be pretty interesting.

Aside from reading, movies were Ruby's greatest passion, particularly thrillers and horror — a passion she shared with Mrs. Digby. Nothing cheered Mrs. Digby as much as a good murder story. *Too bad she isn't prepared to risk a few ghosts*, thought Ruby. Tonight was going to be a bonanza of thriller movie memorabilia.

Ruby took longer than usual to get ready. She'd had to make a couple of minor adjustments to the new dress she had bought — namely hacking four inches off the hem and fixing it in place with tape. She was largely pleased with the overall effect, and once she had her new shades on too, she really looked the business. All in all, she was looking forward to the costume show. At least it would take her mind off worrying about that dumb Spectrum test.

"*That's* what you're wearing?"

Sabina Redfort stared at her daughter, who was attired in a strange misshapen dress with worn-looking shoes and over-the-knee socks. Obscuring her eyes were a pair of huge white square-framed sunglasses.

The dress had very obviously been purchased at a vintage store or possibly off a charity rack. It was on the large side and covered in a loud pink-and-yellow paisley print. She had pulled it together with a wide white buckle belt.

Jeepers! thought Sabina. *Maybe the kid actually pulled it out of a Dumpster.*

"What?" said Ruby, reading her mother's thoughts, which were obvious by the expression on her face.

Her mother closed her eyes and shook her head like she was trying to dislodge the vision.

"OK," said Sabina, "I'm not going to make a thing of it. Let's just go and have a nice time. I'll pretend you're wearing that lovely peach dress I got you at the department store — why *aren't* you wearing that lovely peach dress I got you at the department store?"

Brant Redfort, now dressed in an elegant black suit, walked into the living room to find his wife, a picture in rose with matching accessories.

"You look sensational, honey," he said, kissing his wife. "You too . . . Ruby." He uttered this compliment before he had really taken in the vision that was his daughter. "You look very . . . very . . . " He paused, searching for some word that might not insult but that might also be truthful. He could find no word.

"I'll take *very very*," said Ruby. "No need to get your underwear in a bunch on my account."

Hitch drove the Redforts to the venue. It was a big-deal affair, red carpet, the whole circus.

The costume show was being held at the Scarlet Pagoda—the proceeds from the very expensive tickets and raffle would, it was hoped, raise enough money to keep the old art deco building from crumbling to dust. The place was considered an architectural gem of great historical importance, having been built in the heyday of the Roaring Twenties. Any elderly star worth an Oscar had tripped across this stage.

And many of those stars had left their footprints—literally. Outside the theater was Twinford's own walk of fame, where brass star shapes were set into the sidewalk, commemorating the town's most famous. Next to each star was a cast of the actors' shoes, their footprints pressed into wet concrete.

Ruby and her family walked past the footprints, and as they walked, Sabina gave a running commentary.

"There's Fletch Gregory, what a man, and oh, look at dear

little Arthur Mudge's teeny feet — I always thought he was taller, and goodness, are those *really* Margo Bardem's?"

And on into the theater.

It had begun as a theater for circus and stage productions, then much later it had become a movie theater. But now it was just a room, a large empty space, where each week another tiny gold mosaic tile would drop from the ceiling. A place where the elegant ladies who silently stared out from the murals faded a little more each year. Soon, if nothing was done, their faces would disappear altogether and then the wrecking ball would be called in.

For tonight, though, it was a sparkling extravaganza of a party, a hint of the things to come when it was renovated. Everyone who was anyone was there, champagne glasses in hand, laughing and chatting as elegant young waiters glided around with silver trays of canapés.

As soon as Ruby and her parents walked in, they were surrounded. "It's such a wonderful example of the deco era," said Dora Shoering, Twinford's self-declared expert on all things historical. She had to talk loudly over the hubbub of voices and clinking glasses. "You can touch the history, run your hands over it, breathe it into your lungs." The women all took deep breaths.

Sabina coughed — the Pagoda was a haven for dust mites.

"You know your onions, Dora. I mean, it would be a perfect sadness if it were destroyed," she said.

"I totally agree," agreed Marjorie Humbert, who was now looking for a tissue, having just run her hands over history. "It would be Twinford's bitter loss."

Elaine Lemon joined them. "So what are you ladies talking about? Gossip, I hope!"

"Oh, we were just saying how it would be the most terrible pity if they were to flatten this building," said Marjorie.

"I so concur," said Elaine, opting for a sad expression. "It would be the most awful tragedy." She paused. "A tragic one." In truth, Elaine was not there because she was remotely interested in the Scarlet Pagoda, but had eagerly accepted Sabina's offer of a free ticket because everyone else was going.

Ruby felt this conversation wasn't really going places and so moved off in search of something entertaining. As she circled around the room, she recognized many big names from the stage and screen, including one of her favorites, Erica Grey. She was a star of B movies and had played some of the most curious and monstrous villains on the medium-size screen. She was originally from Alabama and spoke in a drawn-out drawl, her voice rich and deep. Every few sentences, she would throw her head back and laugh — her red lipsticked mouth opening wide to display perfectly white shining teeth.

Ruby weaved her way through the crowd and caught a glimpse of *Crazy Cops* actor Dirk Draylon as he made his way to his seat on the other side of the catwalk. Apparently the show was about to begin.

Boy, Mrs. Digby would love this, she thought.

There were many other well-known personalities mingling in the crowd but none whom Ruby felt eager to shake hands with. Not because she didn't admire them, she did, she just had a wariness about meeting screen heroes; meeting one's hero could be a mistake, a big letdown. This illusionary world that was film often survived better if it was never contaminated by real life.

At least that's what she thought until she met the makeup artist Frederick Lutz. Frederick Lutz was a man Ruby greatly admired — a true artist, he had created some of the most startling monsters, villains, and victims of the screen, as well as making up the faces of the great and beautiful.

They chatted for a while and then he thanked her for her compliments, and as she moved off to find her seat he called, "If you ever need makeup for a very important occasion, then think of me — it would be my great pleasure, Ms. Redfort."

"You can bet I will," said Ruby, who was thinking Halloween. Then she turned and bumped heads with her friend Red Monroe.

"I've been looking for you," said Red, rubbing her forehead.

"Hey, Red, where's Sadie?" asked Ruby, clutching her nose.

"Oh, Sadie's backstage helping the radioactive lobster fix his pincers." She said this as if it was not so very different from mentioning that someone needed help straightening their bow tie.

Red's mom, usually referred to as Sadie, was a costume designer — she mainly designed for thrillers and sci-fi flicks and had done more than her share of B-movie work. Ruby liked hanging out at Red's place because her mother always had something unusual going on in her studio and Mrs. Monroe was often to be found with pencil poised, asking some kind of curious question. *"So, Ruby, tell me, what do you think a Grungemeister looks like? Do you think he would have fingers or grabbers?"*

Ruby and Red made their way to their seats. Elliot Finch was already there, studying the program.

The lights went down. Everyone clapped.

"Clancy not here?" whispered Red.

"He had to smile for his dad," replied Ruby.

"That kid's gonna dislocate his jaw one of these days."

"Tell me about it," said Ruby.

A crabby lady in the row behind them started making shushing sounds.

"Welcome to the opening of the Twinford Film Festival — A Date with Thrills!" said the host, Ray Conner, bounding onto the stage.

Applause from the audience.

Ray Conner was a bit of a cheeseball, in Ruby's opinion.

"As you all know, tonight's extravaganza is a fund-raiser in aid of this beautiful theater of ours, the Scarlet Pagoda."

Pause for more applause. Smiling from the host.

"The title of this year's festival is A Date with Thrills, in other words, thriller flicks, be they comic, romantic, or just plain terrifying. And tonight we are particularly celebrating our wonderful costume designers, all too often unseen."

More clapping, especially from Red, whose mother was a costume designer, after all.

Smiling and nodding from the host.

"During the next few weeks, Twinford movie theaters will be showing some fabulous films from years gone by. The wonderful work of stars such as Betsy Blume, Leonard Fuller, and Crompton Haynes, culminating in a tribute to the wonderful actress Margo Bardem, who as a young thing worked in this theater as a hairdresser and whose career began with a romantic thriller that was both shot and later premiered in this very auditorium in 1952, and who subsequently went on to dominate the romantic thriller genre."

More applause. A tight smile from Betsy Blume.

"Sadly, Margo Bardem can't be here tonight . . ."

A groan from the audience.

"*But* she will of course be joining us for the film festival finale on Friday the fifteenth!"

Applause.

"Thank you, thank you," said Ray, trying to be heard above the clapping. "This, folks, will be a very special occasion, because on that night at this very theater will be the world premiere of *Feel the Fear,* a movie that also features the Scarlet Pagoda in some scenes. A movie shot in 1954 but for some reason never shown, so you lucky people will have the chance to be its first audience!"

Wild applause now.

"Jeepers," whispered Elliot, "I wish this guy would move it along a little."

"Speaking of this wonderful actress, one of the highlights of *this* particular evening will be the fabulous costumes worn by Ms. Bardem in the thrillers *The Truth Will Out, The Last Wish, Catch Your Death,* and of course *The Cat That Got the Canary.*

Yes, tonight you will all be fortunate enough to see those awe-inspiring outfits worn by Ms. Bardem that made those particular pictures such a movie sensation." He paused for suspense.

"The feather dress . . ." Applause.

"The white fur-trimmed gown . . ." Applause.

"And yes, those legendary size threes, the Little Yellow Shoes." Applause.

"The list goes on," said Ray, who was going on a little too much as far as Ruby was concerned.

"You will also be dazzled by costumes from films such as *Fingers from Outer Space, It's Behind You,* and *The Claw at the Window.*

There was a loud whistling—there were obviously a lot of *The Claw at the Window* appreciators in the audience.

"And folks, let's not forget the other of this evening's highlights—the raffle!"

More frenzy, Ruby suspected most of it generated by her own mother.

After a bit more buildup, the show finally began. Music started up, Ray Conner thankfully slipped stage right, and a succession of models started strutting across the stage in a variety of outfits, each one more outlandish than the last. Ruby was engrossed—her favorite movies were coming to life.

Red too leaned forward in her seat. "Isn't that the dress from *Two's Company, Three's a Shroud?*"

"I believe so," said Ruby.

"It looks like it's made from actual cobwebs, and look at that. . . ." As Red stretched her arm out to point toward another costume classic, she knocked her drink right into her lap.

"Oh, cripes, not again!" said Red, violently wiping at her dress.

"If that's a blue slushy, Red, you better go pour water on it," said Elliot. "That stuff stains, man — talk about radioactive."

Red had an accident of this nature most hours of the week, and she was well practiced at dashing to restrooms or water fountains.

While Red made her way to the bathroom to deal with the slushy, Ruby and Elliot continued to enjoy the show — there was so much more to the outfits than one ever saw when just viewing on a screen. It was fair to say, some of the costumes were a whole lot better than the movies they had appeared in.

Fifteen minutes later, Ruby looked up to see Red making her way back to her seat. By the looks on people's faces, she was stepping on an awful lot of toes. As she got closer, Ruby saw that the blood seemed to have drained from her face, which gave her a strange, almost ghostly appearance.

"What's up with you?" Ruby asked as Red finally sat down beside her. "You look like you just ran into the Scorpion Specter."

"Yeah, well, maybe I did—I got lost and ended up backstage, and there is something weird back there. It may not be the scorpion, but it sure to goodness scared the pants off me."

"Seriously?" said Elliot.

"I tell you, I think this place is haunted, just like they say," said Red.

Ruby gave her the once-over. "Look, maybe you should ease up on the slushies, Red—you know they put a lot of chemicals in those things. I think some of them mighta gone to your head."

"I'm not kidding around, you guys. I know I tend to walk into a lot of things, but this time I swear I tripped over something that wasn't there—I mean there was something there, nothing I could see, but there was something—I mean, I couldn't have tripped over nothing, right? And I swear I heard footsteps."

"Red, you are always tripping over nothing," said Ruby.

Red stared back at them both. "Well, this time I didn't," she said firmly. "This time it wasn't just me."

And the weirdest thing was . . . Ruby believed her.

CHAPTER 10
Funny Peculiar

IT WAS SHORTLY AFTER THE INTERMISSION, just ten minutes into the second half of the show, that something seemed to go wrong.

The organizer came onto the catwalk to apologize for the hitch in the proceedings, blaming it on a technical problem.

Then Ray, the host, came back on and made some so-so jokes suggesting it might be something to do with the Claw at the Window or the Ecto Grabber, and everyone laughed good-naturedly.

The organizer returned to announce that unfortunately one of the star pieces had been mislaid but the show would go on.

Ruby and Red looked at each other.

"Told you," said Red. "Something is back there."

"I'll go check it out," said Ruby nonchalantly. By now her curiosity had really gotten a grip, and even if it meant coming face to pincers with the Scorpion Specter, she needed to know just what was going down. Happily, she didn't believe in scorpion specters, so there wasn't a whole lot to fear; besides, she had come through a forest fire almost unscathed, she had survived two encounters with the evil Count von Viscount, and she had escaped the clutches of a sea monster. She was beginning to think she might be invincible.

Ruby slipped out of her seat and made her way backstage. She did it with such confidence that no one accosted her, at least not until she reached the area where the show director was issuing orders.

"You can't come back here!" said an intimidating-looking woman in an asymmetric dress and asymmetric haircut.

"I'm just . . ."

"Scram," said the woman, slamming the door an inch in front of Ruby's nose.

"Darn it," muttered Ruby. As she turned to leave, she spotted a whole stack of fish heads, giant ones. The fish heads were made from papier-mâché. Ruby recognized them; she knew the movie they came from, she had watched it over and over again squished in next to Mrs. Digby on her settee. She had been just three when she first saw *The Sea of Fish Devils*.

Ruby picked up one of the heads and examined it. *Worth a try, I guess.* She pulled it down over her head so her face was totally hidden — she could see out all right but no one could see in. It was uncomfortable but it was bearable. She checked the rack of costumes and found what she was looking for. Pulling it from its hanger she wriggled into one of the fish tails. There was no telling who she actually was now. She was just a short Fish Devil. She opened the door and this time the woman ushered her in.

"About time! Where's the rest of your shoal?"

Ruby shrugged.

"No one's a professional anymore," said the asymmetric woman, shaking her head. She looked more closely at the fish in front of her. "Kinda small, aren't you? Your fins are dragging."

The fish shrugged but said nothing. Then it indicated that it needed to go to the bathroom, and the woman rolled her eyes and said, "OK, but make it snappy, Bubbles."

As Ruby threaded her way between the racks of costumes and boxes full of props and accessories, she overheard one of the models talking to the organizer. "I swear, one minute they were totally there and, like, the next, you know, gone — weird, right? Only, I swear I felt something — like air moving past me. A breeze, you know?" She sighed. "Not that it matters. I could never have modeled them anyway." She looked down at her feet. "No chance of squeezing these size nines into those teeny tiny shoes — that Margo Bardem must have pixie feet."

Ruby slipped out the side door into the labyrinth of

passageways. She shed her fish ensemble and tiptoed along the various backstage corridors. She had no real idea where she was headed but she followed the voices — they were coming from high up in the pagoda. Ruby had once been told that there was a strong room up top there, built long ago for a famously difficult actress who *insisted* on having a dressing room at the very top of the building and *insisted* that her valuables be locked safely away in the room next door while she performed onstage.

As Ruby climbed the next set of stairs, the voices became louder. Using the extendable mirror that was one of the many attachments belonging to the Escape Watch, she managed to peek around the wall. Two guards were explaining to the show organizer how they had not moved one inch from the door of the room that contained prop 53.

"Not only did we not move one inch from the place I am standing right now," insisted one of the guards, "but no one even so much as touched the handle of that door, let alone walked inside, at least not until the stagehand came to collect 'em."

"That's right," said the other guy. "Everything Stan says is exactly what happened — until you unlocked that door, no one went in."

"So you want me to believe that you've been standing here the whole time?"

"Look, lady, I don't want you to believe nothing. I'm telling you, me and Al never moved an inch from where we are stood now."

"Not an inch," confirmed Al. "Everything's been shipshape and exactly as it should be, so far as we're concerned." Al picked up a little piece of paper from the floor as if to illustrate his point. "Everything in the right place." He tucked it into his pocket. "Shipshape, see?"

"So prop fifty-three was just spirited away? Is that what you're saying?"

"It's the only explanation," said Al, "and I don't mind telling you, as of today, I'm never working here again. This place is haunted — no two ways about it. When your stagehand guy came up to fetch your so-called *prop fifty-three,* I felt the weirdest sensation, like someone brushed right by me. So as of tomorrow, lady, you can find another security guard for your grand finale premiere shindig."

The woman shook her head as if she couldn't believe what she was hearing. But despite her protests, Stan and Al were not to be persuaded otherwise.

"Ghosts or no ghosts," she said, "could you at least assure me that all exits have security on them? No one backstage — and I repeat, no one — costumed or otherwise, is to leave this building without being checked for stolen items!" She turned to leave and then added, "And that includes me!"

The security guy nodded. "Affirmative," he said. "No one leaves without our clearance."

If this was true, thought Ruby, then the thief was very possibly still somewhere in the building, lurking, waiting for his chance to escape. But how was he going to do that? She looked around. *Via a window?* she thought.

She ran back down the stairs. There were no windows on the ground floor. The windows on the stairway did not open, and there were no missing or broken panes of glass. *No way out.* She started down the corridor back toward the front of the stage.

It was when she rounded the next corner that she thought she heard something, something a little like soft movements. *Coulda been a mouse . . . or a rat.* She shivered. *Pull it together, Redfort.*

By the time Ruby made it back to her seat, the show was just wrapping up. The raffle had been drawn, the pledges of financial support all collected, and now it was the showstopper finish — atmospheric lights, sinister sound effects, and a parade of the monstrous and villainous were playing out on the stage, complete with a shoal of Fish Devils.

Ruby tried to appreciate it all, but she was understandably

distracted by what she had overheard. As the last outrageous costume left the stage, the theater broke into applause.

Few of the audience seemed to have been bothered by the non-appearance of prop 53, there was so much else to look at. Sabina Redfort, however, was very disappointed.

"Where do you think they got to? I thought they were supposed to be one of the highlights of the evening?"

"I'm sure they were there," said Brant. "You probably just missed them."

"I don't think I would just miss the Little Yellow Shoes, Brant," said Sabina.

"Well," said Brant, "don't be too disappointed — don't forget, *you did* win the Ada Borland prize."

"Oh, yes!" cried Sabina. "Ruby, I won the raffle and you, you lucky kid, are going to have your portrait taken by the great Ada Borland!"

Ruby didn't *feel* so lucky — she was never too thrilled about smiling for the camera. It was usually a very boring activity. But what she said was "Super."

"You had lady luck on your side," said Brant.

"Well," said Sabina, "I cut the odds a little. I did purchase a hundred and twenty-two tickets."

The Redforts, carried by the tide, spilled out onto the street with most of the other theatergoers. Brant glanced up at the old building. "Looking at it, you can't help kind of believing this old place might just be haunted." He winked at Barbara Bartholomew. "Kind of exciting, isn't it, Barb?"

Barbara gave an involuntary shiver. "Gives me the creeps," she said.

Ruby said nothing the whole ride home. Her brain was trying to make connections and bring a little logic into the evening's events. She listened to her parents' conversation, but they spoke of nothing more interesting than their appreciation of the canapés and concern that the theater was understaffed — they seemed to have forgotten about the Little Yellow Shoes already.

Ruby took a juice from the refrigerator, bid her parents good night, and climbed the stairs to her room.

OK, so Red Monroe was about as gullible as they came and no one was more accident prone, but it was weird that Red, the security guards, *and* the model had all experienced something so similar, had all sensed a presence that they just couldn't explain. Ruby might have been tempted to write this off: imaginations stirred by the theater's rumored hauntings, the spooky sensations conjured by the noises and drafts of an old building. People could be pretty prone to suggestion, and once one person described a strange experience, often others would follow suit. Ruby had read all about it in Dr. Stephanie Randleman's book *I Think I Saw That Too.*

On the other hand, it was important not to dismiss a possibility just because it sounded like the far-fetched ramblings of a gaggle of highly suggestible folks. Was it *possible* that the rumors about the Scarlet Pagoda had some substance after all? Ruby remembered back to the case she had worked on involving the Sea Whisperer. In that instance, the people who had claimed they had heard a whispering sound coming from the ocean had not imagined it—it was absolutely true.

She too had heard it, and even seen the creature the sound came from, but ghosts? Ghosts were a stretch. Ruby would need a lot more evidence before she concluded that something from the spirit world was responsible for stealing a pair of size-three shoes.

**She took out her key chain
and set about turning the
five different keys . . .**

. . . in the five different locks. She pushed open the heavy door, stepped inside, and closed it behind her.

Someone was there.

She knew instantly that it was him: she could smell the polish on his Italian leather shoes. He was in the apartment.

She walked slowly along the corridor, her stiletto heels sharp on the marble floor. The door to her study was open, and she could make out a shadowed figure sitting in the armchair in front of the window.

"A long day at work?" he asked.

"You could say that," she replied. Her voice betrayed no fear, yet she was afraid.

"By the way," he said, "red hair suits you. Does your accent match your new look?"

"I didn't want anyone to recognize me, so I opted for another face."

"It's very arresting and an interesting choice," he said. "People will think that they've seen a ghost." He paused. "But enough chitchat. I trust everything is proceeding as it should?"

"I'm not sure," she replied.

He smiled. "Oh, dear. Uncertainty is a terrible drain on one, isn't it?"

She said nothing.

"Not knowing can make one horribly paranoid." He looked at her, his black eyes seeming to fathom her soul. "Best to fix the situation before sleepless nights set in. You don't want to find yourself dead on your feet."

She knew what he was saying, and she had no intention of finding herself dead on her feet—or dead from a nasty fall, for that matter. She would find the traitor, and she would make him an offer. Life or death. There was no in-between.

CHAPTER 11
Wide Awake

FOR THE SECOND MORNING IN A ROW, Ruby was woken by the sound of ringing. This time it *was* the phone, and this time it was a good deal earlier than ten a.m. Ruby checked her alarm clock, but the numerals were fuzzy. She sat up and fumbled for her glasses. *Seven a.m., brother!*

"This better be important, buster," said Ruby into the receiver.

"Sorta," said the voice.

RUBY: *Oh, hi, Red, I thought it was Clance.*

RED: *It was in the paper. It means I wasn't imagining it.*

RUBY: *What was in the paper? Imagining what?*

RED: *The ghost.*

RUBY: *What?*

RED: *They confirmed it had to have been a ghost who took them.*

RUBY: *Took what?*

RED: *The Little Yellow Shoes — that's what were stolen last night.*

RUBY: *I already figured it had to be the shoes, but how do you propose a ghost carries a pair of shoes?*

RED: *It has arms, doesn't it?*

RUBY: *Ghosts can't pick up solid items.*

RED: *Well, that's not what the* Twinford Echo *is saying.*

RUBY: *Hang on a sec, Red.*

She set the phone down, hurriedly pulled on a pair of jeans that were sprawled next to the bed, found a cleanish T-shirt, and moved to the bathroom. Plucking up the soap-shaped phone, she grabbed her toothbrush at the same time.

RUBY: *You still there?*

RED: *Uh-huh.*

Ruby began to brush her teeth.

RED: *You sound funny.*

RUBY: *I'm practicing good oral hygiene.*

RED: *Oh.*

RUBY: *So how sure are they that the shoes are stolen rather than just missing?*

RED: *Definite.*

RUBY: *Definite?*

RED: *Yeah, the shoes are highly valuable 'cause you know they featured in that film, the one that made Margo Bardem a big star.*

RUBY: The Cat That Got the Canary. *Yeah, everyone knows that — it's part of Twinford history.*

RED: *Exactly! Everyone knows. So they had a whole lot of security last night.*

RUBY: *Well, of course.*

RED: *Not just for the shoes. There was a lot of other valuable stuff too. Anyway, somehow someone got the Yellow Shoes out of the locked case and out of the locked room, past the security team, down the stairs, and out of one of the several exits. But what no one can figure is how that person got into that room in the first place . . . so it has to be a ghost. Everyone's saying it is.*

Ruby said nothing; she was thinking.

RED: *Rube, you still there?*

RUBY: *Uh-huh, I'm thinking.*

Silence.

RED: *You still thinking?*
RUBY: *Yeah.*
RED: *OK, I might hang up, then.*
RUBY: *OK.*

Ruby stood there just thinking for about another ten minutes before snapping out of it. She walked across the room and peeked down into the kitchen via the homemade periscope she had constructed when she was six years old. Her parents must have left already — they had some business thing they both had to attend — and Mrs. Digby was probably out at the farmers' market, so she would have to fix her own breakfast. She skittered downstairs in search of food, opened the fridge, and took a slug of peach juice. Then she popped a couple of slices of bread in the toaster and climbed onto one of the high stools at the kitchen bar. She glanced at the *Twinford Echo* and saw a huge headline:

SHOES GONE WALKABOUT
The townsfolk of Twinford are speculating that the shoe thief might actually be a

specter. Despite the fifty-strong security team, the Little Yellow Shoes, famous for their role in the film *The Cat That Got the Canary*, disappeared last night from a locked and windowless safe room at the Scarlet Pagoda. How this pair of size threes made it out of there alone remains a mystery.

THE NO-SHOW SHOES
Stan Barrell (42) was one of the crack security team guarding the door at the fateful moment when the shoes shuffled off.

"It was like they were there one minute and gone the next. They were totally not there. The only thing that coulda taken them is a living breathing ghost."

Really, Stan? Have you given any thought to what you just said? Stan didn't sound like he was the smartest security guard in the deck.

Many of the audience apparently agreed with Stan Barrell's prime-suspect suspicions.

"There is no other explanation for it," said Mrs. Doris Flum from Garden Estates, South Twinford, who happened to be at last night's Scarlet Pagoda costume extravaganza. "That theater is haunted, always has been," she stated emphatically.

"Why are we talking to Doris Flum? What's she gonna know? And how can the theater always have been haunted? Someone must have had to die there to haunt it; it wasn't built haunted." Ruby was talking to herself out loud now, and Bug was looking confused. Was she talking to him? Was she suggesting food? Nothing was appearing in his dog bowl, and she hadn't mentioned the word "walk." Ruby didn't notice the husky's hopeful eyes; she was enjoying being irritated by the paper.

The *Twinford Echo* had a reputation for being a rather sensationalist and silly newspaper; fact wasn't its strong suit. The only interesting thing it had managed to report concerning the event was that the pair of shoes — otherwise known as prop 53 — was the only thing to go missing, apparently stolen.

So why not anything else?

Ruby pulled her yellow notebook from her back pocket and made a note of this — it sure as eggs had to mean something.

She went back to flipping through the *Echo* and saw that the second biggest story was about the weather.

WAVE BYE-BYE TO HEAT WAVE
Twinford's heat wave is set to end in dramatic style sooner or later.

Who writes this stuff?

She read on. It was a fairly overblown piece about the usual storms that fall brought with it, only this year it seemed they were headed Twinford's way a little earlier than expected . . . but maybe not. The meteorologists couldn't agree. She turned the page and was faced with yet another picture of the mayor's statue. The Twinford public was making its feelings known, and some wise guy had dressed it up to look like the Scorpion Specter. The mayor was not amused.

MAYOR ABRAHAMS DOES NOT SEE FUNNY SIDE

The toast popped, and as Ruby extracted it from the slot and dropped it onto her plate, she saw that it was toast with a mission.

Awake?

Good.

Test.

Imminent.

HQ.

Immediately.

"Cut a kid some slack," moaned Ruby. "I haven't had my breakfast yet."

This was one of the downsides to having a toaster that doubled as a fax machine. Few people wanted orders delivered from their place of work directly to their kitchen table, but for Ruby it was an occupational hazard.

Ruby coated the toast in butter, stuck it between her teeth, picked up her satchel with one hand and her juice with the other, and teetered downstairs to the lower ground floor. She could hear one of Hitch's records playing on the turntable, the melody drifting out the open door. She knocked, and on hearing the "come in" call, she entered.

The tiny apartment was, as always, shipshape, not a strewn sock or dirty coffee cup to be seen. Didn't matter what time of day or night, Ruby had never caught Hitch unprepared, asleep, or even on the brink of dozing off.

"Hey, kid, you're up early."

"Spectrum called." Ruby held up the toast.

"Ah, the test," said Hitch. "You ready for it?"

"My choice would have been to eat breakfast first," said Ruby, "but yeah, I'm eager."

"That's good to hear, kid," said Hitch. He looked like he was going to add something, but if he was, then he changed his mind.

"The thing is," said Ruby, "I don't have my bike, so I was wondering if you could see your way to maybe driving me in?" She gave him the Ruby Redfort slow blink and full-on eye hold — but it didn't work.

"Kid, it may come as a shock, but I'm not actually employed by Spectrum secret services to drive you around. The job's more complicated than you think."

"So how am I supposed to get to HQ immediately? It's gonna take me three city buses and a twenty-minute walk."

"Take the subway from Greenstreet," suggested Hitch.

"Greenstreet is closed for maintenance," said Ruby.

"I'm sure you'll think of something. Isn't that what we pay you for? Thinking?"

"That's what I was doing. That was me thinking *you might give me a lift*."

"Think again, kid."

"So how do I make it into the Spectrum elevator? You never gave me the code."

"Sure I did," said Hitch.

"You did?" said Ruby.

"Think about it," said Hitch. "I'm sure it'll come to you. Just add it up."

CHAPTER 12
Skitching a Lift

RUBY LEFT HITCH'S APARTMENT muttering to herself about the gross injustice of it and how it was tantamount to child neglect, etc., etc. She picked up her satchel, slung it across her chest, and walked out the front door, slamming it behind her. She was working up to being in a bad mood all the way down the front steps, until she caught sight of Elaine Lemon, a woman to be avoided at all costs. Mrs. Lemon was always trying to engage Ruby in conversation that was rarely anything but deadly dull and she pretty much always ended up by saying, *"So maybe you'd like to babysit for Archie. I know how much you two enjoy spending time together."*

This was not true: Archie was not quite a year old.

Did he even *care* who he was spending time with? And as for Ruby, was it possible to enjoy hanging out with a baby?

Ruby, for one, thought not, and so in an effort to avoid Mrs. Lemon, she completely gave up on her bad mood and ran as fast as she could down Cedarwood Drive. When she got well out of hollering range, she slowed her pace to a brisk walk. As she made it past the O'Learys' place, she couldn't help but notice that yet again they were having building work done. They seemed to have the place remodeled at least twice a year. There was a Dumpster piled with junk out in front, and sticking out of it was what looked like a perfectly OK skateboard.

This was typical of Britney O'Leary; she would try something for about a week, get bored, and then move on to another activity. Ruby yanked the board out and set it on the ground. It looked fine. She stepped onto it; it felt fine.

Here was her transport. It wasn't as fast as biking or driving, but it was quicker than taking three buses and a three-block walk. Of course it would be quicker still if she grabbed the wheel arch of a moving vehicle. If that guy with the haircut could do it, then she certainly could. Yes, she would skitch a ride.

Ruby had never actually tried it before. If she was totally honest this was because she had always thought it was a dumb thing to do; unless of course it was an out-and-out emergency type of situation or one wanted to end up in the emergency room. But things had changed; she had escaped from the mouth of death, felt its burning tongues of fire, but she'd come out of it unscathed, permanent injury–wise. She felt, well, invincible, and so skitching suddenly seemed like a very good way of getting around fast.

Ruby set off on her newly acquired skateboard. Minutes later she had grabbed hold of an unsuspecting car headed in the right direction and she was on her way. She traveled at high speed, a great deal faster than pedaling a bike. She only had to shift rides twice, when the cars she had chosen peeled off in the wrong direction, and she reached the Schroeder Building parking garage in very good time.

As she snatched up her board, she couldn't resist a smile — quite a blast: the wind in her face, the road speeding so close beneath her feet. Traveling at thirty miles an hour without working for it, yeah, it was a blast all right. If she'd wiped out, it would most probably have been curtains for Ruby Redfort . . . but then, that only made her like it more.

She walked to the elevator, stepped inside, and waited for the doors to close behind her. *Now what?* Now she needed to figure out the code that would take her to Spectrum.

She stood there thinking, *If Hitch told me the code, then it must have been when we arrived in the underground garage.*

What did we talk about?

It couldn't have been very interesting or she would have

remembered. No, it was boring; Hitch was small-talking about the building . . . something to do with cars and levels and floors.

She looked around — somewhere there would be a parking notice.

It was near the ramp where the cars came in.

Level capacity 500 vehicles.

There were three levels, so that meant 1,500 cars. The Schroeder was seventy-seven stories high. She knew that because everyone knew that; it had a big 77 above its entrance, the number referring to where the building was on the street and also to the number of floors it was made up of. She thought of what Hitch had said: add it up.

She added the numbers, 1,500+3+77, stepped inside the elevator, and tapped 1580 into the code panel. The door did not open.

"What?" said Ruby out loud. "Is this thing broken? How do I even call Spectrum maintenance?" And that's when she remembered that she needed to factor in the number of maintenance vehicles — Hitch had mentioned those too, but she couldn't remember the exact number. This was somewhat of a pain since it involved counting the "maintenance reserved" bays, but eventually she got there. Seventeen.

OK, add the maintenance vehicles.

She tapped in 1597, and the door opened.

"Could he not have just reminded me?" Ruby muttered. But she knew what his answer to that would be: *Pay attention, Redfort.*

Despite the almost impossible feat of arriving barely twenty-seven minutes after leaving home, she was still met with an impatient look from Buzz, who told her to sit and wait until she was called.

"Could I maybe go grab something from the cafeteria?" said Ruby. "I skipped breakfast to be here."

"If you're not here when they call you, it's a fail," said Buzz.

Ruby rolled her eyes and went and sat in the atrium for at least as long as it would have taken to eat breakfast.

"Agent Redfort, please make your way immediately to the rainbow office," came the robotic voice over the intercom.

Finally.

She stood up and walked back over to the circular desk where the mushroom woman sat.

"Why the stupid announcement?" said Ruby, "I'm right here. Why does it have to be *announced*? It's not like *you* couldn't just wave your hand."

"It's not my job," was all Buzz said by way of reply.

"*Jeepers,*" muttered Ruby. "You never, like, get tempted to go off script?"

"The announcer announces; I answer calls," said Buzz, pushing a card toward Ruby. "*And* I issue directions."

On the card were some words and some numbers:

```
Test candidate 45902314: Take the elevator to the gray zone,
where you will be issued instructions by the duty agent.
```

The duty agent turned out to be Froghorn, otherwise known as "the silent G"— a nickname Ruby had given him because he was very particular about the pronunciation of his name, i.e., Frohorn, not Froghorn, as it was actually written.

"Hey, Froghorn." She made the *g* sound very clear. "What are *you* doing on bozo duty? They still not forgiven you for lousing up the whole Melrose Dorff robbery case?"

Froghorn gave her a withering look. "Talk about lousing up: I heard you hurt your little arm. Did someone push you over at kindergarten?"

"Er, no, I was walked over a cliff by a psychopath, actually. What did *you* do during summer break? Give yourself an extreme manicure?"

Froghorn gave her a tired expression. "Little girl, if I had time to reply, then I would, but I'm very busy here."

"If you could *think* of a reply, I'm sure you would, but don't sweat it — I can see you're real busy standing there behind a table."

Froghorn smiled a tight smile. "So I hear you're out of the Field Agent Training Program if you flunk this test." He peered down at the slip of paper she was holding. "Test candidate 45902314. Will this be your lucky number? Or the digits that will keep you locked on the wrong side of Agent World forever?"

"Yeah, well, at least I have a shot; no one's exactly falling over themselves to offer you one," said Ruby.

"Why would I want one?" snapped Froghorn. "HQ is where it all happens."

Ruby made a point of looking theatrically around her. "Yeah, I can see it must be very thrilling sitting here behind this nice little desk in this cozy little room."

"Your test," said Froghorn flatly, and he handed Ruby a key attached to a yellow tag. On one side of the tag was the number 5, on the other a pattern of lines and circles. "Let's hope it's a nice quick one. Fail it and LB will have you kicked out of Spectrum before lunch. We don't want to miss nap time, do we?"

Ruby yawned. "You might want to spend time working on your irritating remarks; that one's getting kinda tired."

Ruby walked back to the elevator bank and descended to yellow level, then stepped out and walked the long curved corridor until the yellow key tag perfectly matched the yellow of a door. None of the doors were numbered, so Ruby was unsure what the number 5 on the yellow tag represented. She turned the key in the lock and stepped into a strange inside-outside room: an urban landscape of fake buildings and industrial machinery, cranes and water towers, fire escapes and alleyways.

She examined the maze-like pattern on the back of the tag — a map of sorts, she assumed: the five circles representing locations in the room, the zigzagging lines the route. She considered the tag's printed number five. *Five things,* she concluded. *The task is to retrieve five things.*

There was no indication that she was up against the clock, but she imagined she probably was; time was always a factor.

The task required her to make her way across the varied urban landscape. The lines on the tag gave her the necessary clues as to the direction she should go in; how she managed it was down to her.

And so she began. At first cautiously, assessing the terrain and planning the route that would take her to object one: a small bunch of keys — not easy to spot, particularly for Ruby, whose eyes were not her greatest asset. The keys were lodged in a wall that she had to climb while contending with a fake rainstorm, which drenched her in under a minute — but even so, it didn't present too much of a challenge. Ruby slipped object one into her pocket.

One down, four to go.

The next was a yellow flashlight. It was perched on top of a shattered rooftop; the only way to reach it that Ruby could see was to climb the building's crumbling walls. Bricks and plaster came loose as she made her way up, and a whole section of roof fell away as she clambered onto the rafters, tiles and beams crashing down with an almighty boom.

Oops, thought Ruby.

Ruby grabbed the flashlight and paused to take stock. The tag's map indicated that she should make her way through the room beneath her and exit via a doorway into the adjacent building, but the room was now full of rubble, and whatever doorway there might have been was gone. So she tucked the flashlight into her belt and found another route, much longer and more perilous and involving a certain amount of physical labor in order to uncover a trapdoor.

The third object was hidden in an underground space that Ruby had to crawl into on her stomach. She shivered at the prospect, being no fan of small dark spaces. However, this was where the flashlight came into its own, and Ruby traced the light across the walls, methodical in her search, and although she was not at all at ease, she didn't allow herself to become panicked (after all, **RULE 19: PANIC WILL FREEZE YOUR BRAIN**).

However, she was aware of the time ticking by and was sure it had taken her longer than it should to lay her hands on the copper-colored coin that was object three. She needed to speed things up, and so rather than continue crawling through this long winding tunnel, she decided to resurface and make her way at ground level; that way, she could pick up the pace.

From looking at the map, it seemed that the fourth object was on the other side of the urban set, so she headed for the water tower, which stood fifty feet in the air. It was a gamble, but as it turned out, it was a good gamble. Having climbed the fifty feet to reach the wide platform that held the tank, Ruby chose not to make the final ascent by way of the ladder propped against the tank itself but instead to free-climb up it, using the wooden bands around it for hand- and footholds.

Ruby took off her shoes — they weren't climbing shoes, and she'd have a better grip with her bare feet. She was a good climber, and she shinnied up in no time, never looking left or right. At the top she found what she was looking for: a small penknife fastened to the surface by a metal band. It took Ruby no time at all to figure out that the copper coin would act as screwdriver and she could use it to turn the screw and release the penknife. She stood there on the edge of the tank, surveying the terrain. She could see object five. She didn't need to check her map; it was suspended from a crane, a large silver cylinder gleaming in the light.

Ruby didn't want to lose time by climbing down from where she was, but if she was going to reach the crane by jumping, then she needed to be on the other side of the tank. The only way was to dive into the water and swim.

So she did.

She hauled herself out of the water and barely paused before making the leap from water tower to crane. Her heart lurched as her fingers slipped — she threw up her other hand, gripped the metal, and swung herself monkey-like along the crane's arm.

She could see the cylinder hanging from the end on a sturdy rope. Fall from here and she might cause herself some damage — or certainly end up with more than a few bruises. But she wouldn't fall. Reaching the crane's end, she pulled on the rope, then grabbed the cylinder and used the penknife to slice through its tether. The cylinder was a good deal heavier than she had predicted and also awkward to carry; her solution was to push it up her T-shirt, which worked just fine.

From there she used what was left of the rope and swung herself back and forth until she felt able to let go, flinging herself toward the scaffolding platform at the far end of the urban jungle.

To reach the end zone meant jumping across a gap wider than she had ever jumped; the drop beneath looked to be approximately thirty feet. It didn't look possible, but everything was *possible,* wasn't it? She took fifteen paces back and then ran as fast as she could before leaping into the air, propelling her body forward, touching her toes on the far side, falling forward, and gripping what she could grip.

She had made it.

Just.

She leaned against the wall and dropped her head to her knees; she was out of breath, but she had proved what she needed to prove — she could get a perfect score. A guy in a white short-sleeve shirt and brown tie came out from behind the building she had been resting against and stretched out his hand.

"Thank you, Agent Redfort. You made great time and a pretty good score."

Ruby looked at him, stunned. "What? Did I wobble or something?"

CHAPTER 13
A Must-Have Item

RUBY WAS REQUIRED TO WAIT on the hard metal bench until someone told her otherwise. "About ten minutes or so." They didn't even give her a towel. Or return her shoes.

No doubt she would be debriefed by some brainiac über-nerd who would yak on to her about her skills, ego, motivation, blah, blah. To be honest, Ruby was not looking forward to this. The way she saw it, it was all so much hot air. Could she do it or not was the point. Clearly she could, so why talk it over?

After what seemed like a long ten minutes, someone came to fetch Ruby and she was led to a gray door down a monochrome spiraling passage. On the other side of the door was another agent, also wearing a white short-sleeve shirt and brown tie. He was sitting at a gray desk, shuffling pieces of paper around.

"Hello, Ms. Redfort," he said, getting to his feet. "I'm Agent—"

"Gill," finished Ruby.

He looked surprised.

"I recognize your voice from the phone," said Ruby.

"You have a good ear," said Agent Gill. "Do sit down."

Ruby sat and waited for Gill to speak.

He did some more shuffling and clearing of his throat before he eventually came to the point.

"You took a lot of risks out there," he said. "I have to be honest: a couple of those objects I didn't expect you to reach, given how high they were."

"Are you saying I'm short, sir?" said Ruby, her face in no way making it clear that she was kidding around.

"I'm saying that you obviously took my advice and worked on your fitness; you made some very big stretches considering, well, considering . . . No insult intended, Ms. Redfort."

"Forgiven," said Ruby.

Gill looked a little perturbed but took a sip of his water and continued.

"The thing is, there's a problem."

"What? I made it without falling, didn't I?"

"Yes," said Agent Gill.

"I was fast, right?"

"You were."

"I got all five objects. That's what the puzzle was telling me, five things?"

"Five things, yes," agreed Agent Gill.

"So?"

"You missed something."

"You lost me."

"You needed to collect the *correct* five things." Agent Gill picked up the final item, the silver cylinder — it shone as the light from the desk lamp hit it.

Ruby was puzzled until her eyes took in what was written down one side of the silver item. BOMB, it said.

"How could I have missed *that*?" said Ruby, more to herself than the test supervisor.

"Plenty of people do," said Gill.

"You're talking about change blindness? Focusing too much on the main task — missing the detail?"

"Yes, that's why *some* people fail," said Agent Gill. "But in your case, I think it was because you were being reckless; you lost focus altogether. You got carried away."

Ruby frowned at him. "But I —"

"You also missed this." He pushed a photo over the desk. It showed the water tower Ruby had climbed up and swum through. On its side were large letters spelling the word TOXIC, a skull and crossbones painted beneath.

How could she not have seen *that*?

"If you'd noticed the warning," he said, "you could have used the ladder leaning against the tank, hauled it up, then slid it over the water to create a bridge. I must say, it's what I expected you to do, given your reputation."

"Um . . ." Ruby was all out of words.

But Agent Gill wasn't. "In addition, had you simply walked around the building where you spotted the flashlight, you would have discovered a door. The bunch of keys you picked up would have allowed you access to that door, and you could have simply climbed a staircase to the roof instead of bringing the whole roof crashing to the floor and thus blocking your route to the trapdoor and object three."

"Oh," said Ruby.

Gill peered at her. "Oh indeed," he said. "From observation, I would have to conclude that you have a curious lack of regard for your own life. A certain fearless approach, causing you to be impulsive rather than considered. You are reacting rather than making decisions—your actions are gambles—and it's a dangerous way to be when you are in the field. I have to be frank: this is not how I expected you to fail."

"You *expected* me to fail?" said Ruby.

"Yes. But in quite a different way. We didn't think you would make the final leap. I mean, we guessed you would try, but you see it was set farther than you could jump. Candidates are expected to assess the risk, figure on it being too great, and find a better route. But you made it, and this surprises us very much."

"What can I say?" said Ruby dryly. "I'm a real good jumper."

"Or you got very lucky," said Agent Gill. He coughed and reshuffled his papers. "Ordinarily you'd be put forward for stage three of the Field Agent Training Program and you would be enrolled in free-climb training at Dry River Canyon. But you're not going to be recommended for further field work or tuition at this stage."

"What?" said Ruby.

"I'm sorry," said Gill.

"But I've already been sitting things out. I thought this test was about putting me back in."

"Not possible," said Gill. "Not given your current test scores. You're a danger to yourself and a possible danger to others if you don't respect your own life."

"What do you mean?" asked Ruby, "Because I'm not afraid, this makes me some kind of liability?"

"You *are* a liability," said Gill. "Because your apparent

lack of fear is clouding your judgment, we can't risk you out there — besides, you're someone's kid."

"Isn't everyone? Aren't you?"

"That's different," said Agent Gill. "My folks aren't home waiting for me with milk and cookies."

"What? And you think mine are?" said Ruby, rolling her eyes. "I'm thirteen, not three."

Disappointment wasn't the word for how Ruby was feeling. Furious might be. Agent Gill had shuffled her along to be assessed by the Spectrum psychiatrists, and she was now sitting in Dr. Selgood's calm, book-lined office. Mercifully, she had been handed a towel and was beginning to dry off. Her shoes still hadn't been returned.

DR. SELGOOD: *What you have, Redfort, is a condition — it's a syndrome that survivors of near-fatal accidents sometimes experience. There's no name for it and there are very few studies on those who experience it, but I call it the Miracle Effect. I had a patient who likened it to having an ever-present guardian angel at his side. He feared nothing and no one.*

RUBY: *What happened to him?*

DR. SELGOOD: *He died.*

RUBY: *The angel was on a break?*

DR. SELGOOD: *No one beats death. What you are now dealing with is a sort of euphoria — you don't believe you can die.*

RUBY: *I haven't so far.*

DR. SELGOOD: *Doesn't mean you won't.*

RUBY: *It seems unlikely.*

DR. SELGOOD: *Which is why you take risks?*

RUBY: *The more risks I take, the less dead I feel.*

DR. SELGOOD: *Yet ironically the more likely you are to wind up that way.*

RUBY: *I'm not so sure.*

DR. SELGOOD: *How so?*

RUBY: *I read this book once about this kid who believes in the probability of death, a sort of risk assessment of life. He believes if something unlikely has happened one day, like, say a plane lands on your house or a forest fire breaks out and you fall off a cliff, then that particular risk is dealt with because in all probability that ain't gonna happen twice.*

DR. SELGOOD: *Here you are talking about statistics and yet you know better than most that just because a plane lands on your house once doesn't mean it can't happen again.*

RUBY: *True, but it would seem unlucky.*

DR. SELGOOD: *And you consider yourself to be lucky?*

RUBY: *I'd say not many people escape a giant egg timer.*

DR. SELGOOD: *You're referring here to the time you were almost buried alive in sand.*

RUBY: *I could just as well bring up the time that I was paralyzed by jellyfish and nearly eaten alive by sharks.*

DR. SELGOOD: *And it doesn't occur to you that perhaps the situation you had put yourself in led to your near demise? And that the reason you escaped with your life is due in part to your training and some pretty advanced gadgetry and in part to the luck of being rescued in the nick of time?*

RUBY: *I couldn't have put it better myself, Doc. I am very unlikely to die. I've got everything going for me.*

DR. SELGOOD: *And yet, in your test, you swam through toxic water, then climbed a crane to grab a bomb.*

RUBY: *Oh, come on. It was a* test. *Those things weren't real.*

DR. SELGOOD: *But what if they had been?*

RUBY: *They weren't.*

DR. SELGOOD: *The thirty-foot drop was real.*

RUBY: *You telling me there wasn't a giant inflatable there to catch me?*

The psychiatrist sighed and closed the file.

DR. SELGOOD: *Maybe you should come and see me again. How about I set up some appointments?*

RUBY: *If you enjoy chatting so much, then who am I to deny you this pleasure?*

She smiled but her teeth were gritted.

When Ruby exited the psychiatrist's room, she found her shoes sitting waiting for her, both now quite dry. She put them on, looked around, and thought for a moment. Then instead of turning left and taking the elevator to Buzz level, she turned right and fast-walked her way to the zigzagging emergency stairs and on down to orange level. She stopped at the gadget room door, looked at her watch, and tapped in the exact time — this was the code to open the door, or at least should have been, but the door did *not* open.

Those sneaks.

Click, click went her brain.

Froghorn, she muttered, *I'll bet it was you.*

Froghorn was the go-to guy when anyone at Spectrum was looking to switch a code or speedily improve short-term security. But codes worked best when set by an unknown, and unfortunately for Froghorn, Ruby knew him pretty well. She guessed that part of the reason for resetting the gadget room code was to prevent her from accessing it. Froghorn would enjoy that; it would make him very happy to think the Redfort kid had been locked out. So she asked herself, *What would Froghorn do?*

And recalling the conversation she'd had earlier with him, she suddenly knew. He wouldn't have been able to resist.

45902314: her test number, the digits that spoke of failure.

She punched them in, and the lock clicked open.

People can be so predictable, thought Ruby.

She had no trouble finding what she wanted. She had gazed at them on so many occasions that she would be able to locate them had she been blindfolded. Twenty seconds later, item 202 was zipped safely inside her satchel. She didn't feel one iota of guilt about it — she needed them, should have been issued them, and in any case, who else here was going to wear them? And after all, she couldn't skitch everywhere on that skateboard, certainly not to Dry River Canyon, which was where she intended to go.

GETAWAY SHOES
Depress green button on base of left shoe to
convert to "roller shoes." Depress red button
on base of right shoe to activate power jets.
Maximum speed ninety-one miles per hour for a
distance of approximately seven miles.
WARNING! CAN CAUSE FEET TO OVERHEAT. AVOID USE ON
RUGGED TERRAIN.

They had once belonged to the boy Bradley Baker and were
now gathering dust in a display case. That was all wrong, as far as
she saw it. Ruby closed the glass door, hoping that no one would
notice the empty space. She didn't think they would. **RULE 18:**
PEOPLE OFTEN MISS THE DOWNRIGHT OBVIOUS.

She was about to leave when her eye caught sight of a "must-
have item," as her mother would put it. The item appeared to be
nothing more than a tiny silver backpack, but when she read
the description, it struck her that this was one very cool and
extremely useful piece of gadgetry.

GLIDER WINGS
Simply slip backpack on over clothing. Make sure
nothing covers backpack. To activate fabra-tech

wings, jump (minimum height twenty feet) and,
once falling, hit red button located on the
right-hand strap.

If wings fail—

The note about wings failing was missing, the paper torn,
but she figured that the wings wouldn't fail and if they did,
well, she could figure that out while she was falling. There
was a small orange card to the side of the little glider wings no
doubt explaining that this item should not be removed without
permission, blah, blah.

Ruby figured if she was in trouble for taking one item, she
might just as well be in trouble for taking two. And anyway, if
Spectrum was so worried about her falling off things and so on,
then why not be prepared? Surely by taking the glider wings
she was actually being responsible—well, that's how she saw
it, anyway.

In for a penny, in for a pound, she thought as she headed back
to street level.

CHAPTER 14
Run

RUBY STOPPED BY AMSTER GREEN hoping to catch Clancy — she felt like she needed to see a friendly face after her disappointing morning at Spectrum. But it was a long shot, and when she climbed the oak and reached into one of the many knots in its bark, she found only a small piece of paper, folded into the shape of a bug. She opened it up and read the message.

```
ukuevj't fsge bl wm usxylaptbfc kbvviedw.*
```

"Poor Clance," sighed Ruby. "That Olive kid is something else."

She climbed back down and began her short trip home. The skateboard ran smoothly along the level road of Amster and her tired limbs took it easy.

As soon as Ruby got in, she called Clancy.

"I got your message. Sounds like a drag. Couldn't your sister Minny help you out? She owes you for all those other times."

"You got that right," grumbled Clancy. "Anyway, so where were you today?"

"I had to take my Girl Scout test." Ruby and Clancy had learned from experience to speak in a roundabout fashion on an unsecured line.

"Are you back in?"

"Nope."

"Whaddaya mean? You must be back in, I mean, what was it testing?"

"You know, to see if I was all there in mind and body."

"And?"

"Something was missing, apparently."

"What something?"

"Fear."

"Is that bad?"

"They seem to think so — they figure I have some kind of death wish."

"They said that?"

"No, they dressed it up a bit, called it the Miracle Effect."

"This thing they're saying about you," said Clancy, "is it true, do you think?"

"If it's weird to feel like your number's not gonna come up, then I guess I got some kinda syndrome, call it the Miracle Effect, the Angel Complex, call it any darned thing you want, but it doesn't change the fact that I'm still here and probability says I shouldn't be."

"So what does it feel like?" asked Clancy. "Believing you can't die?"

Ruby paused before saying, "I sort of can't help pushing things to see what will happen, to see how it feels to be invincible, and every time I don't die, it's harder to believe I ever will. But I don't get what the problem is — I mean, I'm a Girl Scout, right? Or at least a trainee Girl Scout, so how can fearlessness be a bad thing?" She paused. "Look, you coming over or what?"

"What," said Clancy.

"That's funny, Clance. You're a laugh a minute, buster, you know that?"

"Yeah, well, if I could I would, you know."

"I know, but there's Olive, right?"

"Yeah, but once I'm done with that, I'm planning on meeting Elliot at the diner, if you feel like it."

"I'll bear it in mind," said Ruby. "Meantime, stay outta jail." She hung up and went down to the kitchen looking for food, but as she was passing the hall table, the telephone began to ring. She picked up the receiver. "Twinford Space Program. Slip into an astronaut suit and make gravity a thing of the past."

"Uh . . ." said a hesitant voice down the end of the line.

"Oh, hi, Quent."

"It's Quent," said Quent.

"I know," said Ruby.

"You did? How come?" He sounded really pleased.

"You have a kinda recognizable voice."

"I do?"

"Yeah."

"Wow, no one's ever told me that before."

"Happy I could make your day. Now, what can I do you for?"

"I was hoping you could make it to my birthday party."

Silence.

"I sent the invitation several weeks ago, but I know you were in the hospital getting your arm fixed, so you might have missed it."

Silence.

"That's why I'm following up with a call."

Silence.

"It's going to be a superhero theme."

Silence.

"I haven't decided on my costume yet, but it might be that one who breathes underwater."

"Aquaman?"

"Yeah, Aquaman, but it's a hard superhero to do out of the pool and our pool's being drained due to the algae."

"So remind me of the date, Quent?"

"It's on Saturday the sixteenth."

"Saturday the sixteenth. That's a tough break — any other day but Saturday the sixteenth and I'd be there like a shot."

"You mean you can't make it?" Quent sounded devastated. Not a tiny bit upset — devastated.

If Ruby could be hard-nosed when confronted by bullies and psychopaths, she entirely crumbled when faced with disappointed, lisping eleven-year-old boys, or disappointed anyone for that matter — all that Ruby Redfort tough-talking, cocksure cool just evaporated.

"Look, Quent, before you let that lip start wobbling, let me see if I can't rejig a few things here."

A superhero party, that's all I need.

While Ruby was contemplating her dilemma, her friend Clancy was figuring a way to wriggle out of his little problem. He was so absorbed by these thoughts that he didn't at first hear the small voice calling out to him.

"I *said,* can you walk me to the party now?" It was Olive, Clancy's five-year-old sister.

"No," said Clancy, "I said I'd hang out with you, but I'm not walking you to any party."

"But Mom said you have to."

Olive was standing in the doorway to his room in her hat, coat, gloves, and backpack.

"What are you wearing Olive?" said Clancy. "You do realize it's still about seventy-five degrees outside?"

"Mom says we are expecting a cold snip any day soon," said Olive.

"Yeah, well, I think you are a little overprepared. And by the way it's cold *snap,* not cold *snip.*"

"I like snip better," said Olive.

Clancy rolled his eyes. Most people seemed to find Olive cute, but he didn't. She was too annoying for cute.

While Clancy looked for his backpack, Olive went down to find their mother and tell on him.

Clancy took the back stairs to avoid the inevitable — maybe he could slip out without Olive seeing — but as he turned the corner, to his dismay there she was.

"Mom says you're in trouble if you don't take me."

There was to be no escape. Mrs. Crew's voice called out, "Clancy, is it really too much to ask that you walk your little sister to her party? She so looks up to you. Can't you just be kind?"

Olive was looking straight ahead, her big eyes blinking at him. She looked as innocent as a Kewpie doll.

Clancy was about to offer Olive a bribe, but his mother marched out from the kitchen followed by Amy, the second youngest Crew sister.

Amy was seven and not a big talker and Clancy, perhaps for this very reason, was especially fond of her.

"OK, OK, I'll take her," grumbled Clancy.

Amy gave him a sympathetic glance.

Mrs. Crew bent to kiss Olive on the nose. "You are a perfect picture!"

Clancy looked at Olive. She was a picture, all right.

Reluctantly he walked her to her friend's party, where she immediately latched on to some other kid and began talking to it as if Clancy had never been there.

"My total pleasure," he called. "Don't mention it."

Olive didn't even hear.

"Is that your little sister?" said a mother on the way to drop off her kid. "I could just eat her up."

"You'll need plenty of relish," said Clancy.

Due to the Olive drop-off, Clancy was now running late and Elliot would already be at the Donut waiting for him. Clancy didn't like to be late; he liked to be punctual. He got anxious when he wasn't on time. So he started to run. It was well past midday and hot, but he would rather be on time than comfortable, therefore he sprinted, not easing his pace for even a minute. Clancy was fast, but despite his running flat-out, he arrived twenty-one minutes late. It was a shame because this was one instance when Clancy would have benefited from being on time; it would have saved him a whole lot of bother.

As he pushed open the door to the diner on Amster Street, he went smack into the back of a kid who was tying his shoe on the other side of the door.

"Whoa, sorry," said Clancy, stepping back.

The boy straightened and turned around, and for just a second looked like he was about to say something along the lines of "No problem," but sort of changed his mind when he laid eyes on Clancy.

It was like he had a choice — shrug it off or make something of it. He took option two.

"You deep-down stupid? Or do you just feel the need to get socked in the face?"

"What?" said Clancy. He didn't get what was going on here. All he'd done was walk into the Double Donut, and now he was about to get beaten up? It wasn't even one p.m.; the day had barely gotten going.

"You deaf too, loser?" said the boy.

Clancy just stared, unsure what to say. The kid's jaw was set in an angry clench and his eyes had narrowed. He was sort of ugly looking, all fists and muscles — looked like he could take on a gorilla.

"Look, I didn't mean to bump into you. It was an accident caused by you being in the way."

"What?" The gorilla looked puzzled.

"But sorry if I hurt you." Clancy knew that that last thing wasn't a good thing to say if he wanted to walk away without getting blood all over his shirt, but the guy was ticking him off and he couldn't help himself.

"*What* did you just say?" said the boy.

"Sorry if I hurt you. I guess you have a low pain threshold," said Clancy. "Some people do."

The boy's face was set like stone. "You aren't even going to *have* a pain threshold by the time I've finished with you," he hissed. "I'm going to snap it right in half."

"That doesn't make sense," said Clancy. "You can't snap a pain threshold, not in half, not in quarters, not in nothing."

But the boy wasn't listening. He had grabbed Clancy by the collar and had his other hand balled into a fist. His face was very near Clancy's, and his breath smelled of something not so fresh.

"If it's all the same to you," croaked Clancy, "I'd really like to apologize. I'm sure it was all my fault. What do you say we start fresh?"

This only served to make the boy even madder. He was about to really punch Clancy when Marla stepped in. She had hold of the kid's arm, real tight.

Marla was known for her strong grip and well-developed biceps; she could open any size of pickle jar, hurl heavy sacks of potatoes into the storage cupboard, and throw brawling men out into the street without breaking a sweat.

Marla looked the gorilla kid square in the eye. "I don't wanna see you again, not in my diner, not outside my diner, not anywhere near my diner — you got that, cookie?"

The boy kind of nodded.

"Sure you do," said Marla as she turned him around and marched him out the door. "Now scram."

Then she looked at Clancy. "Play nice" was all she said before going back to her kitchen. Clancy brushed himself down, then made his way through the tables to where Elliot was sitting.

Elliot looked up when Clancy approached. "Do you know how late you are?"

"Did you see that?" asked Clancy.

"What?" said Elliot. "Did I miss something?" He was looking around now.

"I nearly got squeezed to death by a gorilla is all."

"Really?"

"Almost," said Clancy, "but knowing *you* were there thinking about me made all the difference."

"What do you mean a gorilla?" Elliot looked both afraid and eager to see it.

"This huge guy was trying to kill me; Marla threw him out."

"If only I'd seen," said Elliot, "I would have . . . you know, done something. . . ."

"I'm sure you would have weighed in."

"No way, José," said Elliot. "You're a good friend, Clance, but I like my teeth where they are — in my mouth."

"So what would you have done?" said Clancy.

"Run in the other direction, most likely," said Elliot, and then he began to laugh, so much that the whole table began to vibrate and his milkshake ended up on the floor. At which point Marla handed him a mop.

Clancy didn't mind that Elliot was not prepared to put himself in the line of attack; at least he was honest about it. It was hard to hate someone for *that*.

CHAPTER 15
No Guardian Angel

RUBY WOKE UP EARLY THE NEXT MORNING and got dressed: a pair of shorts, a T-shirt bearing the word *scram,* sunscreen. She stuffed her climb shoes into her backpack, along with a bottle of water, some climbing chalk, and the glider wings, then she took out item 202: THE GETAWAY SHOES.

If Spectrum wasn't going to give her free-climb training, then she was just going to have to do it for herself.

She slipped on the shoes. A perfect fit. It was clear that they had belonged to Bradley Baker back in the day, but they didn't look like they had gotten too much wear and the leather was still in fine condition.

She pushed open her window, swung herself out to the tree, and climbed down to the yard. Then she went out the back gate into the alley and ran until she met the Dry River road, a long gently winding ribbon of pavement. She clicked the green button, and the roller wheels snapped out. Now they looked more or less like traditional roller skates. Then she clicked the red button. Nothing happened. She skated a couple of yards — still nothing — *stupid Spectrum junk!* And then quite suddenly she was moving at incredible speed toward Dry River Canyon.

This was the climb location the Spectrum trainees would be training at, so why shouldn't she give it a try? She was as good as any of them, whatever LB or Agent Gill thought. It was still early morning and it wasn't too hot, a perfect day for a climb, and what better way to test her newly fixed arm than by climbing several hundred feet up a rock face?

Plenty, some might say.

Ruby arrived without injury, but her feet were very hot and a strange smell was coming from the Getaway Shoes. She took them off and placed them in the shade of a rock to cool. There were no trees in Dry River Canyon, just huge boulders strewn along what would have once been the riverbed: vast stone formations marching across the landscape and a huge wall of golden rock towering up and around the canyon's edge. She changed into her climb shoes, fastened her chalk pouch around her waist, and stood looking up at the cliff that rose several hundred feet above her. Then she slipped on the tiny backpack containing the folded Glider Wings, so lightweight that she could barely even feel the straps on her shoulders.

She began to climb.

She was fast, and from a distance it looked effortless as she reached with her arms and legs, feeling out hand- and footholds. She paused now and again but only so she could reach behind her and dig her hands into the pouch and dust them with chalk. Keeping her fingers free of sweat was her only concern. She'd made it a good way up — four hundred feet perhaps.

She was now balanced on the smallest of ledges, just contemplating the view before she made the final ascent. The air was very fresh this morning, only a light breeze lifting her hair. She worked out the direction she wanted to go in — she did not choose the easiest route; she picked the one with the most challenge to it, which meant rounding the rock face under a large overhang and then getting herself up and over. She was counting on there being some pretty decent fingerholds or it was going to get tricky.

This was a dangerous route for the best of climbers, but such was Ruby's confidence in her climbing that she didn't think for one minute, not one second, that she could fall. She felt like Spider-Man as she clung by her fingertips and toe tops, making her way across the face of the golden rock. She had made it all the way under the jutting stone face — now all she needed to do was to get above it. She chalked her hands and without pause began to work her way out and to the edge of the lip. For a few seconds she hung by her fingers from the overhang, four hundred and fifty feet above the canyon floor, then with a superhuman effort she swung her foot up and hooked it over the top. Twisting, she lifted herself up and over the lip.

Once above it, she felt a rush of adrenaline — she had pretty much made it. She was doing well, not a wrong move, and then quite unexpectedly her foot slipped and she was sliding fast, back to the place where the rock cut under and there would be no surface to grab. She dug her fingers in, making claws of her hands, and then, at the last moment, just before she went over the edge, she found a hold and for a moment she hung there by her fingers' very tips just thanking her "Redfort Good Luck."

Phew.

She let out a breath and then almost chuckled to herself. Life and death, so easily exchanged — and currently hanging in the balance, quite literally. She looked around her, calmly gauging her next move, then when she was sure, she swung her body to create momentum and kind of leaped to the right, letting go of her handhold as she did so.

A heartbeat of completely thin air —

and then the warm dry rock was once again in her grasp.

Ten minutes later she had made it, and standing there

drinking in the sun's rays, she felt very alive, the adrenaline coursing through her body. *Perfect,* she thought. She was about to fly. Glide down like some kind of eagle. She unlatched the safety catch on the Glider Wings and felt for the release button. The one thing she had understood from reading the instructions was that you had to jump before depressing it — that was crucial — a hard thing to do, because it meant totally and utterly trusting that it was going to work.

She stepped back from the edge and walked about twenty paces. Then turned to face the canyon she was about to dive into. She ran as fast as she could until she was running like one of those cartoon characters who realize too late that they are running in midair above a giant gorge.

She punched the button.

A horrible split-second of nothing.

She punched again and felt the tiny wings spread out and she was airborne, gliding like a huge bird of prey. She could control direction with her body, leaning from side to side. This was without doubt the most incredible experience of her life; she was several hundred feet up and utterly alone, held only by the air around her. Silent, and surrounded by empty space.

And then a very unwelcome sound — the sound of tearing fabra-tech.

CHAPTER 16
Just Lucky

AS THE AIR PRESSURE RIPPED into the glider wings, some of the fabra-tech "feathers" whirled away into the sky and Ruby began to half glide, half fall, Icarus-like, toward the rock face. She reached out her hands but could not catch hold of anything that would halt her descent.

A sudden gust of wind grabbed at the glider gear and wrenched it from the backpack, and then she was tumbling and turning as she tried to grab air.

Ruby caught sight of the little wings peacefully gliding away — like the wings of an invisible, and forgetful, guardian angel. She caught sight of the ground rushing to meet her and knew that there was no way she would land without making one big dent in the earth, and no doubt an even bigger one in her skull.

What to do? She was all out of ideas, her mind in free fall — no life memories flashing before her eyes, just simply the ground getting nearer.

And then quite suddenly she wasn't falling—she was floating. Had the card describing the Glider Wings not been ripped, Ruby would have discovered that embedded in the safety straps was a panel that contained a tiny parachute. A parachute that had deployed automatically when the wings failed, and was now lifting her back toward the sun and the sky.

Am I lucky or am I just a Redfort? Ruby thought this thought a split second before a gust of wind picked her up and slammed her into the rock face.

OW!

She was stuck, the little parachute canopy having hooked itself on a sharp outcrop a hundred or so feet from the canyon valley base.

She hung there, dangling from the parachute suspension lines.

Yikes, thought Ruby, *now what?* She remembered her survival training. *No sudden movements, that would be a good place to start.*

She slowly worked on trying to unsnag the lines. But that just wasn't a realistic possibility, given that she was attached to them.

She tried swinging herself, to see if she could grab the rock face and climb up, then untangle the parachute. This also proved impossible.

Once she had tried every means of getting herself down,

other than the easiest — cut the suspension lines and see where you land (even Ruby didn't believe she would survive that) — she saw that there was only one thing to do. *Get help or end your days snagged on a rock face.*

Sighing, she pressed the rescue button on her Escape Watch and waited for that help to arrive.

She must have fallen asleep soon after the alarm call went out, because the next thing she was aware of was a voice.

"Do you have some kind of death wish, kid?"

At that exact moment Hitch's voice was the best sound Ruby had ever heard, even though it in fact sounded sort of furious. He wasn't shouting, which made it worse, his voice heavy with disappointment, his expression telling her that at that very minute he wasn't exactly pleased to see her breathing but was relieved that he hadn't had to pick up the Ruby-shaped pieces.

"I was just free-climbing. Keeping my fitness levels up since Spectrum doesn't think I'm worth training," explained Ruby. "How am I ever gonna make the grade if I don't keep practicing?"

Hitch raised an eyebrow. He saw at a glance what had really happened. "Don't give me that baloney. This wasn't about practice; this was about you thrill seeking. You were taking one heck of a risk because you wanted to try out a piece of Spectrum equipment — equipment you haven't been trained to use, let alone *authorized* to use, nor, let's not forget, even permitted to take out of the gadget facility. You have broken so many rules here that I don't know why I am even wasting my breath; *you* sure as darn it don't care."

Ruby folded her arms. It was hard to look defiant when suspended from a rock by a piece of string, but she gave it her best shot.

"Oh, please," said Hitch. "Don't give me the petulant schoolkid act; it's just annoying."

All the time he was talking, he was climbing.

"I ought to haul you down from there and let you walk home. Better still, why don't I just leave you? The eagles might appreciate a little bird food."

Ruby would very much liked to have replied to these various insults but was kind of eager to make it home before supper, so decided it might be wise to keep her mouth shut.

"Do you value life so little?" asked Hitch.

"I totally value life; it's just I don't believe I'm going to die. I mean, it's inconceivable that I would die, will die — I mean, like now, I didn't, did I? The parachute saved me."

"By trussing you up on a cliff face? If I hadn't come along, you'd have starved or been pecked to pieces by vultures. This place is slap bang in the middle of nowhere."

"But you did come along and I'm not gonna die."

Hitch sighed. "Everyone dies, kid. What makes you so special?"

"I don't know; it's just a feeling. I keep not dying when I sort of should."

"And why *is* that, do you think?"

"Just lucky, I guess."

"I don't think so," said Hitch. "I think it's because people keep rescuing you, that and some pretty state-of-the-art equipment—the watch you're wearing, for instance."

"OK," agreed Ruby, "you might be right about the watch, but I wouldn't have been in this position at all if it hadn't been for those guardian wings—they don't work, you know."

"Kid, you wouldn't have been in this position at all if it wasn't for your crazy desire to take life to the edge and peer into the abyss. I've read your psych evaluation, and I happen to agree with it—your lack of fear blinds you to detail. For instance, the little orange card sitting next to the Glider Wings saying, *Do not use—awaiting repair.*"

"Oh," said Ruby. "Well, I was in kind of a hurry, you know. I didn't want to get caught sneaking around in there."

Hitch didn't even bother responding to that.

By now he had reached her and was busy figuring out a way

to get her down. Aware that her life was in his hands, she kept it zipped while he worked on the problem.

Twenty minutes later and she was standing on solid ground.

"How did you even get out here, anyway?" asked Hitch, who was looking around for some clue as to transport.

Ruby opened her mouth, ready to come up with an answer that Hitch might swallow, but before she could speak, he held up his hand.

"You know what," he said, "don't even bother to lie, because I don't want to know."

**The figure in black
walked down the side
of the building . . .**

. . . not exactly Spider-Man–like, but it didn't look like it was causing him a whole lot of effort either. That is to say, it looked entirely natural, in the way it looks natural for a gymnast to *flick-flack* across a mat, or an acrobat to walk on his hands.

Only this guy was walking down a vertical wall.

Not only that, but he looked like he walked up and down walls for a living, and judging by the way he was now running along the narrow parapet, perhaps the balance beam was something he used daily too.

When he reached the ninth floor of the apartment building, its facade decorated with ornate stone carvings, he edged over to a small window, held onto the lintel, and — using his feet — pushed at the glass until it gave.

Then he flipped himself inside.

CHAPTER 17
The Human
Spider-Bird-Fly

MR. AND MRS. OKRA WERE PERPLEXED to find paint chips in the tub. They would probably never have spotted them at all had it not been for Mrs. Okra's bad back and her deciding to have a long hot soak in the tub rather than take a shower. She was about to step in when she noticed the flakes of white paint floating on the surface of the water. How had they gotten there?

She looked up. Of course, the only thing above her, the only thing painted white, was the tiny window high in the bathroom wall. She found the stepladder and took a closer look. The window, which had previously been painted shut, had clearly been forced open, and this was what had caused the sprinkling of white flakes.

Mrs. Okra was mystified. She called her husband, and they searched the ninth-floor apartment for missing items. The only thing that seemed to be gone was a first-edition poetry book, *A Line Through My Center,* by JJ Calkin, which had been on Mr. Okra's nightstand. It was always kept there. Mr. Okra had

a sentimental attachment to the book and often read a page or two when he was feeling melancholy.

There was a handwritten inscription inside: *To my darling Cat from your Celeste*, and Mr. Okra had always wondered who these people were. It was nice to think of this woman giving the book to someone important to her.

The cops were called and they examined the evidence. There had indeed been a break-in, no doubt about it, but who would be brave enough to climb ninety feet up the outside of the Fountain Heights Building to the ninth floor, be strong enough to force a stuck window, be small enough to climb through the tiny opening, and be silent enough to not wake the sleeping Mr. Okra and discreet enough to not be seen by his insomniac wife and get away undetected with a possession kept so close at hand?

THE GHOST OF SPIDER-MAN, ran the headline in the *Twinford Echo*.

Ruby Redfort rolled her eyes when she read this; she was not a big believer in ghosts, and ghosts of superheroes even less so. This was even dumber than the article about the Little Yellow Shoes specter. She tended to opt for the simpler explanation when it came to crimes that couldn't be solved; 99 percent of them were pretty easy to crack if one looked at them logically. **RULE 33: MORE OFTEN THAN NOT THERE IS A VERY ORDINARY EXPLANATION FOR THE "EXTRAORDINARY" HAPPENING.**

Cars and cabs passed by, late-night walkers hurried home, but no one took notice of this human fly, the journalist had written.

Spiders? Flies? What next, birds?

Ruby read on.

"I'm thinking it must have been some type of birdman," Jimmy Long, the concierge at the Fountain Heights Building, explained. "He just swooped in from nowhere and dived in through one of the windows; yeah, it was a birdman, all right."

"Ah, there we go, birds," muttered Ruby.

Mr. Long went on to explain that he had been asleep at the time of the incident and hadn't actually seen or heard a peep, a buzz, or a chirp from the burglar, but that sort of detail didn't seem to bother the *Echo*. If Jimmy Long said it was a birdman, then that was what it was.

But the *Twinford Lark* (Mrs. Digby's paper) had something better than Jimmy Long—they had a witness who claimed to have *seen* the mysterious climber.

Boo White, a guy sleeping in a disused shop doorway, thought he had seen a man scaling a building. "Like Spider-Man," he insisted. "I saw him climb from the roof to halfway down the wall and in through a window, but I never saw him come back down."

"Jimmy says birdman? Boo says Spider-Man? Who should I believe?" asked Ruby, imitating the voice of Elaine Lemon.

She knew Elaine Lemon would love this story.

There wasn't a single other person who had noticed so much as an insect crawl up the building, and no one had seen the intruder come out of the Okras' apartment, and though the cops searched from basement to rooftop, there was no sign of the intruder anywhere in the building.

Clancy and Ruby were sitting up in the oak tree on Amster Green. Ruby had risen early that morning and left the house by climbing out the window and down the eucalyptus tree. She didn't feel like running into Hitch and had decided to stay out of his way for as long as possible, then maybe he would eventually stop wanting to strangle her.

She and Clancy were perusing various local papers; they were actually supposed to be looking for a French polishing service that might visit the Crews' house pronto, no questions asked. This would save Clancy's older sister, Minny, from a month of hard labor and evenings in her room. Minny had trashed their mom's Louis XV dressing table by splattering it with hair dye — she would be suffering a whole lot of grief if something wasn't done about it before Mrs. Crew discovered the wreckage.

Clancy's mom was out of town but was expected back in twenty-four hours. Clancy for one couldn't cope with the stress of the imminent storm and so had decided to take matters into his own hands. However, he and Ruby had gotten diverted from their perusal of the ad pages by yet another sensationalist piece about the Okra robbery.

"Was it highly valuable?" asked Clancy. "This poetry book that was stolen?"

"Ummm,"— Ruby scanned the words—"no, unless you call twenty bucks a lot."

"I do, actually," said Clancy, "but I wouldn't climb up or down the outside of a building for it — so what makes this book so special?"

Ruby read on a little more. Mr. Okra was describing the book's importance to him. "I found it tucked into the seat pocket of a plane I was on. I guess whoever it belonged to had forgotten it when they disembarked. I was traveling back from L.A., I was very depressed at the time, my life was in tatters, but I discovered that book and I began reading—it turned me around. I wrote a piece about it for the Twinford Herald."

"Must be some book," said Clancy.

"I guess things don't have to be valuable to be valuable," said Ruby.

"I guess you're right," said Clancy.

Ruby looked at her watch. "Better go," she said. She and Clancy were heading to meet Mouse and Elliot at the outdoor Ping-Pong table in Harker Square. It had recently been fixed, having suffered a mishap at the jaws of a tiger (it's a long story). They were sort of dawdling; it was just that sort of day. When they finally got there, the same topic was being discussed. *Why would a person break into a swank apartment on the ninth floor of a secure building, stuffed full of super-valuable stuff, and only steal one single book?*

"I guess this person likes reading," said Elliot. Ruby looked at him. "I mean, a lot," he added.

"There's a library down the street," said Mouse.

"Maybe he lost his library card," said Elliot.

"Yeah, but there has to be something about this particular copy," said Ruby.

"Maybe it had cash in it. My mom sometimes does that, hides a hundred-dollar bill in a book," said Elliot.

"Why does she do that?" asked Mouse.

"Because it gives her a thrill when she finds it; she always forgets about it until one day, bingo!"

Mouse smiled. "I might come over later and borrow some books," she said.

CHAPTER 18
The Dangers of Soap

PING-PONG WAS BECOMING increasingly difficult because the wind was beginning to pick up, and the four of them spent most of the time chasing the ball around the park. After a half hour, they gave up. Mouse and Clancy had to head home, and Elliot went over to Del's place. Ruby said she'd join him, but first she had to pop home to pick up Bug.

"He could do with the exercise; he's been taking it easy since I got injured," said Ruby. "Hey, head on over without me. I'll see you in a while, OK?"

Ruby went home and got the dog, then hit the streets. The wind made Bug uneasy. He didn't like it blowing into his ears or ruffling through his fur. It was as if he felt some unknown presence just to his side or close behind him, someone invisible.

He was the same with ghosts, or at least that's what Elliot believed.

Whenever Bug or *any* dog for that matter would stop still and bark for no visible reason, Elliot would say, *"You wanna know why he's barking? Spooky dead things that only dogs pick up on."*

Unluckily for Bug, the Twinford County region was prone to getting these short-lived but violent windstorms. They blew in fast and blew out fast. Hard to predict, but destined to repeat over and over, gaining in force during the season until they eventually moved on. The locals often referred to them as Twinford gusters; they usually began in mid-October and whirled away till November arrived, but occasionally they arrived early and hit in September. When this happened, they usually culminated in a truly *fearsome* coming-together of rain, wind, thunder, and lightning. It seemed that this year was a year when one might want to batten down the hatches.

When it came to storms, Ruby did not feel the same way as Bug. The storm's force, only made visible by what it tore up or tossed into the air, terrified the dog, his animal instinct telling him this was bad news. But Ruby loved it. The sheer energy with which it churned the sea and bent the trees: all this she found exhilarating. Sure, it was dangerous, but somehow it transferred its energy and made her feel invincible.

Ruby called to the husky, who reluctantly got to his feet and followed her out the back door. She put him on the leash, not because he needed to be controlled (Bug was a very well-trained husky), but because the wind was already making him anxious, as if he might be required to do something—the result was one on-edge dog.

They walked all the way to Del's place, skirting through the back streets. The house backed onto the ocean and Ruby could hear the waves crashing onto the beach as she passed through the front gate. She didn't bother to knock on the door, but instead slipped through the gap to the side of the house, where she knew Del would be. Del was an outdoor type and when hanging out at home was usually in her yard fixing something or kicking, throwing, or catching a ball, maybe twirling a Hula-Hoop or standing on her head. Today she was sitting on the wooden yard chairs with Elliot, both watching the ocean. The sea was bringing in some big waves, and there were a lot of surfers out—the sound of the ocean boomed loud, and the wind carried their words.

"Hey, Rube," Del said, patting the seat next to her, "sit yourself down. Bug need a drink?" She was up and walking toward the kitchen.

"Sure," said Ruby, "You got any strawberry milk?"

Del raised an eyebrow. "Your dog drinks strawberry milk?"

"Yeah, funny one, Del. I might crack a smile one day."

When Del came back, the four of them (dog included) sat there contemplating the ocean. The water was dotted with the surfers who sat astride boards waiting for the right wave to roll in.

"Do you think Bug could surf?" asked Elliot.

"Unassisted, you mean?" asked Ruby.

Elliot nodded.

"I've taken him out with me a few times; he just hasn't gotten the hang of getting up on the board."

"But he's interested?" asked Del.

"Oh, he's got an interest, all right. Bug loves the water; he's just not so dexterous. It's hard when you don't have thumbs."

"Yeah," said Del, "I guess he's not really a grabber."

"No, a dog can't grab," agreed Ruby, "not even Bug."

"He's pretty smart for a dog," said Del. "What do you think he would be if he was a human?"

"I think he would do a job that involved working with the general public," said Ruby. "He's a people person."

While Del and Ruby were discussing Bug's human career prospects, Elliot was thinking. Finally he piped up.

"Do you think he could help solve the yellow shoe mystery?"

"What?" said Del.

"Who?" said Ruby.

"Bug," said Elliot.

"How?" said Ruby.

"What?" said Del again. "What are you talking about?"

"You know, the yellow shoes, the ones that got stolen the other night by that ghoul," said Elliot. Del was looking blank.

"How can you not know this? Where have you been? Mars?"

"Florida, actually." Del pointed to her extremely tanned face. "If you hadn't noticed, I've been on summer vacation."

"Yeah, well, you've missed a lot," said Elliot.

"So exactly *how* are you proposing Bug help out with this investigation?" asked Ruby for the second time.

"By, you know, sniffing around and finding that ghost that took the shoes from the Scarlet Pagoda."

"Are you seriously halfway to the planet no-brain?" spluttered Del. "You think a ghost stole the shoes?"

"It's what everyone is saying," said Elliot.

"You're telling me you actually believe in ghosts?" said Del.

"Why not? Animals believe in them; they can sense them. Humans have lost this ability, but dogs and cats can tune into specter vibes," said Elliot.

Del looked at him. "What are you talking about?"

"It's what makes the fur go all upward and stand on end; they just sense paranormal activity and they react."

Elliot said this like it explained everything — ghosts existed because animals' fur stood on end from time to time, and there it was, fact.

"Where do you get your information?" asked Ruby.

"From books," confirmed Elliot, "and this TV show I watched. This man was interviewed about this house he rented. As he was looking around the place, the dog followed him to every room until he got to the bathroom, and his dog, Buswell, refused to step inside."

"Maybe he didn't need to *go*," said Del.

Elliot ignored her. "Buswell stood there and growled, and later when the man spoke to the guy who had rented him the place, the guy told him that someone had actually died in there from slipping on a bar of soap."

"They died from slipping on a bar of soap?" said Ruby.

"Yeah," confirmed Elliot.

"Actually in that bathroom?" she asked.

"Not exactly in the bathroom but about an hour later in the emergency room at St. Angelina's, but it was the soap that did it."

"So why wouldn't the ghost haunt the emergency room at St. Angelina's hospital?" asked Del. "Why would it travel all the way back to the bathroom of its apartment?"

"Because I guess it felt more comfortable there," said Elliot.

"And how did it even get there?"

"I don't know — I'm not a ghost expert. Maybe on the bus?" said Elliot.

"Oh, man, that is the lamest story," spluttered Del. "Rube, is that lame or what?"

Ruby had stopped paying attention and was instead thinking about the evening at the Scarlet Pagoda; would Bug have followed her down that corridor, would *his* fur have stood on end? Red had certainly experienced something weird, something she couldn't actually explain. But still she nodded at Del and said, "It's the soap they should be scared of, not the ghost hanging out in the bathroom."

On her way back from Del's, inspired by the story of the soap ghost, Ruby turned her mind to the poetry ghost. She decided to stop in at the city library and see if she could borrow a copy of Mr. Okra's favorite book, *A Line Through My Center*. However, as it turned out, this was easier said than done.

"I'm afraid we don't have a copy. We used to many years back, but it's long since disappeared and no one thought to replace it," said Mr. Lithgo. He knew a lot about the books the library held, unsurprising because he seemed to have been there since the first stone was laid. Mr. Lithgo made calls to the various smaller

Twinford libraries, but none of them had ever owned a copy. "It was never considered very important, and I have to say, it is very rarely requested."

Next stop for Ruby was Penny Books, a secondhand store that dealt in any kind of literature: popular, unpopular, in print or out of print.

Ray Penny shook his head. "I can do my best to track down a copy, but it may take a while."

"Call me as soon as you find one, would you?" said Ruby. "I'll come right over the second you call."

"Will do, Ruby," said Ray. "Sounds real important."

CHAPTER 19
The Fly Barrette

WHEN RUBY GOT HOME, she went downstairs to Hitch's apartment and found him sitting at the table looking at some blueprints — she had no idea what they related to.

"Look, I'm sorry about yesterday," she said. "I know it was irresponsible."

Hitch raised an eyebrow.

"OK," added Ruby, "I know it wasn't too smart either."

Hitch blinked a slow blink.

Ruby sighed. "OK, if it means so much to you, then I know it was super dumb . . . and . . ."

"Look, before you begin with the groveling, I have to tell you, I agree with Agent Gill and Dr. Selgood, and before you ask, no, I haven't told anyone about your latest dumb-klutz behavior. Those two Spectrum items you stole have been returned, and Hal in gadgets said he'd fix them both on the quiet."

Ruby said nothing.

"You still think you being removed from training is unfair?"

Ruby shrugged; it was the sort of question that wasn't a question.

"Whether you do or whether you don't, it doesn't really change my mind," he continued. "It's just that I happen to know a few agents who caught the fearlessness bug, and they all have one thing in common."

"You're gonna tell me they're dead, right?"

"I don't have to; you know it. Anyone with a grain of sense knows that if you keep playing Russian roulette, one day you have to run into a bullet. The odds begin to stack against you."

Neither of them said anything for a minute, until Hitch took a small silver case out of his top pocket.

He slid it across the table. "It's to keep you out of harm's way," he said, "or at least so I have a way of tracking you when all else fails. You can't rely on just one thing; the Escape Watch is not enough. And besides . . . LB might decide to recall it."

"You think she'd do that?"

"I don't know. Just take the gift, OK?"

She opened the box. "A barrette?" said Ruby. She picked it up — it was a blue barrette and attached to it, very realistically, was an enamel black-and-white housefly. "What does it do?"

"It transmits a signal, helps me locate you, plus it has a tiny radio transmitter so we can communicate. I had Hal in gadgets make it up for me. It's a prototype — he hasn't had a whole lot of time to test-run it, but, well, it's better than nothing at all."

"I'll wear it if it makes you happy," said Ruby, sliding it into her hair and checking her reflection in the dark window glass, "and it looks OK, I guess."

Just then, some toast popped out of the toaster. Hitch went over, looked at it, raised an eyebrow, and slid it over to Ruby. Ruby looked down.

Redfort, Hitch, return to HQ immediately.

"You think they know about . . . my recent . . . activity?" said Ruby.

"No idea," said Hitch. "Could be something else entirely."

"Maybe they saw the light, realized they'd made a big mistake, and are ungrounding me," said Ruby.

"Yeah, that's right, kid," said Hitch. "You stay hopeful."

There was an air of unease in the briefing room, and everyone at Spectrum seemed to be sitting on the edge of their seats.

"What's going on?" asked Ruby. One thing was for sure — it didn't seem to have anything to do with her.

"I honestly don't know," said Hitch, and for once Ruby believed him.

This time the briefing was led by Agent Dixie Deneuve, from Spectrum 9. She wore a suit and she looked serious — no time for light humor, or even the faintest of smiles.

"Is that a made-up name?" hissed Ruby.

Hitch gave her a look that suggested she zip it.

The room went silent.

"A highly classified prototype has gone missing from the Department of Defense development base," said Dixie Deneuve. "As yet we have not even a trace of a clue as to who could have perpetrated this act." She took a sip of water before continuing. "This item was being developed by Spectrum scientists in collaboration with the military and was stored in a secure military location. Its disappearance is *highly* embarrassing for us. All Spectrum divisions have been alerted."

An agent put up her hand, and Deneuve nodded.

"Are we to know what this highly classified missing item is?" she asked.

"No," said Dixie Deneuve.

A murmur traveled through the briefing theater, no one quite understanding what the point of the briefing was if no one was authorized to know what the missing thing actually was.

"I cannot tell you because I do not know," said Agent Deneuve. "I do not know because I am not authorized to know, and if I am not authorized to know, then I must assume that I do not *need* to know."

"So," ventured another agent, "how do we know that this item has actually been taken?"

Agent Deneuve peered at him disdainfully. "Take my word for it, Agent"—she made a big deal of trying to read his name badge —"Dunst. That's your job, after all."

The agent shuffled uncomfortably in his seat.

"All Spectrum 8 need concern itself with is this: make sure security is kept tight and surveillance is maintained at the highest level. We need to bring these criminals in, and swiftly, without an almighty news story — simple as that."

"Given that Spectrum staff know the location of the DOD base and could potentially access the code to enter it, is it possible that the prototype has been taken by a person on the Spectrum team?" asked Blacker.

Dixie Deneuve blinked. "Anything is possible, agent. But at present we are operating on the assumption that it's an outside job. Although the circumstances surrounding the theft are . . . troubling."

She paused. "We know of various criminals who are

interested in our research with the military. It is impossible to keep secrets from everybody. But as far as it is possible, we keep tabs on them, we endeavor to know roughly where they are at any given time. For now what we need to focus on is *how* the intruder gained access rather than *why*. If we knew the answer to that first question, it might help lead us in the right direction."

She clicked a switch and the slide projector came on. The first image appeared.

This face was familiar to Ruby — she remembered it all too well from her first case protecting the Jade Buddha of Khotan.

"Nine Lives," announced Agent Deneuve, "a.k.a. Valerie Capaldi. She's dead, we know this for a certainty, but what we are interested in knowing is the whereabouts of her sometime sidekick."

Click.

"Fenton Oswald, a renowned jewel thief, based in Berlin and as far as we are aware, still there — we had a confirmed sighting of him just yesterday. He without doubt has the ability needed to mastermind a plan of this nature."

Click went the projector; more slides, more faces.

Count von Viscount, last seen walking along the seafront of Nice.

"He has a hideaway there," said Deneuve. "It wouldn't

surprise me if he was involved somehow; he just feeds off a mystery, and the stealing of this item is nothing if not mysterious."

Next came Hog-Trotter, and Agent Deneuve shivered and moved on. It seemed he wasn't a suspect—"Doing a little jail time," said Deneuve, "a minor misdemeanor involving some unpaid parking tickets but enough to put him out of action."

Up came another slide, another familiar face.

"Baby Face Marshall, still incarcerated and unlikely to be released this side of this century."

Click.

"Lorelei von Leyden was involved in our most recent case, and her whereabouts are at this precise time unknown."

Click. "But although we perhaps have many pictures of her . . ."

Click. A picture of a seemingly different woman came up. "We might just as well have none, since she is a human chameleon."

Click. Another woman, now with blond hair. "We might know what she looked like yesterday."

Click. Now she looked Chinese. "But we have no idea what she looks like today."

Click, click, click. Eight slides, eight very different-looking women.

"As for the Australian, a.k.a. the woman with the blue eyes, whom Agent Redfort almost lost her life to, she is still very much an unknown. Apart from one piece of security camera footage we are pretty much scratching our heads here." A very blurry image was projected onto the screen.

"So let me get this straight: we have nothing?" said Blacker.

"For now," said Deneuve. "But all Spectrum agents in all Spectrum divisions in all departments are expected to work every line of intelligence."

"Looks like it's going to be a long night," said Hitch.

"Too bad," sighed Ruby. "There's a *Crazy Cops* double bill on TV tonight."

**The transmitter was
buzzing and working its way
across the steel tabletop. . . .**

He picked it up and accepted the call. "Yes?" he said.

"I know what you're up to, Birdboy."

"I don't follow."

"You don't think I read the papers?"

Silence.

"You're famous. Twinford is enthralled — all this breaking and entering, all this petty theft, yet no sign of who it could be."

"I have no idea what you're talking about."

"I think you should stop lying; it's embarrassing."

"I told you, I have no idea what you are talking about."

"Just hand it over . . . or face the consequences."

CHAPTER 20
An Emergency Call

RUBY WAS DOWNSTAIRS EATING her breakfast — she'd had a bit of a late start, having worked through the night, and was enjoying just hanging out in the kitchen listening to Twinford Talk Radio. She had it turned up really loud and almost missed the sound of the phone ringing in her bedroom. She took the stairs two at a time and reached it just before it clicked through to the answering machine.

"Twinford Pest Control. We spray to kill."

"Rube?"

"Roaches or rats, sir?"

"This is no time for kidding around. I'm in deep trouble, I tell you, deep."

"What is it, Clance? Are you OK? Are you injured or something?"

"No, but I will be if you don't think of something quick and by quick I sorta mean now!"

"OK, but first you gotta explain. I can't help you if I don't know what's going on."

"OK," said Clancy, breathing hard, "so you know how I was supposed to be searching the ads for a restorer to fix my mom's Louis the Fifteenth dressing table because it's not looking so good on account of Minny's hair dye?"

"Yeah," said Ruby patiently.

"So I couldn't get hold of an *emergency* repair service and I'm thinking Minny is going to get grounded for like the rest of her entire life and that kinda sucks . . . so . . ."

Ruby waited for him to finish his no doubt painful sentence; she could hear his arms flapping.

"So I sorta stepped in. Minny got this stuff from the hardware store that was supposed to be some kind of restorer polish, and I didn't get around to reading the label to check that she had gotten the right whatever it was — you know how it is with me and labels. . . ."

"Yeah, you never read 'em."

"Anyway, this stuff turns out to be some kinda paint stripper, and now the Louis the Fifteenth dressing table looks kinda . . . not so Louis the Fifteenth, if you know what I'm saying. . . . My mother —"

"She's gonna kill you," said Ruby.

"She's gonna kill me," agreed Clancy.

"Minny's gonna kill you," said Ruby.

"Minny is also gonna kill me," agreed Clancy.

"Although the whole thing was her fault in the first place."

"Minny's not logical like that," said Clancy.

Ruby said nothing; she was thinking.

"Are you there?" said Clancy, his voice raspy with panic.

"I'm thinking," said Ruby.

"Well, could you maybe hurry it up a little," Clancy urged.

An agonizing pause.

"I got it," said Ruby. "Sit tight—I think I have the solution. Just stay away from any furniture that looks Louis-ish."

Twelve minutes later, Hitch's car rolled up outside the Crews' house. He was wearing dark glasses and carrying a black leather case.

Clancy was there to greet him and opened the door way before he could reach for the doorbell.

"When are you expecting her home?" Hitch asked.

"Um, maybe an hour and a half from now, maybe two."

"OK, so we'll work with seventy-five minutes," said Hitch,

activating the countdown on his Spectrum-issue watch. "So where is it?"

Clancy led Hitch to his mother's dressing room, and Hitch surveyed the damage. He winced, ran his fingers over the wood. "Pear and walnut, made in the French provinces."

He opened the drawers and examined their construction. "Circa 1727, very typical." He looked underneath the tabletop, found what he was looking for. "Surprising." Then he took a magnifier from his bag and held it over the damaged wood of the table. "A quality piece."

He forwarded all this information via his watch — a thorough description of the wood, the polish, the patina, the exact color of the remaining gold leaf, and the precise extent of the damage.

Less than seven minutes later, three restorers arrived. Hitch let them in and directed them upstairs. They said nothing but immediately set to work. Hitch handed Clancy a sponge and Ruby, who had just that minute arrived, a bucket of soapy water. He pointed to his car. "It will calm your nerves," he said. They didn't argue.

When they were done washing the silver convertible, they sat in the kitchen sipping the drinks Hitch had fixed — a couple of mint lemonade sodas. Hitch went up to check on the restorers. Sixty minutes after arriving, they had finished, their tools packed, dust sheets folded. Hitch took a fat wad of twenty-dollar bills from his wallet, peeled off a large number and handed them to the guy in charge, shook them all by the hand, and watched them leave. Then, reaching into his bag, he drew out a silver aerosol can, free of logo or label, and sprayed it across the room.

"What's that?" asked Clancy.

"I think it must be an odor neutralizer," said Ruby.

"I don't smell anything," said Clancy.

Ruby looked at him. "Did the panic affect your brain? It's to *remove the smell* — from all that polish and stuff."

Done with that, Hitch picked up one of Mrs. Crew's perfume bottles, squeezed the atomizer, and let it waft through the air. Now the room smelled as it should.

He checked his watch — seventy-four minutes gone. He took a final look around and, judging everything to be shipshape, clicked his fingers, a signal that it was time to leave, then closed the door and walked speedily downstairs, trailed by Ruby and an awestruck Clancy.

Before he exited, he turned to Clancy and said, "Don't blow it by being all cute and nice to your mom. She'll smell a rat in five seconds flat." He stepped into his car and turned the key. "Adios, amigos," he called, then drove off in the direction of Cedarwood

Drive. He had barely turned the corner of Rose when he saw Mrs. Crew's limousine sail by.

He glanced at his Spectrum-issue watch and smiled as the countdown hit zero.

Clancy watched as his mother pulled in through the gates. "Boy, that's some butler," he said.

"Yeah," said Ruby, "that was impressive."

Mrs. Crew was getting out of the car.

"Hey there, Mom, how are you? Can I help you with your bags? Get you some iced tea?" called Clancy.

"What are you doing?" hissed Ruby.

"I don't know," whispered Clancy. "It's the nerves."

His mother was looking at him suspiciously. That was until Ruby kicked him hard in the shin and Clancy cursed loudly before punching her on the arm.

Mrs. Crew's face relaxed; everything was as it should be.

When Ruby returned to Cedarwood Drive, she walked upstairs into the kitchen. Mrs. Digby's voice called out. "A fellow dropped by to see you."

"Who?" asked Ruby.

"Well, it wasn't Quent Humbert, if that's what's worrying you.

It was that Ray Penny from the bookstore — he left something for you."

There was a rectangular package on the hall table and next to it a scrawled note:

```
Your book came in —
just thought I should drop it off,
you being in such a hurry and all.
```

The poetry book cost no more than a few dollars. It was not a first edition, nor even a second. Its pages were torn and grubby, and its binding was broken, some pages floating free of the spine. It was not signed by the author nor inscribed to anyone of note, but still, the words were there and that was what really mattered.

Ruby began to read. She read it in the order the poems were set out. From front to back, every letter written she read, including the copyright page, the publisher's address, and the information saying where the book was printed. She read it all in case the dullest part of the book held some clue as to why it had been stolen. It didn't seem to.

The weird thing was, there was a poem listed in the

index—poem 14, "You Are a Poem, Celeste"—but when Ruby looked for it, it didn't seem to be there.

She checked the page number to see if perhaps one piece of the book had fallen out, become lost, but no, the page numbers were all in order; nothing was missing.

She remembered the newspaper article. She remembered that Mr. Okra's copy had been inscribed, by hand, by someone named Celeste.

Well, that's certainly a connection, thought Ruby.

"So what have you got there?" said Mrs. Digby, peering over Ruby's shoulder. "Saints preserve us, that school of yours isn't making you study that pretentious book of self-absorbed drivel?"

"You know this poet?" asked Ruby.

"I do," replied Mrs. Digby. She had her hands on her hips. "My cousin Emily had a job at the Scarlet Pagoda, back in the day, and she said that JJ Calkin came in practically every week to watch the shows and gaze at his muse, whoever she might be—drove everyone quite doolally."

"From his poetry I would guess he wasn't a happy guy."

" 'Lighten up' is what Emily told him."

"How did that go down?"

"He wasn't a fellow who took criticism well—he never spoke

to her again. You want a tuna sandwich? You look pasty."

"I'd rather have cake," said Ruby.

"I'll make you a sandwich," said the housekeeper.

It was much later, after supper in fact, that Ruby got a call, something important judging by the fly flashing yellow on her Escape Watch. She excused herself, suggesting she needed an early night, climbed the stairs to her room, grabbed her jacket, and climbed out the window.

Her arm was buzzing — she looked down and saw that the fly was now illuminated red.

Jeepers, she thought. *When do they expect me to sleep?*

CHAPTER 21
Utterly Blank

WHEN RUBY ARRIVED AT SPECTRUM, she went over to Buzz's circular desk.

Buzz was speaking Mandarin, and when she caught sight of Ruby, she paused her conversation and said, "Blacker wants to see you. He's in the cafeteria."

Ruby found him wiping soy sauce off his jacket.

"So what have you got for me?" said Ruby.

Blacker worked in decoding, and for that reason he and Ruby had spent many long hours together poring over bits of paper in small rooms, donut boxes spilling out of the trash can. Blacker gave the impression of a person who wasn't really keeping his eye on the ball, but the truth was very different from the way it appeared. "Don't underestimate Blacker" was something Hitch had cautioned her against right from the get-go. She never had.

Blacker leaned forward in his seat. "You've heard about these weird robberies, right?" he said, pulling a newspaper clipping from his pocket. It was folded several times and looked like it had been read over and over.

The headline read GHOSTLY CRIMES. It was a piece about the Okras and their missing book. The picture showed them clutching hands on the couch, looking stricken.

"Sure I have, but why would Spectrum be interested in this?" asked Ruby. "I'm as eager as anyone to know who this skywalker is, but Spectrum? I heard these burglaries were all domestic robberies, not important financially or security-wise."

"You think getting robbed doesn't matter?" said Froghorn, who had just that second arrived at their table. He sounded very pompous and puffed up about it. "Little Ruby Rich Kid doesn't need to worry about losing a few hundred dollars because she's got her millionaire mommy and daddy to fill her piggy bank whenever she wants a new ballet dress. . . ."

"What?" said Ruby. "What are you babbling about ballet dresses? I'm raising a legitimate point here."

Blacker looked at Froghorn. "Come on, Miles, Rube is actually asking a fair question." Froghorn pursed his lips. "Look, Miles," said Blacker, "why don't you make a start on the data? It would be one big help if we could make a few inroads here. I gotta hand it to you, man, the work you took on yesterday kept the whole showboat afloat."

Froghorn was the one who fed all sorts of data into the computer banks, so he knew a lot about the various cases Spectrum 8 was working on. He was no slouch in the brain department either; you couldn't dismiss him as a lightweight or an upstart, and his combative attitude made him a formidable intellectual opponent. It was just a shame he was such a potato head.

Froghorn stood up, very nearly smiled at Blacker, and, without speaking another word, exited the cafeteria. That was the other thing you couldn't help but admire about Blacker — he was a diplomat.

Froghorn gone, Blacker turned back to Ruby. "Let me explain. So as you know, a few days ago Mr. and Mrs. Okra had their ninth-floor apartment broken into. It would seem that the thief entered via the small bathroom window, which means he is pretty determined."

"It also means he is a heck of a climber too."

"And either very small or some kind of contortionist," said Blacker. "Not many people could fit through a window that size."

"I probably could," said Ruby.

"Yeah, I bet you could," said Blacker, looking at her. "To answer your question, there are two really strange things about this crime that interest Spectrum, the most obvious being, why go to such lengths when all you intend to steal is a poetry book?"

"Yeah," said Ruby. "The only thing I discovered is that the poet used to hang out at the Pagoda theater."

"So we have a connection to the shoes at least," said Blacker. "Both are linked to the Scarlet Pagoda."

"And what's the second thing?" said Ruby.

"Second," said Blacker, "Mrs. Okra claims to have found something at the scene. At first she thought it had been left by the Crime Scene Investigation squad, but when she contacted them they had no knowledge of it."

"Knowledge of what?" asked Ruby.

"Well, Mrs. Okra keeps a very orderly house, no dust, no clutter, but she found something that doesn't make any sense to her."

"Something the cops missed?"

"Easy to miss."

"What was it?"

"A card," said Blacker.

"Like a postcard?"

"No, like a calling card."

"So was there a number?" asked Ruby.

"No," said Blacker.

"An address?"

"There wasn't one."

"A name?"

"Uh-uh."

"Nothing?"

"It was blank."

"So why does Mrs. Okra think this is important?"

"Because it wasn't there before."

"That's a good enough reason, I guess."

"It is if you are Mrs. Okra — boy, is she tidy."

"So this thief accidentally left evidence?"

"I wouldn't say so. This card was very deliberately placed on top of a pile of books. It didn't just land on the floor like it fell out of a pocket."

"A completely blank card?" repeated Ruby.

"Well, blank as in nothing printed on it," said Blacker.

"I don't follow. Is it blank or is it not blank?"

"It has bumps."

"Bumps like Braille?"

"Yes, but no."

"As in not Braille but possibly another form of touch alphabet?"

"Perhaps."

"You mean the thief is maybe deliberately leaving some kind of coded message?"

"That's exactly what I mean," said Blacker. "And that's what brings Spectrum into it. That . . . and the fact that a similar break-in and robbery was identified at that DOD base, the item taken from a secure room, no one seen arriving or leaving."

"So you think there *is* a connection?" said Ruby.

"Well," said Blacker, "could be. It's too big a coincidence for there *not* to be a connection, don't you think? The yellow shoes were taken from a secured room and no one at the theater saw a thing."

They thought about this for almost a minute until Blacker asked, "You wanna split a donut?"

"Let's split two," said Ruby.

Taking a break was a good idea, and the donut was an even better one.

"Boy, is there anything so good as a jelly donut?" said Blacker.

"You got me," said Ruby.

"So, anything come to mind?" he asked. "Case-wise, I mean?"

"I'm thinking, if you were going to steal something as inconsequential as a book, from somebody's apartment — secure, yes, but no Fort Knox — then why be so elaborate about it? Is it really necessary to climb up and down walls? What is this guy trying to prove here?"

"That, my pal Ruby, is a mystery," said Blacker. "Not only do we not know why he does it, but we also don't know *how* he does it. Why is it that not one security camera has picked him up leaving the apartment?"

"So you are thinking of investigating the ghost angle?" said Ruby.

"Not yet I'm not, but I'm telling you, it might come to it," said Blacker. He winked, and wiped his hands on his jacket. He caught Ruby's eye and shrugged. "Ah, it needs washing anyway."

"So this card Mrs. Okra found, did the cops get any fingerprints off it? Or were there prints in the apartment?" asked Ruby.

"Zip," Blacker replied. "The lab technicians are running some tests — UV light, that kind of thing."

"And this Braille-type code," asked Ruby, "is there enough for us to crack it?"

"We'll see, but I don't think so," said Blacker. "It looks like only a handful of characters. Not enough for us to break it with any kind of statistical analysis. We need more cards. More cipher text."

"In other words, we have to wait for him to strike again?"

"And you can bet he will," said Blacker. "For now, stay on standby. I'm gonna have SJ hand the card over to you when she's done her thing. I want your input on the code."

"You know me," said Ruby, "I'm always on standby."

CHAPTER 22
Now You See It

THE SUMMER WAS FADING FAST NOW, the wind beginning to gust through the trees, pulling at the branches in an effort to loosen the leaves. Whatever the townsfolk might be feeling, the authorities certainly weren't sad to see the back of summer, but no one had quite been expecting the season to change with such force.

Clancy and Ruby lay on beanbags facing the large picture window in Ruby's top-floor loft-style bedroom.

"Do you think that by the time we grow up, man will have invented a flying suit — a Superman-type of thing?" mused Clancy.

"Maybe," said Ruby, thinking of the Glider Wings. "It's more than likely."

"It would be pretty cool — I mean, if I could have any superpower, that would be it," said Clancy. "That or invisibility."

"Invisibility is overrated as a superpower," said Ruby.

"There's an art to being invisible — you just have to think yourself into it."

"Yeah," said Clancy. "I saw that guy on TV doing it, you know, the one I was telling you about? The illusionist?"

"Darnley Rex," said Ruby.

"Yeah," said Clancy, "him. I might give it a try."

"Give what a try?"

"Thinking myself invisible," said Clancy, "see if it works."

"You might have to lose the socks," said Ruby, indicating Clancy's neon-yellow footwear.

"Nancy took all of mine; I'm down to wearing Minny's."

"And perhaps the hat should go too," added Ruby.

"But this hat's practical; it's got a good brim and it's waterproof."

"It's pea green," said Ruby. "It practically glows."

"Not if you're against grass," argued Clancy.

"I don't think invisibility's a natural fit for you, Clance."

It was true enough. Clancy was the sort of boy who wanted to blend in but who got noticed, and usually for all the wrong reasons. The only person who didn't seem to see him was his father.

"No, if I could have any superpower," said Ruby, "and I admit flying would be good, I might choose time travel. Imagine being able to teleport yourself from one time and place to another."

"Yeah, that would be kinda useful." Clancy was thinking

about all those French tests he could retake once he had memorized the answers.

"D'ya wanna grab a snack?" said Ruby, pulling herself up.

Clancy nodded. "I could eat."

They went downstairs and padded barefoot into the kitchen, where Mrs. Digby was sitting reading her *Twinford Echo*.

She didn't look up but said, "If you two children think I'm about to up and fix you an ox tongue and sea pickle sandwich, you are quite mistaken."

"I'm disappointed," said Ruby, "but actually I was thinking more along the lines of cheese and ham."

"Oh, well, that I can do you for," said Mrs. Digby, getting to her feet. "I live to serve."

Clancy wiped his brow; he wasn't always sure when the old lady was pulling his leg. She had told him so many stories of the things she had been forced to eat as a young woman growing up during the Great Depression that he couldn't be certain that the housekeeper wasn't about to feed him some alarming part of a creature.

"So what have you children been plotting? Mischief, no doubt," said Mrs. Digby, tutting.

"We have been discussing superpowers," said Clancy. "What kind of superhuman would you be if you could be anything?"

"I've got just about all the superpowers a person could have. Look at the amount I have to do around here. You think you could do all this at my age?"

"I hadn't looked at it that way," said Clancy.

Mrs. Digby threw Ruby a glance. "That Quent called again. He wants to know if you will be attending his superhero party."

"Darn it," said Ruby, "I was trying to forget about that."

"Well, I hope your father doesn't hear you talking that way. You know how he gets about the notion of hurting another mortal's feelings."

Ruby sighed; she knew only too well.

"Jeepers," said Clancy, "so you're gonna have to go!"

"I'll think of something," said Ruby.

They were just about to settle into some solid TV time when Mrs. Digby called from the kitchen.

"Child, did you put this piece of bread in the toaster?"

Silence.

"I just made you a snack, for jeepers' sake," continued Mrs. Digby. "It'll be dinner not so long from now, and you're making yourself toast. You suffering from worms or something?"

"Ah, no, Mrs. Digby, that's Clance's toast."

"What?" hissed Clancy.

"Yeah, you see, he's looking to put on a little weight, so he's eating double."

"Darnedest thing," said Mrs. Digby. "Almost looks like there's words on this toast."

Ruby raced into the kitchen and took the plate from the puzzled housekeeper.

"Must be your cataracts, Mrs. Digby. I don't see a thing."

The message read:

REPORT TO HQ IMMEDIATELY.

A half hour later, Ruby was standing in the Spectrum lab looking at the evidence: a small card in a little plastic Ziploc bag.

"This is it?"

"Uh-huh," said SJ. "We are just conducting one more test before it's all yours."

"What are you testing for?" asked Ruby.

"Toxic substances," said SJ.

"What? You think it's poisoned or something?" said Ruby.

"I doubt it, but you never know."

"I guess you don't," said Ruby. "Mind if I take a look at the card before you run your tests?"

"Sure," said SJ.

Ruby took the card out of the Ziploc bag. It was thick with a smooth back. On the front was some kind of touch code made up of dots; some were raised, and some were cut out of one layer.

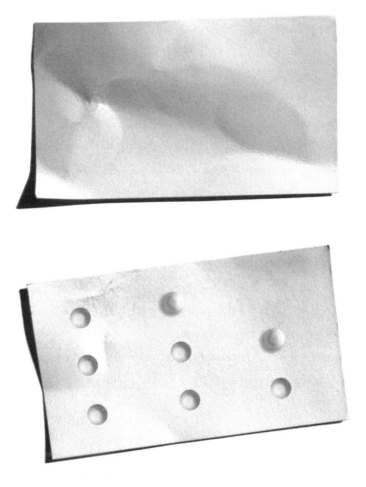

"Any thoughts?" said SJ when Ruby handed the card back.

"Not yet," said Ruby. The dots meant something, but without more code and ideally something to give them some context, there was no way to decipher them.

"OK," said SJ. She put the card back in the bag. "I'll see what I can find."

"I might go grab a drink while you do your thing," said Ruby. "I could use something sugary."

"You know, some people consider sugar to be a toxin," said the young technician.

"Yeah, my mom, for one," said Ruby, "but it sure does taste sorta good."

Ruby was a little weary and was thinking a pep-up soda might be just what she needed. Unfortunately, however, she ran straight into Froghorn by the drink machine and got into a little altercation with him.

"This machine doesn't dispense bottled milk," he said.

"Strange," said Ruby, "because it seems to attract babies."

"You are so childish," said Froghorn.

"You started it," said Ruby.

"I started it? Me? You lowered the maturity level the second you stepped into Spectrum back in April."

"Wow, I managed to get it below your level. Who knew that was possible?"

"Don't you miss the other nursery-school kids?" asked Froghorn.

The sound of fingernails tapping on metal caused Ruby and Froghorn to stop their bickering and turn around. What they saw was LB standing right behind them, her fingers drumming on the side of the fridge. They hadn't heard her arrive due to her bare feet and almost silent footsteps.

"I seem to have stepped into some dreadful version of kindergarten," she said, her nose wrinkled. "I found preschool unbearable the first time around; *do not* make me suffer it again." This was both a demand and a warning.

Froghorn's cheeks colored pink; he did not like getting called out, especially not by LB, the very person he so hoped to impress. Without another word the Spectrum 8 boss turned and continued her silent way along the corridor.

By the time Ruby made it back to the lab, she was feeling flustered. She had wasted a whole twenty minutes on nothing at all, and now she was about to examine a piece of evidence that also offered little in the way of help.

SJ was gone, but the little white card had been placed on the countertop underneath a bright desk lamp. A powerful magnifier was sitting next to it so she could examine the card more closely, but as it turned out, she didn't need to. It was perfectly plain to see that the card was no longer blank. What had been a small area of plain white was now dissected by thin black lines forming a sort of grid.

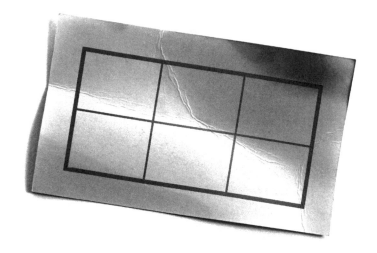

Ruby picked up the phone and dialed.

"Blacker," came the voice down the line.

"It's me. Get yourself down to the lab — something just came to light."

CHAPTER 23
The *Whispering Weekly*

TWO MINUTES LATER, BLACKER was standing next to her — he looked more disheveled than usual, perhaps due to the sprint from the upper floor.

He looked over Ruby's shoulder. "Well, I'll be. . . ."

"It must have been the heat," said Ruby. "It was left under this lamp and I think that's what did it. Boy, I could kiss Froghorn."

"You OK, Ruby?" Blacker was looking concerned. "You sound like you might need to lie down."

"It's a figure of speech — not actually, nah — you know what I'm saying. It's just if I hadn't gotten into this fight with him, then the card wouldn't have been left under the lamp so long, and then it might not have reacted with the heat. . . ." She was staring intently at the card. "So what does it look like to you?"

Blacker didn't say anything for a few minutes and then broke the silence by saying, "Well, on the one hand it looks like how one might draw a window, you know, the rectangle shape with one line down the middle and three cutting across it like glazing bars making six panes of glass."

"And?" said Ruby.

"On the other hand, it looks a lot like a customer loyalty card."

"Exactly what I thought," said Ruby. "So what if it's both? The window image is telling us it's the calling card of the thief who comes in through the window, and the grid markings are also telling us how many things he's going to take."

"So why are the boxes all empty?"

"You got me." Ruby sighed.

"Give me a minute," said Blacker. He walked to the intercom and paged the lab technician.

Two minutes later, SJ was back.

"Something happened?" said SJ.

Blacker pointed at the card.

SJ peered at it and then examined it through the magnifier.

"Very interesting," she said. "It reacted to heat, so you are wondering what else it might react to?"

"Yup," confirmed Blacker.

SJ wasted no time and began setting up various tests using a number of liquids — mild acids, alkalies, various other substances. Drop by drop, they fell onto the card but revealed nothing.

Black light revealed more nothing.

X-rays revealed nothing too.

Same when they took the card to a darkroom and dunked it in a developing bath, as if it were photographic paper.

Finally SJ took off her goggles, peeled off her gloves, and sat down. "That's all I've got," she said with resignation. "Not sure what else I can throw at it."

"Looks like that's all, folks," said Blacker. "Rube, go on home and put your head on a pillow; we can look at this again in the morning."

It was disappointing to make one breakthrough with the grid lines, only to get no further, but since they had hit a dead end, they decided they all might as well head on home.

Once back at Cedarwood Drive, Ruby watched some TV, but she couldn't concentrate. Her book wasn't holding her attention either.

Finally she gave up and went to bed. But—and not for the first time—she found it difficult to sleep; she just couldn't turn off that brain of hers. She pulled out her notebook from the doorjamb and wrote down a couple of questions that she really needed answers to.

The first being:

```
If we are right in our theory that the thief
is leaving loyalty cards in place of stolen
items, then why has the Okras' card been left
blank?
```

```
If this robbery is connected to the shoe
theft, then why no loyalty card there?
```

No answers were popping into her exhausted brain, so she went down to the kitchen to find a snack. She made herself a pastrami bagel and while she ate, she flicked through an ancient copy of the *Whispering Weekly* that she found in a stack of old newspapers that Mrs. Digby used to protect the table when she was polishing the silver. The *Whispering Weekly* was not a very entertaining magazine, unless you were a person who particularly enjoyed reading about other people's misery, both public and personal.

In this particular issue there was a feature on famous people who had been spotted wearing hairpieces — not hairpieces worn to add to the celebrities' general glamour but hairpieces to prevent men from looking bald.

Geez, thought Ruby, *why contaminate your mind with this junk?* She stuffed the gossip mag back in the pile and went back to her room to find something better to occupy her brain. What she chose to read was one of her encoding books, in the vague hope that she might stumble across some clue as to what this whole mystery was about. She climbed into bed with a copy of Sherman Tree's *Unlock My Brain* and read until she nodded off.

It was four a.m. when Ruby's eyes suddenly blinked open and she sat bolt upright, feeling around for her glasses.

Quite out of the blue, she felt an urgent need to get hold of the latest issue of the *Whispering Weekly.*

CHAPTER 24
Did You Spot
the Gorilla?

RUBY GOT OUT OF BED and pulled on the clothes that happened to be piled on her chair (her new jeans and a T-shirt announcing *keep your distance*).

She crept downstairs, her satchel slung over her shoulder, tiptoed into the kitchen, opened the refrigerator, took a quick slug of peach juice, called to Bug, and then set off for Marty's mini-mart.

Ruby skateboarded along Cedarwood, Bug running along beside her. The sped together down Pecan until they reached the little store where four busy roads met. Sure enough, Marty's had what she was looking for. Ruby paid for her copy of the *Whispering Weekly* along with one green apple and one blueberry slushy and some dog bones for Bug, then she went and sat on the bench outside the store.

Looking at the pictures of poor old Jessica Riley and the way the camera had revealed something the mere naked eye could never have seen made Ruby believe in her theory all the more. But she was halfway through her slushy when tiredness took a hold of her — lack of sleep the night before had finally caught up. She placed the *Whispering Weekly* shock-horror journal under her head, curled up on the wooden seat, and closed her eyes. *Just a five-minute nap,* she told herself. Her dog sat watching, never taking his eyes off her.

She woke to the clank of Mrs. Beesman's shopping cart. Today it was full of soup — cans and cans of the stuff — and two war-torn-looking cats.

Bug's fur stood on end; he was wary of one-eyed felines with chewed ears — they could be unpredictable: they had nothing to lose.

Ruby rubbed her eyes and adjusted her glasses.

"Hi, Mrs. Beesman. How are you this morning?"

The disheveled lady peered at her and grunted.

Mrs. Beesman had never said one friendly word to her, not that Ruby minded that. Today she appeared a little more cranky than usual, which might have something to do with the yellow paint sprayed in an arc across her shopping cart. There was even a little on the cats' tails. It didn't seem like the sort of thing she would have done herself, so Ruby figured it was vandals or bullies. Mrs. Beesman tended to run into a lot of them.

※ ※ ※

It was the first day of a new school year at Twinford Junior High, and Clancy was feeling sort of OK about it—not exactly eager for the new semester but happy enough to put some distance between himself and recent past events of the summer break.

As far as the happy stakes went, the summer had been a mixed bag. On the one hand, great weather, a few precious weeks with no school, and even more important, no Madame Loup, so that was good. It had been exciting solving a crime and saving an almost extinct wild animal from a miserable end, so, yes, that had also been a plus.

Less fun on the other hand was the being abducted and nearly murdered by psychopaths, which, combined with the almost being burned alive by a ferocious forest fire, made the summer break far from idyllic, and for obvious reasons it was this near-death experience that dominated Clancy's impression of the vacation.

He got to class a little early, as he just about always did, sat down, and cracked open his new graphic novel, *Snoozer*. The stories were ridiculous but very entertaining, and Clancy felt an affinity with the main character, who was a bit of an underdog.

Clancy wasn't surprised when the school bell rang and still

there was no sign of his friend. She would never be entered for any punctuality contest, and if she was, well, then she would doubtless miss the start.

Ruby finally strolled into her homeroom just as Mrs. Drisco called, *"Redfort?"*

"Present," Ruby called back as she slid into her seat.

"Barely," muttered Mrs. Drisco, her pen hovering over the absent box.

But Mrs. Drisco wasn't in the mood to have a long-drawn-out back-and-forth with Ruby Redfort. It was the first day of a new school year, and she didn't want to start it on a losing streak.

When the bell rang, the students spilled out of their homerooms into the corridor.

"You look awful tired," said Clancy. "Something keep you awake?"

"You could say that." Ruby yawned. "I'm trying to figure out something, something to do with the window thief."

"There are clues?" asked Clancy.

"There are always clues," said Ruby. "It's just a matter of spotting them and then putting them together. I had a kinda brainwave at four o'clock this morning."

"This morning?" said Clancy. "Before school?"

"Impressive, huh?"

"For you, yeah," said Clancy. "Morning isn't really your time of day."

"Which is why I zonked out on the bench outside Marty's."

"You spent the night sleeping on a bench?"

"Not the whole night, Clance. Just a couple of hours."

"You feel like hanging out later?" asked Clancy.

"Yeah but nah. I have to get into Spectrum, work on my theory."

"So what's the theory?"

"I'll tell you when I prove myself right," said Ruby. "Let's just say it came to me in a flash."

Clancy was in a good mood all morning — he had so far been assigned all his favorite teachers and no Madame Loup. He felt there was something about this year that was going to be good — better than the last one, anyway. At lunchtime, he lined up in the cafeteria and managed to get the very last slice of pecan pie. Yes, there was no doubt that this was going to be a *good* year for him.

He took his tray of food outside to one of the wooden tables arranged under the trees.

"Hey," said Del, "I haven't seen you in a while. You been away?"

"Nah," said Clancy, "just lying low."

"You *need* to lie low?" asked Red. "Are you in trouble?"

"No, nothing like that—more of a lifestyle choice," replied Clancy.

Mouse looked at him. "I thought your dad didn't approve of lying low."

"Or choices, for that matter," said Del.

"Yeah, well, normally no, but he felt I deserved some downtime since I passed my French exam and rescued those Whimbrel kids from the forest fire."

"Quite the little hero," said Del. "Did you get a medal?"

"No, but my dad got me a bell for my bicycle," said Clancy. "He even had it engraved."

"Boy, he must have been *really* proud!" she said. "What do you think he would have given you if you had saved a bunch of puppies as well as just those kids?"

"Probably one of those little windmill things that you can attach to the handlebars," said Clancy.

"Hey, you never said what you were doing out there in the first place," said Mouse.

Clancy was knocked off his guard for only a second before

he came back with a convincing enough answer. "Ah, it was just a coincidence, really. I was mad at my dad and so I biked out to Little Bear Mountain. I was going to camp out, get some space to myself — I have five sisters — you know what I'm saying? But then the fire hit." It was part of the truth but not the whole truth, yet they all swallowed it, because why not?

Ruby and Elliot arrived and sat down, and the six of them chatted about vacations and heat waves and anything else that came up.

"So, we should check out some of these film festival movies, huh?" said Ruby.

"Yeah," said Clancy. "I wanna see *The Claw* again. I mean, it's a classic, right?"

"I think it's lame," said Elliot. "*The Sea of Fish Devils* is the one to catch."

"Are you crazy, man?" said Del.

This was a conversation they'd all had over and over since the Twinford Film Festival program had been announced. In fact, they were still in this exact same conversation as they approached the school gates at the end of the day when something quite unexpected happened. Elliot watched Clancy Crew's face change from relaxed and kind of cheery to a mask of something approaching horror. He followed his friend's gaze and instantly knew what the problem was. His eyes flicked back from the object of Clancy's concern to Clancy. Neither of them said anything and no one else saw, not even Ruby, who was busy rooting in her satchel.

"You know what, guys?" said Clancy. "Go ahead without me. I think I must have left my Ping-Pong paddle in my locker."

"You're holding it, duh brain," said Del.

"Ah, no, not this one, my good one — I mean, I thought I had picked up my good one, but this isn't it." Clancy was beginning to sweat. "See you tomorrow," he called as he ran back toward the school.

"That is one seriously mixed-up kid," said Del.

Ruby registered precisely none of this; she was far more concerned about making it back to Spectrum so she could test out her new theory.

CHAPTER 25
The Illusion of
Invisibility

WHEN CLANCY FINALLY DARED to walk out of the Twinford Junior High gates, everyone had long gone. He took the bus back home and went straight up to his room. He sat down on his bed and took a deep, deep breath. *What are you going to do about this, Clance?*

He jumped when the phone rang. "Hello, Elliot." He knew it had to be Elliot; he had probably called about twenty-five times already.

"Hey, howdya know it was me?"

"Probability."

"So what are you going to do?" asked Elliot. "I mean, this is bad, man."

"Do you want to meet?" asked Clancy. "I think I need to get some air."

Clancy and Elliot had arranged to meet at the Donut, mainly because Elliot felt safe there. Marla did not allow brawling or customers beating other customers to a pulp, not on *her* premises, and the gorilla had been told to take a walk. As fearful as he was about being caught in someone else's punch-up, Elliot was very interested to talk about it.

"So, have you seen the kid again?" said Elliot, leaning forward, talking in a hushed voice.

"Do I look like I have?" said Clancy, pointing at his face.

"That's good," said Elliot. "What did he look like, anyway? I didn't get a good chance to see."

"Ugly," said Clancy. "Nasty eyes, you know, unpleasant."

"Probably one of those kids that's got no friends, you know."

"Even Bugwart has friends," said Clancy.

"Yeah, but she's got a sort of charisma; this guy sounds like a loser," suggested Elliot.

"Yeah," agreed Clancy. "No charisma that I could detect, but he sure looked like he had plenty of friends hanging around."

"That's not good; if he has friends at the junior high, then I expect you will run into him again, huh?" said Elliot.

Clancy looked at him with exasperation. "Would you stop sounding so thrilled about it?"

"Sorry," said Elliot. "You think he's gonna hound you for the rest of your school days?"

Clancy took a deep breath in an effort to keep his cool. "Look, I don't think he's even realized I'm at Twinford Junior High, and since he doesn't go there, then if I'm lucky, he won't notice me before graduation. I mean, we only met for like a second. He's not gonna remember me."

"Some hope," said Elliot. "A kid like that sets his sights on you, you are done for."

"That's helpful," said Clancy. "I am feeling a whole lot better after this little chat."

"You got a way of preventing yourself from being socked in the nose?"

"Yeah, I'm gonna avoid him," said Clancy.

"And how do you plan to do that?" asked Elliot.

"I'm gonna try that technique — the one that magician what's-his-name was talking about."

"Which one?" asked Elliot.

"Thingy on Channel Z, with the hands that look like they belong to someone else."

"The magician guy person?" said Elliot. "Darnley Rex?"

"Yeah, that guy," agreed Clancy. "So he was talking about invisibility and —"

"You're gonna make yourself invisible?" interrupted Elliot. "By magic?"

Clancy rolled his eyes. "Are you nuts? Of course not by magic. I'm talking about the illusion of invisibility."

"Well, good luck with that." Elliot started to laugh.

Clancy rolled his eyes again. "You don't sound like you have a lot of confidence in me."

"Oh, I do." Elliot laughed. "It's just, say . . ." He was beginning to lose it now. "It's just — I mean, I hate to be a downer here, Clancy, and throw eggs on your parade or whatever, but what if the kid sees right through your brilliant illusion?"

"Then I guess I get socked in the nose."

Elliot nodded. "So long as we're clear." He continued to laugh so much that he fell off his chair, which caught Marla's attention.

"Could you two kids behave like people who belong in a diner or could you take yourselves to another establishment?"

Clancy and Elliot immediately pulled it together.

"So look," said Clancy, "don't tell anyone about this, OK?"

"Why not?" said Elliot. "What's the problem with people knowing?"

"Because it's my problem," said Clancy, "nobody else's, and I'm going to deal with it my way. Plus," he added, trying to appeal to Elliot's cowardly side, "I don't want anyone else to get this creep's attention. I'm gonna take care of it myself."

"What about Ruby? You gotta tell her, don'tcha?"

"Definitely not Ruby. You know what she's like; she'll only end up trying to punch him, and I really don't think that's a good idea — I don't think her arm's strong enough after the break. You gotta promise me, OK? Don't tell Rube."

"If you say so, Clance," said Elliot, "but let me know if you need a buddy to step in to defend you and I'll try and find a candidate — hey, maybe Muhammad Ali would be interested."

He was back.
The smell of shoe leather,
the not-quite silence
that filled the apartment. . . .

She braced herself and strode into the dimly lit room. He looked up.

"So who are you today, dear thing?" He was smiling, a questioning sort of look playing in his eyes as if he might really be interested. "You seem to have such fun; you see a future in all this. I remember those days—just." His smile faded and a sadness fell across his face. "I try to see the point in it all, but after a while it all becomes so"—he gestured with his hand—"samey."

She almost felt sorry for him; he did look so disappointed.

"Murder, kidnapping, theft? What really lies beyond this, kicks-wise, I mean?"

"World domination?" she ventured.

"A pipe dream," he said. "I mean, does one really ever dominate the world? Can it be done?"

"Well . . ." she began.

He looked deep into her eyes, the cold black of his stare holding her, fixing her; she could not look away. "I hope you are not double-crossing me, my dear. I should hate to sever our friendship."

"I would never," she said. "Never."

"Then prove it. Bring me the 8 key and the other trifle or I will have to assume the worst."

CHAPTER 26
Tap Tap Tap

ON HER WAY INTO SPECTRUM, Ruby took 4th Avenue, which ran close to Radio Street. It had been named that way many years ago, when the big technology boom took hold and one by one all the stores on that street became suppliers of radios, cameras, TVs, stereos, and the like. It was cameras that Ruby was interested in today. She stepped off her board when she reached Photo Cam, a store that specialized in Polaroid instant cameras. She wasn't too concerned about the quality, though she figured it was worth getting a good one. She took the advice of the man behind the counter—he seemed to know what he was talking about. She bought several packs of Polaroid film and stuffed her purchases in her backpack. Then she continued on her way to Spectrum.

Ruby went straight down to the lab and asked SJ if she could study the card. Then, when it was lying on the counter, Ruby loaded the film into the camera, held it above the card, and pressed the button. The camera flashed and spat out a small square photograph. Ruby waited for the required three minutes before pulling off the paper to reveal the print. Ruby wasn't actually expecting it to work—it was what's known as a stab in the dark—but now she was seeing things. What had been invisible was now visible.

What had been a total blank was now a card stamped with three words—or rather, the same word, written three times.

TAP

TAP

TAP

Plus, of course, the customer loyalty card design that had been revealed by the warmth of the lamp the previous day, and the Braille-like code. One card, seven black lines, three TAPs, a whole lot of bumps.

"This guy seems to have access to some pretty sophisticated materials," said Ruby. "I mean this ink? Where would one lay one's hands on such an item?"

"Beats me," said SJ. "I haven't seen it used before. He's either some sort of hotshot who's managed to develop a flash-sensitive ink . . ."

"Unlikely," said Ruby.

"Highly," said SJ. "*Or* he has access to a place where this ink is being produced."

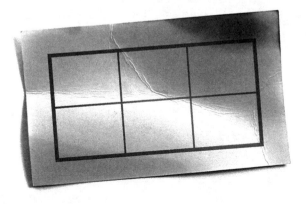

"Where does that lead us?" asked Ruby.

SJ shrugged. "Nowhere that I'm aware of. I'll report it to Spectrum 1, see if they can find a connection — something's always going down somewhere."

The TAPs meant something, clearly, but she had no idea what. The bumps: well, she had no idea what they meant either. They looked like Braille, but the configurations bore no relation to the Braille she had studied. The picture that kept coming into her head was a corridor. It was not like the corridors of Spectrum, but rather was scruffy, with flaked paintwork and chipped stone floor. The image kept coming in and out of focus, then shoes popped into her mind. *Shoes,* she thought. *Why?* The thought *connected* with the Little Yellow Shoes but was *not* the Little Yellow Shoes. The ones she saw were black, men's shoes, work shoes. Not fancy, not scruffy. Then something else. A hand, a piece of paper. A small white piece of paper. Blank.

Ruby opened her eyes. She stared ahead of her, unblinking, and then suddenly activated her watch transmitter and buzzed for Hitch. He responded on the second ring.

"Redfort?"

"We gotta speak to the security guard," said Ruby.

It didn't take more than ten minutes to get the answer to her question.

"It seems you were on the money," said Hitch. "What you saw the security guard at the Scarlet Pagoda pick up *was* a card, just like the one found at the Okras' apartment. He's had it in his pocket since the night of the costume show, didn't think anything of it. Why would he?"

"So we have two," said Ruby. "Are they exactly the same?"

"I guess we better take a look," said Hitch. "I'll go pick it up and bring it on back to the lab. I won't be more than twenty minutes."

He was true to his word, and only a half hour later, Blacker, Hitch, and Ruby were gathered in the lab, studying the new card as SJ went about her business.

"Same results as the other card," she said. "We've got the grid of lines, and look, in the Polaroid shot, we have the taps — but this time only two." She laid the shoe card next to the poetry card, and they all stared down at them. Both had embossed dots and bumps; both had the grid lines. Next to the cards, the two Polaroids. On one, three words revealed and on the other just two. All the words were the same — TAP.

Hitch and Ruby were staring at them; it was a breakthrough.

RUBY: *So one has to wonder, why are there two stamps on the card found at the Pagoda theater?*

HITCH: *They were the second item the thief stole. The book was the third, hence three TAPs.*

BLACKER: *That's my bet.*

RUBY: *So this naturally leaves us wondering . . .*

HITCH: *What was the first robbery?*

BLACKER: *Correct.*

BLACKER: *Also, if we are right about our theory, and I am bold enough to say I think we are, then we are expecting three more high-rise thefts.*

HITCH: *So it looks like what we've got is a serial thief, a very organized one at that.*

BLACKER: *Yeah, and one who seems to want to get caught.*

HITCH: *Or he thinks he's too good to get caught.*

"Or maybe," said Ruby, "he just wants to be noticed."

CHAPTER 27
In Search of the
Little Yellow Shoes

RUBY, HITCH, AND BLACKER had agreed that the main focus should be trying to anticipate the next item on the thief's list — trying to get a step ahead of him.

Ruby had to start somewhere, and since she had gotten next to nowhere with the poetry book, she decided to find out more about the Little Yellow Shoes. She checked the newspaper for the film festival listings and made a note of the time.

She was early to school for once and was hanging out waiting for Clancy. Unusually, he wasn't one of the first to make it through the gates, nor was he dressed at all like himself — he looked kind of *normal*. Ruby was already seated when he finally made an appearance, not late but not overly punctual, as was his style ordinarily.

"Where have you been and what are you wearing?"

"What do you mean? I am on time and I look like everyone else," said Clancy.

"Exactly," said Ruby. "What's going on?"

"Nothing," replied Clancy, "I'm just trying to blend in."

"But why?" asked Ruby.

"It's an experiment," said Clancy; he had anticipated the grilling Ruby might give him for his weird behavior and was primed with his answers. "You know, we were talking about it the other day. I thought I would see if it really works."

"What really works?"

"Becoming invisible."

"Oh, that," said Ruby. "Well, I have to say, I noticed you as soon as you walked in."

"Yeah, but that's different; you were looking for me."

"Maybe," said Ruby. "Anyway, what I wanted to ask you is, do you feel like cutting class?"

"I only just got here."

"Not now, at lunchtime."

"Will we be back for history?" asked Clancy.

"No, duh brain. That's why I said, 'Do you feel like cutting class?' as in not going."

"Rube, you shouldn't ask me to do this. I can't afford to get in trouble."

"It's OK — you won't. I've got a plan."

"You always say you have a plan, but often the plan gets me

into more trouble than the thing you were planning to keep me out of trouble *for*."

Ruby looked at him. "I'm finding you hard to follow. Look, are you in or are you out?"

"Out."

"Aw, Clance, don't say that. It'll be fun — you gotta come." She gave him the Ruby Redfort eye hold. "I'll do your Spanish homework for a week."

"I speak fluent Spanish."

"OK, biology."

"I'm good at biology."

"OK, so you pick."

"Fine, two weeks of French and math and I'll cut class."

"You drive a hard bargain, my friend."

"Take it or leave it."

"Meet me by the bike racks right before lunch," said Ruby. She was already walking away.

"Where are you going?"

"To put my *plan* into operation."

"Oh."

"Don't blab."

"When do I ever blab?" called Clancy.

"Never," shouted Ruby.

At that moment Red and Del came in through the doors.

"She's in a hurry," said Del.

"Yeah, she has to do something," said Clancy.

"What?" asked Del.

"How should I know?" said Clancy.

"You look different," said Red, giving Clancy the once-over. "Really different."

"I've modified my look."

"You've what?" said Del.

"It's intentional," said Clancy. "I've changed my style."

"Nothing about your style is intentional. How can you possibly change it?"

"I'm taking more of an interest," replied Clancy. "This look's on purpose."

"You have changed your look to 'purposely bland'?"

"It's my new style."

"Is bland a style?" asked Red.

After Clancy had spent the hour struggling through math class, he felt a little more motivated about Ruby's plan—he would join her in skipping school and happily allow her to do his math homework.

They met at the agreed time and managed to dodge Del and

the rest of their friends so they wouldn't get caught up in any explaining.

"So where are we going, exactly?" asked Clancy as he unlocked his bike.

"The flicks," replied Ruby. "There's a matinee showing in midtown, and I wanted to catch it."

"So why don't we go after school?"

"Because it's only showing this lunchtime; it's a one-off, all part of the Twinford Film Festival."

Clancy was by now sitting on his bike.

"So how are you going to get there?" he asked.

"You're going to give me a backie," said Ruby.

"Oh, brother! You're gonna kill me, Ruby. You weigh more than you think, you know that?"

"Stop complaining, man. You're beginning to sound like your mother."

"That is a low blow," said Clancy.

They set off at high speed. Clancy was a lot more athletic than he looked, and despite his grumbling, he found it pretty easy transporting Ruby.

"So what's so important about this film?" shouted Clancy as they sped down Avenue Hill.

"It features the Little Yellow Shoes — you know, the ones that went missing the other night?"

"Oh, yeah, what's it called again? Something to do with a cat, isn't it?"

"*The Cat That Got the Canary*. It was made back in the 1950s. I'm scratching my head here, trying to find a reason why someone would take the shoes, other than because they are a deranged fan, I mean."

"OK," said Clancy, "so it's work — why we're cutting class I mean?"

"Oh, yeah, it's work," confirmed Ruby. Clancy looked a lot happier — he didn't mind taking a risk so much if it was for a good cause.

They bought their tickets from the box-office guy — he was young and wore big fashion-type glasses and had a badge with his name on it; Horace, it said. Ruby and Clancy settled down in the near-empty theater.

The film was enjoyable enough. It was an old-fashioned romantic thriller — not that thrilling, but then to be fair it wasn't really meant to be. It was all about the dialogue, very sassy and smart. And Margo Bardem shone.

It was about this dancer named Celeste who finds herself invited out on a date by a suave-looking fellow. The fellow is actually a ruthless criminal who is under the surveillance of some unsentimental killer types. They are hunting for a jewel and rightly figure that he's the one who has stolen it. The criminal plants the jewel in the dancer's handbag before hopping out through the bathroom window, leaving the dancer to pick up the check. Unfortunately for the criminal, the killers find him and as soon as he's blabbed about the jewel's location, they kill him.

"Shoulda seen that coming," hissed Clancy.

"They *never* do," replied Ruby.

Naturally, then the murderers turn their attention to the dancer, and she has to run for it, still wearing her glittery yellow tap shoes, running across rooftops and cable-car cables and you name it. The shoes, noisy and sparkly, made her easy to spot.

One had to wonder why this woman couldn't just stop off and buy a decent pair of sneakers. It would have saved her an awful lot of grief, but then that would spoil the whole premise of the movie.

"Boy, does she have the loudest scream," said Clancy, his ears still ringing as he left the theater.

"The loudest scream in Hollywood was what they said," said the guy from the ticket booth.

"That movie was highly unrealistic," commented Clancy, "but on the whole I liked it."

"I think she's a whole lot better in *Don't Call My Name,* but then it's a much better film," said the guy. "It's a total classic."

"It's OK," said Ruby.

"The only reason *Canary* is so famous," continued the ticket-booth guy, "is because it's the movie that made Bardem famous, and that's only because she does those like totally cool stunts — I mean, without the stunts, I don't think Margo Bardem would have even been noticed."

"I can't agree with you there, Horace," said Ruby. "Margo's got charisma and that goes a long way — she can deliver a comedy line as well as any comedian, and that ain't as easy as it looks."

Horace shrugged. "I guess, but I still think it's a lame film — take away those stunts and the film would have been a total flop."

Ruby and Clancy walked out into the sunlight.

"So, you have a better idea now of who might have taken the shoes?"

"Not a clue," said Ruby.

"Me either," said Clancy.

They rode back toward West Twinford and on to Cedarwood Drive.

"So what's your plan?" said Clancy. "The one you came up with to prevent me from getting another detention?"

"You're taking trumpet lessons," said Ruby.

"But I don't even play the trumpet," said Clancy.

"Exactly, so you can't fail," said Ruby.

"Jeepers," whined Clancy, "some great plan — I mean, totally foolproof."

"What do you mean? No one's gonna ask you to suddenly play the trumpet," said Ruby.

"That's what you think," said Clancy. "Word gets around that I play the trumpet, and suddenly I'm appearing at the junior high school concert."

"And that's when you fake a broken finger or get amnesia," said Ruby. "It's no biggie."

"I think you must have damaged more than your limbs in that fall," said Clancy. "So what's *your* excuse?"

"I've been at physical therapy," said Ruby, holding her arm up. "Damaged arms sure are useful."

"You have a legit excuse, and I have a totally bogus one," moaned Clancy, but Ruby had stopped listening.

"You know what, Clance? Drop me right here on the corner of Lime — I need to get a pack of bubble gum. I'll catch you tomorrow."

Ruby hopped off and Clancy rode toward home, all the time looking out for a possible ambush. He was tired of this feeling: constantly fearing a voice behind him, or worse. Like he needed another stupid Neanderthal patrolling the streets around school, calling him names. Bullies traveled in packs, hunting down the most vulnerable. Clancy fit the bill—he knew he did. He always had. From his first toddler party, his first morning at kindergarten, he knew it.

There were plenty of kids smaller than him, skinnier, uglier (Clancy would actually be considered nice looking, but it didn't count for much when you added up all the other victim check points). He just fit a profile that caught the bullies' attention, and although he had a best friend in Ruby Redfort, this in some ways only served to make his plight worse. They loathed him the more for it—he had this band of cool kids to hang out with, he was close to the toughest, most popular kid of all, but he himself was a loser. What did she see in him? Why pick him when she could hang out with better specimens? This was how they always saw it. He sighed to himself. *Clancy Crew, you are such a loser.*

It was when Ruby was nearing Cedarwood Drive that she heard a sort of familiar voice. "Hey!"

She looked up and saw the good-looking boy hanging by his fingertips from the top of a street lamp.

"Oh, it's you, the boy who goes around asking people personal questions."

"Hi," said the boy. He swung himself back and connected with the lamppost's trunk and shinnied down to the sidewalk.

"What were you doing?" asked Ruby.

"Just testing my nerve, seeing how long I could hang without, you know, falling."

"Sounds like an intelligent pursuit," said Ruby.

"You should try it from a crane," said the boy, whistling. "Really pumps the adrenaline, and, you know, it's something to do."

"That's your motivation?" She looked at him with such an intense expression that he looked away uneasily. "So," said Ruby, "what is it?"

"What?"

"Your name, buster."

"My friends call me Beetle," said the boy.

"If that's what you wanna go by, then that's fine with me." Ruby shrugged.

"You're Ruby, right?"

"Word gets around."

"Last time I saw you, you had a cast — on your arm."

"Yes, I did, and now I don't," said Ruby.

"So they sawed it off?" he said.

"It would seem so," said Ruby, looking at her cast-free arm.

"Did it hurt—when they took it off, I mean?"

"Only when they sawed right through and on into my arm."

He looked alarmed for a second and then nodded. "Oh, you're kidding." He laughed a bit too much, as if trying to show that he *really* got the joke. "Do you maybe want something to drink . . . or eat?" he asked.

"Yeah," said Ruby, "that's why I'm heading home."

"You wanna grab a bite, like, somewhere else maybe?"

"Nope," said Ruby. "I'm not really persuadable that way. Once I've made my mind up about what I want to eat, that's pretty much it."

"Some other time?" ventured the boy.

"Maybe," said Ruby. "I'm not making any firm plans today because I've got a lot on my mind."

"Sure," said the boy. "By the way, what's your T-shirt about?"

Ruby looked down; she had forgotten which one she was wearing today. It read: ***did you spot the gorilla?***

"It's to remind me of something," she said, disappearing around the corner.

CHAPTER 28
One Too Many Coincidences

SO RUBY HADN'T BEEN EXACTLY STRAIGHT UP with Beetle — she was not heading home but was on her way to Spectrum to see how the investigation was going. Although she *was* hoping to eat, she *did* have something particular in mind and happily she found it in the Spectrum cafeteria.

After wolfing down her burger, she hurried to the violet code zone. As usual, Froghorn was in room 324 (the Frog Pod, as Blacker called it). This was where he spent most of his time when at Spectrum; his work involved entering all available data into the Spectrum computers. Newspapers, crime reports, police records, you name it.

Froghorn had been tasked with searching through the records of all crimes committed in Twinford City, looking for robberies that might bear close resemblance to the crimes Spectrum was already investigating. If they could figure out when and where the mysterious thief had first struck, they could recover the first card and then, they hoped, decipher the code.

Froghorn didn't acknowledge Ruby's arrival, but Blacker gave her a smile and a friendly greeting.

"Hey, Ruby, just the person we need on this."

"You found something?" she asked.

"Froghorn has," replied Blacker. "Fill us in, why don't you, Miles."

Froghorn cleared his throat and began.

"Well, I brought up the robbery cases and set aside all the unsolved or unexplained. Of the ones I printed out, the only burglary that made any kind of link with the Little Yellow Shoes and the book of poetry was a break-in at Mr. Baradi's place, on the twenty-sixth floor of the Lakeridge Square apartments, though nothing has ever been reported missing."

Ruby remembered hearing about this on the cabdriver's radio the day she had her cast removed. "I heard about it," she said.

"As far as the way the break-in was conducted," said Froghorn, "it's identical to the Okra burglary."

Blacker was looking at the report. "I visited the scene this morning. Everything about the break-in is the same, so it would suggest that the crimes are connected, though why did the thief not take anything? Did he change his mind?"

"Maybe not," suggested Ruby. "Maybe he *did* take something, but Mr. Baradi hasn't yet figured out what it was."

"Or, just say," said Blacker, "that the robber made a mistake. Imagine you are two hundred feet up in the air, dangling from a piece of string. . . . I mean, it would be pretty easy to lose your bearings, take the wrong turn, get the wrong floor, come in the wrong window. The Lakeridge Building is huge. Maybe he was trying to target a different apartment, say on the twenty-seventh floor rather than the twenty-sixth. Maybe he just counted the floors wrong."

"So you're saying, maybe he broke into Mr. Baradi's by mistake?"

"Yep."

"So . . . what?"

"So maybe he realized his mistake," said Blacker. "And maybe he corrected it. Climbed back out the window, climbed up or down to the *right* level — maybe the twenty-fifth or twenty-seventh — and went back in, stole what he was after, then strolled on down and out the door of the building."

"With the first item . . ." said Ruby.

"Yeah."

"So how come it hasn't been reported?" asked Ruby.

Blacker shrugged. "Could be the owner of the apartment is away, or if he is anything like me, then he wouldn't notice a break-in — I'm telling you, my place is real chaotic."

"You surprise me," said Froghorn in a sarcastic tone. "I had you pegged as Mr. Tidy."

"No, Miles, it looks pretty much like a dump."

"So how sure are you that the thief comes in at the window and leaves by the door?" asked Ruby.

"Pretty sure." Blacker nodded. "There are marks on the *outside* of the Okras' window frame, like someone spent a while trying to get the thing to open — he had to force it — and, well, the front door was unlocked from the *inside*. Mr. Baradi's window was found open even though he swears blind that he is an air-conditioning-all-the-time sorta guy."

"You don't think *he* could have opened it?" said Ruby. "And then *forgot* that he opened it?"

"I have to say, I'm inclined to believe him when he says he never ever opens a window; it was kinda fuggy in there." Blacker made a face at the memory of it. It was then that Froghorn's phone began to ring and he signaled that they should continue without him.

"And the door?" asked Ruby.

"The door *was* unlocked from the inside," said Blacker, "though we have no actual proof that Mr. Baradi didn't unlock it himself."

"You think he could be an attention seeker?" asked Ruby. "Just made the whole thing up?"

"He doesn't seem the type," said Blacker. "He's kinda straightforward, meat and potatoes all the way. It's possible, of course, but my instinct tells me no."

"And the Little Yellow Shoes robbery?"

"If they are linked to the Okra robbery, then how the thief entered the building is more of a mystery," said Blacker.

"You don't think he came in through the window?"

Blacker frowned. "The thing is, although there is a window in the safe room at the Scarlet Pagoda theater and although it is easy to open, there is no way a grown man or woman could make it through—it's too small. You'd have to be some kind of contortionist."

They were silent for a minute, until Blacker added, "What we do know is this thief goes to a lot of effort getting *in* but doesn't seem to waste energy making his escape."

"Why bother climbing down a building if you can walk out the door?" said Ruby.

"Agreed," said Blacker. "But this guy must be pretty confident that he won't get seen exiting the premises."

"So I guess the doorman's always on duty? This is a fancy apartment block the Okras live in, right?"

"Totally," said Blacker. "There are cameras, so anyone using the back stairs would be picked up on film."

"And Mr. Baradi's place?"

"Not so much," said Blacker, "but what it lacks in fancy, it makes up for in nosy neighbors. Mr. Grint on the ground floor spends his whole time in the lobby watching people come and go."

"And what does Mr. Grint *say*?" asked Ruby.

"He didn't see any strangers that evening, not a one."

"So what's your theory?"

"The investigators think the thief must hang out somewhere in the building, a maintenance closet or somewhere like that. Then once it's morning and the building gets busy, he leaves, perhaps disguising himself as a mailman or maintenance."

"So what next?" asked Ruby.

"Froghorn is calling the TCPD, asking them if they could check out the apartments directly above and below Mr. Baradi's."

"You think you might be right about your theory — that the thief got the wrong floor first, and so tried again?"

"You know what, Rube? Yes, I do."

"So you're checking the floors above and below?"

"Yes," said Blacker. "Yes, I am."

When Ruby reached home, her brain was swimming with thoughts; she lay back on her beanbag and stared up at the ceiling and tried to pull them in, stack them up, create some kind of pattern with them.

```
ITEM ONE: Unknown, but possibly taken from
the 26th/27th/25th floor of the Lakeridge
Square apartment building.

ITEM TWO: Little Yellow Shoes worn by Margo
Bardem in the film The Cat That Got the
Canary. Partly filmed in the Scarlet Pagoda.
Stolen from the top floor of the Scarlet
Pagoda.

ITEM THREE: The poetry book A Line Through
My Center by JJ Calkin, a man who spent a lot
of time hanging out at the Scarlet Pagoda,
where apparently he went to see his "muse."
Question: Who was his muse?
```

The book was found by Mr. Okra on a plane
when he was traveling back from L.A. to
Twinford. Previous owner unknown. Stolen from
Mr. Okra's nightstand in #914, a ninth-floor
apartment in the Fountain Heights Building.
Handwritten inscription: *To my darling Cat
from your Celeste.*

This sounded like a reference to the characters in the film — there was after all a cat and a Celeste, the characters played by Hugo Gerard and Margo Bardem.

And one thing was for sure: the Scarlet Pagoda certainly connected both items.

Ruby took the poetry book from her drawer. The way the poems were laid out was interesting in itself. They weren't simply all arranged in verses and lines: some of them traveled across the page, words changing size as they went as if to make a point of what they were saying, the hidden thought, the subtext. None of the poems rhymed, and none of them were straightforward in their meaning.

The poem that didn't seem to be there, poem 14, was called "You Are a Poem, Celeste," so was it merely a coincidence that the handwritten inscription was from someone also named Celeste?

And was it a coincidence that the character in *The Cat That Got the Canary* was named Celeste too? Ruby didn't think so.

She turned back to the cover.

JJ Calkin. *A Line Through My Center.*

Click, click, click went her brain.

A line through the center.

And she set about in search of poem number 14.

**It wasn't difficult
breaking in this time. . . .**

In fact, he didn't have to do any breaking in at all. No forcing windows or contorting through air vents — he just walked right in the door and followed her in.

There was a moment when he thought she might have sensed him, but how could she know that he was there? He had watched her as she placed the 8 key in the little safe box, memorized the combinations, and when she had left the safe room, he had taken it — just like that.

Easy as 1 2 3.

CHAPTER 29
A Crime Scene

OUR THEORY WAS CORRECT," said Blacker. "Our thief *did* make a mistake when he went into Mr. Baradi's. And *did* then break into the right place."

"Huh," said Ruby. She had forgotten to turn her transmitter off on the Escape Watch, and Blacker's voice had pierced through her unconscious and dragged her from her dreams.

"Our theory was correct, re: the window thief."

"*Your* theory," said Ruby. "*I* can't take credit for it." She stumbled to her desk and picked up a pencil. "So which apartment was it that got burgled?"

"Twenty-five C," said Blacker. "I think he came in the window of twenty-six C, couldn't find what he wanted, opened the front door to check that he had the right apartment number, saw he had screwed up, and went back out the window."

"Why didn't he just decide to take the stairs?" She was noting down everything Blacker was saying.

"It's not his style. Anyway, maybe he's no locksmith — maybe to him, climbing in through the window is easier than breaking a lock. Who can say?" said Blacker. "Or maybe he's just making a point."

Ruby stretched her arms out, yawning. "What time is it, man?"

"You're not up? Aren't you supposed to be school bound?" said Blacker.

She reached for her glasses and peered at her bird alarm clock.

"Yeah." She yawned again. "So what are you saying? He climbed down a level and came in the window of twenty-five C, is that it?"

"Yup, so the guy who owns the place, a Mr. Norgaard, is away, but a neighbor noticed the door was unlocked; he comes by once a week to water the plants and check on the place while the owner's out of town."

"Very neighborly of him," said Ruby.

"Isn't it?" agreed Blacker. "So coincidentally the neighbor calls the cops yesterday evening, having popped in for plant-watering duty and spotted that something was wrong — one of the windows was open, and he swears he left it shut."

"Anything missing?"

"Nothing obvious, evidently."

"But did he find a card?" asked Ruby.

"That I don't know. I spoke to the detectives, but they didn't mention anything. That's what we need to check out next." Blacker paused before adding, "So what class were you planning on being late for?"

"You're asking me to cut class," said Ruby.

"Rube, you know I'd never interfere with a kid's education."

"I'll meet you at the apartment," she said. "I'll just go find Hitch; he might wanna come along."

"He's in with LB," said Blacker. "He's been at Spectrum for most of the night."

"What's happened?" said Ruby.

"Beats me," he said, "but something's going down."

Ruby skateboarded downtown, skitching a ride from a yellow cab and then a garbage truck (which didn't smell too pretty).

She met Blacker on the sidewalk outside the apartment building.

"Geez, Redfort, did you switch perfumes or did you fall into something unmentionable? "

"I skitched the wrong ride," said Ruby.

"Huh?"

"Never mind."

Mr. Grint—she was pretty sure it was Mr. Grint—was in the lobby watching folks come and go. He watched her and Blacker as they made their way to the elevator and pressed the button for the twenty-fifth floor. The elevator was not in the first flush of youth, and it made horrible groaning sighs as it climbed. They stepped out and walked along the corridor until they reached Mr. Norgaard's door. Blacker handed Ruby gloves and shoe covers; these looked ridiculous but served to preserve the crime scene from cross-contamination.

For a while, the two agents simply surveyed the scene. It was not a disorganized apartment, not especially untidy either. There were piles of books on the floor, piles of scripts too, but they were not without order. It was clear that Norgaard wasn't a big entertainer, because most of the chairs were also occupied by books, notebooks, and paper stacks—the furniture was more of a filing system than somewhere to sit.

There were a few papers strewn across the floor under the desk, but as Blacker suggested, perhaps the wind had caught these when the thief wrenched open the window. Apart from that, it was all very orderly. It wasn't at all obvious what had been removed from the apartment, but it was safe to say that something had been, for there on the desk was a little white calling card.

"Bingo," said Blacker.

"Only thing is," said Ruby, scanning the desk, "what's missing?"

They both looked at the desk. On it was a spider plant, a cactus, a pen pot, a stapler, a hole punch, a roll of tape in a tape dispenser, five paperweights on top of five different piles of papers, some envelopes, some checks, some typewritten sheets. There was a tin of lip balm, an eraser, a glasses case, and a sheet of stamps.

"A telephone?" suggested Blacker.

"Seems unlikely a thief would steal the telephone," said Ruby.

"Seems unlikely a thief would steal a not-so-valuable book," said Blacker.

"True, but still, a telephone?" said Ruby.

"I agree, unlikely," said Blacker. He pressed the transmitter button on his watch — no answer, so he tried again, and this time the call connected and he spoke into the tiny speaker. "Hi, Buzz, I am trying to locate Froghorn — could you get him on the line? I appreciate it." A pause. "Froghorn, could we ask the neighbor about the phone? I mean, just to be sure — did he have one and if so where?"

They waited. After a few minutes, they got their answer.

"Mr. Norgaard's neighbor said Norgaard never had a phone

on the desk," Blacker relayed, "because he didn't want to be disturbed when he was writing."

"What does he write?" asked Ruby.

"He's a scriptwriter," said Blacker.

"No, I meant *what* does he write? TV? Film — anything I woulda heard of?"

"Nothing I have ever heard of," said Blacker. "I'm not sure how successful he is, maybe not as successful as his father."

"His father is a scriptwriter?"

"Was," said Blacker. "He wrote the screenplay for *The Storm Snatcher* and *The Silver Scream*."

"Two of Mrs. Digby's favorites," said Ruby, impressed. She looked again at the desk. "And the paperweights?" she said. "What a lot of paperweights Mr. Norgaard does have."

It was the papers under the desk that made her think of it. Everything about Norgaard's room was tidy — cluttered with scripts and papers, but all in order, except for the sheets under the desk — just why were they there?

"What did the detectives say about the window?" asked Ruby.

"What do you mean?"

"Just . . . did they say *anything* about it?"

"Well, that's an interesting thing. . . ." said Blacker. "They said that the intruder would have had no problem opening it because it was used regularly, slid up and down with no trouble at all. Unlike our friend Mr. Baradi, it seems this guy liked fresh air, never had air-conditioning installed."

"Which would explain why he used paperweights, not just *decorative* things but actually there to stop paper from blowing around."

"That would be logical," agreed Blacker.

"So . . . the papers under the desk don't make sense — they don't fit with the way Norgaard does things," Ruby said. "Look at the piles." Blacker looked. Every pile of papers was secured by a paperweight.

Blacker smiled. "You think one of his paperweights is missing."

"I do," said Ruby, "but which one?"

"No way to know," said Blacker, "not without talking to Norgaard, and who knows when he's going to resurface?"

"Yeah," said Ruby, "it's too bad." She took her Polaroid camera from her backpack and started snapping pictures of the desk.

"You know the TCPD will pass on a complete set of photographs; they took about a zillion of the apartment," said Blacker.

"I know," said Ruby. "But I'm only really interested in the

desk, and this way I can look and look until I see the answer; it's probably staring me in the face."

She was right about this in a sense, but she was missing the big picture, and without it, she was never going to see what she needed to see. . . .

**"So I see from reading
my morning paper that
you went shopping
again. . . .**

A nice high-rise on Avenue Walk."

"So?"

"No one saw you."

"People only see what they expect to see."

"People only see what they are able to see; you're cheating."

"You are mistaken."

"Don't mess with me, Birdboy — we both know you've got it, and I'm coming after you."

"You're trying to scare me?"

"No, I'm warning you. I would hope that you were scared already. I am the living dead, after all."

"I don't scare. I have nothing to lose."

"How about your life?"

"I lost that a long time ago."

CHAPTER 30
Proper English

IT WAS EARLY MORNING and Mrs. Digby was reading all about it. She had a cup of strong tea and a currant bun (in proper English style) and her copy of the *Twinford Lark*.

Ruby had woken very early, perhaps due to the strange hours she was working and as a consequence of her altered sleep rhythms. She woke hungry and wandered into the kitchen looking for food.

"Howdy, Mrs. Digby."

"Knock me down with a feather, child. What are you doing walking at this hour?"

"Beats me," said Ruby. "So what's the story, Mrs. Digby?"

"Another robbery," said the housekeeper, "this time on the thirty-seventh floor of the Warrington Apartments on Avenue Walk."

"Really? The same guy, they think?"

"Looks that way," said Mrs. Digby, slurping on her tea. "Came in the window, left by the door."

"What did he steal?" Ruby was wondering why Blacker hadn't contacted her about this; it had to be connected.

"Never mind what he took. Those folks are lucky to be alive; they could be dead in their beds."

"That's not his MO," said Ruby. "He's not a murderer."

"Not yet," warned Mrs. Digby, "but just you wait until he gets the idea in his head; that could all change."

"Mrs. Digby, you are getting carried away."

"Well, I'm glad we don't live in a high-rise, is all I can say."

The sound of the doorbell interrupted their discussion. Ruby went down to answer it.

"Hey, Clance, what brings you to my doorstep?"

"Why are you up so early?" asked Clancy.

"I have no idea," said Ruby. "Why are you even here?"

"Oh, I was trying to avoid taking Olive to kindergarten, so I told my mom that I had to leave home super early because I had to pick something up from your place."

"Why didn't you just, you know, like say you were coming here but hang out in the diner?" asked Ruby.

"Because she will probably call you in a minute to check that I wasn't lying."

At that moment, the telephone began to ring. Ruby picked up the receiver.

"Hello, Mrs. Crew, yes, he's here. . . . OK, I will, yes, bye-bye."

"What did she say?" asked Clancy.

"Be sure to come straight home after school; Olive wants you to play hopscotch with her."

"Oh, brother!"

"Well, come on in. Mrs. Digby and I were just discussing the latest high-rise robbery."

Clancy followed Ruby back up to the kitchen.

"Who did the place belong to?" he asked.

"It says here," said Ruby, reading from the *Lark*, "that it was a couple, Pamela and Fabian Thompson, and their fifteen-month-old son, Nileston."

"Nileston?" repeated Clancy, screwing up his nose. "Nileston? What kind of name is that for a kid?"

"Apparently it's a family name," answered Ruby. The *Lark* was the sort of paper that gave out useless information like this.

"Anyway," she said, "Pamela Thompson says, 'The only thing that we have noticed missing is my husband's tie clip.'"

"How does that fit in to any theory you might have?" asked Clancy.

"Mrs. Digby thinks the guy's a wannabe murderer, but I don't have a theory, at least not one that involves a suspect. Sure, everyone knows this thief can climb and that he can open windows and squeeze through small spaces, but no one seems to have a clue about who this bozo is."

"A dangerous man, is who this bozo is," said Mrs. Digby, hopping off her seat and taking her teacup to the sink. "If you want a cookie, there are fresh ones in the tin; I have to get back to my chores." She left them alone.

Ruby picked up a pencil and wrote down the objects that had so far been stolen.

"You see, the shoes, yes, they are valuable, all right. I mean, maybe not in themselves but to a collector, to someone interested in the movies."

"Or someone who's a real devoted fan of Margo Bardem," said Clancy. "I mean, maybe this guy is collecting famous-people memorabilia."

"That's a good point, Clance," said Ruby. "I guess it's possible."

"Yeah," said Clancy, warming to the idea, "I heard them saying on the radio that the tie clip once belonged to the king of the U.K."

"England," corrected Ruby. "Kings of the U.K. are generally referred to as the king of England."

"It must be pretty valuable, right?" said Clancy. "They said it was inscribed with the guy's initials. This window thief could be like a king of England fan."

Ruby smiled. Clance really made her see the funny side. "Yep, it was the king's, all right. It was engraved, and look—there's even a photograph of him wearing it back in the day."

"So," Clancy asked, "did this king of England lose it or something, because what I want to know is how it ended up pinned on a Twinford car salesman."

"Advertising man," corrected Ruby.

"Car advertiser, whatever," said Clancy. "Why is it not back home in the Tower of London?" He caught Ruby's expression. "Or wherever the royal people keep their stuff now."

"You are asking all the right questions, my friend. Thinking like a detective." Ruby gave Clancy a pinch on his cheek.

"Cut it out, Rube."

"I guess we gotta assume that maybe this king gave it away, it's the sorta thing kings do, but it could have changed hands many times before Mr. Thompson got his mitts on it. If Mrs. Thompson bought it at auction or some antique store, then who did it belong to before that and what were they doing selling it?"

"Perhaps the original owner decided to cash it in; it's the kind of piece someone might pay a few thou for—I mean, I would," said Clancy. "I think it would look pretty stylish, but I wouldn't wear it on a tie—maybe on a hat but not a tie."

"What else do we have?" said Ruby, running her pencil down the list.

"Oh, yeah, the poetry book. This messes up your famous-person theory, because the poet JJ Calkin was not a famous poet and the book is not valuable — not enough to make it worth stealing, and risking the chance of getting caught."

"Or splatted," remarked Clancy, who was thinking about the nine floors the thief had had to climb to reach it. "But it might be sentimental. I mean, it has to mean something to someone."

Neither of them said anything for a minute or two, and then Clancy said, "Perhaps it was a commission — to steal these four things. I mean, perhaps the thief was contracted to grab the items, and the money he gets paid makes it all worthwhile?"

"Possible," agreed Ruby. "The thief could have a steal-and-deal business, or as you say, he could have a steal-to-order business, unless of course . . ." She paused.

"What?" said Clancy.

"Unless he's planning on keeping everything for himself."

"Like trophies for his trouble, you mean, like he is saying look how good I am? Like one of those rich gentleman thieves who do it for kicks?"

"Raffles," said Mrs. Digby, re-entering the room.

"Who's Raffles?" said Clancy, wrinkling his nose.

"A rich gentleman thief who steals for kicks," replied Ruby.

Ruby tapped her pencil on her desk — *tap, tap, tap, tap*. She was thinking about the white cards now. Why hadn't Blacker called?

"No," she said. "This guy is not showing off. This guy is tapping us on the shoulder, trying to get us to turn around and look."

The transmitter was buzzing again. He walked over to where it sat, taking his time about it. . . .

"Hello," he said.

"Don't give me 'hello' like we are on genteel speaking terms." The woman spat the words angrily into his ear, and he instinctively pulled the receiver away from his ear as if she might perhaps reach into it and grab him. "How long are you going to make me wait?"

"Not much longer."

"What's that supposed to mean?" she said.

"I have it," he said calmly.

"You have the 8 key?" She took a deep breath. "At last — when will you deliver?"

"Be patient. I just have two small tasks to complete and then both items will be yours."

"Be patient? You are telling me to be patient? You dare to suggest I wait a moment longer, Birdboy? You better count the hours because the end is nigh —"

He smiled and hung up. He felt very secure, safe, out of reach; she could threaten him, but she could not find him. All she could do was call and beg and bully, but that was only because he allowed her this luxury of contact. If he chose to, he could disappear entirely, and as soon as he had executed his plan, that's exactly what he would do.

Wait until it has all played out, he told himself. *Wait for the money and the big finale and then be gone.*

CHAPTER 31
The Tiny File Clerk

AFTER SCHOOL, Ruby took her skateboard and skitched her way to the Schroeder Building and down to Spectrum.

She found Blacker in his office, going through some files.

"So have you picked up the card from the latest robbery," she asked, "the tie-clip theft, I mean? Why haven't you called me?"

"No, there was no card," said Blacker.

Ruby looked at him. "But there has to be."

"I'm telling you, Ruby, there wasn't. Our guys were all over the joint. They didn't find a thing. So I'm thinking maybe it's not our guy."

"But it should have been — I mean, it would have been next to the tie, the tie Mr. Thompson hung up in his closet."

"On the floor, you mean," said Blacker. "Mrs. Thompson was real clear about that; they were having quite a marital spat." Blacker raised his eyebrows. "Mrs. T. is not happy about it, claims he never picks up after himself, just walks in the door, kicks off his shoes, drops his jacket, pulls off his tie, and wherever it lands is where it stays."

"Sounds like Mrs. Thompson is pretty strung out about it," said Ruby.

Blacker nodded. "Is she ever."

"So where *did* Mr. Thompson discard his tie last night?"

"In the dog bowl, according to Mrs. Thompson. She was very upset about it."

"I'm guessing the dog's got something to say about it too," said Ruby.

"Mr. Thompson doesn't remember anything about that, swears it couldn't have gotten there because when he arrived home, the baby was crying and he went straight to the kid's room. Mrs. T. was supervising the nanny while she made a bottle of whatever it is those little guys drink."

"So Mr. and Mrs. T. woke up in the morning to find the tie clip gone?"

"Not quite. The nanny was up with Nileston. She took him into the kitchen and let him crawl around, and that's when she noticed the tie in the dog bowl."

"And no tie clip."

"No tie clip," confirmed Blacker.

"You don't suppose Nileston swallowed it?" suggested Ruby.

"I would say impossible," said Blacker. "If the kid ate it, then he would be in the ER right now; same goes for the dog, I imagine — anyway, it doesn't explain the open window or the unlocked door."

"Unless this is an insurance scam," said Froghorn, who had stepped out of the Frog Pod with a file, which he handed to Blacker. "They could be faking a burglary — maybe they need the money."

"They are living on Avenue Walk in the Warrington Apartments. Why would they need money?" said Ruby.

"Appearances can be deceptive," said Blacker. "Never take anything at face value. It's certainly worth checking out the Thompsons' bank account."

"We'll get someone on it," said Froghorn. "They can check the Thompsons' financial position, see if they are in debt."

"If they were in debt, they would hardly just report one valuable missing," said Ruby.

"Exactly, which is why we are also investigating the more than likely angle that Mr. Thompson simply mislaid the tie clip, left the window open, and forgot to lock the front door when he came home," said Blacker. "However, the police are convinced it's a copycat burglar. Either way, there's not much we can do without that card."

"What are the Thompsons doing while all this goes on?" asked Ruby.

"They're spending a few days out of town," said Blacker. "Mrs. Thompson doesn't feel safe knowing that anyone can just crawl in the window whenever they feel like it."

When Ruby got home, the main house phone was ringing. She answered, "Dentures Dental Service. You got tooth decay, we got pliers."

"Excuse me?" said the voice of Elaine Lemon. "I was trying to get hold of Ruby, Ruby Redfort?"

"I can't help you there, lady."

"Are you sure? She adores my baby boy, Archie. I wanted to offer her some babysitting at his little birthday party."

"That sounds unlikely."

"Pardon me?"

"What I'm saying is, you dialed an incorrect number."

"But that can't be. The Redfort number is programmed into my phone."

"Look, cookie, unless you got some kind of toothy emergency, I'm going to have to ask you to clear the line."

Mrs. Lemon hung up, and Ruby switched the phone so it went directly to the answering machine.

Mrs. Digby peered around the kitchen door. "Child," she said, "I'm sure the king of mischief himself could learn a thing or two from you."

It was just as Ruby was changing into her nightwear, an over-size T-shirt with **superhero** written across the front, that Archie Lemon's face popped into her head.

Why? she wondered. *What are you trying to tell me, brain?*

Somewhere deep inside her mind, a thought was trying to connect with another thought. When Ruby was very small, she had sometimes liked to imagine that there was a tiny person, a little file clerk, in her head, filing facts and sifting through ideas, collecting stray thoughts and joining them all together. When she was struggling to remember something, she would imagine this little figure going off to search for it in one of the many file drawers.

She hoped the tiny clerk would return with something soon.

She went into the bathroom to brush her teeth. Then she washed her face, examined her newly mended arm, and her recently injured foot — the scar was almost gone. She massaged it with some baby oil that Mrs. Digby had bought for the purpose, and then suddenly there it was: the brain clerk had found what she needed — Archie Lemon and Nileston Thompson.

Both babies, both crawlers, both grabbers.

The tie was in the dog bowl because *Nileston* had put it there. The tie should have been where Mr. Thompson had left it, which was most likely not in the closet as he had claimed, but on the floor of Nileston's room. Therefore the card would have been left on the floor on top of the tie.

Nileston must have grabbed the card when he grabbed the tie, so where it was now was anyone's guess. It was only a theory, of course — she couldn't prove it . . . at least not unless she went over there and searched the place. Of course she could wait until dawn, or she could call someone right now and tell them her theory, but she felt the need to do it herself. It was *her* theory, after all.

She wondered what Hitch would say, and decided it was probably best not to imagine.

Ruby changed into her climb gear: black clothes, free-climbing shoes, climbing gloves, and a pouch of chalk dust belted around her waist. She took off her glasses and switched to contacts, clipped her hair in place with her barrette, and found a warm woolen hat — it was bound to get a little chilly thirty-seven stories up. She decided she would take the same route the window thief had taken, to figure out how he had done it, and at the same time avoiding the security guard sitting outside the apartment door — she was pretty sure there would be a security guard, and she just hoped he wasn't authorized to use the Thompsons' bathroom.

She took a deep breath. She was going to climb the outside of an apartment building.

A little voice in the back of her mind said, *This is exactly the kind of dangerous stunt Hitch was warning you about. If he finds out, you might as well wave bye-bye to Spectrum.*

Aw, shut up, little voice, thought Ruby.

CHAPTER 32
Mr. Potato Head

IT TOOK RUBY APPROXIMATELY twenty-three minutes to reach the Warrington Apartments on Avenue Walk. When she got there, she found a place to hide her skateboard, behind a low stone wall to the side of the building, then looked for the easiest way to make her ascent without being spotted.

It wasn't exactly an *easy* climb, and even as she hauled herself up the outside of the building, she tried not to dwell on the possible challenges to come, not least how she was going to bluff it if the security guard decided to pop into the apartment and have a look around. The wind was howling outside the Warrington, fluttering her hair, and it hampered her progress; on the other hand it meant that everyone had their shades drawn and no one would hear her.

Arriving at the thirty-seventh floor, she looked down at the teeny cars and the few tiny nighttime sidewalk walkers below. The air was a little on the chilly side, and she had to admit she wasn't exactly comfortable, but neither was she fearful. She felt sort of in her element crouching there on that windowsill. She hoped it was the baby's room she was peering into. *Give it a try,* she thought, and she set about opening the window, using the laser-cutting device on her Escape Watch; she was in in a matter of minutes. She landed softly on carpeted floor.

There was no doubt about it being Nileston's room — it reeked of baby lotion and talcum powder and all that other gunk people smeared their babies with. First she headed for his crib, methodically looking in between the bedding and even under the mattress. Then she searched the floor, under the shelves, anywhere that was in baby reach, nothing above a couple of feet. After thirty-two minutes, she got lucky while she was rooting through the toy box next to the window.

It was underneath Mr. Potato Head.

"Bingo!" she whispered as she pulled out a slightly chewed little white card.

Ruby made it down to the street without so much as a graze, retrieved her skateboard, and began wending her way through the streets, still busy even though the hour was late. She stopped only to get her bearings, looking around to pick the best route home. It was when she looked up northward that she saw him.

A tiny figure was walking across the sky.

The skywalker.

When the cabdriver had mentioned him the other day on the way to St. Angelina's, she hadn't taken much notice; it sounded like the product of someone's wild imagination or a film festival stunt. But now she thought, *What if the window thief and the skywalker are one and the same? What if he doesn't just climb? What if he walks a high wire too?*

She watched the little figure. He was headed toward the seedier part of downtown Twinford, away from the posher area.

Where are you going?

He wasn't so far away, but as she made it farther into that part of the city where the apartments became offices and the buildings became taller and denser, she began to lose sight of him. She wasn't exactly sure, but she thought he was walking the gap between the Luper Building and the Carrington Apartments, or was it the Berman Block? She managed to sneak into the main entrance of the Luper, taking the elevator as far as it went and continuing up the stairs and out onto the roof. Now she could see clearly: the building the skywalker was headed to was neither Carrington nor Berman — it was the Hauser Ink offices.

She could see where the high-wire cable stretched, and in theory she could follow, but the gap between the roof she stood on and the roof he was walking to might as well have been a mile apart. Her balance was good and she was not afraid of heights, but she knew her physical limits. There was no way she could walk a hundred feet of steel cable.

Ruby watched the tiny figure as he crossed the barely visible wire. He was mesmerizing. It was almost like watching a dancer, so precise, so confident, and for just a moment the beauty of the spectacle became the only thing and Ruby forgot why she was there. She shook herself. *Get a grip, Rube.* He had almost reached the other side. *Should I follow him?* This was the closest she had come to their thief — assuming of course that he and the skywalker *were* indeed one and the same.

The skywalker was tantalizingly close — others had seen him stepping across clouds and air, but no one had gotten near catching him. This was Ruby's big chance. If she followed, then she would be able to identify him — find out if he was their guy. If so, she could inform the Spectrum team — it wasn't like she planned to wrestle him to the ground or anything.

She walked over to the wire. *He doesn't know I'm here. As long as it stays that way, then I am perfectly safe.* She thought about that statement for a second. *As long as I don't fall,* she added. She thought about Beetle and the thrill he got from dangling from cranes and lampposts — he wouldn't think twice, so neither would she.

No sweat, she thought.

She wasn't unduly worried about the possibility of falling, because her finger grip was strong and she knew that if she kept very calm and focused, she would be able to grip the wire and make her way across by edging along one hand over the other. In other words, she would hang on to the tightrope like some kind of monkey rather than step across it. She might be fearless, but she wasn't crazy.

She waited until the skywalker had reached the opposite roof, and then she stepped onto the parapet where the high wire connected to the building. She dusted her hands in chalk and, taking the cable in both hands, slowly lowered herself until she was hanging from the wire. Then she began to edge out across the void. She was soon dangling several hundred feet above the dark streets. It felt OK. She was confident. She would not fall. The sirens below were not reacting to her daredevil act; they were simply the unharmonious music of the city's streets.

She kept her focus forward just as she had been taught by Coach Norov in gymnastics. Her nerves were steel and her confidence unwavering. She was a good halfway across when all that changed. She began to feel a movement in the wire.

What's happening?

Did it matter? Not at that exact moment. All she knew

was she needed to get to the other side as fast as possible. *Don't panic, but speed it up.* She started moving fast, hand over hand. But it soon became clear, as the movement in the wire became more and more dramatic, that something was very wrong. The wire was going to snap. She would have to abandon it before it abandoned her.

Otherwise you'll hit that wall like a wrecking ball.

She braced herself, waiting for the cable to be completely severed from its anchor, waiting for the moment when she would be swung at great speed toward the Hauser Ink Building, knowing that if she timed it right, she would survive, knowing that if she timed it wrong, she would smash into the wall or be dashed onto the sidewalk below. No second chances; make it or die.

Snap.

The wire gave, and Ruby swung at alarming speed toward the Hauser Ink Building. She was planning to leap onto the large ledge just above the Hauser's vast central window. All she had to do was time it right.

The air rushed past. The building rushed closer.

Not yet . . .

Not yet . . .

Now.

She let go.

She wasn't even close to making it.

CHAPTER 33
A Miss Is as Good as a Mile

RUBY'S LEAP WAS AN AMBITIOUS MOVE—the kind of stunt that needed practice.

And Ruby had had very little practice at swinging from buildings on wires.

So where did she land? In true comedy style (not that Ruby was close to laughing), her fall was broken by a flagpole, or perhaps it would be more accurate to say, she was lucky enough to grab the flag as she began her descent to sidewalk level. Now she was hanging on with one hand and looking down at the red and white lights of the tiny cars on Ink Street. More movies than she could recall titles to had a scene like this. She gripped the tough fabric and worked her way steadily up the cloth until she was finally grasping the flagpole it was attached to.

Ruby thanked her lucky Redfort stars that her death-defying window-ledge encounter at the Sandwich Building had in some way prepared her for this moment.

It wasn't easy to edge her way back to the building; the flag was billowing and enfolding her in its massive stars and stripes, but, undeterred, she gradually maneuvered herself closer to the building's ledge, where she hoped there might be an open window.

She heard a voice.

"Kid, where exactly are you? My radar has you placed at three hundred feet above street level. Please don't tell me you are on some rooftop."

"I'm not," Ruby replied in the rather strangled voice of one who is hanging by two hands over a three-hundred-foot void. She couldn't have been more surprised to hear Hitch's voice crackling out of the fly barrette, and she couldn't have been more grateful either.

"You don't sound all right. Are you all right?" Hitch asked.

"Um," said Ruby, "kinda. It depends."

"Depends on what?"

"Whether there is a window open on the thirtieth floor of the Hauser Ink Building."

"Jeepers, Redfort, do you ever obey orders? I'm coming to get you — just stay there!"

"I'll try," said Ruby, her voice betraying the strain of her predicament.

By the time Ruby reached the building, her fingers were feeling the strain. She let herself down onto the ledge, finally daring to let go of the flagpole. There was no window. So she pressed her body firmly against the Hauser's bricks and prayed the wind would not change direction while she waited for Hitch to come get her. She looked up when she heard her name being called. "Grab this and I'll haul you up."

He sounded ticked off, and Ruby had half a mind not to catch the rope but instead sit the night through and figure out another way down.

But, she thought, whatever storm was coming her way, she was going to have to face it sometime or other, and besides, it was cold up on that ledge. She grabbed the rope, slipped her foot into the foot loop, and was pulled back to safety.

She was met by a very unhappy-looking Hitch.

"So why were you tailing me?" she asked.

"I wasn't. I was just testing the transmitter function on my watch and guess who pops up on my radar?"

Stupid Redfort, you should have left the fly barrette at home!

"I can probably explain," said Ruby.

"You always can."

"I think someone just tried to kill me."

"You're looking at the next guy in line — I just happened to be having dinner two blocks away with a very charming meter maid."

"Look, the thing is . . ."

"Let's be clear on one thing, Redfort: don't say one more word."

Ruby nodded.

Hitch was winding the rope back. She waited for him to gather up his rescue kit, and then, in complete silence, she followed him back in through the roof-hatch door and all the way down the stairs to street level.

Ruby said nothing, not in fact because Hitch didn't look like he had lifted the no-talk ban, but because she really couldn't think of anything worth saying.

She picked up her skateboard from where she had abandoned it outside the Luper Building, but Hitch had already hailed a cab and was directing her into it.

"Go home, Redfort," he said. Then he slammed the cab door and walked off in the direction of the restaurant and his no doubt rather cold supper.

**The voice cooed
down the line. . . .**

"I've been following you."

Silence.

"That's right, and not in the papers."

"But you don't know what I look like."

"Why would that matter? You make a real spectacle of yourself. I've got to hand it to you: it's quite a show you put on."

Silence.

"I've seen you walking on air. I've watched you disappear, but I'm right behind you and getting closer."

"I told you, you'll get what you want when I've completed my task."

"Too late, Birdboy. I don't like to wait and I've been waiting a long time." Laughter spilled down the line. "But you know what? It's more fun this way, like a little old game of hide-and-seek, and I'm coming to get you, buddy — you can be sure of that."

CHAPTER 34
A Turn for the Worse

CLANCY WAS IN SURPRISINGLY GOOD SPIRITS the next morning when he arrived at Twinford Junior High. He had been concentrating on his invisibility all week, and it appeared to be working—he was certainly less visible than he had been the day before or the day before that. He had toned down his look and had become "regular"—neither eccentrically obvious, nor eccentrically bland.

Red and Elliot walked right past him at the bus stop and Del stood two places ahead of him in the cafeteria line without noticing he was there. Vapona Begwell didn't even hurl one insult his way for the whole entire basketball game, and Vapona *never* missed a chance to bait him. He was feeling confident and relaxed, at one with the world.

In contrast, Ruby was in a complicated mood that morning. She barely spoke a word before leaving the house and headed for school *without* breakfast. Rare for Ruby not to feel hungry, rare for Ruby not to feel like talking. Clancy, a sensitive kid, tuned in to her awkward state of mind at once and decided it might be wise to give her some space. He didn't mind. Things were going his way, and Clancy had not encountered the gorilla boy once since his first day back at school. He had seen the guy plenty of times outside the gates, hanging with his crowd, but the gorilla had never spotted *him*. However, this good feeling was not to last, and things took a turn for the worse in the afternoon.

Clancy walked into his history class, a little late due to a problem with his locker combination, and by the time he reached class, all the desks near the window and the back of the room had already been taken. In fact only two places remained, both in his least favorite positions: front and center. Reluctantly he sat himself down and took out his books. He was just lining up his various pens and stuff when the door opened.

"And you are?" said the history teacher.

"Bailey Roach," said a voice.

"Well, Mr. Roach, since you're new to Twinford Junior High, I won't wail about your being late. You do know school began on Monday?"

"I had trouble enrolling," said Bailey Roach.

"Well, never mind," said the history teacher. "You're here now — there's a desk next to Mr. Crew."

Clancy looked up and at once knew that his invisibility ruse was not going to cut it. The gorilla was sitting next to him. And when he caught Clancy's eye, he smiled and made a sign to suggest, *I'm going to squash you to pulp,* and then he turned and sat down.

Ruby meanwhile was having problems of her own. She didn't feel like going home, nor did she feel like hanging out; she didn't feel like talking to anyone, and she didn't feel like being in her own company either.

She *especially* didn't want to be at home, since her mother would no doubt go on and on about the Ada Borland portrait and how lucky Ruby was to have this great opportunity to have a picture snapped by this genius woman. Worse still, Hitch was mad at her, and worse even than that, she could see his point of view.

She had followed the skywalker onto a tightrope three hundred feet above the street, and she had *fallen.*

Or rather, someone had tried to kill her. She was certain of it: someone had cut the cable. Not a good feeling to know that someone had tried to kill you . . . *again.*

So on balance, yes, being alone might be the better option, so when the school bell rang, she picked up her skateboard and took herself out to a part of Twinford she liked a lot but rarely found herself in.

Clancy slammed the front door and went upstairs to find his sister Lulu.

"What's wrong?" she said.

"You know Vapona Begwell?"

"Uh . . . that girl at junior high? The one you pointed out to me that time?"

"Yeah," said Clancy.

Lulu nodded. "Sure I do."

"Well, this one's worse." He slumped down on one of Lulu's many floor cushions. He looked depressed.

"Don't tell me you've attracted the attention of yet another bozo," said Lulu.

"Yeah," said Clancy slightly mournfully, "and it wasn't even my fault. All I did was bump into him at the diner."

"Him?" said Lulu.

"Yeah, it's a him and he's kind of partial to socking people in the face," said Clancy.

Lulu made her mouth go out of shape, a sort of visual code for *You're in trouble, my friend.*

"Anyway, I thought it was just a one-off thing, you know, an unpleasant encounter in the diner, and I'd never see him again." He paused, Lulu waiting for him to continue. "But then he sorta turns up at school." Again Lulu waited. "To be accurate, in my class."

"The kid, from the diner? The one who threatened to sock you in the face?" Lulu wasn't actually asking these questions; she was laying it out for him, acknowledging the direness of the situation, and Clancy was grateful for that. Any adult would have played it down, but not Lulu.

"He sits next to me in history."

Lulu let her whole face go with it now. "Dude, you are in seriously deep—"

Before she could finish her no-doubt colorful sentence, there was a tiny knock at the door.

"Go away!" said both Clancy and his sister in unison. They knew it was Olive.

"Mom says you have got to be nice to me," came Olive's sing-song voice.

"We *are* being *nice*," said Lulu. "We are warning you that if you come in here, we will kidnap Buttercup." (Buttercup was Olive's new doll.)

Olive went away. Clancy and his sister continued to discuss his options for future survival. There was another knock at the door, much louder and much more insistent.

"Enter," said Lulu, and in tottered Minny, Clancy's oldest sister. She was tottering because she was not only wearing very high cork-wedge heels, but she also had a very full tray of snacks and sodas. She closed the door with her foot and dumped the tray on the floor.

"Hey, that's not fair," said a voice from behind the door. Olive obviously hadn't gone away after all. "Why is she allowed in and not me?" came the muffled whine.

"Scram!" shouted Minny. "Or Buttercup is going in the blender." Minny didn't believe in taking prisoners, and this time Olive's footsteps could be heard running down the staircase.

"So," said Minny, looking from one sibling to another, "what seems to be the problem?"

Clancy repeated the story, and Minny quizzed him on all the various options. These seemed to amount to: hire a bodyguard, change schools, or start working out — none of them seemed truly viable.

"What does Ruby say?" asked Minny.

"I haven't told her," said Clancy.

"What?" said Minny.

"I don't want her to know," said Clancy, "not after what she's been through."

"Yeah, I get that," said Lulu. "She did almost bite the big one."

"Yeah, and she's gone all weird," Clancy said, flapping his arms now.

"You should take a look at yourself," said Minny.

"Yeah, but that's different. I'm trying to blend in, keep a low profile, but Ruby, she thinks she's indestructible. I mean, it's dangerous, I'm telling you."

"It's kinda dangerous having gorilla boy on your tail too," said Minny.

"On the other hand," Lulu said, "I mean, if Ruby's gone all kung fu warrior and stuff, why not get her to help?"

"I don't know," said Minny. "I think Clancy's right. He's got to sort this out himself. Even if Ruby *doesn't* wind up dead taking on a pack of meatheads, she can't *always* be there, right?"

"So what do you suggest I do?" said Clancy.

"Stop running," said Minny, "and beat the guy to a pulp."

"Maybe go tell Principal Levine," said Lulu. "This guy sounds dangerous. He could knock your block off."

"Great idea — I'll look like a supersissy."

"Better a *walking* supersissy than a bozo without a head in a hospital bed," said Lulu.

"Maybe start going to the gym," said Minny.

But what Clancy actually did was get on his bike and ride around for a bit. He could use the air, though what he wanted more than anything was to find Ruby. If only he could tell her what was going on, then he would feel a whole lot better.

CHAPTER 35
A Solid Punch to
the Solar Plexus

RUBY HAD BEEN THERE for about forty minutes when she was interrupted in her reading.

"Hey," said a voice.

Ruby looked up from her comic to see the face of the kid with the overstyled hair.

She had been sitting in Sunny's, a diner she rarely frequented, mainly because it wasn't on her turf, but also because it didn't do pancakes. Today she had wanted to take a little time to herself, and here at Sunny's she wasn't likely to encounter anyone she knew, so she was surprised when she saw the kid called Beetle.

"Hey," she said.

"Can I buy you a drink or something?" he asked.

"I got one already, thanks," said Ruby.

"Can I get you another?"

"Thanks but no, thanks. I'm on a strict three-milkshakes-a-day program."

"You watching your figure?"

Ruby looked at him like he had lost a few marbles somewhere. "Why would I watch my figure?"

Beetle shrugged awkwardly. "No reason."

"I'm just trying to keep a balanced food intake, you know, dietary requirements? Minerals, vitamins, that kinda stuff."

He nodded again like he had no idea what she was talking about.

"So what's on your mind?" asked Ruby.

"How . . . do you . . . mean?" stammered Beetle.

"You seem like you want to tell me something," said Ruby.

"Oh, uh, yeah, that's right. I got your book, the one you left outside the store."

Ruby gave him a blank look until he pulled a scruffy paperback out of his jacket pocket and placed it on the table. The title was written to look like it was scrawled in blood: *No Time to Scream.*

"Oh yeah, thanks, man," said Ruby. "I forgot about that. I thought I'd never find out what happened to poor old Philippo. Did he make it back to camp or did he get"— she drew her hand across her throat —"axed to smithereens by the maniac?"

"He got away."

"Oh, thanks for telling me, buster," said Ruby, tossing the book onto the next table.

"Ah, sorry, I thought you, like, wanted to know. I only read the last few pages."

"Ah, doesn't matter. There are plenty more thrillers out there."

The boy smiled. "You sure have gory taste in books."

"So you like books about bunnies?" asked Ruby.

"No! 'Course not, but I'm not a girl."

"Which century were *you* born in, bozo?" said Ruby, giving him a straight-up look.

"I just meant, most of the girls I have ever met read about fashion and stuff."

"Sounds like you need to shake up your social life." Something remembered passed through her head. "Hey, what time is it, anyway?" Where was her watch?

"I don't know, like, six?" Beetle shrugged.

Ruby stood up. "I gotta split," she said, then paused before adding, "If you don't mind my mentioning it, you seem a little antiquated in your thinking, Beetle. Maybe you should read a few books, broaden your horizons, you know what I'm saying? Look, see you around."

His eyes followed her as she left, and he hoped she might turn around, perhaps even wave.

But she didn't.

It was as Clancy Crew was making his way home that he felt a solid punch to the solar plexus.

He felt nearly fell off his bike before propping himself up against a wall, taking in gulps of breath. He hadn't actually been struck. In fact, there was no one on the sidewalk. The wind had picked up and it was not the sort of evening for lingering.

The light was fading and the stores and restaurants were brightly lit now, the windows illuminated so each held a little glowing scene in the darkness. It was in one of these windows that he saw something that sent him reeling, something he really couldn't begin to explain. And now he felt completely alone.

CHAPTER 36
Fearless

RUBY BEGAN WENDING HER WAY BACK to Cedarwood Drive. At first she let the board take her at the speed it wanted to go, and then she considered how she might rack up some extra brownie points if she made it home superearly — her mom wanted to yak on about Ada Borland. Sabina wanted to plan what Ruby would wear for the portrait and explain what Ruby should say when she met Ada and impress on Ruby how polite she should be and how lucky Ruby was to have such a great artist give her this unique opportunity and blah, blah, blah.

Ruby maneuvered herself into the center of the traffic and fixed on a suitable car to grab on to. The driver was a little reckless and he ran more than a couple of red lights, but that suited Ruby fine. Besides, she could use the thrill.

Clancy felt dizzy. His mouth was dry and his heart pumping fast; he had to stop for a minute.

Take it easy, Clance.

He needed a soda or something. Just to give him the energy to get home.

The driver of the car Ruby was hanging from the back of hit his brakes without warning, and she was sent careering into oncoming traffic. Her attempt to make a turn on Midtown Avenue failed completely — there was just no way through — and so she went sailing on down the Fountain Park Slopes, gathering speed as she traveled.

Yikes.

She flew through a red light and caused a minor collision, swerved her way through a gaggle of elderly theatergoers as they ventured over the pedestrian crossing, and would have made it all in one piece had it not been for the police car making a left. At this point, she was separated from her transport, sailed over the cop car, her skateboard freewheeling under, and girl and board were destined never to reunite.

Ruby landed in a sprawling heap on the pavement of Fountain Park Slopes, and the skateboard continued on its journey.

Remarkably, apart from the severely grazed arm, an eye that was swelling by the second, and a horrible-looking knee poking through jeans that were ripped to shreds, Ruby Redfort was actually in good shape, as in: not dead.

The cops stood over her like she was an alien who had fallen from her spaceship.

"Hi, Officer," said Ruby.

"Why is this kid not dead?" said one of the officers to the other.

"Beats me," said his partner. "Must have a guardian angel watching over her."

"Something like that," said Ruby, looking down at her still-breathing self. *Boy, am I lucky,* she thought.

Clancy hadn't spotted the kids outside the mini-mart. He'd been too distracted by his breathing trouble and subsequent struggle to open the can. The soda felt good as he gulped it down, cold and sugary and fizzy. He was OK; it was all OK; really it was. He bent down to unlock his bike and when he stood up, they were surrounding him.

"Nice wheels," said the gorilla, "though I think they would suit you better if they was yellow, you know, chicken colored." He laughed and his gorilla friends laughed too, even though it was a pretty pathetic joke in Clancy's opinion.

Clancy looked at all four of them, their big leering faces, their ugly smiles, their dumb comments. Why was he frightened of these losers? And suddenly he found courage, even all alone as he was in the little side alley of Marty's mini-mart. Suddenly he felt fearless.

After she was checked over by a doctor at the ER, Ruby was escorted by the two cops — Officer Nadal and Officer Polpo — back to Cedarwood Drive.

Sabina Redfort practically fainted when she saw the two cops standing there outside the front door, and her expression only slightly relaxed when Ruby stepped out from behind them. The thing was, her darling daughter's face did not resemble the face she had kissed good-bye that same morning. This face looked horrible; it was a funny color and puffy in all the wrong places.

"Oh, my good gosh, whatever happened to you?"

"Skitching, ma'am," said Polpo.

"It's an illegal activity," said Nadal.

"I'm sorry?" Sabina looked puzzled. "Knitting is illegal?"

"Skitching," repeated Nadal, with more emphasis. "It's an activity that involves hanging on to a moving vehicle while skateboarding, roller-skating, or bicycling."

"What?" said Sabina.

"I'm sorry to inform you, ma'am, that your daughter was involved in this illegal method of transportation."

"Who says it's illegal?" said Ruby. "Discouraged, sure, but illegal . . . I don't think so."

Sabina glared at her. "Don't push your luck, pancake! You are already well and truly in the doghouse. You have a *portrait* booked for tomorrow for jeepers' sake, and I can't *cancel* Ada Borland — no one *cancels* Ada Borland — the woman's a genius."

"I'm sorry, ma'am?" said Officer Nadal, who had no idea what was going on.

"Might I be of help, officers?" asked Hitch, who seemed to have appeared from nowhere. "Mrs. Redfort, why don't you take Ruby up to her room? She needs to lie down. And ask Mrs. Digby to fix her some soup, while I talk this over with the officers."

Ruby missed what happened next, but ten minutes later, Hitch was in the kitchen brewing up herb tea for her mother, while simultaneously on the line to a highly regarded masseuse, and at the same time listening to Sabina, who was saying, "What's the kid trying to do, kill herself? Have I failed as a mother? Have we not been there for her? Is this a cry for help? And someone please tell me . . . what are we going to do about her *portrait*? Have you seen that bruise? Have you seen the lip? Geez, the kid could double for the ugliest member of the Addams Family."

❋ ❋ ❋

Clancy heard their footsteps fading off into the distance, their whoops of laughter as they turned the corner. He reached a hand to his forehead and felt the warm sticky blood oozing from the cut on his eyebrow. He tried to stand, his ribs aching from where they had punched him. His arm felt dead. His hair felt funny, smelled funny; that of course was due to the spray paint—how was he going to explain this to his mom? She was unlikely to understand why his hair was now canary yellow, and if he told her the truth, she would no doubt call the police, the school, and Bailey Roach's mom, and Clancy really didn't want that.

He found his bike, the front fender now bent out of shape and its beautiful Windrush blue marred by the yellow sweep of the spray can.

He picked up the bike and wheeled it home. He needed to clean the paint off before it set.

Ruby must not see this.

CHAPTER 37
The Magic
of the Movies

RUBY HAD A VERY SORE HEAD when she woke up the next morning.

She examined her face in the bathroom mirror. *Ruby, you look terrible,* she told herself. She got dressed, went downstairs to the kitchen, poured herself a bowl of cereal, and sat down at the table.

She looked up when Hitch entered the room, but continued to eat her Cheerios.

Hitch said nothing.

"Look, about the skitching—" she finally muttered.

"I'm not interested in that," said Hitch, cutting her off. "You want to kill yourself that way, that's your business."

She resumed her eating.

"But there is something I need to ask you, and I'm pretty sure I'm not going to like the answer."

Ruby looked up just for a second.

"Before I rescued you from that flagpole, where were you, exactly?"

"In the vicinity," replied Ruby.

"As in, near the Warrington Apartments?" asked Hitch.

"If the Warrington Apartments are in the vicinity, then I guess so," said Ruby.

"Funny thing," said Hitch; he wasn't taking his eyes off her. "The TCPD found footprints in the Thompsons' apartment, fresh footprints, in the chalk dust — size threes."

Ruby took another spoonful of cereal. "Must have belonged to the security guard."

"You would imagine so, but you see, the thing that's going through my mind is, what security guard has size three feet?"

"A real short one," said Ruby.

"And what security guard uses climbing chalk?"

"An adventurous one?"

"I think we both know that's a million to one, and so if it wasn't a security guard's footprint, then who might it belong to? And what the Sam Hill was this person doing in the Thompsons' apartment last night? And then I get to thinking." He tapped his head with two fingers. "Ruby wears size threes. Ruby was in the area. Ruby is the sort of numbskull to climb up thirty-seven stories of an apartment building and break into someone else's home when she has been strictly forbidden to do any kind of field work."

Ruby looked up from her breakfast. Her expression said, *OK, you got me.*

"What I haven't figured out, and I would be truly grateful if you could enlighten me, is why."

Ruby put down her spoon.

"I went because I needed to find something: the card, OK? Blacker and Froghorn weren't so sure the Thompsons *had* been robbed, at least not by the window thief anyway, and the police were saying it had to be a copycat burglary, but how many burglars can climb up a building like that and squeeze in through a window of that size?"

"You," said Hitch.

"Right, but you know what I'm saying, man — you know this has to be connected."

"As it happens, I agree with you. What I have a problem with is your methods." He paused a beat. "So, did you find what you were looking for?"

"Yes." She pulled the card from her sweatshirt pocket and laid it on the table. There was a bite mark in one corner, impressions of tiny teeth.

"Nileston had it?" said Hitch, taking the card.

"It would be more accurate to say Mr. Potato Head had it. The kid must have picked it up before the cops arrived; it was in among all his baby junk. I guess his parents were too freaked by what had happened to even notice."

"OK," said Hitch, "I'll take it in to Blacker, see what he makes of it, but his department is pretty busy right now due to another security breach."

"At Spectrum?" asked Ruby.

"No," replied Hitch, "but a piece of Spectrum hardware has gone missing, and as a result, all security codes need to be reconfigured."

He started to leave.

"Oh . . . if someone has time, they might want to take a look at this," said Ruby. She tore the back page out of the novel she was reading. On it were written four sets of numbers.

3	14	1		10	14	8
15	14	13		17	14	15

"What are these?" asked Hitch.

"It's the code from the cards, from the bumps and indents—turns out they aren't words after all."

"You cracked it?"

"Yep."

"*When?*" asked Hitch.

"Oh," said Ruby, "I had a spare moment at three a.m., when the pain from my smooshed face was keeping me awake."

"How?" said Hitch.

"Turn the page," said Ruby.

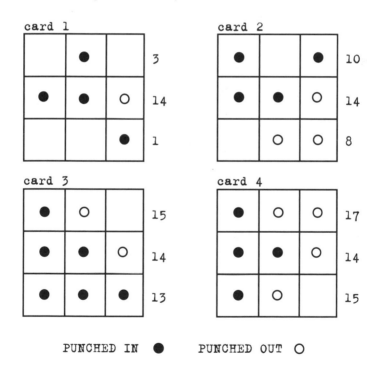

card 1

	●		3
●	●	○	14
		●	1

card 2

●		●	10
●	●	○	14
	○	○	8

card 3

●	○		15
●	●	○	14
●	●	●	13

card 4

●	○	○	17
●	●	○	14
●	○		15

PUNCHED IN ●   PUNCHED OUT ○

"So what do the numbers mean?" asked Hitch.

"Beats me," said Ruby, turning back to her bowl of Cheerios. "That's the big *don't know.*' I've figured out that the code breaks down into those numbers, but I haven't a clue what the numbers stand for."

"So . . . give them to Blacker?"

Ruby nodded. "Might as well — my head's too sore to think about them. Tell him it's a ternary numbering system. He'll understand."*

Hitch turned to go, then looked at his watch. He frowned.

"What's up?" said Ruby.

"A message," he said.

"Who from?"

"Well, you, actually."

"Me?" said Ruby.

"Yes," said Hitch. "Tell me . . . on your little adventure, did you happen to lose the Escape Watch?"

Ruby checked her wrist. "Um . . . yeah."

Hitch sighed. "Well, then, I guess someone got ahold of it."

"Someone like who?" asked Ruby.

"No idea," replied Hitch.

"So what do they want?" asked Ruby.

*TURN TO PAGE 497 TO SEE HOW RUBY CRACKED THE TOUCH CODE.

"How would I know?" replied Hitch. "The message happens to be in code."

Ruby looked at him. "You think it might be the skywalker?"

"The thought is crossing my mind," said Hitch.

"So what are you going to do?" asked Ruby — she was beginning to feel the smallest flicker of panic.

"Sit tight," he replied. "It's one of those Spectrum rules. Bide your time until things begin to make sense — same goes for you, by the way."

And with that, he was gone.

Mrs. Digby wouldn't hear of Ruby going anywhere. Ruby had mild concussion, and as Mrs. Digby so wisely said, "You don't want to play fast and loose with concussions."

Ruby's donut phone rang.

"Hey, it's me," said Clancy. "You wanna meet at the diner this morning?" He was trying to sound brighter than he felt; he needed to see her.

"I can't today," said Ruby. "I had a bit of an accident last night. My whole face is smooshed and I took a knock to the head, so Mrs. D. says I gotta lie low."

"Are you OK?" asked Clancy. He sounded alarmed; Ruby could hear his arms flapping.

"Relax, would you, Clance? I'm totally fine, OK. I don't look so good, but I'm all there."

"You sure you're sure, Rube?"

"Yeah," she said. "I'll call you if I start dying."

"OK, promise you will."

"I promise, Clance."

Ruby's eye was turning a nice shade of purple and she had a fat lip. The graze to her arm was looking OK, but her knee looked gruesome. Ruby looked a long way from picture-perfect. Too bad her mother had booked that Ada Borland portrait — today was really not the day for it.

"You know, I'm going to cancel," announced Sabina, sweeping into the room.

"Why?" said Ruby.

"Take a look in the mirror, Ruby. Have you caught sight of yourself lately?"

Ruby peered at her reflection in the bathroom mirror. "I don't have a problem with getting my picture taken."

"But you don't look how you look," explained her mother.

"What are you saying?" said Ruby. "This is exactly how I look."

"Yes, how you look after you collided with a cop car," said her mother.

"And how many mothers can say that about their kid's picture? That's gotta be more interesting than the usual snap."

"Snap? *Snap!*" Sabina's hands were on her hips, her voice raised unusually loud. Ruby thought she maybe needed another of Hitch's herbal teas. "Do you have any idea what a privilege it is to have Ada Borland take your picture? I was ecstatic when I won that raffle, but *you,* you couldn't just do this one thing for me. You had to louse it up, Ruby, because it's all about you and what *you* want! If my daughter could have just done this *single sweet* thing for me, I swear I'd be happy until Christmas!"

Sabina turned and strode out of the room with such force that the soap fell out of the soap dish. Ruby heard her mother dial the photographer's number and leave a message to the effect that she was very sorry but her daughter had been in an accident and the portrait would have to be canceled. Ruby felt truly bad. As much as she didn't particularly want her photograph taken, even if it was to be by the great Ada Borland, she *did* understand how much it meant to her mother. But what could she do?

She tried to block out these unpleasant feelings by switching on the TV matinee, and strangely it was while watching *The Rise of the Zombies* that Ruby thought of something.

She had a plan.

CHAPTER 38
Not Nice at All

SHE PICKED UP THE PHONE and dialed Red's number. She got lucky — Mrs. Monroe answered. "Sadie, it's Ruby. I wondered if you could help me out."

"Sure, I'll try," replied Sadie. "What is it you need?"

"It's a kinda weird request, but I was wondering if there was any way your friend Frederick Lutz could do me a favor. It's just that when I met him at the Scarlet Pagoda costume benefit, he said if I ever wanted to get my makeup done for a special occasion, then he would do it."

"If Frederick said that, then it's a done deal," said Sadie. "He never backs out of a promise."

"The thing is," said Ruby, "it's kinda time-sensitive."

"How time-sensitive?" asked Sadie.

"Like now," said Ruby.

"Ah," said Sadie, "no wiggle room?"

"None," said Ruby. "I'm kinda desperate."

"That bad, huh? Hang in there, Ruby, and I'll get right back to you."

Ruby didn't have to wait long. Sadie called barely seven minutes later.

"Frederick would be delighted to see you; get over there as quick as you can." She gave Ruby the address and wished her luck with whatever the emergency was. This was one of the things Ruby liked about Sadie: she didn't ask too many questions. When Ruby reached the pay phone on the corner of Cedarwood, she called Ada Borland's studio and left another message with the secretary from her "mother."

"Hi, this is Sabina Redfort again. Sorry for the confusion, but it turns out I was overdramatizing . . . as usual. . . . I know. I'm a total worry worm"— pause for laughter —"really, it's wart? Well, there you go — I'm a worrywart. Anyway, my daughter will be with you after all. Boy, that kid is a real trooper, an inspiration to us all."

Ruby arrived at 119 Derilla Drive to find Frederick Lutz sitting on a lawn chair in his driveway. On his lap was a dachshund. He raised a hand in greeting and slowly heaved himself up from his chair. "Come on in," he said. "This is Paullie," he added, indicating the dachshund.

The dachshund raised its head and regarded Ruby sleepily.

"Hey, Paullie," said Ruby.

Lutz set the dog down on the grass, and Paullie stood on his tiny legs waiting.

"Come," said Lutz.

He led Ruby into his workshop, a spare room that he had converted into a kind of salon, every surface covered with movie memorabilia. He sat her down in a swivel chair in front of a brightly lit mirror and took in the horror show that was her face.

"So I see we are *starting* with Halloween and heading backward. Kind of unusual for me; I usually start off with pretty and head in the other direction."

"Yeah, I know, it's bad, huh? Is there anything you can do with it?"

"Can I do anything? Can I do anything? Kid, you're talking to Frederick Lutz here; 'course I can do anything! Never fear, I'll have you looking like Shirley Temple in the blink of an eye. That's the look we're going for, right?" He winked.

Ruby smiled. "Well, something along those lines."

The Hollywood makeup genius worked on Ruby for a good couple of hours, and while he worked, he talked. Mainly he talked about the old days when the industry was dominated by sirens of the silver screen — Erica Grey, Bette Davis, Lauren Bacall.

"They were some women, I can tell you," said Frederick. "They don't make 'em like that anymore."

The makeup artist's walls were crammed with framed photographs and posters of the actors he had worked with and the movies he had worked on and stuff he had collected over the years. There was no end of big names. One poster that caught her eye was the one for *The Cat That Got the Canary*. The image was of the Little Yellow Shoes, and Margo's lower legs were all that could be seen of the actress. A black cat walked off to the right of the picture, a yellow feather in its mouth. It was a striking image. The poster was signed by the actress herself.

"So did you meet her?" asked Ruby, pointing to the poster.

"Oh, many times," said Frederick. "One fabulous lady. Too bad she married that George Katsel."

"Not nice?" asked Ruby.

Frederick scrunched his face into a sour expression. "Not nice at all, only interested in himself. It was all about him and what he wanted; never did a thing for anyone else."

Ruby winced — the words so closely echoed her mother's.

"He had magnetic appeal, though; it was hard for anyone to resist him when he set his baby blues on something."

"Old George sounds like quite the egomaniac," said Ruby.

"You better believe it," said Frederick, shaking his head. "They called him the Cat, because he was so darned lucky. Katsel always got what he wanted, always the Cat that got the cream." Frederick paused to make a careful adjustment to Ruby's foundation. "I met Margo after that time, long after she broke it off with George and much later on in her career, when she was already quite famous, and I can't think of a bad word to say about her, except I wish she hadn't been so darned tall."

"Funny . . ." Ruby considered. "I always thought she would be kinda small, more like my height — well, taller than me but, you know."

"Are you kidding?" said Frederick.

"She looks little in *The Cat That Got the Canary*," said Ruby.

"Smoke and mirrors," said Frederick, pausing for a minute to review his latest creation. "If I needed to touch up her makeup on set, I had to stand on a crate. I know I'm not the tallest guy in town, but Margo, she must have been five ten, five eleven. Making Margo look small was the magic of the movies!" Frederick Lutz chuckled and dusted Ruby's face with some bronzer. "Meanwhile, making your face look like it never came into contact with a sidewalk is the magic of makeup!"

And when Ruby turned to view her face in the mirror, she saw that he wasn't lying. She looked just like she usually looked, her face restored, not a visible scratch on it.

CHAPTER 39
Picture-Perfect

HAVING THANKED FREDERICK about twenty times, Ruby set off for Ada Borland's studio, which, as it turned out, was located not so far from the Scarlet Pagoda. She buzzed the buzzer, and a stern-looking woman dressed entirely in gray came to open the door. The woman (named Abigail) was actually very friendly and showed Ruby around the gallery while she waited for Ada to appear.

The Scarlet Pagoda had obviously been a huge influence on Ada, and there were many framed photos of the theater taken over the several decades that she had been working there. It was fascinating to see the various changes made to the building, how it had become a popular destination, flourished, and then later was left to rot. There were pictures of many of the famous faces who had performed there, actors, acrobats, contortionists, dancers, and singers. Starlets in extravagant costumes, circus people in fabulous creations. Ruby was lost in this world of performers when she heard a thick croaky voice.

"Ms. Redfort?"

She turned to see a small woman, quite elderly, with dyed black hair that was cut into a neat bob. An enormous pair of orange-rimmed glasses obscured most of her face; her lips were painted the same color and perfectly matched the frames.

"I'm Ada," she said. "Let's take your picture."

It was clear from looking at Ms. Borland's work that the photographer was interested in a lot more than her subjects' physical appearance. She seemed to look beyond all this and capture the uncapturable. The portrait itself became a story, layered with atmosphere and meaning. The more you looked, the more you saw and the more the background told you — the things that just happened to be there were part of the story too.

Ruby was curious about all these people who had sat for portraits: some grand, some ordinary; old and young. Faces strange, ugly, and beautiful. Posed pictures and casual but all had something of the artist, her viewpoint. And as Ruby looked, she asked: So what was Erica Grey like? What was the president like? What was this grocer man like? And every time, Ada replied, "You tell me; it's all there in the photograph if you care to look."

Ruby enjoyed the experience, and although sitting for her portrait took more time than she would have thought possible, chatting with Ada was a rare opportunity and she was glad she hadn't missed it.

"It was a pleasure to meet you, Ruby Redfort," called Ada. "Do visit again."

Ruby sneaked back into the house only to be greeted by Mrs. Digby, who jumped about six inches when she saw Ruby.

"Jumping jackrabbits, child, what happened to your face?"

"It looks bad?" said Ruby.

"I wouldn't say that," said Mrs. Digby. "I'd say it looks the way it oughta look, but where's the black eye and the fat lip?"

Ruby thought it best to explain what she had been up to. Mrs. Digby was not an easy old bird to fool. **RULE 47: NEVER LIE TO SOMEONE WHO IS LIKELY TO SEE RIGHT THROUGH YOU.**

It happened to be one of those times when the truth really paid off, and Mrs. Digby even kissed the top of Ruby's head and said, "Ruby Redfort, I knew your soul wasn't a lost cause. There's good in you no matter how you try to convince folks otherwise."

A half hour later, Ruby was up in her room, the TV on, watching some gymnast contort herself into impossible shapes, her limbs bending in such a way that she became the smallest thing and she began squeezing herself through smaller and smaller hoops. There was a knock at the door and Clancy Crew's head peered around. He had a checked hat pulled tight down over his hair, obscuring the side of his face. He looked odd, more like himself somehow.

"Nice hat," said Ruby.

"Hey, Rube. Mrs. Digby said to come up and see you. How are you —?" he stopped midsentence.

"What?" said Ruby.

"Your face," he said. "I thought you said it was smooshed."

"Ah, this is makeup, Clance."

"I can see that!" he said, his eyes steely. "Where have you been? Hanging out with some *other* friend, or maybe you're going to some party, somewhere free from all the deadwood you used to call friends?"

"Clance, what the Sam Hill are you talking about? I haven't been anywhere. Well, I have, but it was me doing a good deed, trying to do the right thing for once —"

"Don't sweat it," said Clancy. "It's not your style." He turned and walked out the door and down the stairs, his footsteps loud and angry sounding.

"Clance!" she called. "Jeepers, what's with you? Are you having some type of crisis?" She wasn't really up to chasing him down the street; her head was throbbing and she thought she might throw up if she moved too fast.

Instead, she went and had a good long soak in the tub, and washed her face thoroughly. She could explain about the trip to Ada's when he had calmed down. Geez, it was amazing the effect a little makeup could have — as far as Ruby could see, it seemed to make sensible folks crazy.

CHAPTER 40
The Risk/Fear Equation

RUBY HAD SPENT the best part of the night thinking about the thing Ada had said about the photographs: *It's all there in the photograph if you care to look.*

She had thought a lot about the whole big picture, willing the edges to come back into focus. She was thinking about the skywalker, the window thief, the robberies, and — in particular — Mr. Norgaard and his paperweight collection.

Ruby took the subway downtown to Spectrum and went to seek out Blacker. Then she set about pinning up every single photo taken at Norgaard's place — not just her pictures of the desk but also the pictures taken by the TCPD — and she was now sort of standing back there in the screenwriter's virtual room, scanning it for clues.

"What are you looking for?" said Blacker.

"I don't know," said Ruby, "something I missed."

She looked and looked, like she had all the time in the world. She scanned every part of every photograph, taking in the furniture, the drapes, the ornaments, the books, the lamps, and the rugs. An hour or so later, it was a row of old photographs on the wall above the couch that she was most interested in — they were clearly taken many years ago. The picture she was particularly drawn to was of two men — one sitting behind a large desk looking at a script, the other standing behind him. It was a very posed photograph; the title of the script wasn't in focus, but there was no doubt it was a script.

The seated man in the suit and tie, she recognized as the producer and director George Katsel, "the Cat," as Frederick Lutz had referred to him. *The Cat That Got the Canary* was but one of a whole list of Katsel's box-office successes.

The other man, the one standing behind him, she was pretty sure must be Mr. Norgaard *senior,* Mr. Norgaard's screenwriter father. But what really caught her eye was the round glass object on George Katsel's desk. It was a paperweight containing a single yellow feather. She surveyed the other photographs and found another in which the paperweight appeared, but this time it was shown on Norgaard senior's desk, Mr. Norgaard himself looking much older in this photo. *George Katsel must have given it to him at some point,* thought Ruby.

She looked at every picture she and the cops had taken very, very carefully, but in none of them did the yellow-feather paperweight appear. It was no certainty, but she couldn't help but feel this could be the missing item: stolen object number one.

"You figured something out?" said Blacker.

"As a matter of fact, I think I just mighta, but I'm not a hundred percent on it."

"OK, so tell me when you're ready," said Blacker. There was a buzz from his watch. He checked it. "That's kinda weird."

Ruby looked up. "What is it?" she asked.

Blacker showed her his watch. "A message from you."

Ruby just stared. It said:

```
Xb8fnghsmKKshgg
```

"Is this some kind of a test?" Blacker asked.

"I didn't send it," said Ruby. "The thing is, I lost my watch. I think maybe someone found it."

Blacker kind of winced.

"OK," said Ruby. "I mean someone obviously found it, but it beats me who it could be."

"So where did you lose the watch?"

"Somewhere three hundred feet up in the air," said Ruby.

"Sounds like a long story," said Blacker.

"Kinda," said Ruby. "Look, if I start trying to figure out what the message means —" she paused, looking him in the eye —"do you think there's any chance you could buy me some time? Before you . . . you know."

"Report the watch activity?"

She nodded.

"I'll give you a head start," agreed Blacker, "but don't leave it too long."

Ruby smiled. Blacker was about as cool a partner as one could wish for, and at that moment, she felt pretty lucky.

"Now you better head on home," said Blacker, waving her out the door. "Catch you later."

Ruby was almost at the elevator when Buzz called her back and handed her a note, which read:

Meet me at the Charles Burger
— Hitch

Ruby knew the Charles Burger, an upmarket burger grill place with green leather banquette seating and polished wood tables. It was very Hitch somehow. She pushed in through the brass and glass door and found him sitting at a lamplit table toward the back of the room.

"I got your message," said Ruby. "Are you still thinking of strangling me? It's just if you are, I might keep my distance."

"You've got enough problems, kid," said Hitch. "I was thinking about what you said, about someone trying to kill you."

"At the Hauser Ink Building?"

"Yes, when you were monkeying along that piece of cable."

"And?"

"It couldn't have been the guy you were chasing because, as you explained, the cable came loose from the other side. But it couldn't have been an accident either — one of our guys took a look at the wire and it would appear that the steel was cut through with cable cutters. Took whoever did it a while. That stuff is strong — lucky for you — but it means they were determined."

"You're saying someone was following me?"

"I think someone was tracking the skywalker, just like you were, and they ended up on the same rooftop. I don't think it was you they had their sights on, not to begin with — I think *he* was the target, you just got in the way."

"Still," said Ruby, "it doesn't make them an awful nice kind of a person if they are prepared to kill a thirteen-year-old kid who happens to be going about her business."

Hitch looked at her, eyebrow raised in a *Now I've heard it all* expression. "I think what you got to expect here, Redfort, is that people who are prepared to track a guy, and if necessary kill him, aren't going to spend a lot of time grieving about the demise of a nosy schoolkid."

"That is most likely true," said Ruby.

"Your way of going about things I am not crazy about, but your detective work is sharp," said Hitch, taking a slug of his coffee, "so I've got a proposal."

"I'm listening."

"The thing is, you are supposed to be an agent, not just any agent, a Spectrum agent, a trainee agent maybe, but an agent nonetheless. This means you have to look at things the way an agent would — you don't dive in without testing the water, you don't jump without looking at where you're going to land, and you don't make decisions without thinking things through. Agents think about consequences — we have to because that's the point of what we do."

Ruby wasn't arguing.

"You, Redfort, are acting like some kind of movie agent, like there's a writer out there in the real world penning some book all about you and your giant ego. You need to use that brain of yours and jump script. Make a decision: Are you some kid playing superhero in the schoolyard or are you an intelligent force for good, set on making a difference? I guess what I'm saying is, Are you for real, Redfort?"

For once Ruby found she had no smart riposte. She had nothing to come back with; her mind was a scribbled mess of questions — too many to ask.

"Look, kid, I'm going to have to level with you here — no one's too crazy about the idea of a fearless teenager on the loose taking insane risks and possibly leading the rescue crew into unnecessary danger."

"So you're saying don't take risks?"

"What I'm saying is, there's risk and there's risk."

"You mean big risks and small risks," said Ruby. "Well . . ."

"No, that's not it — you are completely and one hundred percent missing the point. I'm talking about dumb risks and not-dumb risks. Calculated risks and impulsive risks. Risks you have no choice about and risks that only a madman would take. You getting this?"

Ruby said nothing.

"OK, because what I've been seeing is a schoolkid making a whole lot of dumb moves and bypassing the brain function — and Redfort, FYI, you were recruited for your brain, not your overweight ego."

Ruby still said nothing.

"Come outside a minute."

CHAPTER 41
Two Across

THEY LEFT THE CHARLES BURGER and Hitch walked ahead
of her, turning the corner into a grubby-looking alleyway, full of
trash cans and fire-escape ladders, the brick walls rising high on
each side of the narrow space between the buildings.

"Kid, I'm going to explain something to you, so listen up. OK,
I'm bending the rules here so help me out."

She shrugged, unsure what he was about to divulge. "OK."

"I have this idea. Now, it might be a wrong one, but call it a
gut feeling if you will."

She looked at him.

"Frankly, I don't see you ever staying out of trouble — am I
headed in the right direction here?"

Ruby sort of winced.

"So we're agreed that you will continue to behave like a
numbskull action hero at least some of the time."

Ruby tried not to smile.

"My deal," said Hitch, "is that I don't bring up the other day's efforts to get yourself squashed and dead, so long as you meet me halfway."

"I'm listening."

"OK, I'm going to have to square it with the doc and I'm going to have to convince Agent Gill—and let's not forget the whole team at Spectrum 8—but I have an idea."

Ruby didn't ask what it was but hoped it was a good one. "What about LB?" was all she said.

"She'll back me if everyone else is on board," said Hitch.

Ruby gave a slow nod. "So what is this idea of yours?"

"You ever been on an obstacle course?" said Hitch, indicating the alleyway, trash cans, and fire-escape ladder.

"Yeah," she said slowly.

"So this is like an obstacle course but with a twist."

Ruby looked around. "I don't see any course, just buildings and walls and stuff."

"You heard of parkour, kid?"

Ruby looked blank.

"Let me explain." Without warning, Hitch ran. He was across the alley in the blink of an eye and headed straight toward a high brick wall, but he didn't stop, and he didn't slow his pace; he ran at the wall and then *up* the wall, and when he got to the top, he didn't stop running. He jumped a narrow gap, grabbed a ledge, hauled himself easily onto a narrow pediment, leaped from the pediment onto a sloped roof, ran along the ridge tiles, vaulted onto a wall, ran to where the wall ended, did a handspring from the wall onto the ground, rolled, and landed back on his feet.

"OK, that's cool," said Ruby. "The last part was a bit showy-offy but all in all, cool."

Hitch rolled his eyes. "Always the smart mouth, but you're right: this isn't about handsprings and acrobatics; it's not about adrenaline or competition — leave that to the free runners. This is a discipline. You have to train and you have to understand the mind-set."

"And you're telling me that's not risky?" said Ruby.

"Sure, there are risks, but these are risks you assess, that you work up to. Never take a risk that isn't worth taking. Be aware of your body's own capabilities. Fear should be respected but should not control you. These are some of the principles of parkour."

"OK," said Ruby.

"You have to feel it — the sensation of moving fluidly through space, mind and body as one. It's almost like meditation. It's not like crane hanging or one of those daredevil pursuits. It is not you pitting yourself against the urban landscape, not you against fear. It is you harnessing your fear, overcoming physical and psychological challenge through training. The more you practice, the stronger you will become, both in body and mind. If your fear is telling you no, then you listen. The aim is not to lose your fear but to work through it — fear is your friend."

"OK," said Ruby.

"You want to know how to run up a wall?" Hitch asked, but before Ruby could answer, they were interrupted by a small buzzing sound and Hitch looked at his watch and then at Ruby.

"A message from me?" asked Ruby.

"Well, a message from your watch," said Hitch.

Ruby made a face. "The skywalker, you think?"

"Could be anyone," said Hitch.

"Anyone who can encode a message," corrected Ruby.

"Doesn't exactly narrow the field as far as the villains we know go," said Hitch. "For all you know, we might have the Count on our tail."

Ruby shivered. She didn't like to *think* the Count's name, let alone hear it spoken out loud. "So what are you gonna do?"

He shook his head. "Whoever this bozo is, it would seem he wants our attention, but for now he can't have it." Then he looked up. "So where were we?"

"You were running up a wall," said Ruby.

"So I was," said Hitch. "Any questions?"

"Yeah, are you going to teach me how to do that or what?"

"Are you going to stop behaving like a numbskull at least some of the time?" asked Hitch.

"It's a strong possibility," said Ruby.

"OK, that'll have to do," said Hitch, rolling his eyes heavenward. "I'll teach you."

Ruby didn't go to school on Monday, or Tuesday, or Wednesday. Hitch had written a very convincing letter explaining that Ruby had been in a car accident (which wasn't actually a lie) and was suffering psychological trauma (which may have been a tiny one). Instead of sitting at her desk in Twinford Junior High, Ruby spent her time in parking lots, shopping malls, alleys, and low-rises, devoting the days to parkour, to practicing the skills and getting into the mind-set. Parkour was about moving in harmony with the city. It was about challenging the self—mind *and* body adapting to the urban environment, rather than competing with anyone else. Running and climbing, jumps, drops, and vaults, fluid balanced moves, and, above all, staying in the now—something that fear actually helped with.

Ruby understood why Hitch had wanted her to learn the *principles,* because it was all about dealing with obstacles in the most efficient way possible, never taking unnecessary risks.

THE DROP

1. Jump

Target your landing; focus on the timing. Keep your legs back and your upper body upright.

2. Drop

Keep your knees bent with feet angled down. Don't land on your heels. Be prepared to absorb the impact!

3. Land

Touch down on the balls of your feet first and bend your legs. Your muscles will absorb the impact.

4. Move

Drop forward onto your hands to avoid knee strain. Push off into a run.

THE TIC-TAC

1. Approach

Approach the wall at an angle and check your distance (about one running stride). Use the leg nearest the wall.

2. Step

Target your foot landing; keep foot pointing upward. Strike the wall with the ball of your foot for good control.

3. Kick

Kick off the wall immediately — pushing up and out to get some height. Don't be too upright or you'll slip down.

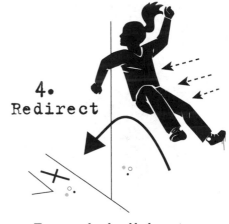

4. Redirect

Turn your head and body, spot your landing, and raise your lead knee to either land on or clear an obstacle.

She found, training with him, that she could drop great distances — farther than she would have thought possible — by perfecting a move called a roll, turning downward force into forward momentum. She learned the importance of building strength and working toward the more challenging jumps, drops, and vaults. Without training and proper preparation, you could injure yourself badly, possibly permanently, and for Ruby, that would mean kissing her dream of making it as a field agent good-bye. She listened to everything Hitch told her; she did not want to blow this chance.

Soon she was leaping from building to building, rolling when landing, running up walls, and swinging herself around stairwells, using her agility and momentum to traverse the city. Her vocabulary now included wall runs, swinging lachés, feet-first underbars, monkey vaults, and tic-tacs.

The more she focused on keeping herself in the moment, the more she began to tune into the rhythm of the city, to see the buildings and parks as spaces she could interact with. No longer were the buildings separate from her; they were her domain, an urban landscape she was now connected to. The amazing thing was that the more Ruby practiced parkour, the clearer things became. The fragments were coming together; she was beginning to see things as a whole again.

Your average busy metropolis? | *Turn the page to see what Ruby sees...*

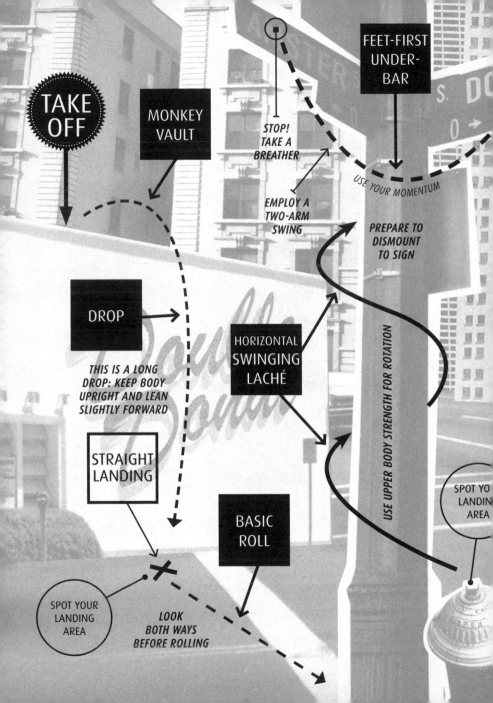

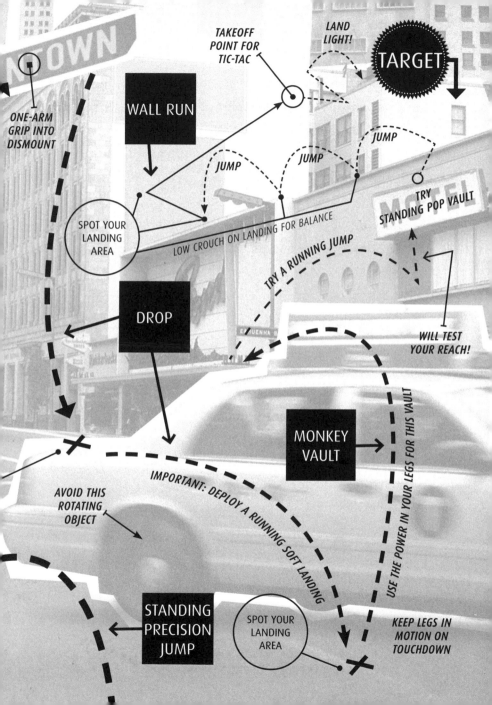

It was when she jumped from the Beyer Building, landing neatly on one of its several flagpoles, allowing herself to drop from it and catch the flagpole directly below, spinning herself around it like a gymnast might, using the momentum to somersault herself down and land gracefully on the sidewalk, that she looked up and saw it.

It was an old faded sign on the side of a building, a ghost sign, with an address at the bottom. But what caught Ruby's eye were the letters above. They spelled out:

TWO ACROSS
THE CITY'S ORIGINAL
CROSSWORD CLUB
EVERY TUESDAY NIGHT AT
THE TIE AND ANCHOR

Suddenly Ruby had an idea about the numbers she'd given to Hitch, the numbers from the cards.

The poetry book was the key to it all.

CHAPTER 42
Click, Click, Click

RUBY ARRIVED AT SPECTRUM, her mind free of the fog it had been clouded in. She grabbed a drink from the cafeteria and made her way to her desk. She took out the four sets of numbers and the book of poems and then she began to work.

She looked again at all four cards, the numbers of each clear to her.

3 14 1   10 14 8   15 14 13   17 14 15

And now she thought the meaning was clear too.

The paperweight, the shoes, the book of poems, the tie clip. Of these the poetry book had been the most mysterious item. It was a book written to hold secrets; the poet had designed it that way—there was the missing poem 14, for one thing, or rather the hidden poem, which Ruby had found as soon as she'd figured out that the title gave the clue.

Looking at it now, she felt sure that this hidden poem also

held the key to unlocking the loyalty card codes.

Blacker found Ruby staring at the poetry book and sitting in exactly the same place she had been sitting five hours earlier. She was so intent on what she was doing that she didn't even hear him enter the room. Spread out in front of her and around her and even under her were scatterings of paper, all scrawled with black ink: lines, numbers, words.

He dropped a brown paper bag onto the desk; the bag oozed donuts, and on any other day, the smell of them would have brought Ruby around like a dose of smelling salts.

"What have you got?" asked Blacker.

Only then did Ruby look up. She was in a kind of daze and answered him as if they happened to be right in the middle of a long conversation and he had been standing there for the past several hours.

"You see, there is another poem," said Ruby. "It's listed in the index, but when I looked for it, I couldn't find it. There should be twenty-seven poems, but I could only count twenty-six. Poem fourteen seemed to be missing." She paused. "But it *is* there; it's just that the poet hid it." She looked at Blacker to make sure he was following. "It's entitled, 'You Are a Poem, Celeste,' and it's buried in the lines of the others, through the center of each page—in other words, line fourteen."

"How do you figure that?" asked Blacker.

"Easy, the title of the book is telling us that."

Blacker smiled. *A Line Through My Center*. Of course.

Ruby opened the book at page three, where the poems began. She wrote down the first word of the fourteenth line (the very middle line), turned the page and wrote down the *second* word of the fourteenth line, turned the page and wrote down the *third* word of the fourteenth line, and so on, until she had one continuous line of poetry stretching across the page.

you are a poem, Celeste, as you tread a barely there line, stolen

in steps am I, transfixed by tiny feet that mar nothing they pass.

"The final line of the poem works differently; it falls down the
edge of page thirty, which is actually the acknowledgments page,
the last word of each sentence reading as one vertical sentence.
Like this." And Ruby wrote it down for him so he could see what
she meant:

What
is
it
about
their
tap
tap
tap
that
makes
me
want
to
fall?

"Tap tap tap?" said Blacker. "That has to relate to the cards."

"Yeah," said Ruby. "And maybe the tap shoes."

"The Little Yellow Shoes," said Blacker.

"Uh-huh." Ruby nodded. "The character in the film, Celeste, *tap*-dances in them, and then of course there's the *treading a barely there line,* which makes me think of a tightrope walker, which makes me think of the skywalker."

Blacker whistled — he could see it all. "But what do the numbers on the cards have to do with this? You said you thought you'd figured them out."

"OK," said Ruby. "Once I figured out that the poetry book contained a hidden poem, it occurred to me that the book might also hold the key to the messages. I mean, this isn't a random steal, right? So I tried something real simple." Ruby set the list of decoded number messages on the table in front of her.

"OK, look," she said. "These are our numbers, three for each of the four cards."

3	14	1
10	14	8
15	14	13
17	14	15

"I thought it was some complicated code at first, but it isn't — it's actually super basic. I mean, this guy's no code freak. It was an old sign for a crossword club that made me think of it — 'Two Across,' the place was called. So I thought, what if these numbers just tell you how to find a word on a page?"

"I see where you're headed," said Blacker.

"Exactly. It's one of the simplest forms of code. The first column relates to the page number, the second to the line number, and the third to the word number."

She picked up a yellow highlighter and drew the color over the first word in the book — page 3, line 14, word 1:

you

Then page 10, line 14, word 8:

tread

Page 15, line 14, word 13:

stolen

And finally, page 17, line 14, word 15:

steps

"You tread stolen steps," said Blacker. "It sounds sorta like a threat."

"That's what I thought," said Ruby, "but just who is being threatened here?"

Ruby looked again at the photograph of George Katsel and Norgaard senior — so many of the clues seemed to involve Katsel.

"I think it's all about George Katsel," said Ruby. "He directed *The Cat That Got the Canary;* he was connected to Norgaard, the current owner of the yellow-feather paperweight; and Mr. Okra's copy of the poetry book was inscribed *To my darling Cat from your Celeste*. Frederick Lutz told me that George Katsel was nicknamed 'the Cat.' Margo Bardem played a character called Celeste in Katsel's *The Cat That Got the Canary,* and I think she must have given him that book, around the time they fell in love or got married or whatever."

"OK," agreed Blacker, "so far your theory hangs together."

George Katsel, thought Ruby.

She looked at the photograph of him and Norgaard again. What else could it tell her? His smart suit, his buttonhole of exotic flowers, his elegant tie held in place with a tie clip . . .

"Do you have a magnifying glass?" asked Ruby.

"You going all Sherlock Holmes on me?" said Blacker, rummaging in his desk. "Here." He handed her the glass, and Ruby held it over the photograph.

"He has a tie clip engraved with the king's crest," she said slowly. "It looks identical to Mr. Thompson's tie clip."

"Well, what do you know," marveled Blacker, taking the magnifier and looking for himself.

Ruby began to draw a spider map, a web of lines that all now led to George Katsel.

PAPERWEIGHT—
the canary feather
contained in it is
from the TCTGTC
filmed at the
Scarlet P by . . .

THE YELLOW SHOES—
worn by Margo Bardem
in the film TCTGTC
filmed at the Scarlet
P by . . .

THE POETRY BOOK—
by a poet who hung
out at the Scarlet
P and dedicated the
book to his muse, who
worked there, and who
could well be Margo,
the wife of . . .

**MR. OKRA'S SPECIFIC COPY
OF THE POETRY BOOK—**
inscribed "To my darling
Cat from your Celeste,"
presumably gifted by
Margo Bardem to . . .

THE TIE CLIP—
belonged to the
king of England and
for a while was
in the possession
of . . .

GEORGE
"THE CAT"
KATSEL

CHAPTER 43
The Celeste

BLACKER STOOD UP. "I'm going to have Froghorn print out all the information we have on George Katsel — newspaper stories, biographical stuff, and what have you."

He stepped out, and Ruby thought he would be gone a while, but she was underestimating the Silent G.

Miles Froghorn might be a very difficult individual, but he was a very efficient and thorough research agent, and before long there was a stack of paper on the desk, all relating to Katsel. Ruby and Blacker sifted through the stories and reports on the life and career of this successful director. He had been married five times, had seven children, and made more than thirty successful movies and many more somewhat less glittering. He had died only two years earlier, having enjoyed a long and — it seemed — happy life.

Many of the newspaper stories were accompanied by photographs of George, his various wives, children, movie collaborators and well-known friends. He was always immaculately turned out, whether pictured on a yacht, on the phone, or on a red carpet. If he wore a tie, then it was always fastened with a tie clip, and if he wore a jacket, he always wore an orchid blossom in his buttonhole.

Ruby sat back in her chair and looked at the pictures spread out as they were, all across the table.

"Well," said Blacker, "to begin with, he's dead, so he's clearly not our thief, and whoever our thief is, he clearly isn't trying to get *Katsel*'s attention — but if not Katsel's, then whose?"

Ruby thought of the cards, the TAP TAP TAP TAP, the hidden message. "No," she agreed. "The messages are not for Katsel, but I think the skywalker is trying to tell us *something* about him. The question is: What?"

Blacker looked at the papers and photos. "Beats me."

"One thing that strikes me about old George," said Ruby. "He seemed to have a bit of a thing for yellow-and-pink-streaked flowers. In every single photo, he's wearing an orchid in his buttonhole."

"Expensive taste too," said Blacker. "That particular orchid is very rare."

"How do you happen to know *that*?" asked Ruby, kind of surprised.

"Ah, once, back when, I had to work undercover tracking

down some orchid smugglers. I learned a lot about the business. You get some highly valuable orchids, I can tell you that much. This one, for example, is worth more than a *few* dollars."

"Oh, yeah?" said Ruby.

"That orchid," said Blacker, "small yellow flowers with those vivid pink markings, it's called a Celeste."

"A *what*?" said Ruby. She'd heard him clearly enough, but she felt the need for him to say it again.

Blacker looked at Ruby, and Ruby looked back at Blacker, and Ruby smiled and then Blacker smiled.

Celeste was a name that was coming up almost as often as George.

"This Celeste orchid, could it be the next item on the skywalker's list?" said Ruby.

"I think it could," agreed Blacker.

Froghorn took no time in calling every supplier and collector in the city — there were five who grew Celestes, and within a half hour all of them were being watched by the Twinford City Police Department.

"Maybe we'll actually catch this clown," said Blacker as he got ready to leave Spectrum 8 and join forces with the TCPD.

"Could I, you know, tag along?" asked Ruby.

"Ah, I wish you could," said Blacker. "But you know how it is with this whole grounded situation. They would probably demote me right back down to coffee boy if I took you along." He gave her a sympathetic look. "You know if it were up to me . . . well, you know."

She did know and she smiled.

"You know, Ruby, you're one darned superkid," said Blacker, shaking her by the hand; then he turned and made for the door.

Now alone, Ruby considered the Escape Watch messages. How did they fit into all of this? She took them out and studied the three coded transmissions, searching for a pattern that might lead her to make sense of them, but she couldn't and her mind wandered back to George Katsel. Her eyes moved over the desk still strewn with papers and photographs all having to do with him.

There was something that hadn't quite clicked into place, but she couldn't seem to put her finger on it. She sifted through the pile of interviews and articles, and two caught her attention, both feature pieces on George Katsel and his gardener. One piece pictured Katsel smiling, a Celeste orchid in his hand. The other showed him standing in a rather ornate-looking greenhouse. She picked up both articles; if nothing else, they would occupy her on her bus ride home.

It was while Ruby was riding westbound on the crosstown bus that it all finally snapped into place.

She was reading the article she had found in a recent issue of *Garden and Gazebo* magazine, which mentioned the recent sad demise of Enrico Fernandez, George Katsel's greenhouse gardener and cut-flower specialist. The article was illustrated with photos of his famous orchids and included quotes from various interviews he had given over the years.

> "I grew every flower that Mr. Katsel wore in his buttonhole," said a proud Mr. Fernandez. "I still have the rare Celeste orchid from which so many of his famous buttonhole flowers came."

Ruby's heart began to beat faster. It seemed that, following Enrico's death, all the plants in the old orchid grower's collection were going to be auctioned off. There was a picture of his ornate-looking greenhouse — it was situated in a pretty spectacular position on the roof of the Acer Street Building.

At the end of the article was a short paragraph listing the date when all the most valuable plants would be auctioned; that date was the following day. Ruby pulled the emergency cord, and the bus screeched to a halt. She pushed through the doors and ran, barely aware of the angry shouts from the driver and many of the passengers. She ran until she reached a pay phone; she felt in her pocket for coins, dialed the number, and it rang and rang, without answer.

She dialed again. "Pick up!" she said.

"Hitch," said the voice.

RUBY: *Where have you been?*

HITCH: *Can't a butler take a shower?*

RUBY: *You're not a butler, and I gotta tell you something.*

HITCH: *OK.*

RUBY: *Can you meet me?*

HITCH: *You in trouble?*

RUBY: *Not yet.*

HITCH: *I'll be there in ten.*

RUBY: *You need to know where I am?*

HITCH: *I know where you are.*

Sure enough, ten minutes later, the silver convertible drew up alongside her, the door opened, Ruby got in, the door closed, and the car shot off into the traffic.

"Drive east," said Ruby. "We're looking for where Seventy-Second meets Acer Street."

Hitch took the next right and headed in the direction of old Twinford.

"You want to explain?" Hitch said. "Because Blacker already updated me about a half hour ago and he said the cops have all the possible targets staked out."

"But that's just the problem," said Ruby. "I read this piece about Katsel's orchid grower and it suddenly clicked — our skywalker thief isn't gonna be stealing just *any* Celeste orchid; he's gonna want the plant most closely connected to George."

"He is?" said Hitch, swerving to avoid a man on crutches.

"Think about it," said Ruby. "Everything about these thefts has been very very personal, all things that were once actually in the possession of Katsel — the paperweight he used to keep on his desk but later gave to his scriptwriter; the shoes from his best-known movie; the poetry book — not just any edition, but the copy signed to him; the tie clip *he* wore . . . There's a whole article about Katsel's greenhouse gardener. I don't have time to actually go into it, but trust me, the important thing is, he *still* had the actual Celeste orchid that George's flowers were taken from. Don't you see? The plant will be stolen from the greenhouse where George Katsel's orchid grew."

"The orchid is still alive?"

"With proper care," said Ruby, "an orchid can live indefinitely."

He stared at her.

"I read that in the magazine," she admitted, "and yeah, I'm sure he had more than one during his life, but the point is, this thief will steal from the greenhouse where Katsel's Celeste was kept."

"So have you called this gardener?" asked Hitch.

"He's dead—he died two months ago, natural causes, but the thing is, the orchid is still there, and the auctioning-off of these plants isn't until tomorrow. The Celeste will be there—if, that is, it hasn't been stolen already."

Without saying another word, Hitch put his foot down and the silver car tore through town.

CHAPTER 44
A Ghost Occurred

THEY ARRIVED AT THE OLD ACER BUILDING and, without wasting a moment, began to climb the exterior fire escape, zig-zagging up the side of the building.

They were out of breath by the time they reached the flat roof where the greenhouse sat. It was a long structure with high-arched glass and ornate fretwork, and most important, it was still full of plants, fruit trees, and, of course, orchids. Even from outside, Ruby could smell the rich scent of earth and pollen.

Quietly, they moved closer. The door was not, as they had expected, locked, nor was the alarm armed — someone had deactivated it.

Someone had gotten there before them.

"Stay here, kid," said Hitch as he pushed open the door. "We don't know where this guy is; keep hidden, OK?"

Ruby nodded.

She did exactly as Hitch told her, crouched on the roof outside the greenhouse, until she heard the most almighty *smash* as plant pots cascaded off the wooden trestles and she heard Hitch shouting, "Kid, watch out!"

She ducked as something, or someone, crashed through the glass, leaped right over where she was crouching, and sprinted over the roof, running fast — a pause, and then more footsteps, farther away now.

"He jumped the roof," shouted Ruby.

"He has to be headed for the Pineapple Building," shouted Hitch. "There's nowhere else to go rooftop-wise. I'll call for backup. I'm going after him — you head him off at street level, make sure he doesn't exit the building."

Ruby did just that, using the fire-escape ladder like monkey bars, swinging herself from level to level until she reached the street. She checked to see where the guy might make his escape, but all the doors were padlocked, bars on the windows, no obvious exit. She ran at the high fence that had been constructed to deter intruders. With her parkour training, her momentum easily carried her up and over, and she dropped into the narrow space between fence and building. She squeezed through a broken window next to the door — a struggle even for someone as small as Ruby.

And then she was in.

The building was deserted. It had formerly been the

Pineapple Building, the large and grand offices of a large and wealthy company that had traded in pineapples. It was an unfriendly old structure — ugly carvings, heavy dark doors, tarnished brass, and cracked marble — a monument to the man who had first imported pineapples to Twinford. He had become very rich, but, like all things, pineapples had finally had their day and M. R. Jonson's empire was now one more crumbling pile of bricks and mortar in a city that could use the land. Everyone still called it the Pineapple Building, though; didn't matter that no one seemed to buy pineapples anymore.

Ruby moved deeper into the shadowy interior. The place was beyond neglected. Some would say spooky, though not Ruby; that word implied something otherworldly, paranormal, but she told herself this was just an abandoned building — it was bound to feel like a lonely place. One of the secrets to managing one's fear was not to let your imagination run away with you. She was always telling Clancy this.

People always got into trouble when they let their imaginations fill in the gaps — even the most unimaginative people could create some crazy possibilities and let their minds run with them. Then they panicked — Ruby had seen it in movies a thousand times. Lone person (about to be victim) enters empty house, hears a creak, sees a shadow, begins to get all creeped out. Soon they are spinning around, running headlong into suits of armor, tripping over stray cats, falling down basement steps, when clearly what they should actually do is turn around and head for the exit. Simple as that.

There was a bank of elevators, but even if they were functioning, which she figured was unlikely, she wasn't going to risk using one — the skywalker would be bound to hear the sound of an elevator car heading up and up from the depths of the building, and tipping this guy off was the last thing she wanted to do.

She would take the stairs. A fine plan, until she reached the second floor — here the stairs were all but gone, though the banister was still in place. She shook it: sturdy enough. So she continued by walking up the disembodied rail.

She paused at each landing to listen for sounds of light feet on marble but heard nothing. It was on the twenty-seventh floor that she heard the unmistakable sound of footsteps. She made herself small and silent, flattened her body to the wall, and followed the sound. It got louder, but still she could see nothing, no one. Strange because the sound was very close; she could have sworn coming from the same long corridor as the one she stood in.

Curiouser and curiouser, Ruby thought.

Then she felt a breeze, a tiny breath of wind, but no apparent open window to cause such a draft. She shivered; a reflex.

Get a grip, Rube.

RULE 8: DON'T LET YOUR IMAGINATION RUN AWAY WITH YOU OR YOU MIGHT WELL LOSE THE PLOT.

She shook herself to rid her mind of fantasy ghouls and specters.

Nothing was there.

Continuing down the corridor, she looked for clues — disturbed dust, footprints, freshly broken glass, anything. A door banged, and Ruby held her breath, waited, and then went in search of the door that had slammed shut. It had to be this one; there was evidence of activity, faint footprints outside the door. She felt a breeze from under the door. . . . There was a window open in that room.

Don't go in, Ruby.

Experience told her not to, wisdom was against it, but Ruby felt no fear; nothing could happen to her. Slowly she turned the handle and eased the door open — it made a horror-movie creaking sound, but she was not afraid. There was little light to see by, but she was reluctant to switch on her flashlight; *keep it dark,* she thought. Her eyes began to adjust to the gloom, and as they did, she saw what caused the broken blinds to clank to and fro — the window was open.

She edged around the room, feeling for the walls in the gloom to steady herself so she could look out. She was unsurprised to see no one at all—the window was a couple of hundred feet up, and although there was a ledge, no one was perched on it, though there was the strangest noise, a sort of breathing, a sense of someone. Was it the ghost Red had talked of? If it was, then it was a long way from its haunt. If it was, then Ruby would take her chances. For now, anyway. Ruby Redfort did not believe in ghosts, ogres, trolls, or things that went bump in the night.

Not yet.

Something clanked, an unmistakable sound, as if someone had knocked into something.

"Hitch?" she called.

No reply. *Who's in the room with me?*

She spun around, reaching for her flashlight, and as the beam appeared, she saw just too late the vast chasm that yawned beneath her—the room had no floor at its center, and the board she stood on began to crumble underfoot. Her hands scrabbled out, trying to grasp something solid that might save her, and the flashlight tumbled and spun into the void and Ruby lost her grip and fell. . . .

Or nearly did.

Because at the moment the floor completely gave way, she felt a yank to her arm, a hand gripping her wrist, and then her whole body was heaved out of the hole. She felt herself pulled out of the room and carried through the air, by what were unmistakably human hands.

And then *BANG*, nothingness.

Ruby wasn't aware of how much time had passed, probably mere seconds, but the space she was in was utterly dark, and when she came back into consciousness, it was voices she heard. The voices, two of them, seemed to come from beyond the cold plaster walls that held her. She strained to hear what the voices were saying, and circled the space, feeling the walls with her fingers, trying to move close so she could pick up their words.

It was a woman's voice she heard. "You are all out of time, Birdboy. You can run but you can't hide."

Her accent was Texan. Her words kept changing in clarity, like the owner of the voice was moving in circles, turning around and around as if searching for something.

"You think because you wear that suit, you are protected, but don't feel *too* safe. I'll find you — be sure of that. And by the way, no more promises. I don't need a promise from some circus act. We had a deal and you let me down and now I got a very angry someone on my tail and I don't see why I should take the blame for your double-crossing. It's too late *for you*, Birdboy — you're about to take a fall like your poor yellow-feathered mama." The woman laughed. "Whole armies couldn't save you now!"

Ruby held her breath, listening for the other person's voice, but only the vaguest sound of disappearing footsteps met her ears.

"That's it, run!" shouted the woman. "Run for all you're worth, but I'll find you and when I do, get ready to fly!"

The woman walked away, sauntering down the echoing corridor with slow, deliberate steps. Every now and then she laughed. A laugh that Ruby almost recognized.

The footsteps melted away, and Ruby was alone in a tiny silent space, with just the dark for company.

Again, she moved her fingers along the plaster walls, until she found the crack where the door met the wall. She felt for the handle, but there wasn't one. She reached into her hair to feel for the fly barrette, but it wasn't there. She got down on her hands and knees and began to feel around on the dusty, rubble-strewn floor.

It has to be here, she muttered to herself. But after thirty-three minutes, she began to lose heart.

OK, she thought. *Now is maybe the time to panic.*

But as it turned out, it wasn't, because a moment later, there was a scraping sound, then light flooded the space and Ruby blinked, blinded. When she could see, it was Hitch who was standing there in the doorway, one eyebrow raised.

"How did you get locked in a storage room?" he said.

"I really have no idea," said Ruby truthfully. "How did you find me?"

"Your barrette," said Hitch.

"I don't *have* my barrette," said Ruby.

"It's right there by your feet," he said. And she looked down and saw that it was.

"I think it got damaged," he said. "The transmitter kept fading out, which accounts for the time it took me to find you. So what *happened* to you?"

"I think ... maybe ... a ghost happened?" She was rethinking her take on the whole question of ghosts — the paranormal as an explanation for all these weird encounters suddenly didn't seem quite so far-fetched. How else was it possible to explain what was going on?

Hitch stared at her. "Did you take another bump to the head, kid?"

"Let me explain," she said. So she told him about the footsteps that belonged to no one, the hand that had caught her when the floor gave way. "I swear no one was in that room," said Ruby, echoing the words of Red Monroe. And then she told him about the voice of the mysterious woman with the Texan accent who kept circling the outside room. "She sounded like she was looking for someone, the same someone she was talking to, but where was this someone? I don't know; maybe she just enjoys talking to herself." Ruby sighed. "So you see, I don't get it. I mean . . . I really don't get it."

Hitch was concentrating on every word said, but he had no explanation either. "So as far as you are aware, you were falling through the floor, grabbed by nothing, carried across the corridor, and thrown into a storeroom. After which you heard some strange Texan talking in the room outside."

"Uh-huh."

"You *saw* no one."

"Uh-uh."

"But you heard footsteps, before you fell?"

"Yes."

"Anything else?"

"The woman's voice, it reminded me of someone."

"Who?"

"Don't laugh, OK, but it reminded me of Nine Lives."

"You're serious?"

"Look, I know she's dead, but I could swear it was her."

"So what you're saying is we are looking for a female jewel thief who died about five months ago?"

"No, I'm just saying the voice reminded me of her, and in any case, what about the someone who wasn't there? The woman who sounded like Nine Lives called him Birdboy. She was angry with him, said he owed her something."

"What?"

"She didn't say, but she told him she was going to find him and when she did — well, it didn't sound like he would be breathing too much longer."

Hitch looked around the large room. "So this guy, where was he hiding? I don't see a whole lot of good cover here."

"Nope," said Ruby.

"So you're saying *he was the ghost*?"

"I don't know, man — maybe they're both ghosts."

"Two ghosts have stolen a paperweight, a pair of shoes, a poetry book, a tie clip, and a rare orchid?"

"I know," said Ruby. "It's kind of a long shot, right?"

"Stranger things have happened at sea," said Hitch.

Ruby looked at him. "I'm not sure they have," she said.

CHAPTER 45
Tap, Tap, Tap, Tap, Tap

THE CARD FOUND AT THE SCENE of the orchid robbery was encoded with the numbers:

25   14   23

Blacker leafed through the poetry book, looking for the twenty-third word on the fourteenth line of the twenty-fifth page.

"Which means that the word on card five would therefore be . . . **mar**," he said.

"Uh-huh," said Ruby.

"So the message reads, **you tread stolen steps mar** . . . You sure about that? It doesn't really make a whole lot of sense."

"Not until you add the rest of the final word," she said.

Blacker looked at her. "You're saying you know what the final word is?"

"I think we can make a pretty good guess." Ruby ran her

fingers across the page. "I can see only one word in the hidden poem that makes any sense."

Blacker: "You can?"

Ruby looked at him hard, willing him to see what she saw. "Think of it as a name," she urged. She wrote the poem out as one long line of words, to make it simpler for him to see.

you are a poem, Celeste, as you tread a barely there line, stolen in steps am I, transfixed by tiny feet that mar nothing as they go. what is it about their tap tap tap that makes me want to fall?

He was silent for a few minutes before he saw it, then he smiled, very slightly, not a happy sort of smile, but the smile of someone who got it.

"Go," he whispered.

Ruby wrote it down:

You tread stolen steps margo

"You thinking what I'm thinking?" said Blacker.

"I think I am," said Ruby.

Whatever it meant, it definitely sounded like a threat. A threat directed not at the long-dead George Katsel but at the very much alive Margo Bardem.

It seemed like the last item that was going to be stolen . . . was an actress.

Blacker was on the phone to the chief of security. "It looks like he's planning to kidnap Margo Bardem." It didn't take long before there was a plan in place to cancel the actress's Scarlet Pagoda appearance. The finale of the film festival, the screening of *Feel the Fear*, could go ahead; there was no need for her to show.

"Do you think she'll agree?" said the chief.

"Why wouldn't she?" replied Blacker.

Blacker had explained to the security team that Margo looked like the last piece of the puzzle, the last "thing" to be stolen, but what no one could figure out was why.

"I mean, what has she done?" said Ruby, looking at the clues on the wall. "I mean George Katsel I get—he sounds by all accounts like an unpleasant guy, but not Margo."

"Perhaps she was too pretty, too nice, too likable," suggested Blacker. "You know how it can be with some folks? Nice people get on their nerves."

It was agreed that Miss Bardem had to be told of the security threat; she had to be given the choice to step out of the festival finale premiere party and get out of town. Everyone hoped she would take this option.

The security team spoke to Margo Bardem later that day. "It can all be handled, Miss Bardem. You don't have to go through with the finale night if you have any doubts about your safety — in fact, we would prefer you not to."

Margo Bardem listened to the experts and considered her options.

"I would like to go ahead," she said finally. "People have gone to a lot of trouble and effort on my account, and I don't want to let my public down. Besides, this is a momentous occasion. *Feel the Fear* is to be screened for the first time, all these many years later, and finally I will have the chance to be seen as the serious actor I always wanted to be."

"You're sure about this, Miss Bardem?" asked the chief of security. "It's your safety on the line here; no one would judge you a coward for stepping out."

"I would," said Margo Bardem firmly. "If I let myself be bullied by this bozo, then I will have let myself down." She smiled. "The show must go on — that's what we showbiz folks always say. It's a cliché, but it's one I live by."

The chief of security nodded. He didn't like it one bit, but he didn't really have a choice.

"OK guys, you heard the lady — let's get to work."

She would be well guarded; that went without saying. They would issue a press release to announce that Miss Bardem would be residing at the Hotel Circus Grande, a favorite of the actress, and well known as *the* showbiz hotel. It would be leaked to the papers that she had decided to prepare for the evening in her hotel rather than in her theater dressing room. The intention was to fool the skywalker, throw him off the scent.

Meanwhile, Margo would *actually* be delivered to the Scarlet Pagoda theater in secret so she could get ready for the ceremony in the artists' room at the very top of the building. The only access to this room was via the stairs; the windows up there didn't open, not even with a crowbar, the glass was toughened, and, just to be completely sure, steel bars had been added. The room had been checked and double-checked; there was no way in, other than through the door, and there were to be two highly experienced heavy-duty security guys outside for the duration of her visit.

There would be no red-carpet walk for Miss Bardem because it was impossible to make the area 100 percent secure. Instead, a Margo Bardem look-alike would wave from her balcony room, exit the Hotel Circus Grande via the main entrance, and step into a limousine. The look-alike (a highly trained special forces agent) would then be hustled into the theater. No one would be any the wiser, and everyone would feel they had been given the chance to lay eyes on the screen idol. This was the compromise. Miss Bardem didn't like it, but the security chief would not back down.

"Miss Bardem, you gotta meet me halfway here," said the chief. "We handle the crowd outside, and you do your thing in the theater. The theater can be locked down; the crowd outside — that's another matter."

"Very well," said Margo Bardem, "we have a deal." She shook his hand. It was agreed.

CHAPTER 46
Yellow

IT WAS THURSDAY AND RUBY was late for school. She had in fact arrived in good time, as she was planning to catch Clancy before class. She was waiting for him to bike in around the back of the building, but after twenty minutes, he still hadn't arrived. Kids came and went but still no Clancy, and the longer she waited, the more she began to think she must have somehow missed him.

She checked the racks again, this time more methodically, and then she saw it: the bike that had formerly been her green bike, given to Clancy and painted Windrush blue, was now yellow. Not entirely yellow but streaked with ugly slashes of the color — the same canary-yellow spray paint that Ruby had seen on Mrs. Beesman's shopping cart.

When Ruby made it into class, Mrs. Drisco marked her down for detention, but Ruby didn't really care — she was too busy looking at Clancy Crew, who had a large Band-Aid on his forehead and a distinctly yellow streak in his hair.

Ruby took her detention during recess with the other unfortunates. Beetle sat in front of her, busy writing two pages on the topic of "respecting school property," while she wrote a very tedious essay on the importance of punctuality. It was while she contemplated the dullness of the topic that she found herself staring at Beetle's shoes. His footwear was predictably self-conscious, him being the sort of kid who wouldn't be caught dead without the correct label on his sneakers. The more she looked, the more she saw, and what she saw was — yellow paint on the sole of his shoe.

It was canary yellow, and Ruby was pretty sure it came out of a spray can.

When the bell rang and they were finally released from the stuffy classroom, Beetle caught up with Ruby in the corridor.

"Hey," he said, "so what bad thing did you do?"

"You have yellow on your shoe," she said.

Beetle glanced down at his footwear. "Yeah, I guess I do."

Ruby looked at him — it was an unsettling look, and the boy began to sense that something was up.

Ruby's voice gave nothing away, her face bore a look it was impossible to fathom, but the question she asked was very direct. "Why did you trash my bike?"

"*Your* bike?" said Beetle. "I would never — I mean, why would I? I mean, I like you."

"That bike was real special to me. That bike saved my life once. Clancy Crew is the only person on this planet I would give that bike to, and you trashed it," said Ruby.

The boy's face slowly began to contort, understanding dawning.

"I didn't know it was yours," he explained.

Clancy, who just happened to be making his way to class, was at that very moment coming toward them, concentrating on not getting bumped by anyone. As a result, he hadn't yet seen his most loyal friend talking to the gorilla kid. It was only when he heard the familiar low-pitched voice that he looked up.

"That Crew kid is a friend of yours? You have to be kidding," said the boy.

"Why do I have to be kidding?" said Ruby. "Do I sound like I'm kidding?"

"It's just you seem like you're, you know, cool."

"I am cool," said Ruby.

"But he's such a loser."

"That 'loser' happens to be a good friend of mine, my closest friend, actually."

"But I mean, how was I to know? He's like a total duh."

"No, I know what a total duh looks like." She was looking at him hard in the face, and it was impossible for this total duh not to get her meaning. "You think it's OK to beat kids up with your three pals, all four of you, bravely fighting one 'loser kid, one skinny loser kid'? You picked the right color, man — yellow, just perfect for a bunch of cowards."

Afterward at the diner, Clancy was feeling a mixed response to what had been said.

"Thanks for sticking up for me and all, but did you have to call me a loser?"

"I didn't call you a loser; I was merely repeating the word he had used to *describe* you."

"Yeah but did you have to do that? I mean what's so wrong with saying, *'He's no loser, OK?'* or better still, *'This kid is the least losery guy I know.'*"

Ruby pondered this a minute before nodding. "Sure, I admit that either of those two options would have been better, but it came out that way in the heat of the moment. So, do you wanna order something? I'm starving."

"I'm considering pancakes," said Clancy.

"I like the way you think, my friend. I'm gonna go with your pancake instinct and double that order!" said Ruby, closing the menu and setting it to one side. Then she looked across the table at him.

"So just how long has this kid been giving you grief, Clance?"

"What kid?" said Clancy, looking around him like there was someone in the diner who was ready to biff him. It was a convincing fake.

"Still got that old Clancy Crew sense of humor, I see." He smiled, and she punched him lightly on the arm.

"Ow," squealed Clancy.

"Good one," said Ruby. "How do you come up with that sound?" She did it again.

"Ow — no, Ruby, that really does totally hurt."

"Oh, jeepers — sorry, Clance — I didn't realize."

"That's OK, Rube. So how come you were all hung up on this guy, anyway?"

"What?" spluttered Ruby.

"I saw you sitting in Sunny's diner chatting with him. You looked real cozy."

"I wasn't *with him,* bozo. He just sorta showed up."

"That's OK, Rube. No need to explain. It's just I wouldn't have figured him to be your type; he seemed like a bit of a phony."

"My type? *My type?* What are you talking about?"

"I mean, I guess if you really look at him, he has got these pretty-boy looks, obvious and a little bland, but that hair — boy, that hair — he has great hair — too much product but you could have changed that."

Ruby was sitting speechless.

"But I mean, a lot of girls get taken in by these kinda bland boys. Don't feel bad about it."

Her face relaxed and then she rolled her eyes.

"Oh, funny, Clance, real funny — are you thinking of comedy as a career?"

"I got ya, Rube — you gotta admit it."

"Did you really think I actually liked that numbskull?"

"For about an hour . . . OK, maybe five days, but now I can see you would rather hang out with a pancake-eating loser than spend quality time with a gorilla."

"Losers don't eat pancakes," said Ruby.

"So let's order," said Clancy.

CHAPTER 47
Such Small Feet

WHEN RUBY WALKED INTO THE KITCHEN, she found a note pinned to the fridge door.

Ruby, I am hanging the pictures for the Margo Bardem exhibition at the Scarlet Pagoda. Please meet me there at four o'clock so we can go shoe shopping — yours, by the way, are a disgrace and you MUST have some decent footwear for tomorrow night's premiere. Please don't argue about it,

YOUR MOTHER

Ruby looked at the kitchen clock — she was already running a half hour late. She toyed with the idea of borrowing Britney O'Leary's latest reject, a brand-new moped that had been sitting for at least a month untouched in the O'Learys' garage and as far as Ruby was aware had only made it out of there five times. It was hardly a crime, was it, to make use of something that a very spoiled someone never even bothered to ride?

She thought for a moment more. Yes, she figured, it no doubt was. In the end she settled for riding the bus.

Stay out of trouble, Rube.

When Ruby arrived at the theater, her mother was still busy directing a team of staff clutching hammers and standing on ladders. The putting-up of the exhibition was taking a lot longer than expected, and framed pictures of Margo Bardem seemed to be leaning against every wall. Margo in costume, Margo relaxing on set, Margo laughing with the crew. It was true what Frederick Lutz had said; she was certainly tall.

There was one of Margo with George Katsel on the set of *The Cat That Got the Canary* — she seemed to be listening very hard to what he was saying. In the background, people were working, moving scenery and setting up lights. At the very top of the photograph, someone was walking a high wire. It was only possible to see their lower legs, but what was interesting about this wire-walker was: she was wearing little yellow tap shoes.

Click, click, click, went Ruby's brain, and she turned and walked out of the theater doors. She ran along the sidewalk, following the walk of fame until she found Margo Bardem's footprints in the concrete, and when Ruby stepped into them, she knew at once the meaning of the message left by the skywalker thief— *You tread stolen steps, Margo.*

Margo Bardem's feet were big. Like, size-eight big.

Margo Bardem could *never* have worn the famous Little Yellow Shoes—they were maybe five sizes too small for her. Therefore, she could not have performed the stunts seen in *The Cat That Got the Canary*. She had never tap-danced on the high wire, or even on a rooftop. The person who *had* was in the background of that photograph—the woman walking the high wire. Who *was* she? Whoever she was, it was her stunts and her tap-dancing that had made Margo a star. Margo Bardem had stolen someone else's limelight—*that* was her crime.

Ruby thought and thought, and as she thought, she walked, and her walking brought her to the door of Ada Borland's studio.

The door was answered by the woman all in gray.

"I'm afraid Ada's not here," said Abigail, "but I would be happy to show you anything if there's something you particularly want to see."

"I was wondering if you had any pictures taken at the Scarlet Pagoda," said Ruby, "around the time *The Cat That Got the Canary* was being shot?"

"Well, yes," Abigail said. "We have a lot of photographs relating to that film. You looking for pictures of Margo?"

"Well, actually," said Ruby, keeping her tone casual, "I wondered if you have any pictures of her stunt double."

Abigail paused for a second. "You mean the acrobat?"

"I guess," said Ruby, "if she's the one who danced on the high wire and ran across the rooftops?"

"The Little Canary." Abigail nodded.

"So you knew Margo never did the stunts?"

"Oh, yes. They kept it quiet," said Abigail, "but people in the industry knew, and in those days I worked for the studio."

"So you have pictures of the Little Canary?" asked Ruby.

"We don't actually have any photographs taken during filming," said Abigail. "Rumor has it that George Katsel banned photographs on set and destroyed any that *were* taken. I think the Cat wanted to build the myth of Margo — he wanted people to believe that she was actually capable of tap-dancing on a high wire."

"Could she *walk* a high wire?" asked Ruby.

"Couldn't even tap-dance on terra firma, not at that time, anyway. She was originally a hairdresser working at the theater. She learned to dance later on, of course."

"So who was the canary?" asked Ruby.

"Come with me," said the woman. She led the way to the space at the back of the gallery where spiral stairs went up to the archive room. Here hundreds of photographs were stored in wide shallow drawers. Abigail paused just a minute before selecting the correct tray and then lifted out a folder, tied at the sides with binding ribbon.

She laid it out on the white table and then, after checking that her hands were clean (they looked like the sort of hands that always were), she went through the folders one by one, first lifting the tissue paper from the photograph and carefully laying it aside so Ruby could see.

"Is that her?" asked Ruby leaning closer. "The acrobat?"

"That's her," confirmed Abigail. "The Little Canary." The feet were blurred like the lights behind her, a tiny figure on an almost invisible wire. "This was taken when she was in the circus, long before the movie was made."

"She's small," announced Ruby.

Abigail was examining the picture with a magnifying glass. "I'd guess about your height."

"Small," said Ruby.

"She was a mere child back then," said Abigail, "but she didn't really grow much taller than that."

The pictures had been taken in the early 1930s and were

all in black and white. You could sense the atmosphere from the expressions on the faces in the crowd, the excitement and wonder, but it was hard to get a real impression of the spectacle it must have been.

"No color pictures?" asked Ruby.

"As it happens, yes; they were taken a few years on, sometime after 1936 — color film wasn't widely available before then."

The color was beautiful, almost super-real. The shoes, though, were still only visible as a sparkling blur of light.

They had a little heel to them and dainty ankle straps and were designed to look as much like tap-dance shoes as was possible, considering that they were actually high-wire shoes.

"It was rumored that she had terrible eyesight," said Abigail. "I don't know if it's true, but they say she even devised her own sort of Braille-like language — a sort of number code, to help her learn her dance steps."

Ruby was looking so intently at Abigail that Abigail asked if she was all right.

"Yes," said Ruby, "just really interested, is all."

"You see, this way she could feel the numbers with her fingers and practice the steps of the routine wherever she was. Who knows if she did or not — it might just be another myth, but what is true is that life to her was just a blur. Though I guess her near-blindness gave her another talent — she could feel her way across a high wire better than anyone I ever heard of or saw since."

"How come the shoes ended up appearing in the movie? Was the film inspired by the high-wire act?"

"Not exactly. It was inspired by her, the Little Canary."

"So why didn't she play the lead?"

"She had originally been set to star in it," said Abigail. "The story goes that one night the director George Katsel went to the circus with some friends; it was all the rage, and everyone wanted to see the avant-garde circus troupe, Cirque de Paradiso, and it was there on this particular night that he saw something that delighted him." Abigail's hands made theater of what she was describing, almost dancing as she spoke.

"The spotlight settled on a tiny yellow-feathered thing high on a trapeze. And then the trapeze began to move, flying back and forth so the feathers started to flutter, spinning in the air until a tiny figure in a yellow-sequined costume was revealed, dazzling as a human mirror ball. The trapeze moved faster and faster, then with a sudden screech of music the room went to black just for a second, a drumroll . . . and when the spotlight returned, there was the same tiny jeweled woman tap-dancing on the high-wire. The audience would gasp."

"How did she do that?" asked Ruby.

"The tap-shoe sound was conjured with sound effects — that was easy enough to explain — but the high heels on the high-wire? No one ever quite knew how she did that. Some kind of illusion — the shoes she wore on the wire were probably flat but designed to appear heeled. No one ever saw them close up. The ones she wore when she stepped onto the ground were regular heeled shoes, but people never saw her make the switch — it was clever. Anyway," continued Abigail, "dashing George Katsel, celebrity of the moment and hero of the movie industry, was dazzled, besotted by this dancing imp and her beauty, and he insisted on meeting the tiny acrobat. She was billed as the Little Canary, and though she was well known as an act, no one outside the circus community knew who she was — which as it turned out was how she liked it."

"Not a fame seeker?" said Ruby.

Abigail shook her head. "This girl liked the shadows. She was reluctant to become visible, to step out from the public's imagination. But George Katsel was not the toast of the silver screen for nothing — he was the very embodiment of glamour and charm, so they met, and fell for each other instantly, the usual pattern for him, but not for her. She was, as far as we know, a serious sort; never took life lightly. She adored him. The circus rolled on, but she stayed behind, mesmerized as a rabbit in headlights, gazing at this man who lived in a permanent spotlight."

"Then what happened?" asked Ruby. Abigail had a way of telling a story — Ruby was rapt.

"Beats me," said Abigail. "George was set to marry her and *she* was set to star in a movie he had commissioned just for her. *The Cat That Got the Canary.* But when it came to the Canary's big moment, she sort of froze, couldn't do it. She wasn't an actress; she was an acrobat. So they replaced her with Margo Bardem. Only . . . the Canary still did the dancing and the high-wire stunts. They just cut the film so you couldn't see her face. They never credited her, of course."

"That's uncool," said Ruby.

"Anyway, next thing you know, the wedding is off."

"Why?" said Ruby.

"Because George Katsel married Margo Bardem."

"Super uncool," said Ruby.

"That's showbiz for you," said Abigail. "Here today, gone tomorrow. Poor Celeste."

"What did you call her?" said Ruby.

"I said, poor Celeste."

"The Canary's name was *Celeste*?"

"Yes. Why? Does that mean something to you?"

The buzzer buzzed. "That's a customer," said Abigail. "You'll have to excuse me." She went to greet whoever it was, and Ruby made her way back onto the street.

So the poet's muse was Celeste the acrobat, the Little Canary, and she was the one who gave the poetry book to George Katsel. Ruby thought these thoughts as she worked her way back home to Cedarwood Drive.

The picture was coming into focus . . . but the edges were still a blur.

CHAPTER 48
Doing the Right Thing

THE NEXT DAY WAS THE DAY of the grand premiere of Margo Bardem's lost movie at the Scarlet Pagoda, and the actress's long-awaited star turn — assuming her security team could prevent her from being kidnapped.

Ruby woke up that morning to find an interesting garment draped over her chair. She blearily stumbled from her bed, fumbled for her glasses, and went to take a closer look. What she saw was a black-and-red jumpsuit, and a pretty cool one at that.

There was a note pinned to it.

Try this on for size. If you are planning on being dumb and dangerous, you might as well look good.
—Hitch

The suit fit perfectly and looked pretty cool, but what, she wondered, was it about this suit that might make Hitch think she should wear it?

She went downstairs and was greeted by Mrs. Digby, who looked her up and down and said, "Well, if those aren't the cat's pajamas, then I don't know what a feline wears these days."

"I have no idea if that's a compliment, Mrs. Digby, but I can tell you this jumpsuit is awful comfortable; you might like one yourself."

"I might indeed, but where would one presume to purchase an outfit of that description?" asked Mrs. Digby. "ShopSmart?"

"I don't think Hitch shops at ShopSmart."

"Well, I guess he knows where the stylish folk purchase their garments. I'm sure I don't."

Ruby took a carton of banana milk from the fridge and climbed onto one of the high stools at the kitchen counter.

"Yes, be sure to eat before you go out tonight," warned Mrs. Digby. "All they serve at these dos is finger food and hot air."

"Why don't you come, Mrs. Digby? I am sure it will be very entertaining."

"I told you, you're not getting me inside that Scarlet Pagoda — not for all the corn in Iowa."

"You don't really believe it's haunted, do you?" said Ruby, slurping her milk.

"I most certainly do," said Mrs. Digby. "A poor unfortunate

circus act met her end there, and my own cousin Emily was present when it happened."

"Sounds gruesome," said Ruby. "What happened? Was she murdered?"

"Goodness me no, child."

"Was she just not up to it?" asked Ruby "The acrobating, I mean?"

"Oh, no, she was the best, she was, the Little Canary," said Mrs. Digby.

Ruby almost spat her milk. "You're not serious?" she said.

Mrs. Digby put her hands on her hips. "What's got you so animated?"

"Strange as it might seem, the woman at the photography gallery just happened to be talking about the very same person, and it's kinda a coincidence is all."

"No such thing as coincidences," said Mrs. Digby. Mrs. Digby was fond of saying things like *No such thing as coincidences* — she was a fatalist.

"Anyway," she continued, "no one quite believed it when she fell."

"She fell?"

"It was tragic," said Mrs. Digby, sitting down on her stool.

"She was engaged to be married to George Katsel—oh, how she adored *that man,* gave him everything she ever had, which was a lot considering she had been given a million gifts during her career—by everybody from the empress of China to the king of England, from poets to politicians. One botanist even named an orchid after her—the Celeste, he called it—of course she gave that to Katsel too."

Ruby was wondering why she hadn't quizzed Mrs. Digby about the ghost of the Scarlet Pagoda before; it would have saved her an awful lot of trouble. **RULE 62: SOMETIMES ALL THE ANSWERS YOU ARE LOOKING FOR ARE UNDER YOUR OWN NOSE.**

"And so," continued Mrs. Digby, who was now well into her stride, "when Katsel left her for Margo Bardem, it was like the life force left her; she just sort of fell off her tiny perch . . . almost like she wanted to."

"You don't think it was an accident, then?" said Ruby.

"Cousin Emily didn't think so. She witnessed the whole thing, poor dear. The Little Canary had returned to the Cirque de Paradiso, and the whole troupe was appearing at the Scarlet Pagoda to perform in sellout shows. Emily said the Canary was even more dazzling than usual, swinging back and forth on her trapeze—beautiful, she looked—then she waved to her audience,

almost as if she was saying farewell. The light went out"—
Mrs. Digby paused to sniff—"then the drums rolled, and when
the spotlight returned, it shone on an empty wire."

Ruby shivered.

"Yes," Mrs. Digby continued. "She simply wasn't there. The
crowd gasped, afraid to imagine what had happened. As the
spotlight searched the Scarlet Pagoda, it fell upon this cruelly
arranged bundle of sequins and feathers—such a contortion
of limbs sprawled on the sawdust floor. It makes one weep to
think of it," said Mrs. Digby, dabbing her eyes. "The question
on everyone's lips was—was it an accident or was it her broken
heart that brought about her death? We will never know. All I
can say is, that George Katsel has a lot to answer for."

"You blame him?" said Ruby.

"I most certainly do. Margo Bardem was a fool to marry him,
but there were many fools before her and there have been a good
many since. At least Margo Bardem came to her senses *eventually*."
Mrs. Digby looked at Ruby. "Too bad for the Little Canary, though.
They may have buried her in that circus cemetery under that
fallen star, but her spirit's not at rest. She still haunts the Pagoda."
The housekeeper stood up and smoothed her crumpled apron.
"Anyway, that's why I'm never stepping inside that old theater.
Now you go find something useful to do."

※ ※ ※

Ruby left the kitchen and went in search of her mother — before she left for school, she was going to have to explain why she had not waited around for the trip to the shoe store. There had been no chance until now. But as it turned out, her mother didn't seem the least bit bothered.

The storm the newspapers had been promising was finally blowing in, growing fiercer and more determined by the hour, whirling the trees in every direction like it was playing with them, pulling branches like a kid in the schoolyard pulling hair. From what the meteorologists were saying, the storm was building and was set to batter the Twinford coast over the next few days. Sabina Redfort was standing in front of the huge window in the dining room.

"Boy, is this one mother of a windy day." She was sipping a cup of herb tea and had her other arm wrapped tightly around her waist as if holding herself together. "Where on earth did this storm spring from?" she asked the great gray sky.

"They've been talking about it for weeks, Mom. Haven't you been paying attention to the weather reports?" Ruby was always amazed by her parents' lack of ability to tune into what was going on around them. What was plain to most people on the street was strangely difficult for Brant and Sabina Redfort to grasp.

"Do you think I should get the patio furniture in?" asked Sabina.

"Yeah," said Ruby, "unless you wanna see how it looks in Mrs. French's yard, five blocks away."

Sabina looked at her daughter, suddenly alarmed. "You really think it's going to come to that?"

"Come to what?" asked Ruby, taking a large gulp of milk.

"Come to us having to chase our lawn furniture down the street?"

"Sure I do. You might wanna put the car in the garage too. They are forecasting tornado conditions."

"Oh, my," said Sabina, "that's really going to mess with my plans for the Scarlet Pagoda do. I wanted to wear that floaty pink dress of mine."

"Yeah, well, you may find yourself floating to Kansas if you wear that little number. My advice: think sou'wester."

"Oh, that really is too bad," said Sabina. "I'm going to have to rethink the whole evening: maybe a heavy brocade or dense velvet."

"Mom, I think you should be thinking 'raincoats and tornado bunker.'"

Sabina wasn't getting it, but thankfully the conversation reached a natural stop when Ruby's father walked in.

Brant followed Sabina's gaze, which was fixed on a couple of plastic bags weaving their way between the arms of swaying trees.

"Something bothering you, honey?"

"Only what the Sam Hill I'm going to wear to the do if that tornado hits!"

"Don't worry about it, honey — it's just a little windstorm, nothing you can't handle. Wear whatever you want to wear."

"Thank you, sweetheart, you're so wise! I'm going to take your advice and go floaty."

"Good choice," he said, handing her a large cardboard envelope. "This was just delivered," he said. "It's addressed to you." He kissed his wife and went downstairs.

Sabina looked puzzled. "I wasn't expecting anything." She pried open the envelope and pulled out the tissue-wrapped photograph it contained. She stared at it, amazed, and then quite suddenly sat down. The photograph was of Ruby, and it was unquestionably the work of the great Ada Borland.

"But how?" she said, looking up at her daughter.

"I called her," said Ruby.

"But I mean your face . . ."

"A touch of makeup," said Ruby.

"You know what, Ruby Redfort? You are one terrific kid," said Sabina.

"Mom, there are better kids out there," said Ruby. "*You* know it, and *I* know it."

"All I know is, I have a portrait of my beautiful daughter taken by the great Ada Borland and no other mother I know can say that—so they can keep their better kids."

"Thanks, I think," said Ruby.

Sabina went off to call Marjorie; she would no doubt be on the phone a long time.

On her way to school, Ruby noticed that one of the plastic bags had been snagged by the tree's twiggy fingers and was flapping this way and that, unable to work its way free.

Ruby was doing the right thing for the second time that week, and her mother beamed with pride when she saw her daughter come downstairs that night in a floaty peach-colored dress. Ruby was trying hard not to scowl: peach was not her color and floaty was not her style.

"You look adorable!" cried Sabina, trying hard not to spoil the moment by mentioning the sneakers that Ruby was wearing with it.

What her mother did *not* know was that under the silk peach number, Ruby was dressed in the black-and-red jumpsuit that Hitch had given her. Like Superman, she wanted to be prepared for every eventuality—to be truthful, she was praying that an eventuality would come along quickly and she would be able to ditch the dress before the finale even began.

"Your father and I will be traveling there early so we can greet all the guests as they arrive at the Circus Grande. Bob will pick you up, Ruby, and drop you at the preshow party—be sure you're ready on time. I don't want a repeat of the Jade Buddha fiasco."

Clancy would be there with his whole family. The evening would be star-studded, and every famous face in Twinford was on the invitation list—it was the sort of night that Ambassador Crew would not want to miss.

Bob, Mr. Redfort's chauffeur, arrived exactly on time, and Ruby got into the car without delay. She was doing the right thing. No lateness, no sidetracks, no getting waylaid or getting into trouble.

The only thing was that the story Mrs. Digby had told her just kept going around and around in her head....

CHAPTER 49
The Fallen Star

THE TRAFFIC WAS HEAVY. It seemed as if every person in Twinford was heading down to the Scarlet Pagoda for the premiere, and what with all the extra security in place, Bob was concerned that he was never going to get her there on time. "I'm going to take a detour," he said. "It's a back route and should be less snarled up."

As it turned out, he was wrong and the little back street behind the Hotel Circus Grande was closed to all nonofficial cars.

A cop was standing in the road. "No vehicles, sir, on account of the film festival security."

"Don't concern yourself, Bob," said Ruby in a reassuring way. "Let me out here and I'll walk the rest of the way."

Bob looked anxious; he had been given strict instructions by Mrs. Redfort to drop Ruby at the hotel door, but given the circumstances, leaving her here seemed to be the only possible course of action.

Ruby hopped out of the car and began walking up the street. It was a street Ruby had never been down before; a high brick wall ran along one side of it, and she could see treetops rising up behind it. What, she wondered, lay on the other side?

She followed the wall until she reached a pair of twisty iron gates. *A cemetery,* she said to herself. There was a carved plaque on the wall that explained everything:

The Circus and Performance Artists' Cemetery

It was the cemetery Mrs. Digby had been talking about, and now here Ruby was, right outside its gates.

"Fate or coincidence?" said Ruby to herself.

Ruby had always known it was located in the heart of Twinford's theaterland, but she hadn't realized that it was right here behind the Hotel Circus Grande.

They buried her in the circus cemetery, under a fallen star.

With Mrs. Digby's words still fresh in her mind, Ruby figured she really ought to take a look — it wouldn't hurt to take ten minutes; her mother wouldn't even be missing her yet.

The gates were locked, but that wasn't a problem; she climbed them so swiftly that had you so much as blinked, you would have missed her.

It was perfectly still within the walls; even the wind didn't seem able to disturb the serenity of this green space. Large leafy plane trees towered high above the twisting paths, and on every side huge buildings looked down on the silent stones.

But how to find Celeste's grave? If it was indeed star shaped, then it would be easier to spot from above.

She looked up at the huge tree that stood where all paths met — from there she thought she would be able to make out a tombstone that looked like a star. She bunched her dress up as best she could, knotting it at the side, and ran at the tree, jumping to reach the high branch, and then heaved herself up. The rest was easy, and she was soon standing twenty-five feet in the air. She could see the banners of the film festival; she could see the Scarlet Pagoda and the Hotel Circus Grande and hear the excitement of the crowds as they waited for the celebrities to arrive.

Ruby moved from branch to branch, scanning the gravestones, searching for Celeste's fallen star, when suddenly her eye was caught by a figure all in black. He seemed to have appeared out of thin air. *Did he also climb the gate?*

She watched him move across the graveyard before stopping and stooping to place yellow flowers on a gravestone that was not standing but lying flat in the grass.

The figure in black stood there for just a minute and then slowly, slowly made his way back along the path. Ruby dropped silently to the ground and, when she was sure he would not see her, ran to the place where he had stood. The grave was not neglected; the weeds and leaves had been removed, and the stone, a five-pointed star of marble, lay on top of neat clipped grass, so it was easy to read the words carved into its surface:

HERE LIES

THE LITTLE CANARY

A BEAUTIFUL ACROBAT

WHO FELL FROM THE SKY,

STOLEN FROM THIS WORLD

Ruby reached out her hand, running her fingers across the carving and tracing around the deep stone shape of the star, only to discover another message. A message carved into the marble that could only be read by touch. A message written in Braille.

She closed her eyes and read, her fingers traveling over the bumps that together formed words:

**I will bring you orchids until the day when those who
brought you low have fallen and you light the skies again
- your adoring son, Claude**

"You have a son, Celeste?" said Ruby to the grave. "So is it
him you haunt?"

She looked around her — where was Celeste's visitor now?
As Ruby rose to her feet, she focused on the flowers that he had
left; they had beautiful spiked pink lines running like veins along
the intense yellow of the petals — small, delicate, and almost
unreal.

They were unmistakably flowers of the Celeste orchid,
flowers from Claude to his lost mother.

Ruby rose to her feet, turned, and reached for the fly barrette,
but it wasn't there. *Darn it, Ruby!* Then she was running down
the winding leaf-strewn path, past ornamental urns and praying
stone angels, through the little cemetery, and as she neared the
gates, she saw him. Instead of scaling the twisting metal, he was
feeding himself through the curly ironwork like a contortionist
might.

Ruby took another route — over the wall, her dress made a
horrible tearing sound as it caught a sharp stone lodged in the
wall. *"Darn it,"* she hissed.

She waited until it was safe, then silently dropped to the street. He didn't see her; he was walking fast, moving like a dancer or gymnast, back straight, feet slightly turned out. When he reached the Hotel Circus Grande, he stopped and stared straight up as if contemplating a climb. He smiled and then the most curious thing happened — he made an action as if pulling something out of his jacket, yet nothing appeared, then he whirled his arm above his head as if to wrap himself in a scarf or blanket . . . and he was gone, in an instant. Disappeared.

What just happened?

He had vanished into thin air. How he had achieved this illusion she did not know, but she knew why he was there — he was the skywalker, the son of the Little Canary, and, like his mother, an extraordinary acrobat and wire-walker, and he was heading to kidnap Margo Bardem.

Ruby ran as fast as she could, pushing through the gathered crowds, flashing her invitation at the clipboard-holding greeters, and on through the Circus Grande's heavy doors. She heard her mother's laugh and Ambassador Crew's pompous voice booming across the room. But there was no sign of Hitch.

She moved on through the crowd until she reached her parents' group. They were chatting with the Humberts and Dora Shoering.

"Have you seen Hitch?" asked Ruby.

Her question went unheard.

"I am wildly curious about the notion of this movie," Sabina said. "I just can't imagine why *Feel the Fear* was never screened. I mean, who wouldn't want to see a Margo Bardem picture?"

"I quite agree," said Marjorie Humbert.

"Mom," said Ruby more insistently.

"Hi, Ruby," said Quent. "Are you coming to my superhero party tomorrow?"

"I'm working on it, Quent," said Ruby. "Mom," she said again, even more forcefully.

"Well, of course that was a big secret," said Dora Shoering. "I mean, hardly anyone knows this, but the film has been locked all these years in the deepest studio vault. No one dared to screen it."

"But whyever not?" said Sabina.

"Mom!" said Ruby, a lot louder. But Sabina could hear nothing but Dora Shoering.

"Because," said Dora Shoering, "the test screening went so badly that they decided this was a film that should never ever be shown for fear that it would destroy Bardem's career."

Now even Ruby was listening.

"But how could it?" said Sabina. "Margo was a huge star."

"Well"— Dora Shoering was really enjoying holding

forth—"for the simple reason that Margo Bardem, darling of the silver screen, is murdered in the movie. This is no comedy thriller, this is high drama, and her character is pushed from a high wire—a sort of nod to Bardem's debut movie *The Cat That Got the Canary,* but this time sinister—and, let's be honest, no fan wanted to see Bardem take a fatal fall."

"So they canned it?" said Sabina.

"They did indeed," said Dora Shoering.

Ruby was staring at Dora Shoering. She was also thinking of the words in Braille on the grave. *When those who brought you low have fallen.* Suddenly the horrible truth was dawning: Margo Bardem was not going to be kidnapped; she was going to be *murdered.* Life would imitate art, and Margo's premiere would be her finale, when she fell to her death.

"He's going to kill her," whispered Ruby. *"He's going to make her fall."*

"What?" said Sabina.

"Where is Hitch?" demanded Ruby.

"Why, I don't know," replied her mother, somewhat alarmed by her daughter's expression. "Is everything all right?" But Ruby had already begun weaving her way through the cocktail party and was making for the main stairs. As she hurried, she heard her mother call, "Don't be long, honey! It's all about to begin!"

The main stairs were roped off, and as Ruby ducked under the barrier, a security guard stuck out his arm. "I'm sorry, little lady, no one goes beyond this point."

Ruby immediately adopted the face of a tearful child. "But I'm staying at the hotel; I left my autograph book in my room," she said, making her voice wobble slightly, "room two fifty-five. You can check with the main desk if you don't believe me."

The man's expression softened. "OK, sweet-face, but make it quick; I'm not supposed to let anyone through."

Ruby darted up the stairs and when she reached the second floor ran along the corridor and slipped through the exit to the back staircase. She ditched the peach dress and stuffed it into a bucket abandoned by the cleaner. Now attired in the more practical and much cooler jumpsuit, Ruby continued up the stairs.

She was just one story from the roof when a burly security guard stepped in front of her, black suited and equipped with earpiece.

"No access to the roof," he said. "All exits have been sealed off. This floor is for authorized personnel only."

"But I'm looking for —"

"No access . . . Hey, wait a minute. Are you a kid?" He peered at her. "You shouldn't even be here. I'll get someone to escort you down."

Ruby didn't wait for that. "It's OK, sir — I'm going." And she turned back before he could march her down to the hotel lobby. Once on the floor below, she began searching for a window that might open. The only way up to the roof was to climb out the window and scale the outside of the building. It was as she was trying to find a suitable window to exit from that she felt a strange vibration down her spine, and then she could have sworn she could hear a tiny voice, tinny and insistent, and it seemed to be calling her name.

"Ruby?"

She stopped and reached her hand down the back of the jumpsuit. What she pulled out was the fly barrette.

"How did you get there?" she said to the barrette.

"What?" said Hitch, his voice crackly and distant.

"Where have you been? I've been looking for you," hissed Ruby into the fly transmitter.

"What are you doing, kid? You should be in the ballroom of the Circus Grande, but you seem to be heading for the roof."

"He's here," she said.

"Who's here?"

"Claude."

"Who's Claude?"

"The Little Canary's son."

"Who's the Little Canary?"

"Celeste, the acrobat, the one who did all Margo's stunts," said Ruby. "Look, it doesn't matter; all you need to know is that I know what's going on. Claude is the skywalker, and he's here to avenge his mother's death. He's got this wrong idea that Margo Bardem's the one responsible for destroying his mother's life."

All the time Ruby was talking, she was working on the window, trying to force it open. *Where was her watch when she needed it?*

"Kid, what are you doing?" said Hitch. "I'm getting interference."

Ruby had taken the barrette and was picking the window lock. "Claude has been collecting things that used to belong to his mother — the paperweight, the shoes, the poems, the tie clip, the orchid. Celeste gave them to George Katsel when they got engaged — he, being less than a lovely person, either lost them or gave them away."

HITCH: *I hear weather. Are you opening a window?*
RUBY: *I'm trying to prevent a crime.*
HITCH: *We're on it, Redfort.*
RUBY: *You're not — you don't understand.*

HITCH: *What exactly don't I understand? There's no way the skywalker or Claude, whatever you want to call him, is going to kidnap Margo.*

RUBY: *He's not here to kidnap her.*

HITCH: *He's not?*

RUBY: *No, he's here to* murder *her.*

HITCH: Murder *her? How do you figure that?*

RUBY: *The movie tonight,* Feel the Fear, *is about a character who plummets to her death from a high wire. Margo plays that role; Claude is gonna ensure that life imitates art.*

HITCH: *Why?*

RUBY: *He wants to make his mother visible again. Don't you see that's what this whole thing is about? He's collecting Celeste's things, tapping us on the shoulder, reminding us who she was, and Margo is the final tap on the card because Margo stole Celeste's spotlight and now Claude is taking the light back. Everyone will remember Celeste the Little Canary.* Until the day when those who brought you low have fallen — *he wrote that on Celeste's grave, and Margo is going to be the one who falls and Claude is going to make it happen.*

HITCH: *He can't get near her, kid, not a chance. There is no way he can get inside either building; we have it covered.*

"You don't get it," said Ruby, her voice clear and steady. "He's already here."

CHAPTER 50
Go

MISS BARDEM?"

The actress turned around.

"Why, yes . . . but where did you appear from?" She looked him up and down, this man dressed entirely in black. "Are you part of the security team?" she asked. "It's just, well, I only opened my door for a moment, to ask for some tea, and I didn't see anyone come in."

"No, but then you wouldn't."

"I don't understand."

"That's not important."

"You shouldn't be here," said the actress.

"Neither should you," said the figure in black.

Margo Bardem looked puzzled. "Is there something I can do for you?"

"That depends: do you know how to bring back the dead?"

"I'm sorry?" she whispered. "I don't understand."

"No, you're not sorry—how could you be sorry? You stole everything from my mother, all she loved. First the applause, then the man she adored, and then worst of all you stole *her*"—his voice cracked—"from me."

"I think you must have confused me with someone else. I don't know your mother; I have no idea what you are talking about." She had played this role so many times on the screen, it was second nature to her. *Keep calm,* she thought. *Never show your fear.*

"Let me jog your memory," said the man. "Those yellow shoes, were they ever really yours? Did anyone ever ask you to actually try to slip your foot into them?"

Miss Bardem turned pale. She was feeling around for the phone; it was somewhere under all the bouquets and well-wisher cards. "You are clearly out of your mind. I would like you to leave, young man."

"I know, Miss Bardem, but we can't always have things our own way. At some point our luck must run out."

"My audience is expecting me; I have to be onstage very soon."

"Not quite yet. You have almost one hour."

"But somebody will be up any minute, to do my hair, my makeup, any minute now. . . ."

"I've read your biography, Miss Bardem. You like exactly one hour all to yourself before you appear in public, and don't you always do your own hair? Of course you do — you used to be a hairdresser before you were a big star, remember?"

Margo Bardem bit her lip and nervously twisted the bird-shaped ring on the fourth finger of her left hand.

"That ring, for instance, wasn't it meant for someone else?"

"It was a present from George Katsel — for my work in *The Cat That Got the Canary*."

"And you did get the canary, didn't you? And when you got her, you killed her."

"What can you possibly mean?"

"You killed the Little Canary."

"What are you talking about?"

"The Little Canary, Celeste — you killed my mother."

"But I hardly knew her. She filmed the dancing scenes, sure, the stunts on the high wire but —"

"You don't have to know someone to destroy them."

"But how could I have destroyed her? I mean, I wouldn't. I couldn't."

"You stole her role. You pretended it was you dancing on the wire — *you* made her disappear."

"But I didn't," pleaded Margo. "You must know I had no say in it." She was almost begging now. "Don't you see? That's the movie business; they don't want to break the illusion. The producers said it would ruin my career if I let it be known that it wasn't me up there. They said that I would be fired. It's just *acting,* just a job."

"Just a job?" spat the man. "Just a job, you say. Perhaps you work for money, but my mother was an artist — walking the high wire was her art!"

"What do you *want* from me?" she pleaded.

"I want you to bring her back, make her visible."

"But how?"

"You admit the truth, tonight. Instead of introducing that film of yours, show everyone that *she* was the one who danced on the high wire, that she was the talent and you were just the face, a spineless puppet."

"And then . . . you'll let me go?"

"Oh," he said, "I'll let you go. Don't you worry about that. I will most definitely let you go."

Her eyes widened as she caught his meaning. "I can scream," said Miss Bardem.

"Louder than anyone in showbiz," said Claude.

Margo Bardem nodded, a slow, knowing gesture; she

understood what he was saying. "You mean they will assume I am practicing for the show tonight . . . and no one will come?"

Claude nodded. "Why would they? They know you are perfectly secure."

She put down her yellow gloves; she didn't think she would need them after all.

"Let's take a walk, shall we?" he said.

"Where are we going?"

"Out," said Claude, his eyes looking up.

The actress gulped. "I have a fear of heights, you know."

"I know," he said. "That's why you never did your own stunts." He looked at her. "But that's all about to change."

He pointed to the dressing table. "Get climbing," he said.

She didn't argue; she didn't see the point. Instead she stepped onto the table and looked at him with pleading eyes.

"Where do you expect me to go?" said Margo. "There's no exit in this room, none but the door."

"You are mistaken. There is one right above your head; it leads to the roof. I used to play up there when I was a boy."

He took the broom leaning against the wall and climbed up beside her, and, using the handle, he pushed at a section of the ornate ceiling, dislodging one of the panels and revealing a trapdoor.

"Liars first." And as he said these words, he dropped a perfectly blank card onto the table. The final loyalty stamp invisibly in place.

Tap tap tap tap tap tap.

The coded bumps and dips spelling out the numbers:

29   14   27

The final word would be *GO*.

CHAPTER 51
Interference

HITCH WAS RUNNING UP THE STAIRS of the Scarlet Pagoda. He had already alerted the security team — Ruby couldn't be right about this, it didn't make any sense, but still he ran.

"Kid, what do you mean he's already here?"

"I saw him in the cemetery," said Ruby. "I followed him to the Circus Grande; I watched him stare up at the building. I felt sure he was preparing to climb. I figure he's going to skywalk over to the Scarlet Pagoda from the hotel rooftop."

"Kid, you're out of your tree here — for one thing, how could he know Margo isn't at the Circus Grande? Not even the Twinford PD has *that* information."

"He knows everything, don't you see that?" Ruby by now was leaning out the window, her face turned skyward, assessing the climb. "He grew up with performers. He met Margo a long time ago; he knows her superstitions about where she has to be before a performance, knows which dressing room she will be in . . ."

He just . . . knows." Ruby hauled herself up onto the windowsill and ducked out onto the ledge.

"Your voice sounds weird, kid. What are you doing? I'm getting a feeling that you might be about to do something dangerous."

"Security has closed off the roof access, so I'm going out the window."

"In a dress?"

"Relax," said Ruby. "I've changed. I'm wearing the jumpsuit you gave me."

A pause.

"Why do you need to get up on the roof?" Hitch asked.

"I need to find the wire. He'll be walking a tightrope to the Pagoda; he'll climb in from the roof. He knows this building like the back of his hand."

"Kid, the place is surrounded."

Ruby ignored him. "If I can just locate the wire, then I can follow."

"You don't need to follow," reasoned Hitch. "If you're right about this, the skywalker will be spotted before he gets close."

"You could have the whole army out there, and he would still get past them," said Ruby.

"How do you figure that?"

"Because . . . he's *invisible.*"

Hitch stopped running. "What?" he said. "Are you talking about ghosts again, Redfort?"

"No, I'm talking something state-of-the-art; I saw it with my own eyes. I saw him wrap himself in something and then he disappeared. He can make himself invisible."

Silence.

"Hitch, you there?"

"Yeah . . ." Hitch was sending messages to all agents.

"It must have been what Nine Lives meant when I heard her in the vacant building talking to the skywalker. She talked about the suit that protected him. She meant an invisibility suit; it's why I couldn't see him, it's why *she* couldn't see him, it's why no one has caught him, and it's why he can make it into the Scarlet Pagoda — into Margo's dressing room — without being seen."

"You're serious, kid?"

"What, don't I sound like I'm serious?"

Silence. But not a shocked silence. A thoughtful silence.

"Does this have to do with that prototype that went missing?" said Ruby.

Silence.

"You not talking, that means yes, right? This *is* what was taken from the Department of Defense. . . ."

He paused. "Listen, kid, let me handle this. Just hang tight; stay right where you are. I'll be —"

"No," said Ruby. "I'm going after him."

"Ruby, don't do that — just wait for backup. I'm on my —"

But she just continued to climb. The wind whistled around her. The ground was very far below, but she didn't look down.

"Ruby —"

"I'll see you up there," she said.

"Kid, what is it with you and orders?"

They were on the roof now, the birdman's light feet tripping across the jade tiles, the actress stumbling and slipping, firmly gripping her captor's arm, eager not to slide to her death.

"Where . . ." she gasped, "where are we going?"

Margo Bardem turned to face him, but he was not there. He was gone, vanished. For one solitary second, she thought he had abandoned her there on the roof — she looked up at the dark sky and thanked whatever force might be watching over her — until, that is, she realized that her arm was still in his firm grip.

He was gone from her sight but not gone from her side, and she felt herself pulled toward the roof's edge, stepping closer and closer to the dizzying drop between the Pagoda and the Hotel Circus Grande. She could see the clusters of fans standing outside the hotel—autograph books in hand, waiting for their star to exit and walk the red carpet.

Little did they know she was about to make the exit of a lifetime—she was about to fall screaming from the sky.

Who could have imagined how closely Margo Bardem's final seconds of life might imitate her art?

There weren't a whole lot of footholds on the upper tier of the Circus Grande, and Ruby was relying on her finger strength to pull herself up and onto the large ledge that ran around the building a couple of feet below its top. Ruby hauled herself up and over and crouched behind the parapet, trying to figure out what her best move might be, and then she saw a very strange sight indeed.

Margo Bardem, holding on to a man who wasn't there, and stepping toward the almost invisible wire that ran between the Scarlet Pagoda and the Circus Grande.

Claude pushed her to the roof's edge. "You fooled everyone into thinking you could do it once—do it now. Your fans want to see you walk the high wire."

Looking down, Margo could see the crowds gathered to watch the guests and VIPs, the celebrated actors, directors, assorted movie people, all making their way along the red carpet.

Then she looked across and saw the thin wire stretching to the hotel roof. It couldn't be more than an inch thick. "You're not serious?" she said.

"Deadly," said Claude. He looked at her, puzzled. "You must know that has to be your destiny?"

"My destiny?"

"If you can walk all the way across, then you deserve to live; if not, then it is only fair that you meet my mother's fate."

Margo glanced down at her public. "This can't be happening," she whispered. "I'm sorry about your mother, I'm sorry you lost her, I'm sorry she had her heart broken by George Katsel, but you must see that it was not my doing. The Cat never loved anyone; he was only interested in himself—your mother lost nothing when she lost him."

"She lost me. Is that nothing?"

"Of course not . . . I didn't mean . . ."

"Walk, or I'll make you fly."

Margo, not knowing what else she could do, put one foot on the high wire. For a moment she thought she saw a young girl on the roof of the hotel opposite. She must be going half crazy with fear. The wind was a gale, and she was walking to certain death. One foot wrong and she would be lost.

Searchlights were skating across the sky, announcing the finale of the film festival, flashbulbs popping as the stars arrived, and all this happening as the thriller above them played out unnoticed.

The fly barrette crackled, and Hitch's voice came through.

"You there, kid?"

"Yeah."

"There's no time to clear the area; there's no time to set up a safe fall," said Hitch. "I am going to have to try to grab her, but I need a little more time."

"OK," said Ruby.

"You feeling fearless?" asked Hitch.

"What do you want me to do?" said Ruby.

"How good's your balance?"

"Excellent."

"You trust me, kid?"

"Totally," she said.

CHAPTER 52
What a Spectacle

MARGO BARDEM WAS TRYING not to whimper — she was an actress from the good old days of moviemaking and was considered a tough cookie, a lady who could roll with the punches, but this was no ordinary role. This was life and death.

"You have to pull it together," said Claude, "or you will definitely fall. Whatever you do, don't look down."

"What, are you crazy? I'm not even looking up." It was the sort of line Margo Bardem had become famous for.

Suddenly the searchlights swooshed across them and for a split second the players were caught in its glare. Then darkness, but there was a gasp from the crowd and then applause.

"They won't be clapping when you tumble to your death."

What the crowd saw was Margo Bardem walking across the wire, her kidnapper invisible. She was spotlit now; the crowd gathered in awe to see what they thought was all choreographed, a wonderful finale to the film festival, all building up to the world premiere of the lost classic *Feel the Fear*, featuring Margo Bardem.

"My, what a spectacle," said Brant Redfort. "I gotta hand it to them; they know how to put on a show."

"Who knew Margo Bardem had it in her—*how* old is she?" said Sabina.

"If only Ruby could see this," said Brant.

Ruby was doing exactly what Hitch had told her to—she was standing on the very edge of the hotel's parapet and reaching a toe to the high wire. She sent a message through the steel: *tap, tap, tap.*

She could feel the tension in the wire change; she knew he had registered her presence. He was invisible, but she could feel his fear. "Hello, Claude," she shouted. "Looking good."

Another searchlight caught hold of a small figure standing on the very edge of the Circus Grande Building.

"Goodness, this is fabulous. How do you think they manage in this wind?" Sabina was finding her dress hard to control. "Ruby told me not to wear the pink dress, but would I listen? No siree, Bob."

"I know what you want," shouted Ruby, her voice carrying on the wind. "You want recognition for the Little Canary. I found the cards, and I happen to agree with you — she *should* be seen."

He definitely heard that. She couldn't see him, but she could see poor Margo Bardem, edging ever farther out onto the thin cable. Claude was presumably in front of her, holding her hands, waiting for the right moment to let her go.

"George Katsel took everything from her. He broke her; he might just as well have pushed my mother from that wire himself," shouted Claude.

"So why punish Margo for Katsel's crime?" shouted Ruby.

"Because she took my mother's place, stole what was rightfully hers, stole her from *me* — and made her disappear. No one even knows her name. She is invisible to this world."

"If you kill Margo, then all anyone will ever remember is how the Little Canary's son became a murderer. No glory in that little tale."

Silence.

"You know, you don't strike me as the murderous type," shouted Ruby, "and trust me, I've met some psychopaths in my time, and what I know about those guys is they don't go around catching people who are falling through floors — it was *you* who saved my life, *wasn't* it, Claude?"

"You were in the way—a coincidence, not a choice, just an accident of fate."

"There's no such thing as coincidence," shouted Ruby. "You saved me because I can change your destiny."

"You?" shouted Claude. "What can *you* do?"

"I can make Celeste visible again."

"What are you? Supergirl?"

"I wouldn't say that. I know people, is all. I have a hotline to a superwoman. She's on the film festival committee. Say the word and your mother will be celebrated for all time. They'll be commissioning sculptures of her. Trust me."

"How can I?"

"I don't know," said Ruby, stepping both feet on to the steel cable. "But I'm trusting you; I'm standing on a high wire one hundred and fifty feet in the air—you jump up and down, and I fall."

The wind was getting up—the storm was about to break. She needed to get him down from there. More important, she needed to get Margo Bardem down from there.

"You have to let Margo go—just walk her back to the roof and I will keep my promise."

If the stakes had not been so high, this exchange between

girl and invisible man would have been comical, but the stakes were VERY high, could not have been higher — a steel wire was all that separated life from death.

"Do I have your word?"

"Girl Scout's honor," she shouted.

"I think they lost the sound on this," said Brant. "I can't hear what they are saying."

"The little one is very good," said Sabina. "Do you think she is a professional actress? She is very small, almost looks like a child."

And as Claude turned, preparing to lead Margo back to safety, the most almighty crash resounded.

A huge gust of wind had caught the Pagoda's fragile spire, knocking it over and sending it scudding down the jade tile roof. It hit the carving that held the cable, sent a shock wave through it.

Then the people below heard a spine-chilling scream as Margo Bardem fell from the wire and into the night air.

Ruby cried out.

The crowd gasped as the woman flailed in the sky, and then they gasped again to see a figure all in black fly across the spotlight's beam to snatch her from the dark. It all happened so quickly that no one could really quite understand what they had seen.

"Was it just me," said Brant, "or did that guy look a lot like Hitch?"

"I wish!" said Sabina. "I'm telling you, Brant, if Hitch ever catches me when I fall off a roof, I'm giving him double pay."

The force of the wind that had torn off the spire had flung Ruby backward, lifting her from the wire to the roof. She was lucky — always lucky. She got to her feet and peered over the parapet.

"You see, Hitch?" she said out loud. "I'm still not dead."

"Not dead — yet."

Ruby spun around. She knew that voice.

"Nine Lives?"

The figure laughed. "Who else?" she said as she grabbed Ruby's arms, wrenching them behind her back — *click, click,* she snapped her wrists into handcuffs.

"Geez, not you again," whined Ruby. "How many lives you *got*?"

CHAPTER 53
Finest Italian Leather

WHAT RUBY SAW WAS A WOMAN dressed to kill. She was clad in a black catsuit, long red hair loose and blowing across her face, skin of ivory and eyes of blue. In her hand, something twinkled brightly.

Ruby remembered that laugh, that voice, the cold weight of that tiny diamond revolver. She remembered Nine Lives Capaldi very well indeed.

She also remembered, distinctly, her being dead.

"What are you doing here?" demanded Ruby.

And Nine Lives laughed and tossed back her beautiful red hair, and just for a second revealed the scar that ran across one eye and disfigured her elegant face. "Do I need an invitation? Is this a private rooftop showdown?" she drawled in her slow Texan drawl.

"What I mean is, why are you not dead?"

Nine Lives smiled. "Being dead is boring — you'll find out for yourself soon enough."

"I'll just take your word for it," said Ruby. "So what are you here for?"

"Not for you, little girl, you can be sure of that, though I'm happy to kill you just for old times' sake. But no, I'm here for the very thing that your Department of Defense and your little *spy guys* are so busy looking for."

"The invisibility suit . . ." said Ruby.

"The suit, the skin, bravo," drawled Capaldi. "The skin's the thing, little girl. That amazing prototype stolen from under your own sophisticated high-security noses. My gosh, how secretive Spectrum is — they really should have kept you in the loop when the skin went missing from the Department of Defense. It mighta made your task a little easier had you known what you were looking for."

"How do you know they *didn't*?" countered Ruby.

"A little bird told me." Nine Lives laughed.

"So Claude stole it? But how?" She needed to keep Nine Lives talking. She didn't have a plan; she was just buying time. **RULE 44: WHEN IN A TIGHT SPOT, BUY YOURSELF SOME TIME: ONE MINUTE COULD CHANGE YOUR FATE.**

"The security room is made of steel; without clearance, the only way in is via an air vent so small that you would—"

"Have to be a contortionist? That's right, he's quite the little circus act. He could get in through a crack in your door. Isn't that right, Claude?" Nine Lives laughed again. "Then once he had the skin, he was able to get his hands on the main attraction."

The main attraction? thought Ruby. *What's the main attraction?*

Nine Lives turned and looked at the wire. "Hello, Birdboy!" she called in a false-bright voice. "I've come for what's mine!"

The wind was picking up again, and the sound of its whistling only added to the theater playing out on this twenty-nine-story stage. Whistling: the very soundtrack of fear.

Ruby heard footsteps on stone: Claude, stepping invisibly from the wire to the parapet. She couldn't see him, but she could feel him, just behind her.

"There you are, Birdboy. I smell you now." Capaldi was sniffing the air. "That skin may be invisible, but you should have stood downwind; its odor is such a giveaway." She aimed the little diamond revolver.

She has quite a nose, thought Ruby, who couldn't smell a thing.

"Give me what I came for or you can make the skin your shroud," spat Nine Lives.

"Let the girl walk," hissed Claude.

Nine Lives threw back her head and laughed her Texan laugh. "Claude, baby, I knew you were sentimental about the past and your dear dead mama, but are you really about to give up everything to save one raggedy little girl?" She tutted. "Honestly, I am disappointed; you have lost focus, honey." Then she laughed some more.

This was an odd situation — here was Ruby, her fate in the hands of a murderer, and the person pleading for her life was a thief and a would-be assassin.

"Let the girl go, Capaldi, or your treasures will be lost forever."

"I don't think you are in the best position to make deals," Nine Lives snarled, dragging Ruby to the parapet. "So looks like you'll be waving bye-bye to your little friend here."

"You want this?" shouted Claude. He ripped the invisibility skin from his body, and there he stood — the skywalker, a mere mortal dressed in black, the son of an acrobat. "And this?" He produced, from his pocket, a small object that Ruby couldn't quite make out.

"You look so much taller when you're invisible," said Nine Lives, and she shoved Ruby another step toward the edge. "Hand them to me! Or watch her fall."

Claude did the only thing he could — he held out his hand — and as Nine Lives stepped toward him, Claude looked into Ruby's eyes and shouted, "Catch."

And as he tossed the invisible thing into the wind, he threw something else — a slight shimmering as it flew — and Ruby heard a clink as it landed somewhere in the darkness. Nine Lives's scream was of fury and frustration, both things flying from her grasp. She lunged at what she could not feel, desperately grabbing at nothingness as the skin whirled away unseen.

In that split second while Capaldi clawed the air, Ruby Redfort lost no time; her wrists still cuffed behind her, she ran along the parapet, tic-tac'd off the stairwell housing onto some piping, then ran along it before somehow leaping onto the roof and ducking into the darkness behind an air-conditioning vent. From the safety of the shadows, she scanned the rooftop, willing herself to lay eyes on the small shiny object Claude had thrown. She slipped her feet over her handcuffed wrists so now at least she held her arms in front of her, and then she began to caterpillar her way forward on her stomach.

"Where are you, bubble-gum girl?"

Lorelei? said Ruby to herself. *Of course you're Lorelei!*

Nine Lives was not Nine Lives, because Nine Lives was dead. This woman was Lorelei von Leyden — the woman of a thousand faces, the perfumer.

But what did it matter? This woman, whether Nine Lives Capaldi or Lorelei von Leyden, was an assassin and Ruby was not feeling fearless.

Just find whatever it is and get out of here.

She closed her eyes, took a breath and blinked them back open, and then she saw it — a small thing like a clear plastic rectangle attached to a cutting-edge key of some kind. A small thing *just like* the thing she had seen in LB's hand that day when she was debriefed at Spectrum. It was lying on the roof just a yard or so away.

Was this the "main attraction" that Lorelei had talked about?

If Ruby could grab it then, she could run; if she could run, then maybe she could drop to a safer rooftop, let someone else tackle the undead. She reached out her hand, almost able to close her fingers around it. She felt she was nearly home free when she heard a familiar sound — a sound that sent cold fear shooting through her veins.

The *tap tap tap* of the finest Italian leather shoes.

CHAPTER 54
Staring into the Void

SHE DIDN'T WANT TO TURN HER HEAD, she didn't want to look, but she couldn't help herself, and when she did, when she stared into those cold black eyes, she gasped to see the void.

The Count raised a finger to his lips. "Shhh, Ms. Redfort, let's not get Ms. von Leyden in another of her tempers. I'm only here for this."

He stooped to pluck up the tag attached to the silver thing. "Good," he said. "All that fuss, all that hanging around waiting for that unreliable girl to bring it *to* me . . . *but* if you want a job done, well, then do it yourself, isn't that what they say?" He smiled. "Let's catch up soon, Ms. Redfort; don't go dying until then." He turned and stepped over the edge of the building.

Ruby didn't have time to wonder where he had gone, she didn't have time to think what next, because what she heard was this:

"Oh, there you are — so it looks like it's just you and me, bubble-gum girl. And I've got nothing left to lose."

"Long time no see, Lorelei," said Ruby. She backed up against the air-conditioning vent as Lorelei walked slowly and deliberately toward her.

"Oh, bravo, so you actually figured something out. I thought you were never going to get there." Her Texan drawl was gone in a second. "Did you really think dear Valerie had returned from the dead?"

The storm was whirling in, and the gale was battering the roof, noisily lifting and dropping anything that it found. But Ruby could feel something else, a strange vibration, more rhythmic than the wind.

"Well, I have to hand it to you," said Ruby. "You are quite the mistress of disguise."

"And you the smart kid's smart kid," said Lorelei. "I'm flattered, really I am."

"Oh, don't be," said Ruby. "I'm merely buying time." She glanced above her and saw them, like black beetles in the air.

"Ah, time," said Lorelei. "Invisibly it slips through the fingers...."

"Rather like Claude," said Ruby.

"Rather like you," said Lorelei, and hauled Ruby to her feet.

The beetles were hovering, suspended by threads.

"Come enjoy the view," said Lorelei von Leyden, shoving Ruby to the edge. "A cliché, I know, but don't the people look like ants?"

"I'll take your word for it," said Ruby, glancing up.

Now the beetles looked more like humans as they silently landed on the roof.

"DROP YOUR WEAPON AND HIT THE DECK!"

Lorelei spun around to see a dozen or more armed Spectrum agents advancing on her.

You took your time, thought Ruby. She couldn't see Hitch, but he'd obviously rallied the troops.

Lorelei turned her head anxiously, looking for an escape route where there was none, her eyes blazing and her fists clenched, but what could she do when faced with an army?

Well, she did the only thing she could — she got her revenge on the kid who had screwed it all up for her.

And Ruby

fell

through

the

sky.

CHAPTER 55
Falling

RUBY'S HANDS WERE CUFFED, no chance to grab, no chance to discover if it was possible to fly.

She fell *fast*.

Plummeting down through the cold air, the concrete sidewalk waiting to greet her.

She closed her eyes. *Not invincible after all.* All that Redfort luck used up.

Then the strangest thing—she felt a weird sensation sort of around her shoulder blades, like she was sprouting wings, which was a coincidence because she seemed to be flying . . . well, gliding, but the effect was the same, since the sidewalk was not getting nearer and the people outside the Scarlet Pagoda were becoming more ant-like again.

As the wind carried her, Ruby thought about the jumpsuit—a gift from Hitch, a gift that, as she had so correctly predicted, had a lot more to it than at first met the eye. *Boy, is he some butler!*

She drifted down from sky to sidewalk, almost without incident, except for the final fifteen feet, when the wind ripped one of the wings off, and had it not been for the Dumpster full of garbage bags, Ruby would have no doubt broken another limb.

She climbed elegantly out from her landing place, not easy to do when exiting a trash can, then she jumped from the top of the Dumpster and landed with a perfect parkour roll.

People were bustling by, but few offered her more than a glance. A schoolkid had fallen from the sky, but Twinfordites took things in stride, shrugged, and walked on.

It was probably a stunt, something to do with the film festival—ignore it and go about your business; it was no big deal.

CHAPTER 56
The Night Mayor
Returns

THAT NIGHT THERE WAS A HUNT led by Spectrum to recover the invisibility skin, but given that it was impossible to *see,* it proved impossible to *find.* It was only when Ruby, unable to sleep, switched on the radio and caught a TTR five a.m. news story about the theft of the mayor's statue — which had seemingly gone missing from its Skylark Building plinth located just down the street from the Hotel Circus Grande — that she figured out what might have happened.

Not stolen, she thought. *Just shrouded.*

After all, the statue was heavy — compressed stone — and without a tow truck, which no witnesses had seen, there was no way the mayor's unfortunate likeness could have been carted out of there.

Tempting as it was to leave the skin exactly where it was, draped over the ugly statue, this would not be considered the right course of action for a Spectrum agent to take, and Ruby was working on her agent professionalism. So instead she took the subway straight there, while it was still dark, and retrieved the invisibility skin from the grip of the stone mayor.

Twinfordites were mightily disappointed to discover that he had reappeared and was once again leering down at them from the Skylark Building.

"Jeepers." Brant winced. "I thought that had gone for good."

"Oh, my," said Sabina. "It sure could give a person nightmares; someone should throw a blanket over it."

CHAPTER 57
Falling over Himself

ON HER WAY BACK FROM DOWNTOWN, Ruby decided to pay Clancy Crew a visit; she thought he would get a big kick out of the invisibility skin. He did — he jumped about two feet into the air, and it took some time before he regained his composure.

"Too bad we have to return it," said Clancy, who was still flapping his arms in disbelief.

"I know," said Ruby, "but we do."

Ruby was about to contact Hitch and tell him that she had located the skin, when she had an idea. It was one of those ideas that was so good that it was worth the risk of being exiled to a desert island or even jail for the rest of all time — or at least a few weeks. Ruby looked at Clancy.

"Well . . ." she said, "maybe we could hold onto it for a couple of hours. . . ."

It was Saturday morning, and they had a pretty good idea where Bailey Roach would be.

Sure enough, he was hanging out with his three friends in front of Marty's mini-mart. Clancy and Ruby walked toward them, though as far as the gorilla boy and his gang were concerned, Clancy was alone.

"Look who it is," he jeered. "Ruby Redfort's little pal, and he's all by himself . . . not such the tough man now."

The gorilla's friends fell over laughing at that one. Bailey Roach really thought he was a funny guy. But Clancy just stood there looking at him. He said nothing at all, and his face read blank. That bothered the gorilla. Why was this shrimpy kid not shaking in his shoes? Why was he not running or begging for mercy?

"What's your problem, Crew? Did I punch you a little too hard the other day? Did that yellow paint get all clogged inside your brain? Are you not all there?"

"Oh, I'm sorry, Bailey, I didn't mean to make you nervous or anything," said Clancy. "I drifted off for a second."

"You wanna drift off, Crew? I'll make you drift off," said Bailey Roach, stepping closer.

"Boy, your hair smells nice," said Clancy, "though I would imagine all that styling you do is a good deal of work. Your hair must take up a lot of your time. No wonder school is a challenge." A little muscle in Bailey Roach's jaw was twitching, but Clancy

Crew just went right on talking. "But you're right, hair *is* important. I've heard it can really open doors. I mean, who needs brains when you have hair that says, *I just stepped out of the salon?*"

That was it; that last insult was the trigger. Bailey Roach lunged at Clancy, his right fist balled, ready for the punch, but a strange thing happened: as he reached to grab the shrimp by his shirt, he felt himself pulled backward, then for no apparent reason that his gorilla friends could see, Bailey Roach fell over. How did the kid do it? Roach sprang to his feet and this time he aimed a kick at Clancy, the sort of kung fu–style move that might have caused some damage had it actually met its target. But it didn't, and instead the gorilla felt his leg grabbed by something, something that had to be, could *only* be, paranormal activity. He completely lost his balance and went slap on his behind. His friends began to laugh.

"Nice move, Beetle," shouted one of them.

"Yeah," said another, "you look like you got the skinny kid exactly where you want him."

The gorilla glared at them and scrambled to his feet, his eyes narrowed. "You're dead meat, Crew." And then quite suddenly he ran at Clancy, but Clancy stood his ground; the only move he made was to raise one hand in front of him like he was batting away a fly. But that was all it took because Bailey Roach, the gorilla of Twinford Junior High, was knocked right off his feet and sent sprawling to the ground.

The gorilla's friends were impressed.

"Are you like some kinda karate black belt, Crew?"

"You look shrimpy but you got some moves, man."

"Kid, do you want to teach me that hand thing?"

But Clancy was done here. There was a donut with his name on it waiting back at Marla's diner, and he really couldn't waste more time on these duh brains.

Epilogue

RUBY WAS SITTING at her desk in the code room, books and papers spread all around her, decoding devices of all sorts cluttering its surface, and yet she was making no progress. None at all.

The door opened behind her, but she didn't turn around, and it was only when she heard the sound of softly padding feet that Ruby actually looked up.

LB looked different today somehow. Perhaps it was a trick of the light, perhaps it was because she looked like she should get some sleep, but to Ruby her face looked less composed, as if one might actually have a chance of fathoming her thoughts.

"Redfort," she said, "I find myself having to congratulate you, even though I have not the faintest idea what you were doing last night standing on a high wire between the Scarlet Pagoda and the Hotel Circus Grande."

"I can explain," offered Ruby.

"I'd rather you didn't," said LB. "Your explanations, I find, are very tedious and more often than not tend to lead to a severe headache, and I have left my aspirin in my office, so if you don't mind, let's skip to the chase."

"OK with me." Ruby shrugged.

"You did well to recover the skin. The Department of Defense is very grateful—this is not the sort of prototype one wants to wind up in the wrong hands."

"So why didn't they brief us all about it?" asked Ruby. "It doesn't make any sense not to; they want something recovered but refuse to tell anyone what we are supposed to be looking for."

"I agree," said LB. "It doesn't make any sense at all, and last night when I spoke to the officer who issued this directive, he denied all knowledge of it."

"Meaning?" said Ruby.

"Meaning that he issued no such order; in fact he went as far as to say that he had particularly requested that *all* Spectrum 8 agents be fully briefed about the nature of the break-in and the prototype stolen. Which is odd because the message that came to us was that only senior agents should know—agents even more senior than me."

"And the other thing that Claude stole?" said Ruby. "What was it? I think I recognized it on the roof; I mean, I saw it in your hand the other day when you were . . . um . . . you know, grounding me."

"The 8 key," said LB.

"The 8 key?" said Ruby.

"A Spectrum 8 security coder," said LB. "It was stolen from my safe-deposit box when I paid a visit to the DOD research lab. The safe box was inside the safe room. Which is code protected. The theft of the invisibility skin explains how someone, I guess Claude Fontaine, whereabouts still unknown, was physically able to steal it, but it doesn't explain how he knew what it was or where it would be. To know that would require . . . inside information."

"You think there's a mole . . . in *Spectrum*?"

"I don't know," said LB, "but it's looking more and more like maybe."

"The 8 key," said Ruby. "Why would anyone want that? I mean, given that Spectrum would just disable it the second they know it's missing . . . I mean, I'm right, aren't I?" said Ruby. "It's useless once disabled?"

"That's correct," replied LB. "The 8 key is useless once disabled."

There was something about LB's reply that stuck in Ruby's mind; it was very deliberate, as if she was trying *not* to say something.

"So you're not looking to retrieve it?" she asked.

LB paused. "There's something I need back," she said. "Not the 8 key itself, but the tag it's attached to."

"Why is that important?" asked Ruby.

"It was mine," said LB. "I mean, always mine. I've had it since I was, well, very young. It was given to me by someone."

"Who?" asked Ruby.

But LB was through with sharing. "It's just a memento," she said finally. "I want it back is all."

Silence.

Neither of them said anything for a minute, and then LB asked, "So what are you doing here, anyway?"

Ruby sighed. "I still haven't figured out those messages, the ones sent from the coder on my Escape Watch." She looked at LB. "I mean, I'm guessing you know about them?"

LB nodded; LB knew everything.

"Hitch and Blacker received them, and I can't tie them into this recent case and I am no nearer to cracking them, but, well, they have to mean something."

"Why?" asked LB.

Ruby looked at her, puzzled. "Everything means something, right?" she said. "At first I thought it must have to do with the skywalker, but now I'm guessing it doesn't—so what if it's in the hands of someone a whole lot worse?"

"My guess is that you are correct; my guess would be that your watch *is* in the hands of someone a whole lot worse," said LB.

Ruby gulped; this was not the news she wanted to hear.

"But," continued her boss, "have you considered that perhaps this individual doesn't want *anything*?"

"I'm not following," said Ruby, who really wasn't following.

"Let's start with a simple one. Where exactly did you last see the Escape Watch?"

"I had it the night I first spotted the skywalker. I remember, because that's the night I returned to the Thompsons' apartment. I know I shouldn't have been there, but I had to see if I could find that card."

"These would be the Thompsons on Avenue Walk—they reside in the Warrington Apartments?"

"Yeah, that's them."

"The parents of Nileston?"

"Yeah." Ruby didn't get why LB was going on and on about the Thompsons. She was beginning to sound like the *Twinford Echo*.

"And where exactly did you find the calling card?" asked LB.

"It showed up in the toy box, a big wicker hamper basket," said Ruby. "The thief wouldn't have meant it to be there, but the kid musta crawled off with it — it was right there underneath a whole lot of plastic junk."

"*You*, I guess, had to rummage through this, when you searched for the card, am I right?"

"Yes, it took a while but I found it under Mr. Potato Head."

"Exactly."

"Exactly what?"

"I think that clears up that mystery." LB turned to leave.

"I don't want to be the one who says I don't get it, but I don't get it," said Ruby.

LB sighed. "Redfort, I think you need to get some sleep; you're really not at the top of your game. Do you really need me to spell it out?"

Ruby blinked dumbly. So LB continued.

"I think it's safe to assume that you lost your watch in Nileston's toy hamper and therefore unless Mr. Potato Head has taken up spy work, it's likely that Nileston was the one sending those 'coded' messages."

"What? You're saying that year-and-a-half-old kid is sending encrypted messages to Spectrum agents?"

"No, Redfort, I'm not saying that at all. Use your noodle for five minutes — this kid has got ahold of your watch and has somehow, via a series of random button-pressing moves, accessed the coder function and is sending gobbledygook to anyone and everyone you have ever been in touch with. I myself received one. You have been failing to see the gorilla here. Don't overthink things; that should be a rule of yours."

Ruby's mouth fell open. After all, it *was* a rule of hers, **RULE 71: WHEN IN DOUBT, THINK THE OBVIOUS.**

"This isn't code," said LB. "These are the random fiddlings of a drooling toddler."

Ruby slapped her forehead with the palm of her hand.

"Oh, quit giving yourself a hard time, kid," said LB as she walked to the door. "It happens to us all. Gorillas, elephants, they're all easy to miss in a place like Spectrum, and I happen to know you're pretty good at spotting gorillas."

She was in the corridor and walking back toward the elevator before she called out, "You should get some sleep, Redfort — you start training on Monday."

Epilogue 2

RUBY TOOK THE ELEVATOR BACK UP to the Schroeder underground parking lot. When the doors opened, she was met by a familiar face.

"I thought you could use a ride," said Hitch. "Where can I take you — home?"

Ruby glanced at Hitch's watch.

She sighed.

"The Humberts' place," she said.

"You sure about that, kid?"

"It's Quent's birthday. For some reason, I feel I gotta be there."

Hitch looked at her, really looked at her. Was she kidding? No, she wasn't kidding.

"You're a better kid than I had you down for, Redfort."

"It's a superhero theme," said Ruby. "I don't suppose I could borrow . . ."

Hitch looked at her, one eyebrow raised — the look said, *You must be out of your mind.*

"So what am I gonna wear?" asked Ruby.

"Ah," said Hitch, "just go as yourself, kid."

From the *Twinford Echo* . . .

MARGO BARDEM ANNOUNCES:

I OWE IT ALL TO THE LITTLE CANARY!

Ms. Bardem announced that the subject of
the much-anticipated Louisa Parker sculpture
will be *The Little Canary,* in honor of the
circus acrobat and tightrope walker, the
original Celeste.

The artwork will stand outside the
Scarlet Pagoda (now saved from demolition)
and will be a worthy tribute to Celeste
Fontaine, the Little Canary of Twinford.

Margo Bardem said, "It is only right that
this artist be celebrated. She caught the
attention of kings, poets, and the people.
She felt the love and applause of all
who saw her—it is high time she was made
visible again."

THINGS I KNOW:
....

The Count is out there somewhere,
and he has the 8 key.
The Count knows Lorelei von Leyden.
LB has a lot of experience with babies.

THINGS I DON'T KNOW:
....

WHY the Count took the 8 key when he
must know it's been deactivated.
Whether Claude is alive.
What it is about that key tag that makes it
so important to LB.
If there's a mole in Spectrum.

Ruby Redfort

How Ruby Decoded Claude's Touch Code

*by Marcus du Sautoy,
super-geek consultant*

Braille is the most famous code that is read by using your sense
of touch. Each letter is represented by a series of raised dots
arranged in a 2-by-3 grid. For example, here is Ruby's name in
Braille:

Although Braille is aimed at helping rather than hiding communication, the idea for the code came from a secret touch code developed by Napoleon's army at the beginning of the nineteenth century. Called a night code, the dots allowed soldiers to communicate at nighttime without a light.

Both Braille and the Napoleonic night code use something called binary notation. When you apply your fingers to each position of the matrix, you can either feel a dot or no dot. Computers use the same idea, where dots are replaced by switches that are either on or off. The digital revolution has turned words, pictures, tweets, and e-mails into a series of 0s and 1s.

It was the seventeenth-century German mathematician Gottfried Leibniz who was the first to realize the power of 0s and 1s as a good way of coding information. Ordinarily, when we write numbers down, we count in powers of ten. The number 234 represents 4 single units, 3 tens, and 2 hundreds. The choice of ten relates to the fact that we have ten fingers. (Presumably the cartoon characters in *The Simpsons* who have eight fingers count in powers of eight rather than ten.) We call this decimal notation, and it needs ten symbols to make it work: 0, 1, 2, 3, 4, 5, 6, 7, 8, and 9.

Leibniz realized, though, that if you used powers of two rather than powers of ten, you could get away with just two symbols: 0 and 1. This is called binary notation. So the number 110101 stands for, reading from right to left: one unit, no 2s, one 4, no 8, one 16, and one 32, making $1 + 4 + 16 + 32 = 53$.

Braille and the Napoleonic night code are actually examples of binary codes done in a touch format, where 1s and 0s are replaced by raised dots or no dots.

Ruby, however, is faced with trying to decode a new sort of touch code that is based on ternary numbers rather than binary numbers. These numbers use powers of 3 rather than powers of 2 to record digits. They require 3 symbols to represent them: 0, 1, and 2. So, for example, the number 16 is represented by 121, which — reading right to left again — means one unit, two 3s, and one 9, making $9 + 2 \times 3 + 1 = 16$.

To render this into a tactile message that can be read using your fingers, Claude has created the code in the following way. First, each number is defined by a row of three dots, punched either up or down into the card. A 1 is represented by a dot punched down into the card while a 2 is represented by a dot punched up out of the card. A zero is represented by no dot. (See diagram.)

Then Claude simply uses three such rows to encode three numbers on each card. The key realization for Ruby was this use of three numbers, as well as the rows of three dots. This made her think of the number 3, which in turn gave her a lightbulb moment when she realized that the whole code was a base-3 — or ternary — numbering system. For his final card, Claude needs the numbers 29 and 27. To get these, he simply adds another column. The touch code on the sixth card would look like this:

Claude's Sixth Card *(with an extra column)*

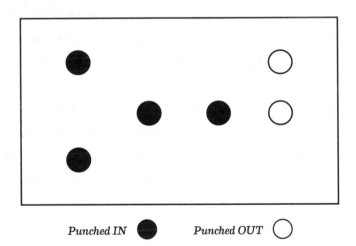

If Braille is based on binary, then perhaps this new touch code based on ternary numbers should be called Traille. The numbers from 0 to 30 are written in Traille on the following pages.

Traille:
Ruby's Ternary Touch Code

The table has been filled in up to 30. Can you crack the last two yourself?

Punched in ● Punched out ○

				0
			●	1
			○	2
		●		3
		●	●	4
		●	○	5
		○		6
		○	●	7
		○	○	8
	●			9
	●		●	10

			○	11
		●		12
		●	●	13
		●	○	14
		○		15
		○	●	16
		○	○	17
	○			18
	○		●	19
	○		○	20
	○	●		21

	○	●	●	22
	○	●	○	23
	○	○		24
	○	○	●	25
	○	○	○	26
●				27
●			●	28
●			○	29
●		●		30
				31
				32

A Note on Parkour

Parkour is a way of moving around one's environment without limitations on movement. The name comes from the French word *parcours,* meaning "way through" or "path." It was originally developed in France in the lead-up to World War I as an obstacle-course military training exercise and has since become standard military practice. In its modern, popularized form, it dates from the 1980s — but Ruby is ahead of her time!

These days parkour is an activity, a youth movement, even a philosophy, usually practiced in and around urban environments, as can be seen in the thousands of videos on the Internet showing seasoned parkour practitioners leaping huge distances, up and over walls. The idea is to use the obstacles in your path to increase your efficiency of movement, the rail that you leap onto becoming the object you use to propel yourself forward.

Some forms of parkour concentrate on this aspect of efficiency and speed of movement, others more on fluidity and self-expression, but for all those that practice free-running and parkour, it is more than just a physical activity — it is a philosophy and a way of life. It accepts fear as a useful warning and an essential part of being in the moment, but through practice, training, and awareness, offers a way to move through fear. It is a new way of seeing one's surroundings — the belief that there are no obstacles in your path, physical or otherwise, that cannot be overcome. No true parkour practitioner is a thrill seeker — but rather someone who seeks to master herself or himself in all environments.

☞ **Parkour is a highly skilled discipline and should not be attempted unsupervised. To find courses and classes near you, try the organization Parkour Generations:** *www.parkourgenerations.com.*

THE ROLL

1.
Stance

From a crouch or stand, turn forty-five degrees in the direction of the roll, with one shoulder and leg forward.

2.
Drop
and
roll

Drop forward, touching the ground with your hands first; roll forward onto your lead shoulder and over onto the opposite hip. Tuck your legs beneath you with your chin to your chest.

3.
Exit

Continue the roll onto your thigh, then onto your toes; stay small like a ball and keep your limbs under control.

4.
Move

Come out of the roll with the lead leg and shoulder forward as you began. Use your hands to stabilize as your legs push off into a run.

THE MONKEY VAULT

1. Approach

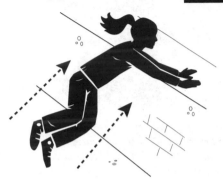

Start head-on, use your momentum, and split your feet at takeoff. Don't take off too close to the obstacle.

2. Dive

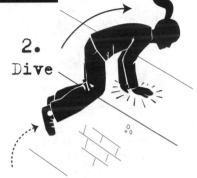

At takeoff, raise your hips and bring your knees up to your chest; plant both palms down flat on the obstacle.

3. Pass over

As you pass over the obstacle, your back should be horizontal. Keep your knees close together.

4. Exit

Push with your hands as you clear the obstacle. Land on one foot to run, or on both for a soft landing.

THE WALL RUN

1. Approach

Approach head-on; the last two steps should be the most powerful. Angle your body back and look up at the wall.

2. Step

When about a stride away, jump at the wall, placing your lead foot on the wall at waist height. Push up from your lead leg, surging upward.

3. Reach

As you push upward, stretch your arms to the top of the wall. Getting your fingertips over the top is enough.

4. Climb up

With both hands on top of the wall, pull yourself up using your arms and shoulders. Aim to get your feet on top so you can make your next move.

A Note on   *

While U.S. military stealth technology has succeeded in creating materials that can hide a tank or a fighter jet from radar, full invisibility — that is, invisibility to the human eye — has until recently proved impossible, involving as it does a different part of the electromagnetic spectrum: light.

In 2007, a team of engineers at Purdue University in Indiana made the first big breakthrough when they developed a "metamaterial" made out of nanoneedles that create an electromagnetic field with the ability to bend light around the object, in much the same way that water moves around a rock in a stream. Unfortunately, however, this metamaterial does not grow on trees. It has to be engineered at the nanoscale (one billionth of a meter), which means that so far the problem has been creating an "invisibility cloak" big enough to hide anything that isn't already too small to be worth hiding.

In 2014 a major breakthrough was made in the race to

achieve full invisibility. Researchers at the University of Florida announced that they had developed a means of mass-producing metamaterial using a type of 3-D-printing process. Though the printed material itself cannot serve as an "invisibility cloak," the printing process does allow for the faster creation of a material with that capability.

At the same time, Professor Chen Hongsheng at Zhejiang University, in China, announced a similarly huge breakthrough when his team succeeded in making a goldfish and a cat seem to disappear, also using a device that bends light. The professor's team is one of more than forty research teams currently funded by the Chinese government to develop full invisibility.

Who will win the race, however, remains to be seen. While the mood in China is confident, former U.S. Navy SEAL officer Chris Sajnog commented, "The general public doesn't know how far the U.S. has really gotten with this technology because it is — and will remain — classified."

* *Invisibility*

A Note on the Gorilla Test

The Gorilla Test, or Invisible Gorilla Test, originated in the mid-1970s and was updated in 1999 by Christopher Chabris of the University of Illinois and Daniel Simons of Harvard. The test involves showing a short video in which two teams of three people, one in black shirts, one in white shirts, pass a ball among themselves. People taking the test are asked to silently count the number of passes made by the white team. At some point during the video, a man in a gorilla suit walks into the center of the room, beats his chest, and walks off again — hard to miss, you would think. However, when the test was originally administered at Harvard, half the people who took the test and correctly counted the passes missed the gorilla. The test was created as a demonstration of selective attention — how, if you are focusing hard on one thing, you may well miss something else, even something big, like a gorilla.

www.theinvisiblegorilla.com/gorilla_experiment.html

Acknowledgments

As always, thank you to Rachel Folder for good ideas and writing things in neat handwriting on little cards all spread out on the floor. Also to: A. D. and T. C., who for many months had to step over and around little cards covered in neat handwriting spread out on the floor. Awsa Bergstrom, who talked me through the principles of parkour and many of the various moves — monkey vaults, tic-tacs, and corkscrew pops — she is so inspiring that I feel as if I could actually do a corkscrew pop. Maisie Cowell, who popped in for a few days' work experience and left having solved a very important plot twist for me — one smart girl. Marcus du Sautoy, because whether he is in a tent deep in the Guatemalan jungle or taking breakfast in Hay-on-Wye, he is never fazed by a question and has never failed to come up with the answer. Rachael Stirling for reading the Ruby stories out loud for audio and doing such a perfect Consuela Cruz that I am writing her back in, and such a funny Quent Humbert that I can never write him out. Thank you to Philippa Perry because I always forget to thank her even though I can't imagine being able to do any of what I am meant to do without her — plus she is super nice. To Mary Byrne, Geraldine Stroud, and Sam White in HarperCollins publicity for also being super nice and never grumpy (at least never when I am in the room). My editors Ruth Alltimes and Nick Lake for a zillion reasons but particularly because even when a book isn't finished when it is meant to be finished, and looks like it never will be finished, they manage to stay very calm and do absolutely no shouting and make out that it is actually a good thing. David Mackintosh, who knows his way around the tightest of deadlines and can still produce a beautifully designed book with perfect illustrations. And finally my publisher Ann-Janine Murtagh, who talks me through a problem even when I know she has somewhere else to be and somehow makes time stretch even when there seems to be none left.

I am very grateful to them all.